SOLACE HOUSE

A gripping crime thriller full of stunning twists

JOY ELLIS

DI Jackman and DS Evans Book 9

Joffe Books, London
www.joffebooks.com

First published in Great Britain in 2022

ISBN: 978-1-80405-557-1

This is to say thank you to Laura Hurt, Penny Attwood and the incredible team of volunteers who run the charity 'Save Our Spaniels'. The fantastic work that they do to rescue and find loving homes for terribly treated, abandoned and homeless spaniels is above and beyond. It's people like this, who pick up little lost and damaged souls and give them a new life, who rarely get acknowledged, but to you, and to all the fosterers and lovely people who have opened their homes to rescue dogs, thank you — you are amazing!

CHAPTER ONE

DI Rowan Jackman dismounted and stroked his horse's neck affectionately. He wished he had more time to spend here at his mother's stables. It was the one place he could be free of the darker side of life — the world of crime and the people who committed it.

Talking gently to the beast, Jackman walked it over to where his mother was speaking to one of her stable staff. 'This boy is really coming along, Mum. We had a great ride today.'

Harriet Jackman nodded in satisfaction, watching the groom lead the chestnut gelding away. 'Just proves it doesn't do to give up on a horse. Bart Cummings didn't have the time or the patience to spend on him. The old rogue knew I was a soft touch, so he sold him to me.' She smiled. 'I always thought he'd suit you, son. He still needs an experienced rider, but he has all the makings of a lovely all-rounder.'

'And I like a challenge, as you well know,' Jackman said. He put an affectionate arm around his mother. 'Before I forget, Laura told me to ask you and Dad to dinner on Friday night, if you're free?'

'That would be lovely, darling! I'd better just check your father's overflowing social engagement diary before I commit us. I'll ring you tonight to confirm.'

1

She walked with him to his car. 'Oh, I must tell you the latest gossip. That old house called Solace is back on the market. The present owners only lasted six months.'

Jackman wasn't surprised. 'They should demolish the place. Fell all those old overgrown leylandii conifers and start again.' He'd always thought that would be the only way to dispel the bad memories the old house held.

'I'm sure it will come to that one day,' said Harriet, 'but everyone who takes it thinks they'll be the ones to make it home sweet home.' She gave a cheerless laugh. 'Fat chance of that!'

With a kiss for his mother, Jackman got into his car. It had been a great start to the morning. Now it was home to Mill Corner for a shower and a change of clothes and then he had the rest of the day to himself for once. Laura, who was the force psychologist, was working over at Greenborough all day and he and his team were catching up on some long overdue days off, something that had been impossible during their last major investigation.

As he drove towards Amberley Fen, a village about a mile from his parents' home, he was suddenly taken with the idea of having another look at the house called Solace. He hung a swift left and turned into a narrow farm drove. After about a quarter of a mile of twists and turns along a single-track lane, he saw a thick, dark cluster of unkempt trees looming up. He slowed down and pulled up about 100 metres short of the drive.

All he could see of the house itself was a single chimney stack rising up through the trees. Even from this distance, he could feel the melancholy atmosphere that hung over the place.

'You lost?'

He hadn't noticed the woman and her dog emerge from a field path just behind the car until she was level with his window. He wound it down. 'No, I'm fine, but thanks anyway.' He smiled and looked down at the young black Labrador standing at the woman's side. 'Oh my! Is that a Sandringham Sydney?'

The woman drew the dog closer and backed away from the car.

'It's okay, honestly. I'm a police officer.' He pulled his warrant card from his pocket and held it up so she could see it. 'I didn't mean to frighten you.'

She visibly relaxed. 'So many dogs are getting stolen these days, you can't be too careful.' She pulled a small can of hairspray from her pocket. 'It's not exactly pepper spray, but it would sting like hell if you got an eyeful.'

'And I can't arrest you for carrying it.' He smiled again. 'Unlike pepper spray. That has the same legal penalties as carrying a gun.'

'To protect my dog, I'd chance it, but maybe I shouldn't be telling you that.' She gave a little laugh. 'And you're right about the breed. You are the first person I've met to have even heard of it, let alone recognise one. You a dog breeder?'

He shook his head. 'No, but I had a beautiful lad like yours when I was a kid. I thought I'd never get over losing him and I was right, I never did. My Ozzie was a very special boy.'

'Like Rory here.' She looked down fondly at her dog and tickled his ear.

'Great name,' Jackman said, thinking of their Home Office pathologist, Professor Rory Wilkinson. Was there maybe the slightest resemblance?

'My husband has a Scottish mother and an Irish father, and he wanted a good strong Gaelic name for the puppy.' She looked at him inquisitively. 'So, why are you out here? And if I might say, you don't look exactly dressed for work, or is that what you'd call plain clothes?'

'Oh no! It's my day off. My mother owns the livery stable about a mile or so back down the drove. I've been riding.' He looked towards the old house. 'I was involved in an enquiry out here many years ago and just wondered what had happened to the place. I guess I hoped it had been completely restored, or maybe—'

'Bulldozed and razed to the ground?' Her tone was harsh.

'So you live around here?' he asked.

'For my sins, I'm the idiot who lives in Solace. But only for as long as it takes to sell it, believe me.'

'I'm sorry,' said Jackman. 'It does have a pretty grim history, doesn't it?'

The woman snorted. 'Hah! That I could cope with. We knew all about the murder when we bought it. We're not superstitious people, Officer. It's just a house. It's people that do terrible things, not bricks and mortar.'

You're not wrong there, thought Jackman. 'So what's the problem?'

She didn't answer, just heaved a sigh and stared at the dog.

He filled in the silence with, 'My name is Jackman. I'm a DI at Saltern-le-Fen. Can I ask, are you having problems with anyone out here? Because if you are, I'd be happy to get one of our people to come and chat with you.'

'No, no, it's nothing like that.' She looked thoroughly miserable. 'It's just no place to bring up children. My name is Holly Stewart, by the way, my husband is Hugh, and I've got two children, Poppy and Aaron.' She gave him a searching look. 'Have you got time for a coffee?'

'Sure. Love to. If you'll forgive the riding breeches and rather ancient horse-smelling gilet?'

'This is the country, DI Jackman, not Mayfair. Park anywhere in the driveway. I'll go and unlock.'

As he drove between the straggling bushes and tall uncared-for conifers, he felt exactly as he had when he first saw Solace — a heaviness of heart and a sense of foreboding.

Without a doubt, it was the most austere house he had ever come across on the Fens. It rose up from the end of the drive like a prison block. There were no windows on this side of the property, just dark red brickwork. It was quite unusual, three storeys high, and nothing like the conventional Fenland farmhouse. The fact that it was facing sideways onto the road made it look as if it was turning away, hoping to be ignored by anyone passing. And anyone with any sense would do just that, drive on past. He had never come across a more inappropriately named house in all his time on the force. There was no solace of any kind to be found here.

He parked and walked around to the left-hand side of the house, where he found the front door open. He experienced an odd feeling of déjà vu. It had been open like this the first time he had come here. But on that occasion, he had found a distraught man sitting next to the body of his dead wife and saying that he had had to kill her, he had had no choice.

Jackman mentally gathered himself, tapped on the open door, and hearing Holly call for him to go in, made his way to the kitchen.

'How do you like your coffee?' she asked, switching the kettle on.

'White, no sugar, thank you.'

She took mugs from a decorative mug tree on the counter, and a cannister of coffee from a cupboard.

Jackman looked around. They had clearly made an effort to cheer up the old place, and it had been freshly painted in a light lemony colour. Some of the work surfaces and cupboards had been replaced, there was a new stainless-steel sink instead of the worn and stained old Belfast sink that he remembered. Children's attempts at artwork and colourful photos were stuck with magnets to the doors of the big fridge-freezer. But still it felt dark and rather depressing.

After having given Jackman a welcoming sniff and a tail wag, Rory had taken himself off to his bed and immediately closed his eyes. Even the dog seemed to be in low spirits now he was indoors again.

'Where are you from,' asked Jackman, 'if you don't mind me asking?'

'Out of the area, DI Jackman. We came here so that the kids wouldn't be brought up on a rough estate on the outskirts of a big town.' There was a resentful edge to her words. 'We had all these hopes for a peaceful rural way of life, but now . . .' She shrugged and gave a rueful smile. 'I wish to God we'd stayed put and chanced our luck with poor schools and maybe a drug dealer for a next-door neighbour.'

'It's really that bad here?' He knew the answer already, but not the reason for it.

She nodded mutely and finished making the drinks. She handed him a mug and sat down opposite him at the kitchen table. 'To say we didn't think this through properly is an understatement, but we really believed it was the best thing that had happened to us.' She leaned forward, her elbows on the table. 'We didn't start out in a rough area, we both come from decent homes and families, but you know how it is sometimes, a run of bad luck, an unwise investment, a business venture folding under us, poor health and so on, and we found ourselves sliding down the ladder.'

Jackman could almost see the exasperation rising from her like steam. But he knew that sometimes events conspired against you and there was little you could do to stop the downward spiral.

'Then Hugh's mother died, and we inherited some money. Not a fortune, but enough for a very small place of our own. Then we wondered if we'd get more for our money if we moved right away from town and into a different area. A friend suggested Lincolnshire, and he was right, the prices are much lower here. Hugh spoke to an estate agent in Saltern, and he sent us a whole load of information on some pretty nice small properties in this area.' Holly gave a little groan. 'Then he told Hugh about this place, almost as a joke. He said, "Mind you, if you are prepared to live in a property with a very dark history, we could offer you a five-bedroom detached house in an acre of ground for the price of a two-bed semi-detached new build on an estate."'

'Ah,' said Jackman, wondering if the estate agent had seen them as a couple of gullible incomers, and had deliberately thrown them a carrot. 'And you simply *had* to view it.'

'Of course! Wouldn't you? As I said, we're townies, but we're down to earth. We just wanted fresh air, a bit of space so the kids could play in safety. We wanted a garden to grow our own vegetables and I wanted to see flowers when I looked out of the window, not overflowing rubbish sacks and car tyres.'

'And when you visited? What was your impression?' Jackman was recalling his own first take on the place, one of gloom and despondency.

'We saw one whole lot of house for very little money, and what we could do with it as the years went by. We never saw it as it was, only what it could become in the future. It was just too good to let go. Or so we thought.' Holly stared into her coffee. 'We didn't bother with proper searches, and worst of all, *we* might not be superstitious, but we never took into consideration what other people thought about a murder having taken place here and the impact that could have on us.'

A murder? thought Jackman. *But it wasn't just one.* Or perhaps she didn't know that. He decided not to take it further right now. 'How does that affect you, Holly?'

'How long have you got? Oh, I won't bore you with the list of ways, but the one that really hurts is how the children are treated at school. They're both bullied and called the Creepy Kids from the House of Horrors. Even their journey on the school bus to Cadring Eaudyke is a nightmare for them. Children can be so spiteful.'

'I'm sorry things have gone so wrong for you. I have to say most Fenlanders are really kind and welcoming, it's not like them to be inhospitable.'

Holly looked thoroughly miserable. 'It's not everyone, of course, we have met a few nice people. Bottom line, it's the house that's the problem. Everything's gone wrong since we moved in. My Hugh had the promise of a really well-paid job in Saltern — he's a skilled welder and a good one — but it fell through at the last minute and he's still not found permanent work yet, so money is tight. Hence, we've been living on the money we'd put aside for the house, so we can't move forward at all.'

Holly looked anxiously at Jackman. 'I'm so sorry. I have no idea why I'm pouring all this out to you. I'm usually a really private person and goodness, I don't even know you!'

'You do now.' Jackman gave her a reassuring smile. 'It sounds like you've bottled this up for too long. Tell me, what has made you abandon your dreams and sell up?'

She sighed. 'There's something about this house, DI Jackman. It's so depressing to live here. It's always dark and it seems to leach all the joy from your life. Sounds stupid, I know, but the children aren't thriving, they sleep badly and have terrible dreams. Hugh and I have started arguing and we never did that before. We love each other dearly, but it's as if all the sunshine has left our lives.' She stood up and walked to the window. 'See all these horrid, overgrown, half-dead conifers?' She gave a sweeping gesture. 'Our first job was to clear them, take them down and get the roots out, let the light in and plan a proper garden.' She pulled a face. 'Then we got the quotes. It was out of the question, especially with Hugh struggling to find work.'

'It would make a huge difference to the light,' said Jackman. 'Maybe doing them in bite-size sections would be cheaper? One small area at a time?'

'Hugh started to do it himself, but it was too dangerous on his own and hiring the right equipment was really costly.' She gave Jackman a sad smile. 'He gave up, and nothing grows in the area that he did clear. I think the tree roots took all the goodness from the soil. It's like everything we do is a failure. Now we're in limbo — every penny we have is tied up in this property. If we can't sell it, we can't move on, or even look at anything else.'

Holly's eyes filled with tears.

'We used to be such a happy family, full of ideas and plans and, well, hope for a better future, and now . . .' Her voice trailed off. 'Now we are living in a nightmare.'

He wished there was something he could do. This woman was a complete stranger, but her sadness and frustration at seeing her dreams slip away and her family suffer was very real indeed. He wondered if there was some small thing that he could do to lighten their life a little. He had an idea. 'How old are your children, Holly?'

'Seven and eight. Aaron is exactly one year older than Poppy.'

'Do they like animals?'

'Oh, they love them, especially Rory. They dote on him.' She dabbed at her eyes with a tissue. 'In fact I don't know what they'd do without him. They tell him all their worries when they feel they can't speak to us.'

'So how would they like to spend a few hours with the horses at my mother's stables? She's got a couple of great little ponies if they feel they'd like to get in the saddle.' Jackman had started riding at three, and still experienced the same thrill every time he sat on a horse.

'That's very kind, DI Jackman, but we really couldn't afford it.'

'Oh, no charge, just a little treat to cheer them up. Horses are brilliant therapy, you know. I used to volunteer at Riding for the Disabled, and the benefit it brought to some of those people was really heart-warming.' He grinned. 'As long as you bring Rory along too. Being a staunch royalist, my mother adores Sandringhams. I'm sure she thinks they're all direct descendants from the Royal Family.'

'That's exactly what I tell the children — that Rory has royal blood in his veins.' This time Holly's smile was genuine. 'And if you're sure it would be no inconvenience, we'd love the kids to see the horses.'

'Saturday morning, ten o'clock. I'll call by here and you can follow me back to the stables. It's a date.'

He took her phone number in case of any change of plan and thanked her for the coffee. As he was leaving, Holly said, 'You mentioned you were involved in the murder investigation that took place here? We've heard so many terrible stories about it and guess that most are hugely exaggerated, but was it really as horrific as people say? I never thought I'd hear myself say this, but I do wonder if it has cast some sort of shadow over the place.'

'No, Holly, it was just a man who had serious psychological problems that hadn't been diagnosed. He had some

9

kind of episode and killed his wife. Afterwards he was grief-stricken. It was desperately sad, not horrific.'

Later, sitting in his car, he thought about what he had said. Regarding the case he had investigated, it was completely true. But the same could not be said for the other murders that allegedly took place there long before Jim Smith strangled his wife, Eleanor. If the old stories were true, they *were* horrific, and it would appear the estate agent had conveniently omitted to mention those.

In stark contrast to Solace, Jackman's home at Mill Corner was a warm and comfortable old farmhouse whose old mill was now converted into a private consulting room for Laura. He went in, still thinking about Holly Stewart and her beleaguered family, and immediately rang his mother to tell her about them and his suggestion for helping the two children. She readily agreed. There were plenty of yard staff there on a Saturday to show them around and let them meet the horses. She'd make sure Debbie Quinton, the riding instructor, was there too. Debbie loved nothing more than teaching the younger kids to ride. 'Poor little mites,' his mother exclaimed when he told her about the bullying. 'Don't you worry, son, we'll make sure they have a lovely time.'

Well, that was something, he supposed. An unexpected surprise would be great for the kids, but what about the parents? A trip round a stable was hardly going to lift their spirits. He frowned, then a thought came to him. He scrolled through his contacts and made a call. 'Gerry? Rowan Jackman here. Have you got a minute?'

His old friend shouted that he was in the workshop and couldn't hear a thing. 'I'm heading for the office, mate. Hold on a mo. Right. That's better. How's it going then?'

They brought each other up to date, and then Jackman said, 'Look, Gerry, this is a bit of a long shot, but do you know anyone who might need a welder? It's your line of business. I don't know the man personally, but I'm told he's good. He was let down on a job offer and he and his family are struggling. Can you help?'

Gerry Keane chuckled. 'He could be in luck if he's as good as you say, and he's prepared to work some long hours. Dad's just landed us a contract for a whole lot of new veg packers and harvesting equipment. I'm prepared to give him a trial here, if you like. No promises, though. You know my dad, he's fair and he pays good wages, but he doesn't suffer fools or people who aren't prepared to work hard.'

'Sounds good to me, Gerry. Shall I get him to ring you? His name's Hugh Stewart and he lives in Amberley Fen.'

'Not too far away, then. Yes, give him my number.'

When they'd finished catching up, Jackman rang Holly with the news.

'Oh my God, DI Jackman! Are you some kind of guardian angel? I only met you today and I feel happier than I have in months! Hughie will be so pleased, and he won't let them down. He'll work his socks off for his family if he's given a chance.'

'Gerry and his father are good employers, Holly. They make and repair agricultural machinery, and they both recognise and appreciate a hard worker when they see one. But tell Hugh to do it sooner rather than later; Gerry is expecting a call.'

Jackman showered and changed his clothes, then decided to have a quick lunch and tackle a few odd jobs he'd been putting off. So far, his precious day off had been spent trying to mend a stranger's life, not the broken catch on the garden gate or the puncture in Laura's electric bike tyre. As he took the makings of a sandwich from the fridge, he smiled to himself. Well, he hadn't excelled at being a handyman, but he felt he'd done rather well to be labelled a guardian angel.

CHAPTER TWO

The man and woman sat opposite each other at a long dining table. At one end were a tidy pile of reports, at the other, a stack of brightly coloured box files. They both had laptops in front of them and were staring at their respective screens, completely engrossed. From the concentration on their faces and the occasional flash of a satisfied smile, an observer could have been forgiven for believing that they were playing an absorbing computer game.

The man closed the folder beside his laptop, saved his work, sat back and stretched. 'Not a bad morning's work. I'm going to put the kettle on, Janet. Fancy a cuppa?'

'Not the kind that you make, thank you,' she replied, smiling. 'I'm sure tea shouldn't look so much like brown sauce.'

The man stood up. 'Well, I prefer that to those herbal infusions you like. They have a strong resemblance to urine.'

She laughed. 'Touché! But all the same, I'll have a camomile tea, please.' She returned to her screen and typed in a few words before saving and closing the file. She backed up her work onto a removable hard drive and slipped the small device into her Mulberry handbag.

They generally only worked in two-hour stretches, but today they'd run on for almost three. The task was important, and they both knew that rushing through it never worked. This had to be done properly, no shortcuts. It was exacting and tiring, but the reward was set to be substantial.

When John returned with the drinks, Janet pointed to a thick file bulging with papers. 'Another one for you. All transferred successfully.'

'Excellent.' He picked it up and sauntered over to the power shredder standing in the corner of the room. In no time at all he was emptying a mass of shreds into a thick compactor sack. 'I'll incinerate it as soon as next door take their washing in. We don't want any complaints, do we?'

Janet took the empty plastic folder ready for reuse. She peeled off the label that read *Dr Laura Archer* and wrote a new one. Her writing was clear and neat, each letter carefully considered — a little like her personality, really. This time the label read *Superintendent Ruth Crooke*.

* * *

It was a strange time at the Saltern-le-Fen police station. Having come through a period of turbulent action in the last big investigation, they had suddenly found themselves becalmed. They never used the Q-word — it never stayed quiet for long in the world of the CID — but it felt to DS Marie Evans as if they were in a kind of bubble, with no serious cases pending and all the paperwork from the last one signed off and sent up the ladder.

Her colleague, Gary Pritchard, kept saying they were in the eye of the storm. 'Any minute now,' he would mutter ominously, as if prophesying a new Armageddon, causing Marie to ball up a sheet of paper and lob it at him, calling him a pessimistic old sod.

'You just wait, Marie Evans! Not long now and we'll be back in at the deep end, I guarantee it.' Gary looked smug. 'Wanna take a little bet on it?'

'I'll pass this time, Gary, thank you.' She pulled a face. 'I know exactly what this place can be like, but right now,

I'm enjoying the luxury of having lunch breaks and getting home on time.'

'Oh my! That was the kiss of death, if ever I heard it. Bet you we have a murder by nightfall now you've said that.'

Marie shook her head in exasperation, but nothing was going to dispel her good mood. For the first time in a very long while, she was happy. In fact, it didn't get much better than this. She was in a job she loved, with a boss she'd walk over hot coals for, surrounded by the best team ever, and to top it all, she had a partner.

Trying not to get too soppy, Marie allowed her thoughts to dwell on her new lover. Both detectives, albeit at different stations, they hadn't been sure if the relationship would work out. Their decision to take it slowly had paid off. The best thing about it was that they understood and appreciated what was involved in being a dedicated police officer, and that there were times when your relationship had to take second place to the job.

'Marie? Gary? Have you two got a minute?'

Jackman was beckoning from his office door.

'Several actually, boss,' she said with a grin. 'For once.' She stood up and followed Gary.

Once inside, Jackman closed the door and they sat down. 'Don't worry, this is nothing serious — well, actually, it's nothing official at all. I just want to pick your brains.'

Marie looked at him with interest. 'Fire away, boss.'

'Remember the Smith case? Jim Smith from the house called Solace in Amberley Fen?'

They both nodded. 'I certainly do,' Marie said. 'Killed his wife, tragic affair. It wasn't even a proper case, was it? He admitted to it and was diagnosed with some psychiatric disorder.' She frowned at Jackman. 'Why? Has that one reared its head again? Did we miss something?'

'No, no, nothing like that, Marie,' said Jackman. 'And it's not even that case I'm interested in. Can either of you recall anything else that happened in that same house, many years before Smith bought it?'

Marie pulled a face. 'Oh yes. I seem to recall the papers jumping straight onto that old story as soon as it was made known that Eleanor Smith had been murdered there. Some Victorian Gothic tale involving several deaths, I think? Not that I can remember any details.'

'That one passed me by, I'm afraid,' said Gary. 'I was still at Harlan Marsh when the Smith case occurred. As I recall, it never made much impact. The husband coughed to the killing, so that was that. The old case means nothing to me.'

'Okay, well, in between the minor cases that you are handling at present, would you two fancy doing a spot of trawling through the internet for me? I want whatever you can dig up on the history of that house.'

'No problem, boss,' Marie said, 'but can I ask why?'

He shrugged. 'I guess I'm not used to having spare time on my hands, so I've embarked on a small crusade. I've heard that some of us Fenlanders have been less than charitable to a family of incomers, and I think, as a gesture of goodwill on behalf of the Fenland Constabulary, it would be nice to make some small reparation.'

'Sounds good to me. Any details, boss?' asked Gary hopefully.

'Get me that history and I'll fill you in. No rush, and don't let your own cases slip. Just when you can, okay?' He glanced at his watch. 'Ah, I need to be upstairs in five minutes. Ruth Crooke wants to see me. So, if you are all right with that, my friends, I'll see you later.'

Marie and Gary returned to their desks via the vending machine and sat drinking coffee while Marie told Gary what she remembered about the more recent murder at Solace House — the one the press had made such a meal out of.

'Sounds like a journalist's dream come true,' said Gary. 'A second murder in a house already known to have been a crime scene. Juicy stuff. Bet they really went to town on that.'

'I recall someone saying most of it was garbage. The papers blew it out of all proportion. Frankly, I had a lot

15

going on at that time and I didn't take too much notice.' She now wished she had paid more attention. 'Actually, I'll be interested to see what the true story was.' She grinned at him. 'My desk is pretty clear, how about you?'

'Nothing pressing, that's for sure. Shall we start now?' He grinned back at her. 'I do love a creepy Victorian murder.'

'Okay, Sherlock, let's see what we can find.'

* * *

Superintendent Ruth Crooke seemed deep in thought, but then she usually looked that way. She didn't smile readily, even at Jackman, who was one of her favourite officers.

'Ah, Rowan, come in and sit down.' Ruth indicated to a chair. 'Boring, I know, but I've just been to a meeting at Headquarters. Frankly, it was same old, same old until we broke for coffee and I met up with Superintendent Ashley Carpenter. Do you remember her at all?'

Jackman nodded. 'Impressive lady. She went after the Friary Fen Killer back in 2012, didn't she? Got injured but still caught him.'

'That's her. She was a DI back then and one of the best officers I've ever worked with. We go back a long way, and I trust her judgement implicitly. She's the superintendent over at Locksford now, further up the county, and she had a rather odd story to tell me.' Ruth leaned back in her chair. 'Well, they recently arrested a man on suspicion of abducting a schoolboy. Although they soon realised he wasn't the man they were looking for, he acted strangely, being much more agitated than his brief arrest warranted. When it was brought to Ashley's attention, she immediately remembered coming across someone with the same name many years before in connection with a murder, one that was never solved.' She looked at him. 'The Shelley Harcourt murder?'

'Oh yes,' Jackman said. 'The teenager who went off one evening to meet some friends for a girls' night out and never made it to the venue. She was found in a churchyard by an off-duty paramedic, I think. It was particularly gruesome, wasn't it?'

'That's the one. A twenty-year-old case which, strangely, was just about to be reviewed for the umpteenth time because of advances in DNA technology. Ashley decided to lean as heavily as she dared on this man, to see if he would say more than he did originally. Even though he was clearly edgy, he said nothing new, so she let him go. Then, in an unexpected turn of events, a couple of days later he rang her and told her he had had enough of protecting someone who cared little for him and that he was prepared to come in and talk to her. Her people are working that case right now and, if this man is kosher, it's looking as if Shelley's family might finally get the answers they've been praying for after all these years. However, it was something else this man said that she thought I would be interested in.'

Jackman heard an unusual note of excitement in Ruth's voice.

'At around the same time as Shelley was found, there was another shocking discovery made, not far from here, on a remote farm at Birch Drove.'

Jackman knew the one she was talking about. It was way before his time but had gone down in the annals of Saltern's history as one of the weirdest unsolved cases the county had ever seen.

'I see from your expression that you know what I'm talking about,' said Ruth with a wry smile. 'And who knows, Rowan, you and your team could be the ones to finally solve it. Ashley's man intimated that, should his cooperation be taken into consideration, he might also have information as to who the victim was and, possibly, more details that could point them to the killer. He denied any involvement and couldn't say if the two cases were actually connected, but he had heard some very interesting pieces of information and was prepared to talk about them. Ashley said she'd go and talk to him but he said he wasn't at home at present. He promised to go to Locksford police station at ten o'clock on Monday morning. They checked his home address and found it to be correct. His neighbour said he had gone off in his car the night before and she hadn't seen him since. She said this wasn't unusual, he regularly visited an old friend and sometimes stayed over for a day or so.' Her eyes were still bright. 'Ashley thought he knew something at the time, but could never pin anything on him. She believes that what he has to tell them could be crucial to solving both cases.' She looked at him, an unspoken question on her lips. 'So . . . ?'

'I'll brief the team, shall I, Ruth?'

'You do that, Rowan,' she said. 'And let's win Saltern-le-Fen some brownie points, okay?'

* * *

'Chuffin' hell, Jackman. What is this? National Nostalgia Day?' Marie laughed. 'First we have the bloody Victorians, now you want us to revisit a twenty-year-old unsolved murder.'

'Well, at least that's one case I *do* know about,' said Gary. 'In fact, everyone does.'

'I'm not sure the younger detectives will know too much,' commented Jackman. 'I'll wait for the others to get here before I give everyone the background.'

'So we are really going to tackle a cold case?' asked Marie, wondering about the logistics of solving a two-decade-old crime.

'Oh yes. A change is as good as a rest, as they say. It'll be interesting and not quite as risky as our last few investigations. This one should be more "cerebral," if you know what I mean. Lots of research, going over old reports and running new tests, so hopefully a little less physical than of late.'

'And a bucketful of kudos should we solve it, no doubt,' added Gary enthusiastically.

'Absolutely,' said Jackman. 'Our revered leader, Superintendent Ruth Crooke, is counting on us. Get a satisfactory conclusion on this one and we'll shoot up the league tables.'

'One thing's for sure, it will make headlines all over the world,' said Gary, sounding slightly overawed. 'It's one of the twenty strangest unsolved murders in the UK.'

'Then let's hope the intel that could be coming our way is correct,' murmured Jackman. 'And in case it's a crock of shit, as our Max would say, don't start practising your best smile for the cameras just yet, Gazza.' He glanced at the wall clock. 'Did the others say how long they'd be, Marie?'

'Half an hour tops, boss. Max and Charlie are out getting statements in connection with the thefts from those High Street shops, Robbie's down in IT getting his phone checked out, and of course, Kevin Stoner is on leave this week.'

'Okay, well, come and get me when they're all here. Meanwhile, clean off the whiteboard and put up the heading "The Birch Drove Farm Killer." Here we go again, guys!'

'Told you so,' said Gary triumphantly, nudging Marie. 'A new case before nightfall.'

'New? You are joking, Gary Pritchard. It's positively archaic!'

'It's still a murder and it's all ours.'

Back in his office, Jackman found himself staring out of the window. Try as he might, he couldn't keep his mind from wandering to that gloomy house and the effect it had had on him. He wanted to be fully committed to their latest case — Gary had been right, it would make the nationals if they finally solved that strange and gruesome mystery, as well as giving closure to any remaining relatives, so why wasn't he excited and firing on all cylinders?

A knock on his door brought him back to the here and now.

Marie came in and laid some printouts on his desk. 'Gary and I thought you might like these to take home for your bedtime reading. They're only a very quick Google search on your 'orrible Victorian murders, but never fear, we'll dig deeper as and when this new case allows. There's too much sensationalist crap surrounding it, boss — we could do with finding some historian who might be able to provide factual evidence of what really happened, not all this "Tales from the Crypt" stuff that has grown up around it.'

'Ah, thanks, Marie. I appreciate that. Are the others back yet?'

'Charlie and Max have just arrived and Robbie's on his way up from IT. We're more or less ready whenever you are.' She smiled at him. 'Cold cases can be tricky, but if this potential witness — or maybe he's a suspect — does know something and is willing to talk, that could really kick-start the whole thing.' The smile widened. 'I'm looking forward to it.'

'Yeah, me too.' He hoped he sounded convincing, although from the quizzical look Marie gave him, he thought he might have failed. 'I'll be out in a few moments. Tell the team to grab some coffees and I'll give you all a briefing on the original case.'

She stopped at the door. 'I know you of old, Jackman. Say if I'm wrong, but I have a feeling you'd just got your head around helping out your "wronged" family when someone dumps this huge case in your lap. You're scared you'll let them down, right?'

'Bang on, you Welsh witch!' He sighed. 'I'm afraid my "crusade" will have to be an off-duty one. I know where my priorities lie.'

'Well, if it helps, you can count Gary and me in for a bit of off-duty research. The little we have dug up is pretty hair-raising and we've both said we'd like to find the truth of the story.' She frowned. 'I'm guessing your family of incomers have bought Solace and are less than thrilled with their purchase?'

'You can say that again.' Jackman shook his head. 'They're desperate to get out, Marie, after only six months. And they aren't a couple of superstitious wimps, I assure you. The estate agent dutifully told them about the Smith murder but seems to have omitted the main reason for that house having such a reputation. At the moment, they believe that all the scaremongering by some of the locals is just Chinese whispers, old wives' tales that came about because of a murder having taken place there. Someone at some point is going to have to tell them a whole lot more.'

'They'll be very lucky to get a new buyer for a place like that,' said Marie grimly. 'Most people wouldn't even consider living in a house where a murder has been committed.'

'And they sunk all they had into buying Solace.'

Marie groaned. 'That's seriously bad news. Then, basically, they are stuffed.'

Jackman straightened up. 'Looks that way. But right now, we have a very different case to attend to. Lead on, Marie. I have a nasty tale to tell my children!'

He took his place in front of the big whiteboard in the CID room. Along the top were the words "*Unknown Female,*" and beneath that, "*The Birch Drove Farm Murder.*" Before he began, he added the date when the girl's body had been found.

He turned back to the eager faces. 'It was twenty-one years ago, on a cold December night. Sounds almost Dickensian, doesn't it? Okay, well, this is an old mystery, but it's new territory for us as a team. We've never dealt with a cold case like this one before, and certainly not one with such a high profile. These investigations are notoriously difficult to solve. The nearest we've come is unearthing background histories to current investigations and we've done those very well, so I have high hopes that we'll nail this one once and for all.'

He stared at the name on the board, memories of newspaper articles beginning to drift back to him. He looked around at his team, who, from their expressions, appeared to be recalling them too.

'We have one major advantage over all the other detectives who have been tasked with revisiting this case over the years. Although it could turn out to be a false trail, we now have the name of a man who professes to know who the victim was and, just possibly — because he referred to protecting someone else — he might also know who is responsible for her death.'

'Sounds too good to be true, boss,' said Max. 'We aren't usually that lucky.'

Jackman grunted. 'Very true, Max. Frankly, I'll only believe it when we are clapping the cuffs on. But let's not be too pessimistic — the super is convinced that the man in question really does know something about it. The question is, is he trying to shift the blame from himself to another party, or has he truly carried a dreadful burden all these years?'

'So when do we get to see this man for ourselves, boss?' asked Gary, an enthusiastic glint in his eye.

Jackman pulled a face. 'He has volunteered to go to Locksford nick on Monday morning. When Superintendent Ashley has spoken to him regarding her own cold case and ascertained the veracity of his information, she has promised to let us talk to him about Birch Drove Farm. I'll keep you all updated as to how this goes, as soon as I know myself.'

'As long as he doesn't get cold feet and bugger off,' murmured Max.

'That's always a possibility, of course, but then he'd have Ashley Carpenter tearing the county apart to find him. She's certain something has happened recently concerning someone he knows who is connected to Shelley Harcourt's death and he's had enough of carrying a secret that's too dark to live with.'

'Carpenter is a real terrier,' laughed Robbie. 'I've been following her career from way back and I wouldn't want her on my tail!'

'Agreed,' said Jackman. 'Now, while we wait with bated breath until this guy starts to actually talk, I've requested that the case notes and whatever is in the evidence store be shipped here so you, my friends, will have plenty of time to acquaint yourselves with the truth of the matter, and not what the newspapers decided would make a good story.' He paused. 'One thing I do know is that it was a ritual killing which, thankfully, is very rare in these parts.'

'Is it true that they never found her head?' asked Charlie Button in a rather hushed tone.

Jackman nodded. 'Afraid so. Which naturally added to the difficulties of identifying the body.'

'Apart from that dreadful case of the boy they called Adam — the one whose torso was discovered in the Thames back in 2001 — I know nothing about ritual murder, sir,' Marie said.

'I doubt you are alone in that, Marie,' he replied. 'I can tell you a little, but we need to do some homework prior to talking to our informant, whose name, by the way, is Martin Bennington.' Jackman had been interested in anthropology at university and now endeavoured to dredge up a few facts from a lecture he had found particularly interesting.

'As far as I can recall, all ritualistic murders — killings that are basically human sacrifice, although anthropologists believe there *is* a difference — have their basis in religion.' He held up a hand. 'But, please, don't start thinking in terms of the Church. I'm talking about personal belief systems, which may be very sinister indeed. However, they all have the aim of providing some sort of benefit to the person or persons who do the killing.'

'What, like way back, when the ancients sacrificed the eldest child to the gods in order to win a battle, or something like that?' asked Robbie.

'Exactly. And some drank the blood of the sacrificed child to give them extended life.' He pulled a face. 'In ancient times, the practice was linked with cannibalism.' He turned to Marie. 'You mentioned Adam, the boy — well, the torso — pulled from the Thames. It is thought that he was brought from Nigeria specifically to be ritually killed and that the level of expertise used to dismember him meant that it was executed by a priest or magician who would have had to be brought in just to carry out the ritual. However, it is believed that our girl, who has always been referred to as Angel, was murdered by a cult. She could have been a member, or just some unfortunate who was taken as a sacrifice. We will only know that if we manage to achieve a successful result — which so many other detectives failed to do over the years.'

'But they didn't have Mr Bennington, did they?' said Marie. 'If a cult was involved, he might have been a member, which is why he knows so much. Plus, Superintendent Ashley is one smart woman. She wouldn't have given us this information if she didn't believe there was a chance of advancing the case further.'

Jackman agreed. 'And one more thing. Although I don't know exactly what Bennington said when he rang Superintendent Carpenter, Ruth Crooke suggested he might have mentioned something that had never been made known outside the original police investigation.'

'Looking good, then,' said Gary, clearly relishing this particular inquiry. His expression became serious. 'Can you tell us the basics of what happened to this Angel?'

Jackman glanced down at the notes he had made from the old files. 'Birch Drove Farm had been empty for about three months. The old boy who had farmed there for most of his life had died suddenly and, as he had never married and had no children, it went to probate. One of his neighbours kept an unofficial eye on the place and made several calls to the police after seeing a group of people, whom he believed to be squatters, hanging around the old farmhouse. Then one evening, his daughter was returning home after visiting a friend and saw a light in one of the barns. Her father, a man named Arthur Leech, drove out there with his two sons. The place was deserted. The intruders most likely had seen the daughter's headlights and left. They checked the barn and made a horrific discovery — the headless body of a young woman.'

Marie grunted. 'Not what they were expecting to find.'

'They were all very badly affected by what they saw, Marie. They might have been a tough farming family, fully prepared to take on trouble if they found it, but to find a mutilated body, well . . . as soon as all the old reports arrive, pay careful attention to what the Home Office pathologist at the time had to say about the victim. There were some post-mortem disfigurements to the arms, legs and torso by way of cuts into the skin forming a cross-like mark or symbol. This mark had never been seen anywhere else, so it was assumed it must be specific to a particular cult.' He took a marker and drew the symbol on the board. 'It's not exact, but it was something like this.' His sketch showed an inverted cross with a diagonal line through it and a double wavy line beneath. When he had first seen this design, it had reminded him of something, but he couldn't think what. They were probably right. It was just the mark of the cult that killed her.

'Has that symbol ever cropped up, either before or since, boss?' asked Max. 'In another case?'

'No. Apparently the last team that worked the case ran a computer comparison check and it's never reappeared. It seems to be a one-off.'

'So how are we going to tackle this, sir?' asked Marie.

'We'll read through the files thoroughly while we wait for Bennington. Then, when we get the chance, we interview him and ascertain if we are dealing with a reliable source or a flake. Then we'll take it from there and either act upon his information, or hand him back to Carpenter, who will probably bang him up for wasting police time.'

'And if his info isn't viable, boss?' asked Gary. 'Do we still proceed to look at the case again?'

'We do. It was almost time for another review anyway.' Jackman shrugged. 'It wouldn't have come to us as a matter of course, but we have no major enquiries at present, so why not us? Fresh eyes and all that.' He looked at them thoughtfully. 'I've got a good feeling about this, Mr Bennington or not. I think we are going to solve this old puzzle. We'll treat it like any new case we are presented with, and we won't be influenced by what past teams have assumed or surmised. Let's give Angel her real name back, shall we?'

There was a murmur of assent. From their chatter as they filed out, he got the feeling that the team were looking forward to a new sort of challenge.

CHAPTER THREE

While they ate their evening meal, Jackman told Laura about his visit to the house called Solace, and about meeting its owner, Holly Stewart.

'That poor family!' said Laura, taking a sip from her glass of wine. 'It just proves that when you embark on a massive undertaking like buying a house, you need to look really carefully at what you're purchasing.' She raised an eyebrow. 'What do they say? "If it seems too good to be true, it probably is."'

Jackman laid down his knife and fork. 'Oh, I agree and, to be honest, I'm not sure how they missed picking up on the oppressive atmosphere of the place. Even when you enter the drive it's as if a dark and threatening cloud hangs around the place.' He gave a little laugh. 'And that's coming from a hard-nosed, pragmatic copper. Imagine what it'd feel like if I were some fanciful, impressionable soul.'

Laura sat back, nursing her glass thoughtfully. 'Actually, you are very sensitive, Jackman. Oh, I know a lot of your perceptiveness comes from your skills as a police officer, but even so, I've always noticed that you have the ability to sense what people are feeling, and you are very responsive to situations.'

'Like you said, it comes with the territory. If a copper doesn't have a good nose for things like that, they won't make a very successful detective.' He stood up and collected their empty plates. 'No, the pervading mood of that house is quite real. I defy anyone not to feel it.' He rinsed the plates and put them in the dishwasher. 'But I do understand where Holly was coming from. They were desperate to get their kids away from a rough area. Both her and her husband came from decent homes and, reading between the lines, I think they believed they'd let their family down and wanted to make up for it. As Holly said, it was a whole lot of house for the money, and the rural location is idyllic.'

Laura topped up their glasses. 'From what you say, it sounds to me as if being surrounded by tall, dark, half-dead conifers isn't helping the atmosphere any. A house can be completely transformed when you let the light in.'

Jackman sat down again. 'Absolutely! That job was first on their list but when Hugh's job offer fell through, it went on hold. Jesus, Laura, Solace gives dreary new meaning to the word.'

'I'd like to visit it, sweetheart. It'd be interesting to see if I get the same vibes as you.'

'Then come with me to the stables at the weekend. They're following me to my mother's place. You can get a look at it then.' He paused. 'Oh, and Mum is ringing tonight about dinner on Friday. She was checking my father's engagements diary first, but she was delighted with the idea and said to say thank you.'

Laura laughed. 'It's usually the women that have these busy social lives after retirement — not in your father's case.'

'That man has more committees, meetings and old boy networks than anyone I know.' Jackman rolled his eyes. 'And since they've assumed a more hands-on role with my nephews after their mother's death, he's now involved with their schooling. He's now a school governor and has joined a whole lot of boards and groups looking at finance and education.' He shook his head. 'And believe it or not, all this is nothing compared with what he used to do. We never saw him when we were boys. I still don't know how my mother managed to juggle James and me *and* a workaholic, high-powered businessman of a husband.'

'It comes as part of the job description of being a wife and mother.' Laura looked smug. 'Women tend to multitask considerably better than men. It's a proven fact.'

He picked up his glass. 'In which case, I'd better try to emulate my mother, as I have a possibly very taxing investigation opening and I'm also determined to find a way to help our struggling family of incomers. Which brings me to this little lot.' He went to the kitchen worktop and picked up the folder of notes Marie and Gary had printed off. 'I'd like you to cast your eyes over them too, if you would. It's "The Macabre History of Solace" — well, according to the popular press and the media. Are you up for it?'

She took another drink of her wine. 'So, gruesome murders it is. I guess my relaxing evening with my feet up can wait.'

* * *

In Sutterthorpe Village, another couple were just finishing their supper too.

'Well, Ralph, I have to compliment you. That was delicious! What you can do with an aubergine defies belief.'

Ralph Enderby laughed. 'You ain't seen nothing yet. Just wait till tomorrow. You'll be amazed at what I can do with a sweet potato.'

'The mind boggles. I have to say that these days off you're having are suiting me a treat.' Marie looked at her empty plate and sighed. 'And I really appreciate you cooking me my meals.'

She and Ralph had settled into a very comfortable relationship, something that a year or so ago she would have found inconceivable. Convinced she would never get over the death of her husband, Marie had been resigned to dedicating the rest of her life to work. Then she met Ralph, and now she was happier than she had ever been in her life. They had kept their own homes and migrated between the two, but rarely spent a night away from one another unless they were called upon to do a night shift, which was rare for a detective sergeant these days.

'I'm just delighted that you seem to enjoy my vegetarian food, Marie.' He looked at her earnestly. 'But I won't object if you want to eat meat, you know. It's up to you.'

'It's funny really,' she said. 'Remember me telling you that Gary lodged here before he got his own place in the village? Well, he loved good old home cooking, so I was regularly presented with puddings and pies and every imaginable variety of stew. It was the other end of the spectrum.'

'But you enjoyed it?'

'I loved it!' exclaimed Marie. 'I'm beginning to think I just love food, in all its forms.'

'Well, you're a joy to cook for — clean plate every time. Now, fancy a walk around the village after we've cleared up?'

Marie smiled. 'And drop into the Cross Keys for a swift half?'

'Perfect.'

They cleared away quickly. 'Let's take the path across the fields that brings us out to the old cemetery, then we can walk down Ferryman's Lane to the pub,' suggested Ralph.

They walked together regularly now if the weather was good, and sometimes even if it wasn't. And they talked. They talked as if they'd each been marooned on a desert island, starved of companionship. Marie sensed that Ralph, too, felt as if an important part of his life had been missing. Now they were both catching up on lost lonely years.

'Jackman's got himself a private crusade,' she said as they left her cul-de-sac behind. She went on to tell Ralph about Solace and its unhappy occupants.

'That's not like us Yellerbellies at all,' said Ralph with a frown. 'People usually chat to incomers and make them feel welcome. Most times you can't shut 'em up.'

'Jackman reckoned they were making the kids' lives a misery. He's even taking them to his mother's stables at the weekend for a few hours with the horses.'

They headed down the long field track that led around to the other side of the village. On either side were fields of sweet-smelling clover, which was much nicer than the usual crop of cabbages, or even worse, onions. She had asked one of the local farmers why they planted clover and had been treated to a lecture in organic field management. So now she knew that it was "planted to improve the soil quality and provide nitrogen and reduce the need for artificial fertilizers," a fact she took every available opportunity to regale the uninitiated with. She breathed in the scented air. 'Gary and I have volunteered to do a bit of unofficial research into the history of the place, going back to the old murders, not the more recent one.'

'I might be able to help you with that — I've got two more days off after the weekend,' Ralph said. 'Someone who really knows the subject is my old crewmate's wife. She's a local historian who wrote a book about historical murders that took place in the Fenlands. I heard her give a talk once, and she managed to make it sound really interesting and exciting.'

Marie slipped her arm through his. 'There you go. My mum always says it's not what you know, but who. That would be brilliant! We're bound to get bogged down in this cold case that's come up, so I'd love your help. It's really got to Jackman for some reason. I've never seen him so distracted by something so apparently insignificant.'

'No problem. In fact it sounds like fun, plus I've been meaning to look up my old mate for ages. He's older than me and retired last year, but you know how it is, you mean to keep in touch and then life gets in the way. It's time I contacted him.'

They walked on in companionable silence for a while. Marie still couldn't believe how easily they got along. Okay, they weren't much alike in their interests — Ralph would never get on a bike, and for her part she couldn't see herself spending days standing in a river patiently waiting for a fish to take the bait. But somehow their differences made it all the nicer.

'Would you buy a house that had seen something awful happen in it?' asked Ralph suddenly.

'No way!' she said at once. 'I've been into houses that had terrible atmospheres but I still can't make out why. I mean, I've never believed in ghosts and spirits and all that.' She looked at him. 'What about you?'

'Me? No. I like peace and quiet when I finish a day's work. My surroundings have to relax me.' He looked across the vast stretch of fields and sighed appreciatively. 'Just like this. I wouldn't want to go home to a place that gave me even more stress than I get at work, thank you.'

'My mother has the idea that houses retain something of the people who lived in them, and that they absorb sadness just as much as happiness.' Marie always spoke of her wonderful mother, Rhiannon, with a smile on her face. She had never left her native Wales where she seemed to provide support for her entire village. If it wasn't running a local food bank, it was collecting and delivering prescriptions, or making up herbal remedies. It was saving abandoned dogs and cats, offering bereavement counselling and generally providing a haven for all those who needed help. 'I kind of see where she's coming from. I mean, as a pragmatic copper everything tells me that an inanimate object constructed out of concrete, bricks, wood and other solid materials *cannot* have a memory, yet I still can't explain those bad vibes you get when you walk through some doors.'

Ralph pointed to where a small gaggle of red-legged partridges were running frenetically to and fro across the path ahead of them before disappearing into the clover. 'I think you've inherited a little more of your mother's intuition than you give yourself credit for, Marie Evans. Everyone says you have the most accurate "copper's nose" in the Fenland constabulary. I'm sure some of it comes from Rhiannon and is

not just a skill honed through constant dealings with villains.'
He gave her an amused smile. 'My own view is that those
bad vibes come from within us, not the building itself. Half
the time we already know the dark history of the place, and
our imaginations take over and give flesh to the bones of a
past occurrence. Even so, whether our uncomfortable feeling derives from the stories we've heard or something more
supernatural, it's real to us and I wouldn't want to live in
that place.'

'Oh dear,' Marie said. 'It's all getting a bit heavy for a
pleasant summer evening stroll, isn't it? I know I brought it
up, but can we talk about something else now?'

Ralph took her hand and squeezed it. 'Okay. Like what?'

'How about clover?'

'What? Again?'

Marie cuffed him smartly and, laughing, they strolled on
beneath the big Fenland sky.

* * *

Janet walked from room to room, securing the windows for
the coming night. It was too warm to close them but always
risky to leave a window open, and Janet never took risks. She
left nothing to chance — every move was calculated, and
she liked it that way. It was why she lived alone. Her only
attempt at a live-in relationship had been a disaster and she
never repeated the attempt. Being in control was paramount,
which included keeping other people out of your living space.
To Janet, the pluses of living alone outweighed the minuses
a hundredfold. She could tolerate John, but only for short
periods of time, and only because he was as single-minded
as her. They made a good working team. John had a fine
mind. His strengths included intelligence-gathering in the
field while hers lay in the careful collation and interpretation
of the information he provided.

Satisfied that all was secure, Janet retired to her bedroom. It was her favourite room, and as in the rest of the

house, everything had its place. Janet preferred to think of her obsession with order as a manifestation of her organised mind rather than OCD. She didn't have rituals, but she did need everything to be just so. *Neat as a pin*, her mother used to say of the young Janet's pristine childhood playroom. Her motto was *attention to detail in all things*.

She folded down the tapestry bedcover, checking that the corners met perfectly, pulled back the duvet and smoothed the crisply ironed bottom sheet. In the en-suite, she washed, placed all of her day clothes into the linen basket and put on her nightclothes. It had been a good day; much had been achieved. She was sure their client would be delighted with what they had managed to pull together during the past month. She would be meeting him next week to deliver a progress report and was confident that he'd be impressed by their commitment and thoroughness.

Janet lay in bed thinking how fortuitous it had been for her and her client to meet when they did. She had been looking for a new challenge and he had needed a very specific job done. With John's involvement, it had come together perfectly. Of course, there was the added benefit of the very generous financial reward.

Janet closed her eyes and turned her thoughts to what she might do with all the money once her job was completed. What a wonderful way to end the day.

* * *

Jackman lay awake and listened to Laura's steady breathing. He wasn't sure exactly what he had expected to learn from Marie and Gary's initial internet search, but it certainly wasn't what he and Laura had read about earlier.

No one had ever been brought to justice, so he wondered how much of it was the truth and how much hearsay. It seemed that Solace had been a Victorian baby farm. It had started as a legitimate business, providing a place to which women could take their infants, to be cared for in exchange for a small fee. A forerunner to the orphanage, where most of the children were illegitimate and were left there until homes could be found for them. It wasn't uncommon for married middle-class parents to place their youngest children with a wet nurse in a pleasant rural setting during their infant and toddler years. It was considered healthier for a young child than life in the polluted cities. Jackman recalled that Jane Austen had been brought up in just such a setting. However, the practice was horribly open to abuse by unscrupulous women. Babies were taken in, money changed hands and the infants died soon afterwards. What had been a successful business benefiting both mother and wet nurse spawned a new breed of money-grabbing murderesses.

Had that really happened in Amberley Fen? Or had an honest woman been accused of murder? Had bodies really been found in the grounds of Solace? Or was it gossip?

Jackman closed his eyes and tried to sleep, but now his mind was racing. Holly and Hugh had two young children. How would they take the news that the home they already regretted buying had possibly been the site of multiple infant deaths? And now he had the seed sown in his brain, he wanted to know the whole truth. Were there more bodies buried in the grounds at Solace? The timing couldn't have been worse. He should be fully engaged with the Birch Drove Farm killing, but instead, he was mulling over a haunting and worrying about a family he hardly knew.

He moved closer to Laura and tried to think only of the peacefully sleeping woman and the love he felt for her.

CHAPTER FOUR

Jackman awoke to a bright, sunny Saturday morning. He was looking forward to meeting the rest of Holly Stewart's family, and glad that Laura was going with him. Her opinion, not just on the house but on the husband and children as well, would be invaluable. Added to that, he had Saturday and Sunday free, he and Marie having decided to take the weekend off so that on Monday morning they'd be raring to go with the Birch Drove Farm murder. It would be nice to have Laura with him for two whole days.

Taking his casual clothes from the wardrobe, he smiled to himself. He had been pleasantly surprised that both his mother and father had made it to dinner the night before. They had spent a delightful evening together, enjoying some rare family downtime. He had been delighted to hear from his mother that his nephews, Ryan and Miles, would also be at the stables when the Stewart children arrived. It might help to break the ice, she said, especially as Ryan seemed to be following in Jackman's footsteps where riding was concerned.

He dressed, his thoughts still on the day before. Friday had passed quickly. The team had spent hours excavating every piece of information they could get on the Birch Drove Farm murder and carefully checking all the new findings from the last review. It reminded Jackman of cramming for his exams. The case had never been closed — it was a murder, after all, and a particularly nasty one. But over the course of time it had been scaled right down to a biannual appraisal in case new advances in forensic science could shed more light on it. Jackman had stipulated that they work the investigation as they would any other new murder inquiry and not take any previous conclusions as gospel. It was easy to make assumptions and they needed to review the whole background history before starting anew. He just hoped Bennington would be as good as his word and go to Locksford police station on Monday morning as he had promised. It was fifty-fifty to his mind — if the guilt really was too much to take any longer, Bennington would be there, but if his fear of repercussions took over during the weekend, he could well change his mind. Either way, on Monday morning their case would begin in earnest. Now it was time to start making amends for the less-than-friendly treatment the locals had given the Stewart family.

He took a quick glance in the mirror.

'Will I do?' Laura stood behind him and he looked at her reflection beside his. She was wearing blue jeans, a navy and white Breton T-shirt and navy trainers. It could not have been a simpler outfit but on Laura it was breathtaking.

'Darling, you look amazing. What? No riding breeches?' He laughed, knowing what she would say.

She gave him a reproving look in the mirror. 'Horses are lovely to look at and I'm happy handing out the odd carrot, but ride one? I think not. It's a long way down to a very hard ground, thank you.'

'You'd love it! There's nothing like it. Mum has a wonderful armchair pony called Petal who would no more throw you off than fly in the air.' Jackman was ever hopeful that one day he'd see his Laura on horseback.

'I'm sure she's an absolute angel, but I'm staying on terra firma. Now, let's go and see this sinister old house.'

As they drove, Laura commented that they weren't far from Jackman's brother's home. 'I'm surprised no one has mentioned this infamous house before, considering that James lives just up the road. Reading that stuff last night made me realise that I've never even heard of it, or the murder you dealt with.'

'Probably because there was no manhunt and no major media fest over it. It was very low-key as murders go — an undiagnosed mental health problem. The husband believed voices were telling him to kill his wife — and you've heard the rest. It was a sad, sad case with no scandal or dirty dealings for the press to have a field day over.'

'But it did occur in a house with a dark history,' she said.

'Oh, they mentioned that all right, but there was no real mileage in the old story, and it petered out very quickly.' Jackman accelerated out of Cartoft village and onto the main road. 'It's just that the locals have long memories for the bad stuff.'

'Like the old haunted house mysteries. Every town has one and each generation adds a bit more to it, until the origins are lost.' Laura stared out of the car window. 'I do hope the local kids haven't filled these children's minds with too many nightmares. They're very young to be fed horror stories. It can have a lasting effect.'

Jackman felt the same way. Poor kids. In his case, he had been one of the lucky few who had enjoyed a good childhood. Not perfect, maybe; money and a loving mother didn't compensate for absolutely everything — like a distant father who gave his son little or no affection. His privileged upbringing had had its darker moments too. Old fears sometimes never left you, they remained with you into adulthood like an unwanted and ever-present shadow. 'You're right, Laura. I suppose you could say that we've both spent our working lives dealing with the aftermath of childhood trauma and abuse.'

'Indeed we have.' She sighed, then patted his leg and brightened. 'But let's not assume the worst. Kids can be remarkably resilient.'

Ten minutes later, they were slowing down and turning into the driveway of Solace House.

'Ah,' said Laura, pulling a face. 'Not the most attractive and welcoming facade I've ever seen.'

Jackman experienced the same dampening of the spirits that had assailed him on every previous visit. The first occasion had been as SIO of a serious crime, a murder, so he would naturally have been in a negative frame of mind. Then there was the austere design of the house itself. He was pretty sure that anyone with the slightest inkling about feng shui would run screaming from the place. The blank, imposing, windowless wall that faced the driveway seemed to loom higher than three floors. Worst of all were the conifers. Unkempt and straggly and far too tall, they formed a prison wall around Solace, keeping the occupants in and the sunlight out. Jackman suddenly felt easier. That's all it was — a completely understandable reaction to a badly designed house and an overgrown garden. And if Hugh got the welder's job that Jackman had organised for him, they'd be able to get rid of those damned trees and let some welcome light in.

'I think your new little friends are rather looking forward to their excursion.'

Laura's voice brought him back to the present and the sight of Holly with a youngster on either side of her, all three gazing excitedly in their direction.

They got out of the car and went across to where the little trio waited. Jackman introduced Laura and spoke to the children. 'No Hugh?'

Holly beamed. 'He's working! Thanks to you, DI Jackman, he officially starts next week but he's helping them out this morning with a rush order. He said to tell you he's more than grateful and he'll thank you in person as soon as he can.'

Jackman glowed with satisfaction and Laura gave his arm a little squeeze. He smiled at the children. 'Okay, let's go and take a look at those horses, shall we?'

Jackman's mother had pulled out all the stops for the Stewart children, and in no time at all they were having the time of their lives. Both found the courage to get in the saddle and receive their first riding lesson, courtesy of Debbie

Quinton and Jackman's very grown-up fourteen-year-old nephew, Ryan. Harriet had been right about the boy. Ryan was completely comfortable with the horses and had a natural rapport with them that Jackman, with no little pride, recognised as belonging to a true horseman.

Having seen that the children were in safe hands, Holly and Laura took themselves off to Harriet's kitchen to have a cup of tea, while Jackman went to check on the new horse. He wasn't going to ride today but wanted to spend some time with the gelding. He had felt an affinity with the animal from the moment his mother brought it home. The horse had some weaknesses, but Jackman could see its potential and wanted to spend as much time as he could with it, so as to build a strong and trusting relationship. He had a good feeling about Hector and from the way the horse responded to him, he was pretty sure they were going to make a brilliant team — just as long as Jackman's day job allowed him enough time to make that happen.

Harriet had organised a whole programme of activities for the children that included a picnic lunch, so Jackman and Laura were happy to leave the Stewarts to enjoy themselves and head back to Mill Corner. He kissed his mother and thanked her for making such an effort on his behalf, but she waved his thanks away, saying it was a pleasure. They were lovely children, and it was a delight to see them interact so well with the people and animals they met.

They were walking back to the car when Jackman heard Miles call out to them. Miles was a little younger than Ryan and of a completely different temperament to his brother. He loved the horses too, especially their own pony, Sherbet, but he was not a confident rider. Instead, he preferred to care for them, and was most happy spending hours grooming and talking to them. Above all, he liked to draw them. Miles was very creative, a talent he had inherited from his mother. Jackman knew that so long as Miles was around, his late mother Sarah would be with them too. They were alike in so many ways it was uncanny.

Miles showed them his sketch pad. Jackman took it, then passed it to Laura. The boy's pencil drawing of the horse's head was exceptionally good.

'It's Hector, Uncle Rowan. He's your favourite, isn't he?'

'I can see it,' said Jackman. 'You've captured him perfectly, even that wicked gleam in his eye. You really are very talented, young man. I do hope your art teacher appreciates you.'

'He's great, Uncle. He says I should aim for the University of the Arts in London, but I think I'm too young to know what I want to do when I leave school.' Sarah's sweet smile lit up his face. 'I might like to just have this as my special hobby and do something important, like you.'

Jackman could no more envisage this sensitive and creative lad as a copper than he could see him as a nightclub bouncer. 'Whatever you do, Miles, never lose that talent, that's really important too. And don't forget, very few people can draw and paint like you can, so don't waste the gift you've been given.'

'I agree,' said Laura, ruffling the boy's hair. 'But whatever you decide, make sure you do something that makes you happy.'

Miles nodded sagely. 'I will. And you can keep the sketch if you want, Uncle.'

'I'd love it! Thank you, Miles. It will have pride of place at Mill Corner.'

Looking pleased, Miles tore it from the sketch pad. But as he handed it over, the smile faded. 'Actually, I came to tell you something I think you should know. It's about Aaron and Poppy.'

Jackman tensed. 'Ye-es?'

'They're frightened of something.'

Jackman exhaled. 'I know, Miles. Some of the other children at school are being unkind to them because of where they live and probably because they're outsiders.'

'Oh, it's not that, although it does upset them. They've seen someone in their garden at night. But, please,' he looked imploringly from one to the other of them, 'don't say I told you. They told Ryan and me about being bullied, but later I overheard little Poppy talking to her brother about "the man who comes at night," and from the way she spoke, sort of whispery and frightened, I thought I should tell you. You being a detective and all that.'

'How did that conversation come up, Miles? What did Poppy say exactly?' he asked, a chill creeping into his bones.

'They had just met a couple of the little ponies. Poppy loved them, she said she wished she could live in a place like this all the time. Then I heard her whisper to Aaron that the man who came into the garden at night wouldn't find them here. Aaron shushed her and said she wasn't to talk about it, it would make things worse and anyway, no one would believe them.' Miles gazed up at him seriously. 'You won't tell on me, will you?'

Jackman didn't like the sound of this at all. 'Of course not. You did the right thing by letting me know what you'd heard. But Miles? If you hear anything else, will you ring me? And maybe keep it to yourself for a bit?'

'Will do. Better get back. Glad you like the picture. Bye, Uncle. Bye, Laura.'

Jackman stared after him as he hurried off. 'Now what was that all about, do you think?'

Laura frowned. 'I don't know, but I don't think you can afford to write it off as childish imagination.'

He had no intention of doing that, but how to find out more?

They drove out of the stables, both deep in thought.

'What did you make of Holly, Laura?' he asked, slowing down at the flashing red lights on a level crossing.

'Nice woman. Friendly, well-balanced but desperately confused about the situation they've found themselves in with their white elephant of a property.' Laura gave Jackman a loving look. 'But so relieved about Hugh finding work. She's really appreciative of what you, a complete stranger, did for them. She was quite emotional about it, darling.'

'I'm just glad I thought of Gerry and his dad's farming equipment business — and that it seems to have paid off,' he said.

'Today will be a real lift for Holly and the kids. You do the Good Samaritan bit rather well, you know.' Her smile faded. 'Now we just need to figure out if something odd is going on at Solace during the hours of darkness, or whether their contemporaries' scary stories have caused Aaron and Poppy to start imagining things. Not that I think the latter is likely. The children are obviously suffering from the name-calling the other pupils in their school are subjecting them to but basically, they are well-adjusted, nicely mannered children. Aaron seems a very sensible little boy and Poppy is obviously a loving child. You could see that from the way she was with the animals.'

Jackman agreed. 'Holly told me the children weren't sleeping well and were having bad dreams. Now I'm starting to wonder if they really have seen something in the garden at night, and it's not the house or its reputation that's worrying them but a real intruder.'

'It's possible,' said Laura. 'But why would anyone want to wander round that place at night? It's not exactly the perfect spot for a midnight assignation and it's rather obvious that the new owners aren't rolling in money and don't have anything of value to steal.'

'You'd be surprised why people sneak into other people's gardens at night, believe me. I've heard every excuse under the sun.' He gave a little laugh. 'And one or two of them are definitely not suitable for your ears.'

'Rowan! I'm a psychologist. I've heard as many, if not more, bizarre and downright gross reasons for doing things as you have. But you have to admit that Solace is a pretty grim spot to wander about in, not to mention quite overgrown and hence dangerous in the dark.'

'Oh, I agree all right. I just don't want my mind to go into overdrive. The thought of someone watching a home with two young children in it gives me the screamers.'

'So do you have an idea of how to approach it without scaring anyone?' Laura asked.

Jackman watched as a single-carriage train from Spalding rumbled past in front of them. The gates rose up, the lights turned green and he pulled away onto the Cartoft road. 'Actually, I think I do. It'll be a downright lie, but you have to be devious sometimes, and it is in a good cause. And if I think there really is something to be concerned about, I'll get someone out there straightaway.'

'Okay, so what is this lie?'

'I'll call over there tomorrow and tell them that we've had reports of people seeing someone hanging around in their gardens. It's probably a vagrant looking for an open shed to doss down in for the night but even so, we don't want him frightening anyone, especially children. It might work and get either Aaron or Poppy to tell us what they saw.' He wasn't certain it would, but it was the best excuse he could come up with. 'If nothing else, I can watch the kids' reaction to what I say and gauge where we go from there.'

'Sounds good to me.' She paused. 'I wonder why they didn't go straight to their parents if they saw someone hanging around?'

'Holly said they don't always confide everything. It's possibly made worse because of the stress that Hugh and Holly are under at present. The kids would know.' He chuckled. 'I know who they'd have told.'

'Who?'

'Rory.'

'Rory?' she exclaimed. 'They know Professor Wilkinson?'

'No. Rory the Labrador. Apparently, they tell him everything.'

'Oh, right! He'll be a great help, I don't think!' Laura laughed. 'Suppose I went with you tomorrow? I'd love to get a look at the family dynamic when Hugh is there as well.' Laura sounded thoughtful. 'Some of what Holly said to me when we were having our cuppa did betray a deep concern

43

about the way that they were dealing with the situation. I got the feeling she could badly do with a friend and confidante.'

'Perfect,' said Jackman. 'There's no better listener than you, so please, do go with me. I'd welcome your opinion.'

They drove on a little further, then Laura said, 'This is not a criticism, sweetheart, but don't you think you're getting a bit too caught up with the Stewarts' problems? You are almost as keyed up over this as you are with a major investigation, and knowing how demanding your job can be, I don't want to see you overstressed.'

Jackman wasn't sure how to answer. He knew it looked as if he had his priorities screwed up, but Holly's plight had hit a nerve. Maybe it wasn't quite rational, but he was determined not to walk away until he'd done all he could to help her, and that was that. Now there was the chance that there was another very real threat to them, in the form of some stranger watching the house. That was *not* acceptable. Then he felt Laura squeeze his leg.

'It's all right, you don't need to explain. Your silence speaks volumes. And I'll help you all I can.'

He heaved a sigh of relief. 'Thank you. And I love you.'

* * *

Marie had spent the morning cleaning and tidying her house. She always kept it nice, but she found herself making much more of an effort since Ralph had been staying over, and almost enjoying the chores. She had just finished and was making herself a welcome mug of tea when her phone rang.

'Are you up for a trip out this afternoon, Marie?' Ralph asked.

'Depends where to. Paris? Amsterdam? Saltern-le-Fen Flea Market?'

'Would Peterborough tempt you? If I threw in a slap-up meal in the city?' He sounded hopeful.

'Doesn't have the romantic, Continental air of the other three destinations, with the possible exception of the flea market, but the meal does rather clinch the deal. So yes.'

'Excellent! I'll pick you up in half an hour.'

'Whoa! What are we doing? Where exactly are we going? What should I wear?' Her questions tumbled out.

Ralph laughed. 'Oh, I forgot to mention, we are visiting my old crewmate Ollie and his wife, Anna. They're really laid back, so don't wear anything special, mainly because they have four dogs.'

'So what about my slap-up meal, Detective Enderby? Jeans with a liberal coating of dog-dribble are not generally the accepted attire for dining out.' Marie tried to sound miffed but couldn't hide the amusement in her voice.

'Relax! The place I have in mind will welcome us with open arms, even covered in a layer of dog hair. Now, go and get ready. I'll see you in thirty.'

She hung up, laughing. She was starting to embrace this new, spontaneous way of life. After living alone for so long, other than the brief period when Gary had lodged with her, it felt so refreshing, almost intoxicating.

As Marie pulled what she hoped would be suitable clothes from the wardrobe, she found herself remembering how differently she had felt when their nemesis, the psychotic killer, Alistair Ashcroft, had been stalking them. Whereas now her main emotion was happiness, back then it had been fear. It had clung to them all, from dawn until dusk and all through the long and frightening nights. She now wondered if that old terror would ever really leave her, no matter how happy she was. After all, Ashcroft was securely incarcerated with no chance of parole, but how do you lock up a memory? There were nights when she still woke in a cold sweat, the leg that had been damaged in her encounter with the killer throbbing mercilessly, and her whole body shaking with distress. It wasn't Ashcroft that caused those moments of terror — he was gone — but his ghost still drifted back to haunt her sleep.

She pushed these thoughts away and pulled out a light purple crew-neck sweater and a pair of chino trousers. 'Let's hope this'll do,' she murmured to herself. 'And if it doesn't, well, tough!'

An hour later, they pulled up outside a character cottage — quite different from the property Marie had been expecting to find.

'This is gorgeous!' she exclaimed. 'When you said Peterborough I imagined the busy city, not this lovely village on the outskirts.' She looked at Ralph. 'Are you sure this belongs to a retired copper? Surely this is a listed building? It must have cost a fortune.'

'Let's just say Ollie made a good marriage. This was Anna's family home. Her parents moved abroad when they retired and left the cottage to Anna. She's quite a bit younger than Ollie and works from home, writing magazine articles on Fenland mysteries, and she still gives talks and lectures.'

Ollie Baker, his face a creased mass of smiles, was already standing at the front door and waving to them. Around his feet milled a cluster of dogs, not one of which was a breed Marie recognised.

'Meet the Misfits!' he called out. 'Rescue mutts, every one of them, not a purebred in the lot!' As soon as they got within touching distance, he clasped Ralph in an enormous hug. 'Been far too long, mate, far too long. My fault, I know, I've got time on my hands and you haven't, but I'm going to blame you anyway.' Then he let Ralph go and turned to Marie with an approving look. 'Well, whatever this jammy little git ever did to discover you, I can't begin to guess. But good for him.' He pumped her hand up and down. 'Come on inside.'

This effusive man didn't gel at all with the kind of policeman that Ralph had described. Was this really the tough guy who had once single-handedly floored and arrested two armed drug dealers? The shrewd and athletic copper who had, in the course of a drugs raid, sprinted over 200 metres in record time, catching the ringleader before he made off in his Porsche?

Ralph was nodding at her. His look said it was indeed the same man.

'Come and meet my wife, Marie. It's too nice to sit indoors, let's go out into the garden.' Ollie was striding ahead of them through the cottage, his faithful troop at his ankles.

Anna was a petite woman with soft brown hair cut in an attractive layered bob. She had an intelligent face with sharp hazel eyes and a ready smile. She gave off an air of utter contentment, as of a person completely happy with her lot in life. And why not indeed? Her home was one of the most delightful properties Marie had ever visited, a clever blend of modern decor and beautifully restored original features. Marie suddenly had a picture of Ralph and herself living in such a home. The thought brought her up short. The idea of a future shared with another person hadn't featured in her life since the death of Bill, her husband.

Anna was asking if they'd like tea or coffee.

'Tea, please, Anna. White, no sugar,' she said, coming back to the present. 'Sorry. I was just admiring your lovely home.'

'Even I,' said Anna, 'never take it for granted. We've been extraordinarily lucky to find ourselves here and there's not a day goes by when I don't give thanks for it.'

They sat around a circular table in front of a well-stocked garden pond. While Hugh and Ollie chatted and laughed, Anna turned to Marie. 'Now, I guess you haven't just come for a spot of mess-room banter, have you? I believe you're after the truth about evil Sally Pinket of Solace House.'

Marie nodded. 'We'd appreciate anything you can tell us. The media coverage of the time is awash with supposition and hype, with very little truth in it as far as we can see.'

'You can blame that on a man called Rupert Larkham.' Anna looked fierce. 'A pompous, self-opinionated hack or, as he called himself, "a feature-writer extraordinaire," who filled the journals of his time with sensationalist *crap*.' The word sounded almost shocking coming from this gentle little woman. She sat back in her chair. 'That awful man was obsessed with female murderers and made it his job to expose and vilify every possible accused woman he could find. Guilty or innocent, it made no difference to Larkham, who understood the snowball theory very well. He formed an original idea about a woman, then concocted the twisted stories and built exaggerated, scandalous, situations to suit his depraved imagination, then set the ball rolling.' Anna grunted. 'As you can imagine, it gathered momentum until all truth had been totally obscured.'

'And you believe he got his teeth into this Sally Pinket?' asked Marie.

'I know he did! There is clear, documented evidence that he spent time in one of the local hostelries, plying the locals with drinks and regaling them with stories of what the "fairer sex" was capable of. Plus, he offered considerable remuneration for information about Solace House and its occupants.' Anna raised a knowing eyebrow at Marie.

'Ah.' Marie understood exactly where this was going. 'So our impoverished locals, struggling to get bread on their tables, suddenly remembered all manner of dark goings-on.'

'Exactly. They invented any story they could think of . . . "Me little brother saw 'er buryin' a babe out on t' Fen. She gave 'im this terrible stare that turned 'im to stone, 'e didn't speak for a week, Mr Larkham, and that's the God's honest truth as I stand 'ere before yer!'

Marie smiled at the thick Lincolnshire accent. 'I can imagine. And all that rubbish found its way into the papers.'

'And books and magazines, and even TV programmes and websites.' Anna shook her head. 'Sadly, that's the dross you'll have found yourself wading through.' She stood up abruptly. 'However, Marie, all is not lost. Back in a mo.'

While they waited, Ollie said, 'So, I see you have chanced upon my wife's *bête noire*, the woman-hating bigot, Mr Rupert Larkham.'

'Anna really doesn't like him, does she?' Ralph said. 'Sorry if we inadvertently lit the blue touchpaper.'

Ollie laughed. 'Oh, don't worry, we get a flare-up once a month at least. And she enjoys slagging him off to anyone who'll listen.'

'I heard that, husband dearest,' said Anna, emerging from the house carrying a red plastic folder. 'Come on, even you have to admit he was a total arsehole.'

'Forgive my wife. She used to speak *so* nicely before she met me.'

'Oh shut up, Ollie.' Anna handed the folder to Marie, grinning. 'While that great oaf sitting next to you was stationed at Fenchester, we lived in one of the outlying villages and one of our neighbours was a descendant of Sally Pinket. When he heard I was studying local Fenland history and particularly murders, he said I might like to know something of the real truth about his great-great-grandmother.' She beamed at Marie. 'I almost bit his hand off!'

'Then it became a major investigation, believe me!' Ollie added. 'She spent every hour following up on this old guy's stories.' He gave a loud guffaw. 'I thought CID were thorough but hellfire, they had nothing on my Anna!'

Anna pointed to the folder. 'That's the basics — well, the notes for a chapter in a book I intend to write about all those who were maligned and discredited by Larkham. A few were indeed guilty, but dear Rupert turned every instance into a single act of violence, a dreadful, vengeful, premeditated murder committed by a wicked woman who, according to him, had probably slain a dozen others in her vile past.' She threw up her hands. 'The man was a malignant liar and a disgrace to journalism, and it's time someone outed him.'

'Even if he has been dead a hundred years,' added Ollie. 'But like me, my wife believes in justice, and I, for one, will toast the author on publication day!' He lifted his mug of tea in salute.

Marie skimmed through the contents of the folder. 'Oh my! I see what Ollie means about attention to detail. You should come and work with DI Jackman, Anna.' She stared at the woman in admiration. 'This is seriously impressive. Are you okay with my taking these with me? I'll get them copied and return the originals as soon as.'

'Keep them for as long as you need, Marie. I've got everything on the computer. There's no rush for the hard copy for a while yet, I'm now on another case that he butchered.'

Marie did not miss the glint in her eyes. This was going to be one book that she would definitely read if it ever made it onto the bookstore shelves. Mind you, she could be visiting Anna in prison if it turned out to be as damning as it sounded — and if the man had descendants who took umbrage at her revelations.

They stayed for another hour, followed by a guided tour of the house and garden. Marie fell in love with the cottage, and with one of the dogs, a lanky little terrier mixture called Flo who glued herself to Marie's side. To her delight, they were both invited back the following weekend for a barbeque in the garden.

It was only just over three miles to the city centre, and in ten minutes they were parking up in the multi-storey car park.

'I thought a walk around the cathedral would be nice, then we'll go to the restaurant I told you about. What do you say?' suggested Ralph.

'Lead on,' said Marie, slipping her arm through his. 'I've been here often, but never actually been inside the cathedral, so that's perfect. Let's forget we are police officers for the rest of the day and just be tourists.'

'Fine with me, but I bet you a tenner you mention something about work before I do.' He squeezed her hand.

'Mmm, you could be right there . . . anyway, right now, I'm just Marie, not DS Evans, and I'm about to look around an amazing Norman cathedral, one of the finest in England, I'm told, founded as a monastic community as far back as 654 AD.'

'Hell, Marie, that's impressive. I never had you down as a history buff.'

'You are standing next to a big colourful tourist poster, Ralph. I was reading from that. Now, let's go and grab some culture.' She smiled angelically. 'And then we can eat.'

* * *

As the evening drew in, John went up to what had been intended to be the spare bedroom, but since no one ever stayed with him it served as his office. It was pretty spartan as home offices went, but that suited him. He had never been a fan of ornaments or nick-nacks, and certainly not of photos in frames, so other than regimented lines of books, office equipment and stationery, the desks were clear.

He turned on his computer. John was the only one who ever used it, but he was meticulous about online security. In his line of business, you couldn't afford to take any chances.

He slipped an SD card from his camera and pushed it into the slot on the tower. In moments he was uploading photographs into a folder marked with the date. He watched as they flashed up on the screen. They were good, but the ones he took always were. He had an exceptionally expensive top-of-the-range camera and a bloody good eye. As soon as they had finished loading, he went through them picture by picture and scrutinised them carefully. Some he deleted but most he kept. This was a good cache. Janet would be pleased with these, and if she was, he was pretty sure their client would be too. That was what this was all about. The client came first, always.

He pulled his thoughts back to the images. He took his time and went through them once more, then, when he was satisfied, he saved the folder, and renamed it Detective Constable Robbie Melton.

CHAPTER FIVE

At ten thirty on Sunday morning, Marie and Ralph were sitting at Marie's dining table poring over the strange history of Sally Pinket.

'Three words sum this lot up,' said Marie, sweeping a hand over the papers. 'Painstakingly detailed research. Anna Baker is something else!'

'I guess if you are going to write a book that decimates someone's character, even if they are dead and buried a century ago, you need to be absolutely sure of what you say.' Ralph picked up another printout. 'But there's no denying her thoroughness. I thought that when I heard her speak. She had the answer to every question, every time.'

'Well, we've only skimmed the surface. Anna said there are a lot of areas to be taken further, if that's humanly possible after so long, but I get the feeling she is absolutely right about this hack, Larkham, muddying the waters and perhaps condemning Sally Pinket to a life of misery she didn't deserve.' She stared at all the papers. 'This will take a while to copy, so I'll get the office manager to run it all off tomorrow at work. And I'll get him to do three of each. We can have a set and I'll give one to Gary, as he's also well into getting this straightened out for Jackman.'

Before Ralph could answer, Marie's mobile rang.

'Marie, I'm sorry to ring you on your day off, but . . .'

Marie heard the edge of concern in Jackman's voice. 'Boss? What's occurring?'

'Oh, nothing work-related,' he gave a short joyless laugh, 'so don't panic. It's just that I've been speaking to Holly Stewart on the phone. When the family were with us at the stables yesterday, one of my nephews overheard the youngest Stewart child whisper something to her brother about a man being in their garden at night. Miles was anxious that we didn't land him in it for telling tales, so Laura and I decided to call over to Solace today. We were going to use the excuse of reports of a vagrant trying to get into people's sheds and tell them that we didn't want the children frightened if he tried it in their garden.'

Marie listened, wondering what was coming next.

'It turns out that after a lovely day, the kids were on a high, and she and Hugh were over the moon about him getting back to work. All seemed great for once. That was until Poppy woke everyone at three in the morning, screaming her head off over a nightmare. Apparently, she was terrified of a man who lived in the trees and only came out at night.' Jackman paused. 'Laura and I are going over there now, but I wondered if you would ring in and have a quiet word with someone in uniform, off the record, as to whether there really have been any sightings of Peeping Toms or Travellers, or anyone really, reported in that area?'

'Of course I will,' she said. 'Shall I ring you directly I have anything?'

'If you would, Marie. You might well come up empty-handed, but if this isn't the child's imagination, it's very worrying.'

'I'll say! That place has had enough dark deeds going on without any more. I'll do it now.' She hung up and told Ralph what Jackman had said.

'Makes you wonder whether one of the locals is trying to scare this new family off for some reason, doesn't it?' he mused. 'Sounds like scare tactics to me. That's if the kid isn't just freaked out by all the horror stories she's been fed by the school bullies.'

'But no one wants that old place,' said Marie. 'It's not the sort of area that a property developer would be interested in, and the house itself would certainly never feature on the cover of *House Beautiful*.' She sighed, perplexed. 'Want to make another cuppa while I have a word with an old mate at the station?'

While Ralph made the drinks, Marie rang PC Simon Laker. He was a good copper and they got on well. She knew she could trust him not to let her unofficial enquiry go any further.

'To be honest, there's nothing specific been reported from the Amberley Fen area over the last few months, certainly no Travellers, DS Evans, although . . .' He paused. 'There's just one thing that I do recall. It could well be a fool's errand, mind, but there's an old couple called Spriggs who live out there, quite close to that house where the murder took place a while back. They have a bungalow down Stone Lane with a tiny parcel of land attached. I think it's called East Winds. They've been a bit of a thorn in our sides over the years, think they own the area. They don't like strangers in their lane, even if they're just walking a dog, and they do have a bee in their bonnets about incomers "taking over". The old girl, Eva Spriggs, has rung in several times over the last few months reporting a car regularly travelling past the end of the lane late at night. She believed it was a poacher setting night traps. As I said, DS Evans, it's probably nothing, but that's it, I'm afraid.'

Marie thanked him. 'Keep your ears open for me?'

'Will do, Sarge. Enjoy your day off.'

Marie rang Jackman straight away. He answered from his car. 'I've heard about the Spriggs from my brother,' he said, after she had relayed Simon's information. 'Real mardy faces, never crack a smile and they're always complaining about something or another, but . . .'

'Exactly. But. We have an aversion to coincidences, don't we, sir? And as the Stewarts have lived there for almost six months and Eva Spriggs never saw this poacher of hers prior to that—'

'We can't ignore it. Maybe we'll call in at the Spriggs place after we've had a chat with the Stewarts. Thanks, Marie, sorry to intrude on your day.'

Marie laughed. 'Well, as we are both up to our armpits with the "Life and Times of Sally Pinket of Solace House," it's not exactly unconnected.' She wished him good luck with the mardy-faced Mrs Spriggs and rang off.

Ralph placed a mug of tea down next to her. 'I had to laugh at you and that little dog Flo yesterday. She really took a shine to you, didn't she?'

Marie smiled. 'I almost felt like dog-napping her, she was so sweet.'

'Would you like a dog, if you could have one?' he asked.

'If I wasn't working, oh yes. A dog and a cat — perfect.'

'I've always fancied two dogs myself, but as you say, it's not an option with this job when there's no one at home when you're working. Shame, really. Seeing all those rescue dogs yesterday and how contented they were, well . . . one day, maybe?'

Once again, Marie found herself contemplating a future — a future with Ralph. 'Yes, one day.'

* * *

Jackman liked Hugh Stewart immediately. Hugh struck him as a solid, dependable man. He grasped Jackman's hand in the warmest of greetings. 'My wife said you were our guardian angel, DI Jackman, and after I met your friend Gerry and his father, I started to believe her. I like people who are forthright like old man Keane. You know exactly where you stand with them. I know I could work with them and do a good job.'

Holly went off to make drinks and Hugh took them into the lounge.

The room was as gloomy as ever, any view from the window obscured by the ubiquitous leylandii. Hugh put the lights on and this cheered it up somewhat, but not much.

'The children are watching a cartoon upstairs,' said Holly from the doorway. 'They'll be down soon, I'm sure, especially if they know you're here.' She rolled her eyes. 'They said that yesterday was the best day ever, and we've heard about nothing but horses and ponies ever since. Now Poppy has her heart set on a pony of her own.'

'My mother said they're free to ride Sherbet anytime they like, Holly. Ryan has moved up to a bigger mount now and Miles prefers to groom rather than ride them, so that little Connemara pony is almost always available.' He accepted a mug of tea. 'And before you say anything, my mother expects no payment from you.'

Hugh looked dubious. 'We can't accept that, DI Jackman. We're very grateful for yesterday, but we'll pay our way if we go back.'

Jackman recognised a proud man when he saw one. 'I understand, but Mother said it would really be doing her a favour. That little pony needs stimulation and right now the people who go there either have their own horses or ride the bigger ones.' He sipped his tea. 'Anyway, I'll leave that with you. The offer is there, and she means it.'

Jackman then gave the couple his story about the possible vagrant, adding, 'So when you told me about Poppy's nightmare, Laura and I wondered if she might really have seen something.'

Anxiety clouded the parents' faces.

'She'd have said something to us, surely?' questioned Holly.

'Not necessarily,' said Laura. 'Children often remain silent about things that upset them, for a host of reasons. She'd be aware that there's a lot of stress in the family at present, so she could have been afraid of making things worse, or simply worried that she wouldn't be believed.' She smiled gently at Holly. 'Kids also tend to blame themselves if things go wrong in their families. They ask, "Is it something I've done that makes Mummy or Daddy so sad, or so angry? It must be my fault."'

Hugh bit on the side of a nail. 'Poppy's been quite withdrawn lately, hasn't she, Holly? We put it down to the kids on the school bus, but I suppose it could be something else. But an intruder in the garden? I've not been sleeping well myself and I swear that if there was someone around, I'd have seen him.'

'Look, if it's all right with you, I'm going to ask two favours,' Jackman said. 'Do you think you could bring the children down and tell them what we've told you about the tramp in people's gardens and ask them if they might have seen anyone they didn't know around here? Don't frighten them, keep it casual and, whatever you do, if they do admit to seeing someone, don't make them feel guilty because they've kept it from you. Then, before we go, I'd like to do a check of your garden, if that's okay?'

Holly went to fetch the children. Jackman heard her calling up the stairs, and a few moments later, Aaron and Poppy rushed into the room, all smiles and still enthusing about their stables adventure. He let them chatter on for a while then looked to Hugh and Holly.

Holly took the lead. 'Kids, listen up for a moment. DI Jackman needs our help with something.'

Two curious pairs of eyes fastened their gaze on him. Hugh spoke first. 'The police have had calls from people who live around here. They're complaining about someone, probably a tramp, hanging around in their gardens. It's nothing to be frightened about, he's probably just looking for an unlocked shed, somewhere dry to spend the night. They want us to keep a lookout for him.'

'Or if you think you might have seen him already, do tell DI Jackman,' Holly added. 'It would help him a lot. Mummy and Daddy would be very proud of you if you were brave enough to help the police.'

The furtive glance that the little girl gave her brother and his almost imperceptible shake of the head told Jackman all he wanted to know. So what now?

All their previous animation had left the children. 'We've never seen anyone, have we, Poppy?' stated Aaron flatly. 'Sorry.'

Poppy remained silent.

'Okay, well, if you do see anyone, you know who to call.' He smiled at them and handed them each one of his cards. 'My private mobile number is on there and it's special, okay? You can talk to me without anyone else knowing. And I don't give them to just anyone, so look after them.'

The children took the cards and stared at them. 'Can we go and watch the end of our film, please?' asked Aaron.

Holly nodded. 'Off you go.'

When they heard the upstairs door close, Hugh said, 'Oh my God! They've seen someone, haven't they?'

Jackman and Laura nodded. 'I'm afraid so,' Jackman said. 'I guess it's time we checked that garden.'

* * *

Laura couldn't help laughing as they drove away from the Spriggs's place. 'Oh my! Not exactly jolly, friendly country folk, are they?'

'You can say that again! They live in their own little world out there. It's like a small country with borders that "frim folk" cross at their peril,' said Jackman, using the Fenland term for foreigners. 'But even though they had no idea what kind of car they've been seeing — other than that it was "a dirty old silver thing," it does seem suspicious.' He frowned. 'What worries me is the fact that it's always evening or night when it's seen, and there's nowhere to go in the direction it was heading other than Solace and a few more scattered properties. If we weren't starting on a time-consuming case tomorrow, I'd be tempted to come out here one night and follow him.'

'Yes, I can imagine,' Laura said. 'And the timing really does coincide with the Stewarts moving in.'

As they drove on towards home, Laura gave Jackman her impressions of the visit to Holly and Hugh. 'Despite their relief at Hugh having found work again thanks to you, that family is under enormous pressure. The air around them almost vibrates with it. I'm actually not a bit surprised that the children aren't talking about what they saw. Kids are very receptive to atmosphere and, even if they don't mean to, their mum and dad are giving off anxiety by the bucketload. It's difficult enough for children when their family ups sticks and moves to totally different surroundings, without finding themselves in hostile territory.' She stared out of the window across a wide drain, its greenish water edged with a bank of high reeds. 'Normally I'd have coaxed Poppy to talk rather than Aaron. She's the one most likely to open up, but,' Laura sighed, 'it would have distressed her further, which is not what this is all about.'

'I wish something more concrete had turned up during the walk around the garden,' Jackman said. 'The ground is disturbed in so many places it was pretty well impossible to see if anyone had been there or not. Rory the Labrador digs holes, Hugh admits to hacking down branches and trying to clear small areas before giving up, and wild animals and birds haunt the place. Even though I found no litter, no footprints other than Hugh's, and the garden is an overgrown shambles, still I was left with the distinct impression that someone had been there, staring up at the children's bedroom window.'

'I think that if we are to get that little girl to talk to us without disturbing her further, we should try at the stables. That seems to be her "safe place" at the moment. So, now school has broken up for the holidays, what if I ring Holly over the next day or so and tell her I have to go out to see your mother about something? I could suggest she meets me there with the children. It's probably the best time to do it — they're not at school, so that's one stressful situation out of the way for a while, and Poppy will be a bit more relaxed. Then I'll try out a bit of undercover psychology on her.'

'Great idea! I'll ring Mum later and let her know. I feel better knowing that you feel uneasy about what's going on at Solace too, and I'm not just being neurotic. I was starting to worry about my ability to read situations,' Jackman said.

Laura squeezed his arm. 'Darling, that grim old house and its occupants are giving off every bad vibe you could imagine. It would be easy to blame it on the fact that you know the place's terrible history, but there's something far more than that going on there.' She paused. 'The only thing I can think of is that someone doesn't want the Stewarts living in that house at all.'

Jackman grunted. 'Then the question is, why?'

Laura had no answer to that one.

* * *

Marie and Ralph decided that they had accumulated as much information as they could thanks to Ralph's friend Anna, and gathered it all together to return it to its folder.

'Let's grab some lunch and go for a drive, shall we?' Ralph said with a smile.

Marie narrowed her eyes. 'Fine with me. I'm all for a bit of lunch, but there's a look in your eyes that tells me I'm in for more than a scenic tour of the Fens.'

'Oh dear. Either I'm being far too transparent, or you are as psychic as Rhiannon.' He looked at her, still smiling. 'Actually, I want to see Solace for myself. Don't you?'

'I've seen it,' she said. 'The night Jim Smith strangled his wife. It's a right Addams Family house if ever I saw one. All it needed was Lurch the butler.'

'I want to see it even more now. So, what do you think?'

Marie shook her head. 'Ralph Enderby, how come you make saying no so difficult?'

'Do I really?' His face lit up. 'In that case I can think of a whole lot more questions I'd like to ask.'

'Well, you can forget those for now, sunshine. Let's concentrate on the old house, shall we?'

He jumped up. 'I'll go and get some lunch together.'

Marie smiled. She wasn't going to admit it to Ralph, but she rather wanted to get another look at the old place herself.

As she slipped the last batch of printouts into the folder, she saw a handwritten message on the last one. There was an asterisk either side of the sentence to draw her attention to the words, *"*See if you can follow up the name Ivy Pettifer in conjunction with the wet nursing organised by Sally Pinket of Solace House. She bothers me."*

And if she bothers you, Anna, then Ivy Pettifer bothers us too, thought Marie. 'Ralph?' she called out. 'After our scenic drive, I've just found our next challenge!'

A theatrical groan emanated from the kitchen.

* * *

Linda and Claire wandered slowly out of the village and onto the fen lane, chatting as they went. The afternoon was bright, and they were pleased to be getting some exercise. In their late sixties, they were pushing a shopping trolley, conspicuous in their orange high-vis vests and the bright red refuse sacks they carried along with grabbers. Linda had joined the Wombles, an organisation of volunteers helping to clean up Britain, the moment she heard about them. As was her wont, she roped in everyone she could, and now they had enough litter pickers to be able to extend their reach beyond the village itself and into the surrounding fen lanes.

'Why on earth is this stretch always worse than the others?' grumbled Claire. 'It only goes to Amberley Fen, and that's miles away.'

'Ah, but there's Lyttons Lane down here on the right, which connects directly to the Saltern road. The lazy sods who can't be bothered to go to the council tips to dump their rubbish see this as a great little place to jettison their junk.'

Fly tippers were a constant bugbear of Linda's. She loved to walk the fen lanes, especially at the beginning and end of the day, and finding this waste spoiled their beauty and made her blood boil. 'Last week I found two different models of vacuum cleaner, a fridge, a roll of underlay and an unopened tub of tile grout in one place alone.'

'Doesn't look too bad today,' commented Claire, deftly picking up a crushed plastic bottle with her grabber.

They walked on, debating which was the best farm shop to buy local produce. Linda was just extolling the virtues of the one on the Saltern–Greenborough road when she stopped, mid-sentence. 'Well, that's a first!' She pointed ahead to something protruding from the dyke that ran alongside the roadway.

'What on earth is it?' exclaimed Claire.

'I'd say it's something that needs reporting to the police as well as the council. It's a gaming machine!'

They stared at the twisted remains of a large slot machine decorated in brilliant colours to look like something from Las Vegas. The words "*Golden Millions*" spilled out from an open treasure chest. Protruding from the duckweed and reeds in the bottom of the ditch, it looked about as incongruous as it was possible to get.

Linda stood, hands on hips. 'I'm ringing this in right now.'

Angrily, she pulled out her mobile phone and found the number of the police station in her contact list. 'I could be wrong, Officer, but I think it's the one from the public house on the bridge over the river — the Lytton Arms. It's been ripped apart, so I reckon someone hit the jackpot in a rather unorthodox manner.' While she spoke, she saw Claire frowning, shaking her head and leaning forward down the bank to tug at a black plastic sack. Claire hauled the bag up onto the bank, gasped, let go of her grabber and jumped back.

'Hold on, Officer! Don't hang up!' Linda rushed to her friend's side.

They stood side by side, staring at the bag which, now gaping open, had slid back down to nestle beside the gaming machine. Close to the pull handle of the big old machine was a human arm. The fingers of the hand appeared to be reaching out to try their luck at Golden Millions.

Claire retched. Linda took a deep breath and spoke shakily to the police officer, still on the line. 'I think you should get out here straight away. This is more than just a robbery!'

CHAPTER SIX

After their whistle-stop tour of Amberley Fen and the house called Solace, Marie and Ralph drove home via a local bird reserve, where they had a long walk along the riverbank.

Marie had barely put the kettle on when her mobile rang. Before she even saw who the caller was, she knew it signalled the end of her relaxing day with Ralph. 'Okay, boss, this had better be good.'

'I'm not sure that's the right word, Marie.' Jackman sounded serious. 'I have to interrupt your day off, I'm afraid, and this time it really is police business.'

With an apologetic glance at Ralph, she said, 'Okay. Where and what?'

'Lyttonville Village, about two miles from Amberley Fen. I'm on Five Posts Lane, about a quarter of a mile outside the village itself. We have body parts dumped in the dyke.'

She groaned. 'Oh lovely, you've just made my day. On my way!'

Marie went across to Ralph, hugged him and didn't want to let go. She took a deep breath. 'I'm sorry.'

He took hold of her shoulders. 'Stop that right now! We agreed, didn't we? This is going to happen all the time, to both of us. You just take care, while I do that homework you set me — Ivy Pettifer.'

She kissed him and pulled on her leathers. 'I'll take the bike. I'll get back all the quicker that way.'

Two minutes later she was riding out of Sutterthorpe Village and heading towards the main road. She reckoned ten minutes on Tiger, her beloved bike, should see her on the outskirts of Lyttonville and, as she knew the shortcut down Lytton Lane, she'd be with Jackman in no time.

He was standing by his car and greeted her with a look that said it was even more serious than he had made out on the phone. A chill ran down her spine. 'So what have we got, boss?'

'Two ladies out litter picking found a nicked fruit machine dumped in the dyke, duly reported it to us then pulled a black plastic sack out of the water and it tore open.' He pulled a face. 'I don't think they were expecting to see a human arm sticking out.'

'Oh, poor women!'

'They only live a few minutes away in the village. They're neighbours, so I've sent them back to one of their houses with a uniformed police officer to make them a cup of tea and calm them down. We'll go and see them when we've finished here, but it's pretty clear what happened. Come and take a look.'

Marie accompanied him to where the uniforms had set up cordon tape.

'Forensics are on their way and believe me, we are going to need them,' Jackman said grimly.

'Call me Mystic Marie if you will, but there's something you've not told me, isn't there?'

'See for yourself.' He lifted up the tape. 'But don't go too close, we don't have any protective suits or shoe-protectors yet.'

'Not too close is fine by me,' muttered Marie. 'Viewing human body parts is a long way from my favourite part of this glorious job.'

She stopped short and stared down at the strange collection of articles in the ditch. It took only moments to see why

Jackman looked the way he did. The severed arm, which was the only limb completely visible protruding from the torn sack, had a familiar symbol cut into the flesh of the upper arm. It was identical to the one on their whiteboard back at the station — on the picture of the headless body of a teenage girl. The one they called Angel. Thoughts tumbled around in her head. The same symbol as a twenty-year-old ritualistic murder? And one that they were a day away from reopening? She exhaled loudly.

'You've reached the same point as me, I see,' Jackman said softly. 'This spells trouble, Marie, big time!'

'Never a truer word,' she whispered. All thoughts of returning home to Ralph and a peaceful end to their day vanished.

* * *

Jackman and Marie sat in his office and stared at each other across his leather-topped desk. It was one of several items acquired in secret from a local house clearance many years ago. These had been smuggled in under cover of darkness in order to make his place of work, where he spent most of his time, more inviting.

'It's a chicken-and-egg thing, isn't it?' said Marie. 'It will be a million to one that the arcade machine and the bag are connected. So did the thieves dump the stolen machine first? Or did the butcher dump his black bag of goodies first?'

Jackman shrugged. 'My guess is that the machine went in first and our butcher popped his sack in close to it, or . . .' He frowned. 'There was quite a bit of water in that dyke after heavy rainfall the night before last, so the bag could have gone in further along, drifted down and been caught in the machine.' That last supposition wasn't likely, though. There was no real flow on the dykes that edged the fields and the lanes, although the wind that cut mercilessly across these fields did push detritus along in front of it.

'So we wait for forensics.' Marie sat back in her chair. 'It was a woman's arm, wasn't it, Jackman?'

'From the slender hand, I'd say so,' he said. 'And going from the lack of serious discolouration, it can't have been there long. This was a recent dismemberment, and I could make out other limbs in the bag, but didn't disturb them. As you say, we desperately need forensics.'

'One of the two women who found the sack said she walks that way with her dog early every morning and makes a mental note of anything the Wombles can pick up later in the day. She said there was nothing on that stretch at all at around seven this morning.' Marie checked her notebook. 'So it happened between then and around two o'clock in the afternoon.'

'I've asked uniform to go house to house on the three routes into that spot — Five Posts Lane, Lyttons Lane and Lyttons End Road, the one that starts in Amberley Fen. I reckon there are no more than twelve dwellings of any kind on all three put together.' Jackman knew that area well. It was nothing but fields and more fields, with just a scattering of little homesteads dotted about. 'I've told them that their best bet will be Slate Farm. The farmer's old mother sits at the window for hours on end, watching the birds in their front garden and clocking passers-by. She helped us spot a vehicle that we were interested in a while back, when that gang was nicking diesel oil from the farm tanks. Do you remember?'

Marie smiled. 'You told her she'd make a damned good lookout and you might hire her next time something big was going down.'

Jackman remembered the old girl chuckling to herself at the thought. 'If anyone drove out here that she didn't recognise, I bet she'll have remembered it. Last time she even logged a car number plate using her birdwatching binoculars.'

They were both silent for a while until Marie said, 'One of us has to ask the question, even though neither of us will have an answer.'

'I know, Marie. Why now? Why now, after twenty years with nothing even vaguely similar to that killing and that symbol?'

'And is it the same killer, two decades on?' Marie said.

Jackman raised an eyebrow. 'It has been known. Serial killers have suddenly stopped killing and then, years later, something happens to trigger another killing spree.'

'As in something traumatic, I suppose?'

'Yes. In one case I read about a man who killed four women over a couple of months, then he abruptly stopped. The killings resumed some ten years later and when he was caught, it transpired that he had actually fallen in love and married, but his wife was killed in an RTC, after which he went off his head and killed three more.' There were other cases, too, mainly in the States or Europe. He had found the concept difficult to understand and had discussed it at some length with Laura.

'Okay,' said Marie thoughtfully. 'Let's assume it's the same killer. The Birch Drove Farm murder was believed to have been a ritual killing conducted by a cult, but as nothing has been seen or heard of them since, they must have disbanded.' She frowned. 'But if they still kept in touch, perhaps our killer heard about Martin Bennington being questioned by the police.' Her eyes lit up. 'He might not realise it was to do with a completely different matter, something Bennington wasn't even involved in. He could have thought his world was about to be blown apart, saw the red mist and killed again.'

Jackman considered the idea. 'You could be thinking along the right lines, Marie, especially regarding the killer. Or maybe other ex-members of the cult found out that Bennington had been taken to the police station and thought he was about to blow the whistle on them. What I don't understand is why they immediately killed again. I would have thought they'd have kept their heads well down, maybe even done a runner.'

'Yes, I see your point,' Marie said. 'If I had got away with murder, I'd have a contingency plan ready just in case the police ever came knocking on my door. Wouldn't you?'

'Oh, I certainly would. Plan B would be ready to roll the moment I caught the slightest whiff of uncertainty about my safety.'

For the next quarter of an hour they toyed with various suppositions. The one thing that linked them all was that someone knew about Martin Bennington and realised that the police were about to resume the old investigation.

Jackman was intensely frustrated at not being able to speak to Bennington. It would only be a matter of hours before they learned whether he'd turned up to the station or not, but there was information that maybe only Bennington had, and Jackman wanted it now. Then another thought crossed his mind. 'This new killing could mean that Bennington is in grave danger. It could have been a warning — *keep your mouth shut or you know what will happen.*'

Marie grunted. 'Or in another scenario, Bennington told someone he thought he could trust, or someone overheard him calling the police. Maybe that someone is desperate enough to simply have Bennington taken out before he can talk.'

'Possibly, although where does our new death come into it? Why kill someone else, in that case? Leave out the overheard phone call for a minute and think about Bennington being pulled in for questioning regarding an unrelated incident of which he was innocent. These things happen all the time. And he was let go again pretty quickly. I don't know why anyone would suspect that after being silent for twenty years, he would start talking about the two old cases, especially the Birch Drove Farm murder. So it doesn't quite follow.'

'Unless the two old cases are actually very closely connected, and the same killer carried out both murders, Shelley *and* Angel.' Marie looked at him. 'Didn't Shelley die in a creepy old cemetery?'

Jackman nodded.

'Well, if it was a satanic cult of some kind, wouldn't that be the perfect place to carry out a ritual murder?'

He thought about it. 'Yeah, maybe. The manner of death was different and there was no symbol on the body, but it was a very unpleasant and gruesome death. It is possible, I suppose, and they could have been disturbed before they cut the symbol into her arm.' He sat back. 'Bennington denied knowing of an actual connection when he phoned in, but maybe he wasn't ready to say too much at that time. We have to consider that, and, in the light of our suspicions, we need to talk to Superintendent Carpenter and find out what Bennington has told her that was never disclosed to the press. If we are on the right lines, there's a chance that Bennington will never be seen again.' Jackman thought for a moment, then picked up the phone. 'I'm ringing Ruth at home. She's friendly with Carpenter, I'll get her to have a word.'

Instead of being annoyed about the disruption to her Sunday, Ruth seemed almost pleased to have something to do. 'What you tell me about this latest dismemberment is very worrying indeed, Rowan, and I can see the connection between the two cold cases. I'll ring her immediately and get back to you.'

Marie went out for coffee, leaving Jackman alone with his thoughts, which were rather dark. They had more or less decided that the cult had disbanded, since there had been no more crimes that could be attributed to them, but was that necessarily the case? Their county was massive, it had countless lonely places, rivers and marshlands. He thought of the huge population of foreign workers, not all of whom were legal. How easy it would be to select a victim, carry them off, kill them, dispose of them and no one would ever be the wiser. So maybe the cult still existed, even if Bennington was no longer involved in it. Maybe it thrived, somewhere. Even somewhere close.

Jackman didn't like where this was going.

Just as Marie was setting down his coffee, his desk phone rang. Ruth sounded apprehensive. 'I've given Ashley Carpenter your mobile number, Rowan. She needs to talk to you personally. She agrees with you that Bennington is hot property, but I'll let her tell you about him herself. I'll see you tomorrow morning, first thing.'

Jackman hung up and almost instantly his mobile rang. He switched on loudspeaker with a glance at Marie, who looked as tense as he felt.

'Hello, Superintendent Carpenter. Thank you for calling.'

'DI Jackman, actually I was going to ring you tomorrow, but as Ruth has contacted me, it's all the better we talk now.'

Her voice was brisk, no-nonsense.

'It would seem that our chance pickup of Martin Bennington has set off something of a chain reaction, with repercussions both here and in your division. And Ruth tells me that you have another, probably connected case breaking right now?'

'Body parts, Superintendent. Dumped in a black sack in a watercourse. One arm has a distinctive mark on it, exactly the same as the one on the body at Birch Drove Farm, twenty years ago. There is no doubt about the connection, and if your man really knows something about it as he professes to, we are very concerned for his safety.'

'No more than I am, believe me,' she exclaimed. 'I decided earlier today that I'm not prepared to hang around until Monday when he might or might not turn up. I've already started a hunt for him. And in light of what you've just told me, I'm bloody glad I did.'

'Any luck so far, ma'am?' Jackman asked, already guessing the answer.

'Sweet sod all, Inspector. What makes it more difficult is the fact that we are trying to keep it low key. We don't want the wrong people alerted to our interest in him. Our cameras picked his car up only once, heading south out of Locksford, and we've found nothing since.' Ashley Carpenter sounded angry. 'I had him in an interview room, sitting right opposite me! It's so galling that I never found a way to make him open up to us right there and then. He is the key to finding the killer of maybe two people, and I had to let him walk out of there.'

Jackman could hear the frustration in her voice.

'When he did ring me, I felt absolutely certain that he knows who killed that lass in our churchyard, and that he does have something, although I'm not sure what exactly, on your old ritualistic killing at Birch Drove Farm.'

Jackman considered this for a moment. 'Superintendent Carpenter, did you feel that his offer of help was genuine?'

'Yes. Without a doubt. And before you ask, I believe he will come in tomorrow, so long as nothing has happened to him in the meantime.'

'Well, that's something. As long as he's able to lie low and find a way to get to you safely, it could go our way after all. As you can imagine, after today's unpleasant find we are pretty desperate to talk to him.' He gave a short laugh. 'And that's aside from our interest in solving the Birch Drove Farm murder. He's the first person for twenty years to shed a light on that case.'

'Oh, I'm sure he does know quite a lot, Inspector, so I'm going to suggest that you come up here first thing tomorrow morning and, assuming he turns up, interview him with me. I've cleared it with Ruth Crooke. It can be a joint effort.' She paused. 'Er, for what it's worth, it's quite tricky talking to him, DI Jackman. Mr Bennington is rather highly strung. I believe he is angry — possibly he feels desperately hurt and let down by someone, most likely the killer. We might need a psychological evaluation before we proceed, but I hope not. He's coming in voluntarily and he'll be treated considerately.'

'Until you discover the extent of his involvement,' added Jackman. 'His dark secret could be a guilty one.'

'Of course, although what that might be remains to be seen. Then we'll have twenty-four hours to question him, thirty-six if I deem it necessary.' She paused. 'You know, our conversation on the phone unnerved me a bit. One minute he sounded manic, the next almost pleading, sub-servient. I think someone exerted an awful lot of power over Bennington for a very long time, and now he's either been cut adrift or he's run away. I had a similar case once where a woman had been brainwashed by her husband. I reckon Bennington has been living with a terrible secret for so long that it's finally got too much for him to bear. He is going to be talking to us willingly, and I believe he knows he'll have to pay the price for what he has done but has decided that's better than life as it is.'

Jackman was relieved to at least get a chance to talk to Bennington. 'I appreciate your offer and we'll happily come to Locksford, Superintendent, but before I ring off, can I ask you two things?'

'Certainly, go ahead.'

'Did you get the impression that he might have been a member of a cult?'

Her reply surprised him. 'Oh yes, DI Jackman. The moment he spoke of this person he was tired of protecting, and considering his strange, submissive way of speaking, I wondered that very thing.'

Jackman saw a smile spread slowly over Marie's face as she heard those words.

'Music to my ears, Superintendent. We are certain that both the old murder and whatever happened to the unfortunate victim whose body parts we found today are ritualistic. We also think your Shelley Harcourt might have fallen foul of the same cult, and that Bennington wasn't exactly truthful about not knowing of any connection.'

The superintendent gave a little laugh. 'A cult or secret society connection has been my private supposition for a long time. *If*, and it's a big if, the helpful but decidedly flaky Martin Bennington turns up, we can start to fill in all the gaps in the old investigations.' She paused, then added, 'From past dealings with this man, DI Jackman, it will take longer than usual and a shedload of patience too, but we can't push him.'

'Patience is one of my greatest attributes, Super.'

'Glad to hear it, especially as it's not usually mine, but I'll give it my best shot. Now, what was the other question?'

'What did he tell you that wasn't common knowledge?'

Carpenter grunted. 'Oh yes, that. He mentioned a single name—'

'Damon?'

'That's the one, the only lead the team at the time had. A witness saw a group of people hurrying away from the churchyard on the night that Shelley was murdered, and he heard one of them call out for Damon to wait for him. He then heard cursing, as if someone was furious that his name had been used. And that was it. But it was never made known, other than within our own ranks.'

'Then he's a very valuable commodity indeed, isn't he?'

'He is, and if anyone finds out that he's confessing to his part in the crime and naming the killer, he is in extreme danger.' Her voice hardened. 'And hearing about what has happened in Saltern-le-Fen, I'm forced to consider that the killer does know.'

'May I suggest that we keep this latest development from Bennington when we speak to him, ma'am?' asked Jackman.

'Oh, he won't be told about that, believe me. If he's as nervy as I suspect he will be, it could push him right over the edge.'

Jackman ended the call with a promise to travel up to Locksford early the next morning.

'I'll leave you to report all this to Ruth, set up an action plan and talk to forensics, Marie. I know they'll pull out all the stops for us but keep on at them.' Jackman let out a low whistle. 'We're out of the starting block, aren't we?'

'And if the angels are on our side, we have a star witness,' added Marie. 'As long as he doesn't freak out before we get some answers.'

'Fear not, he'll be treated with kid gloves, I promise.' Jackman was feeling pretty optimistic. 'I'll be back before close of play tomorrow afternoon, hopefully in a very good mood.'

'Are you with Carpenter on the belief that he'll actually turn up?' asked Marie cautiously.

He thought for a moment. 'It depends how clever the killer is and how much he knows. And because Bennington took off from his home to an undisclosed location, I reckon he is thinking exactly the same thing.'

'So, it's in the lap of the gods.'

'Looks that way.' He smiled at her. 'Right now I'm going to chase up uniform, see if they've made any more nasty discoveries in the fen lanes, and then I suggest we go home. We'll get nothing from forensics today, so there's little more we can do. I'll go direct to Locksford tomorrow, if you wouldn't mind getting in early, briefing the team and getting the investigation under way?'

'No problem. I'll text you if anything interesting crops up. I won't ring if you're deep into the interview.'

'I'll keep you updated as to how things pan out, don't worry,' he said.

'You'd better! This is edge-of-the-seat stuff.' Marie stood and picked up the empty beakers. 'I'm just going to check the rotas and see who's around for the beginning of the week.'

After she had left, Jackman called downstairs to check on the progress of the search.

'Nothing so far, DI Jackman,' said the desk sergeant, 'although your old lady at Slate Farm saw several vehicles that she didn't recognise go past during the time frame we're looking at. One interests us, a small blue car, very possibly a Mini from the way she described it. That went down just after seven this morning and returned some ten minutes later. She said it was hammering along that lane like the hounds of hell were after it. As that road leads only to Amberley Fen, there are no cameras, but we are checking all main junctions out of the village to see if we can pick it up again.'

Jackman thanked him and hung up. He doubted that would be the vehicle they were looking for. You didn't use something that distinctive when you were sneaking out to dump body parts. But it had to be followed up, and he was glad they were checking everything so carefully. Right now, he was haunted by the fact that there were two arms and two legs sitting in the mortuary and they still had to locate the head and the trunk. The thought was nauseating, and he felt deeply for the poor soul who finally made that discovery.

Marie arrived back in the office. 'We have a full complement as from Tuesday. Kevin Stoner is back off leave then and no one else has anything booked for a week or so, so we'll be firing on all cylinders.'

He pushed some reports into a folder. 'Since nothing else has been found out on the lanes around Lyttonville, I suggest you get home, Marie, and try to salvage what's left of today.'

She lifted an eyebrow. 'We'd spent the whole day, until you rang, deeply involved with your Victorian mystery and some very interesting tales about the people who lived in the Amberley Fen area. I have no idea what Gary might have unearthed, but thanks to Ralph, we found a brilliant historian. One of her case studies was the infamous Sally Pinket, one-time owner of Solace House. We have a whole dossier on her, Jackman, and I left Ralph researching another name that cropped up with a big question mark, a woman called Ivy Pettifer.'

'Really? That's amazing! You should become a detective, Marie!'

She gave him a withering look. 'Talk about taking your work home with you. My dining table looks like the nerve centre of a major operation.'

He looked at her fondly. 'And I really appreciate it, Marie, honestly. It's important to me to find some answers for that poor family.'

'I know that. Why do you think we are occupying ourselves with a mini-investigation instead of, er — well, instead of doing things other people do in a new relationship, if you get my drift?' She grinned broadly at him.

He laughed. 'Let's not take that any further, Marie. I understand completely. Now I'm feeling guilty.'

She made to leave, then turned and winked at him. 'Well, don't. We are actually thoroughly enjoying ourselves. And who knows? When you get back from your trip to sunny Locksford, I might even have some interesting facts ready for you to look at. We'll get you the answers you need, Jackman, I guarantee it.'

He believed her.

CHAPTER SEVEN

As Gilly — his lady friend, as he liked to refer to her — was away for the weekend visiting an elderly relative down in Essex, Gary had occupied himself playing amateur detective on the internet. He didn't want to spoil Marie's weekend, so rather than keep ringing her to see how she was getting on, he worked alone and rather enjoyed himself.

He had concentrated on learning more about the subject of the notorious Victorian baby farms and how they had mutated from the acceptable, used even by royalty like Queen Victoria, to a despicable practice that involved murder. He read that Jane Austen had been sent away to be nursed, so he had looked this strange practice up and was shocked to find that it was quite commonplace. It appeared that well-off city families really did ship their young infants off to a wet nurse, preferably in a peaceful rural location, for a small payment. The nurse would provide milk and basic care. Some stayed for three months, some for much longer and returned to their families as toddlers. The very rich brought the nurse into their home to assist with the birth and then stay on for the first couple of weeks to feed and care for the baby. These were called "monthly nurses" and were often recruited from adverts found in the "lying-in hospitals," the forerunners of today's maternity hospitals. But, as the popular belief at the time was that a baby developed its future character from the milk it drank, they had to be sure that the nurse providing said milk was honest, healthy, of sound morals and of a kind and gentle disposition. Since these were qualities that were not easy to prove or disprove, and as references could be falsified, it was a risky business.

Gary stared at his screen, wondering how being removed from the family for such a long period in those early days would have affected someone. It didn't bear thinking about. It had been proved beyond doubt that those first months with the mother are vital to forging a bond. He tried to imagine a small child being formally introduced to his mother and father, two total strangers.

He shook his head, leafed through more papers and began looking at an altogether darker side to this suspect "profession." This was a list of wicked women who had all been hanged for murdering infants. He scanned the names. Amelia Dyer hanged in Newgate Prison, 10 June 1896, convicted of murdering hundreds of babies. Amelia Sach and Annie Walters, the first two women to be hanged at Holloway Prison on 3 February 1903 for killing over twelve infants. Frances Lydia Alice Knorr, hanged in Old Melbourne Gaol, Australia, on 15 January 1894. Minnie Dean, hanged in 1895 in New Zealand.

The list of names ran on. Not all were hanged, as at one time, infanticide did not carry the death penalty. Annie Took, Catherine and John Barnes, Jessie King, Ada Williams, Leslie James . . . Gary sighed, got up and went to make a cup of tea. 'I had no idea,' he muttered to himself as he boiled the kettle. 'And I haven't even looked at the States or Europe yet.'

So, was Sally Pinket such a woman? She had never been convicted, he knew that much, but the accusation had been made, and something must have happened to spark off the witch-hunt. He'd found little on the internet, nothing of interest on websites or blogs, and what there was seemed to have been gleaned from unsubstantiated twaddle in the local rags of the time. He hoped that Marie had had more luck. He'd certainly had his eyes opened to the terrible infant mortality rate of the time, but he'd produced nothing of importance about Sally, or Solace House.

Gary sat at his desk and stared at his screen, wondering where to go next. 'Ah, I know,' he muttered. Before he met Gilly, in order to pass the time when he was off shift, he had signed up to an ancestry search site and had tried to trace his family history. It had been quite addictive, and he'd discovered all manner of small surprises along the way.

He'd become pretty good at it too, so why not forget all the tales about her dark deeds and concentrate on the woman herself, her personal history?

He skimmed through a couple of newspaper articles and found one that featured her full name — Sally Martha Pinket. He typed it in.

'Here goes nothing. Now, let's see what we can find.'

Two and a half hours later, Gary was still sitting at his computer. When he finally took a break, he stared at the notebook lying next to the keyboard. It was covered in scribbled notes. He stretched, then realised he had missed his supper. Not to worry, he'd grab something light in a minute.

So, what did he have? Between the ancestry site and others he'd learned about through his work, he had quite a lot.

He read through the notes: Sally Martha Pinket, née Giddings. One of seven children born to Arthur Giddings, a gamekeeper, and Cicely Giddings, née Cowperthwaite, both of Saltby Eaudyke. Sally was married young, to Jonathon Pinket, a trainee doctor, and they moved to Amberley Fen. She had three children, one of whom died young of diphtheria. He could find little about the other two apart from their names — William and Emma. Jonathon did exceedingly well for himself, specialising in tropical diseases, which, thanks to the expanding empire that thrust many British people into unfamiliar climates, was becoming an important area of medicine. They then purchased Solace House, but within a year, Jonathon contracted typhoid from one of his patients and died at forty one. Sally, it seemed, had been left just enough money to keep the house going and feed herself and the children, but little more. A year after her husband's death, she placed an advertisement in *The Times* describing herself as a healthy, abstinent and experienced young widow who was seeking engagement as a wet nurse.

Thus began her new career at Solace House. Gary found nothing in the records that showed either her or any of her family to be anything other than well-respected and of impeccable character.

He ambled out to the kitchen to get himself some supper, his thoughts on a young widow with two children looking for a way to make life a little easier for them all. Where did it all go wrong?

Gary foraged through the freezer and pulled out a microwave chicken tikka masala. Not the most exciting of evening meals but it was quick, so tonight it would do.

He stared at the slowly revolving plate. Maybe something happened to Sally when she lost her husband. Depression? Anger at the unfairness of his being taken so young? Had it set off thoughts of her dead firstborn? All these things were possible. He'd dealt with cases of traumatised women who'd stolen babies from prams or back gardens after they'd lost their own child. If the accusations were true, there was a very good chance that Sally had suffered a serious mental breakdown which had escalated to the point of murdering her young charges.

Gary ate, hardly tasting the spicy food. He was trying to fathom how to move on from that advert in *The Times*. There was no record of Sally Pinket after then. After a yawning five-year-long gap, the gossip and allegations started. Gary had no idea where to go to fill it.

* * *

Janet unlocked the door, went inside and hung up her jacket. She had just returned home from a meeting with their client.

He had been pleased, more than pleased in fact, even though he was never very demonstrative.

Janet went into her lounge and opened the door to a heavy wooden sideboard from which she took a crystal balloon glass and a bottle of Rémy Martin brandy. The only time she allowed herself any alcohol was when she'd paid a visit to their client. If the meeting went badly, the bottle would stay in the cupboard, although that had never happened yet.

She sank down onto her recliner and took a long sip of brandy. The meetings still made her nervous. Every time she approached the building, she felt her stomach turn over, yet he always greeted her cordially and made her feel she was important to him. Even so, she always fretted until she was back at home in her own lounge, her glass of brandy in her hand.

One more sip before it was time for the next step in her evening ritual. She picked up her phone and called John, who answered immediately. He always did.

'He sends his very best wishes to you, John, and asked me to congratulate you on your excellent work.' She exhaled. 'He was very pleased with what we have achieved since our last meeting, more so than usual. I think we are ahead of the schedule, which pleased him greatly.'

'That is good news, although we already know that what we produce is more than satisfactory,' said John, his voice betraying nothing of the anxiety she guessed he felt. That he must feel. 'And he gave you our orders for the next month?'

'Of course, and I understand that our money for expenses will go into our accounts tomorrow morning, as usual.'

'Good, good. Then I shall call tomorrow morning and collect my assignment. The sooner I start, the better it will be for all of us.'

They said goodnight and Janet put down her phone. What the client called "expenses" was a generous sum, of which she touched barely a quarter. She had even said it was far too much, but he had insisted her work was worth every penny, and she had to admit that it was an incentive to do a good job. He was so good to them that he deserved their loyalty, which they gave in the form of weeks of hard work.

Janet took another sip of the Rémy. She knew she would never find another client like Stephen. In truth, she idolised him, although she'd never admit it to anyone. They were speeding through the job in order to please him, but at the same time she dreaded it coming to an end. The thought of never seeing him again was unbearable. Somehow, she would have to make herself indispensable to him. John, of course, would move on to pastures new, which was fine with her, but Stephen was a very different matter.

She stared into the last of the brandy. She was a very bright woman, enterprising, even ruthless if the need arose. Surely she could think of something?

* * *

Marie rode into her drive and turned off Tiger's engine. It still gave her a thrill to see Ralph's car parked outside and lights on in the house. It made coming home such a pleasure.

She garaged the bike, said goodnight to it as she always did, thanked it for giving her another safe ride and went into the house.

Ralph greeted her with a hug and a kiss. 'You're earlier than I thought you'd be. How was it?'

She took off her boots and hung up her jacket while she told him what had been found and filled him in concerning the cult that probably connected the three cases.

'Phew! We had a cult thing once on our patch. Not murder, but the abduction of teens. It turned out to be an elaborate scam to extort money from the kids' families. Absolute shysters. I don't think I've ever been more delighted than when I shut the slammer door on the ringleader. I see red when people mess with kids' heads.' Ralph glowered angrily then brightened. 'You haven't eaten, have you?'

'Not a morsel. We just wanted to get home, it's an early start tomorrow. Jackman's heading up-county to Locksford and I'm in charge of setting up an action plan for the troops.'

'Good, because I whipped out to the supermarket and bought us a picnic.' He grinned at her.

'A picnic at a quarter past eight in the evening? Er, did I hear you right?'

'Yes, it's a picnic. Go into the lounge.' He pointed to the door.

Marie shook her head in confusion, went into the lounge and burst out laughing.

On the floor in the middle of her living room was a large tartan blanket with two big soft cushions on either side. Spread over the blanket was an array of plates and bowls, all forming a colourful display of, yes, picnic food. She saw at least three different kinds of salad, hunks of crusty bread, eggs, cheese, smoked salmon, dips and sesame bread sticks, and fresh fruit. To one side was a ceramic plant potholder filled with ice and holding a bottle of champagne. Two glasses stood next to it.

'A picnic, Ralph Enderby-style,' he said with pride. 'And it has the advantage of no ants creeping into the butter, no wasps to spoil the ambience and definitely no chance of rain.'

Tears welled up in Marie's eyes. It was the most thoughtful thing anyone had ever done for her.

Ralph looked at her in dismay. 'Oh dear, that wasn't quite the reception I expected. Is it because I pinched your plant pot? Sorry, but you just don't have a proper ice bucket, Marie Evans. I searched everywhere.'

She buried her head in his shoulder. 'You are something else, you really are. This is absolutely wonderful!'

He breathed a sigh of relief and kissed her forehead. 'Then let's eat!' He flopped down onto a cushion and gestured to the other.

Of all the "firsts" in her life, this one took some beating. This man was continually taking her by surprise. He had an extraordinary spontaneity that was like a breath of fresh air. After more years than she cared to remember, she was having fun. One of the strangest things was that, somehow, they were managing to fit this in around one of the most demanding and unpredictable jobs in the world.

'Oh, and I've managed to get a handle on Ivy Pettifer.' Ralph looked well pleased with himself. 'It wasn't easy, considering that it's all way back in the past. I brought up some parish records online and found a local family called Pettifer who lived about two miles from Amberley Fen. I managed to find an Ivy who ties in with the period Sally Pinket took in children at Solace House. If it's the right one, and I'm sure it is, she would have been in her early twenties.'

Marie wiped her lips on a napkin and took another sip of her champagne. 'What kind of family did she come from? Was there any record?'

'I located a birth register which said her mother was "in service," and the father was a farm labourer. They weren't on the breadline, but I suspect life wasn't easy as there were ten children. Ivy was one of the older ones. And that's as far as I got.' Ralph helped himself to prawn salad. 'It made me realise just how much work Anna does. It's not easy trying to unravel events from so long in the past. I found it really difficult and I'm a detective.'

'We need to find out what her relationship to Sally was, don't we? Anna seemed to believe she was important for some reason.' Marie was thinking of the bold asterisks and the words "*She bothers me.*"

Ralph agreed. 'I've been through all of Anna's notes and the name isn't mentioned at all, so I don't understand why she should be of interest to Anna. I think I'll ring her in the morning and ask.'

'Good idea.' Marie pulled a face. 'I'm afraid you're on your own with it tomorrow. I'm going to be run ragged getting the ball rolling with this dismembered body investigation. I'm really sorry. We've been so quiet for weeks, now when something really interesting comes along, we get a high-profile cold case to resurrect *and* a butcher of humans, all in a matter of days.'

He shrugged. 'That's the way it goes with our job. I could get a call tomorrow saying, "leave cancelled, all hands on deck, we have a major crime."'

He was right. She had the feeling that no matter what, they were going to weather it together. '*Que sera*, I guess.'

'Whatever will be, will be,' he finished off, rather out of tune.

The "picnic" was one of the most enjoyable meals of her life. Marie knew she'd remember it forever. It wasn't just the food, although that was lovely, it was the thought behind it, the imagination.

As they cleared away the dishes and restored the lounge to its usual order, Ralph said, 'Would you mind if I bring a few more of my things over from Fenchester? I seem to be spending more time here than at home and I don't want to keep turning up at work in the same clothes.'

'I'll clear a space in the wardrobe,' she said. 'Bring whatever you want.' She smiled to herself, liking the idea. 'And I think I can find a way of saying thank you for a surprising and *very* nice evening.' She gave him a look that meant only one thing.

'Who am I to refuse, DS Evans?'

CHAPTER EIGHT

Josh was in his second week on the carts and being shown the ropes by two old hands at waste collection. Bernie, the driver, was a bit of a grouch and had strong opinions, not just on the job but on everything from running the country to the space programme. Owen was less opinionated. He said very little, other than to give Josh his orders. Josh preferred Owen out of the two but looked forward to being on a regular round with a crew he'd be working with permanently.

'It's not domestic collection today, mate. This morning we're collecting the roadside stuff,' said Owen. 'We have an extra early start and do the main roads — the lay-bys and so on — so we get away before the commuter traffic builds up.'

Josh could have laughed. He came from a city and in the ten years he'd lived in the Fens he'd only seen traffic hold-ups when there was an accident or a diversion for a road closure. They didn't know what morning traffic was, especially around Saltern-le-Fen. It had its busy moments on a market morning, but nothing like the main towns or the cities. He didn't argue the point, though. He was the new boy, and he needed the job.

'We've had a load of fly tipping in the lay-bys recently,' went on Owen. 'The one we are coming to next, on the Fenchester Road, is by far the worst.'

'I know what I'd do to 'em if I got me 'ands on 'em,' growled Bernie. 'And it ain't pretty. The thing is, there ain't no deterrent, is there? The police are never around and it's easy for them dickheads to load their vans and cars with their crap, drive to the nearest lay-by and dump it. Now, if it was down to me, I'd . . .'

As Bernie droned on, the big lorry growled to a halt, and Josh saw what Owen had meant. In the centre of the lay-by was a large, lidded council refuse bin, rubbish piled all around it. Some of it was in plastic bags and sacks, and other stuff, including old tyres, bits of carpet, cans and even a threadbare armchair, had been thrown into the bushes that ran along the back of the grass verge.

'We take all the bags and small stuff, lad,' said Owen, hopping down from the cab. 'We have to ring in and report the rest, then they get an open-back lorry out for the stuff that won't crush.'

Josh dropped to the ground and hurried after Owen. It wasn't the best job in the world, but it was regular work if he made the grade. Plus, Josh had one big advantage. He had no sense of smell.

Eager to look like a hard worker, he wrestled a lot of the smaller bags into the back of the big truck, then returned to help Owen, who was struggling with a couple of the hefty ones.

'Reckon this one can stay,' Owen muttered. 'Too heavy to fling up into the cart.'

Josh nodded. He could see chunks of dried cement or plaster sticking through the plastic. He tested the next one. It was heavy too, but he didn't want to look like a wuss. He gave it a tug to release it from the bag of cement and it tore.

Josh leaped backwards, gasping.

Bernie laughed as he looked out of the open cab window. 'You'll have to cultivate a stronger stomach than that if you want to do this job, mate! What, has someone stuffed a nice bit of roadkill in a bag and left it for us?'

Owen moved towards Josh and poked at the bag with his gloved hand, then he too retreated, gagging.

Bernie stopped laughing and climbed out of the lorry. He stared down at the partially open sack. 'Fucking hell!' He clapped a hand over his mouth.

In some part of his shocked mind, Josh thought this was the longest he'd ever gone without hearing Bernie's voice bleating on in the background.

Owen was trying to get his phone from his pocket, but his hands were shaking so much he dropped it. Finally, he managed to dial 999.

The police arrived so swiftly that even Bernie couldn't complain. Josh found himself leaning against a patrol car, stuttering, trying to explain what had happened. 'I thought it was one of those mannequin things you see in clothes stores but it was too heavy, then I realised that it was . . .' He stopped, gulped, still sick at the thought of what he had seen.

'It's all right, sir.' The woman police officer smiled at him kindly. 'You don't have to say any more about that. Can you just tell us if the bag was in the same position as it is now?'

'I pulled it out a bit, but not far,' said Josh, wishing he didn't have to repeat the story of his grisly find. 'It was stuck under a bag of old builders' materials, you know, hardened cement and stuff.'

She took his name and address and said they would be wanting a statement from him. She also told him that she could arrange for someone to have a chat with him, help him deal with what had been a terrible shock. He agreed to give a statement, but declined the help, thinking that several pints of lager would probably be a better way to sort his head out.

He retired to the dustcart cab, where his two companions waited in silence, having been asked to remain where they were. The bags they had loaded prior to their macabre find had to be taken out again and their contents checked. Rather them than me, Josh thought.

He leaned out of the window as he was still feeling nauseous, and heard muffled curses coming from the two policemen charged with going through the other sacks.

'Just what we needed. Last shout before the shift ends and we get this one, sorting through bags of dogshit. They really don't pay us enough.'

'Oh shut up, Bob. I don't like it any more than you, but it's got to be done. We both know it could be in a separate bag.'

"It?" thought Josh. What was "it" and what were they looking for?

He climbed out of the truck and went towards the back, intending to ask them. His question was answered before he opened his mouth.

'Come on, Bob, we're done here. No head in this lot.'

Deciding that this job might not be quite right for him after all, Josh promptly threw up.

* * *

Jackman was halfway to Locksford when Marie rang him.

'The torso turned up early this morning, sir. In the same black plastic as before, this time dumped in a lay-by with a whole load of rubbish. The SOCO tells us it's a young woman, and Rory has promised to confirm whether it's ours as soon as he gets to see it for himself.'

'Are you okay with seeing this through, Marie?' Jackman asked. For some reason this had come as a surprise to him. He had believed that the rest of the body would probably never be found and certainly wouldn't appear so soon.

'No problem, boss. I've already been out to the site, and very smelly the whole thing was, I can tell you. We had open bin bags everywhere and some of the contents were very ripe indeed. I reckon you timed your early-morning trip rather well.'

He laughed. This was her way of coping with what must have been very unpleasant for her. 'It's highly unlikely to be a different body, so I'm assuming we have all but the victim's head now and, as the last one never materialised, maybe that'll be the case here too.'

'I agree,' Marie said. 'Hell, boss, I'm on tenterhooks here, waiting to see if Bennington makes it to the police station. None of us can concentrate properly and we keep looking at the clock. Please ring us one way or the other, won't you?'

He assured her he would, and she ended the call. He felt the same way. So much hung on what Bennington had to say. The man was obviously in great danger, and this could turn out to be a wasted journey. Yesterday he had been convinced that Bennington would make it to the appointment, now he wasn't so sure.

He arrived early, but Superintendent Ashley Carpenter was waiting for him, her expression grave. Something was wrong, and he hardly dared ask what.

She took him into her office and closed the door. 'There was an RTC at around six this morning, on the main road into Locksford from the north. Three-car smash, but one did a runner from the scene. Bennington's car was involved, DI Jackman.'

'Oh shit! Sorry, ma'am.'

Unfazed by his language, the super echoed his words. 'Too right it's shit. The worst thing is that he's disappeared from the crash site.' She rolled her eyes. 'And how he did that without a vehicle is either a mystery, or—'

'He was taken,' Jackman said. 'Damnation! That man was so important. Do we know if he was hurt?'

'It's unclear, and of course it happened on a stretch of road with very few cameras. We're hoping that another driver might have caught it on a dashcam, but that's a big ask.' She gave an exasperated sigh. 'I hope you don't mind that I didn't cancel your visit, DI Jackman, even though I knew this had happened, but I really wanted to go over the cases with you in person.'

'Absolutely. I'm pleased we can talk it through together, though of course I'm bitterly disappointed about Bennington,' Jackman said.

Before she could answer, there was a knock on the door and her office manager appeared. 'Super, I think you should get downstairs right away. You have someone asking for you. He says his name is Bennington and he's covered in blood.'

Jackman hurried through the old building after the superintendent, down flights of stairs and along corridors. They found Bennington in the medical room. The duty sergeant and a uniformed police constable were with him.

'We've brought him here for his own safety,' said the sergeant, who was watching as the PC tried to apply a large sterile dressing to a nasty gash on the man's arm. 'Just temporary, to staunch the bleeding. The doc is on his way.'

So this was their "star witness". Jackman wasn't sure what he had expected, but Martin Bennington was a bit of a surprise. He was a tall, wiry man, with long, dark, wavy hair. He had very pale eyes. The fact that he was dishevelled, and his clothes stained with both blood and mud, added to his rather unconventional appearance. Jackman was delighted to see him.

A look of intense relief appeared on Bennington's face when he saw Ashley Carpenter. 'It was deliberate! They tried to kill me,' he said at once. He spoke in a soft voice which bore a hint of a local accent.

The superintendent introduced Jackman, took the dressing from the PC and gently and expertly applied it to the wound. 'Are you hurt anywhere else, Martin?' she asked. 'There's an awful lot of blood for just one injury.'

He touched the back of his head using his good arm. 'I'm not sure how that happened, but it bled a lot.'

Jackman saw that Bennington's hair was matted with blood at the spot he'd indicated. This man needed hospital treatment, although it would be extremely risky to move him. He guessed it depended on the on-call doctor's verdict. He glanced around the room and saw that it was spotlessly clean and considerably better equipped than Saltern's. Hopefully, the doctor would be able to patch him up.

Without prompting, Bennington said, 'There were two of them, two cars. They forced me off the road, but it didn't go as they expected. My car spun and clipped one of theirs.

It did more damage to him than to me, and the driver got trapped.' He shivered. 'Thank God! I'd be dead if that hadn't happened.'

Ashley Carpenter took a foil blanket from a cupboard and wrapped it around Bennington's shoulders. The room was very warm, but Bennington was shivering.

'The second driver went to help, and I think he managed to free him, so I took my chance and ran. I went through the trees and bushes along the edge of the road and across some allotments and found an old shed to hide in.' Bennington exhaled. 'I knew I was hurt but I was alive, and I wanted to stay that way.' His eyes flashed. 'And I still do!'

Jackman noted the sudden change of mood. Up until now Bennington had seemed a sensible, albeit frightened man. Now he saw what the super had meant.

The man was twitchy, shifting constantly in his seat and looking extremely anxious. 'Am I safe here? I mean, really safe?' he asked, his eyes darting around the room.

Ashley spoke softly to him. 'You are safe, Martin, I promise. No one will get to you in here.' She smiled gently. 'Now, the doctor will examine you, photograph your injuries and do all he can to make you comfortable. If you need further treatment at hospital that will be arranged, or, if he is happy to treat you himself, he will, and then we'll get you a hot drink and maybe some food if you're hungry. After that, we'll talk, okay?' Bennington was still now, responding to her calm voice.

There was a knock on the door, and the doctor came in.

He was obviously well known in the station, clearly an old hand at this sort of thing and was soon ushering them out of the room and making reassuring noises to his new patient.

Ashley Carpenter asked the sergeant to call her the moment Bennington was fit to be interviewed and reiterated the need to keep him under constant close surveillance. 'Now we've finally got him,' she muttered to Jackman, 'I'm not losing him again. He's the principal character in this drama and we're stuffed without him.'

They returned to her office. 'Get us some drinks, Geoff, please,' she called to her manager.

'Coming up! Tea? Coffee? Chocolate? Large Scotch?' He grinned.

She glanced at Jackman.

'A coffee, white, one sugar, please.'

'And the usual for me, thank you,' Ashley said.

The civilian manager nodded. 'Okay, one coffee, one double whisky on its way.'

She shook her head and smiled apologetically at Jackman. 'It's worth putting up with all that, I'll tell you. Believe it or not, he's actually a model of efficiency and runs this office like a well-oiled machine.' Seating herself, she pointed to a chair. 'Well, that's a turn-up for the books. I was certain Bennington would have been spirited away, only to reappear without a pulse.'

Her words reminded Jackman about Marie's news of a torso being found. He relayed it to Ashley Carpenter, adding, 'And because of the symbol found on the arm and the missing head, there's no doubt about the connection to the Birch Drove Farm murder.'

'I know very little about that case, Jackman.'

'And I'm not fully up to speed on Shelley Harcourt's death either.'

'Then while we wait for the doc to patch up Bennington, I suggest we do a bit of cramming. You first. Tell me what you know about your girl, Angel.'

* * *

'Is the dear boy skiving off again, Marie?' Professor Rory Wilkinson seemed to materialise out of nowhere. 'And I've made a special trip to share a few moments of his congenial company. I'm devastated. Utterly devastated.'

Marie patted his arm. 'There there, Prof, you'll get over it. And in the meantime, will I do?'

'Admirably! Where can we talk?'

She led him to the "dear boy's" office where as soon as the door closed behind them, the joviality ceased. 'Jackman is with the Locksford team. A man might be coming in who was involved in, or at least has knowledge of, one or both of the old murders. We're all hanging by our eyelashes until we learn if he's shown.' At that very moment her phone beeped. 'Yes! He's there! Seems as if he only just made it, though.' She stared at Rory. 'Someone tried to eradicate him on his way in.'

'So long as they failed, that's very good news,' said Rory. 'If someone thinks it's necessary to prevent him talking, he obviously has something worth listening to.'

'Exactly.' Marie felt a huge weight lift from her shoulders. She had been wondering if they'd ever see Bennington at all, and now they had him. That was massive!

'I can see that the news has made your morning, Detective. And this small offering might add to your good mood. You certainly only have one dismembered body. Your find of earlier this morning arrived just before I left for a meeting here with dear Ruth Crooke. So I took a cursory peek at it, and it was quite clear that our jigsaw pieces make up one single victim.'

'No more than we expected,' Marie said, 'but as you say, it's a relief to have it confirmed.'

'As soon as we're through with the meeting upstairs, I'll get back and do an in-depth examination, but I can tell you something already — unpleasant as it is.'

Marie tensed.

'The victim, a young woman most likely in her early twenties, was not hacked to death in a frenzy. She was certainly dead when the dismemberment took place, which is a blessing of course, but it was done methodically and with great skill.'

'Skill?' she asked, wondering where a killer picked up that kind of knowledge.

'I would say that this is certainly not the first time our killer has done this kind of thing, although I need to do a lot more work on this poor girl before I can elaborate on that. I've never seen this kind of work before, but I've been consulting with a colleague who has.' He gave Marie an unusually serious stare. 'He is an expert on "muti" murder, where humans are killed for their body parts. It is still a common practice in many parts of Africa. Organs are removed and rendered down to make potions that are believed to confer good luck and power on the recipients.'

'Oh Lord. You mean like Adam, that child they found in the Thames?' Marie felt queasy.

Rory nodded. 'My colleague, Noel, told me that in that kind of ritual murder, removal of the head and limbs is the norm, but in Africa it is done while the subject, usually a child, is still alive. Our young woman was at least spared that horror.'

Marie squeezed her eyes shut against the images this conjured up.

'Sorry, dear heart,' said Rory, 'but you need to know what's involved. In the case you mentioned, an expert medicine man was brought in from abroad to carry out the murder in the prescribed manner. It was noted that the flesh was expertly cut to reveal the bone, which was cleanly sliced with a very sharp implement, most likely a well-honed meat cleaver. It was the same with our victim.' Rory tilted his head to one side. 'Please don't think I'm insinuating that our murderer has any connection with African "medicine" killings, just that he knew exactly what he was doing.'

'As in a master butcher jointing meat,' said Marie.

'A good analogy. Although I was going to say an anatomist, or maybe even a pathologist.' Rory grinned.

There were times, thought Marie, when their pledge to protect life and property led them down some very unpleasant roads indeed. This was certainly one of them.

'And now I must away to my meeting, my lovely friend.' Rory stood up and made for the door. 'Please pass this on to the dear boy himself, and I'll let you have a report on our victim forthwith.'

And Marie was left alone to wonder, with an increasing sense of foreboding, who they might meet in the course of this investigation.

CHAPTER NINE

Holly Stewart had taken the children to a farm park not far from home, where they had a great time meeting the animals and exploring the activity centre. With Hugh at work again, Holly felt she could finally relax and unwind. He had told her that this job was far more interesting than the one that had fallen through, and if he managed to get through the probation period, he would enjoy working with them — he preferred smaller family businesses to big impersonal ones.

For once, her mood didn't fade as she approached the house. She was starting to believe that this might be the turning point, that their low spirits had simply been down to their run of bad luck and lack of funds. Even Poppy and Aaron's nocturnal intruder might have been nothing more sinister than a vagrant in the neighbourhood.

Before she had even got out of the car, she heard Rory barking furiously. It wasn't like him, but he had been left longer than usual. They all hastened into the kitchen, apologising to the dog for being so long. 'Okay, kids. Drinks and biscuits. Then you can watch a film while I prepare lunch. What's it to be, *Kung Fu Panda* or *Peter Rabbit*?'

'What's that smell?' asked Aaron, ignoring her question.

Holly sniffed. It did smell odd, kind of musty and metallic. 'Hmm. I don't know. You two stay here for a minute.' She stood outside the closed lounge door, suddenly afraid.

Her heart thundering in her chest, she opened the door and stepped inside.

Her blood turned to ice. Two words were written in red letters a foot high, across the wall that faced her. *GET OUT!* Beneath them, the words "Or Sally Pinket will come for your children."

Now she knew why Rory had been barking his head off. Without as much as a second glance, Holly shut the door, gathered up the children and the dog and put them in the car, roared away up the drive and then stopped. Where to go? She had no friends here. She daren't go to Hugh's place of work — he had pinned all his hopes on keeping that job, and a hysterical wife turning up would hardly help his chances. She didn't want to take the children to the police station. Police? Jackman. Of course! Not the detective but his mother. She put the car in gear and set off for the stables.

* * *

The doctor assured them that Bennington's wounds looked worse than they were, and apart from some bruising there was no serious damage. He had stitched him up and dressed the wounds properly, and now saw no reason why the interview could not go ahead.

'He's shaken, naturally, but I've given him something to calm him. I'm sure you are aware that he does have a lot of deep-seated anxiety issues, but he has expressed his strong desire to talk to you. Just tread carefully, won't you?'

Ashley assured him they'd be careful not to push him.

When they finally got back into the room, they found Bennington calm again.

'Is it all right with you if we take this to a proper interview room, Mr Bennington? Then we can get you something to eat and drink.' Ashley spoke in a relaxed, friendly manner.

Bennington said he would like a cup of tea.

When they were settled, a new tape was inserted into the recorder and the formal introductions were made. The superintendent kept precisely to the official phrasing, and Jackman guessed she was being very careful not to have the interview declared inadmissible because of some slip-up on her part.

'Do you have any idea how the people that tried to run you off the road knew where you were?' Ashley began. 'We believed you had gone into hiding.'

'I had. I went to a bolthole I've had for years, a friend's caravan that he rarely uses. The thing is, I've been watched for a while, so I knew I was in danger from the moment you picked me up.' Bennington nibbled on a thumbnail. 'I thought I'd managed to lose them soon after I left home, but they must have followed me to the caravan. I guess when I made an early-morning dash in this direction, they must have decided to stop me — for good.'

'Do you know who they were?' she asked.

'I'd never seen them before, but I know who sent them.' His voice dropped to a whisper. 'Daemon.'

'Do you have this Damon's full name, Martin?' Ashley asked.

'No. But it's spelled D-a-e-m-o-n, with an A. None of us used surnames. We rejected them.'

'We?' she asked softly. 'Can you tell us who you're referring to?'

Bennington shifted around on his chair. 'Is this it, then? Is this where I start to tell you everything? I don't yet know what I'll get out of this, do I? Except maybe my sanity.'

Ashley explained that volunteering to tell the truth always counted in your favour. She said that at this point they knew nothing about what he had seen or knew or even been a part of, so there was no way they could comment. 'You said you'd kept a secret for too long, Martin. I believe you need to share it now.' She pointed to his dressings. 'This is bad, I know, but think what they were actually trying to do to you. They tried to *kill* you, and they will try again if you walk out of here.'

The sigh that followed contained a world of pain. Jackman's heart went out to him. 'Just talk to us, Martin,' he said. 'We're not here to judge you, we just want to catch whoever killed and mutilated Shelley and Angel.' *And our "black bag" woman too*, he thought.

'And if you were part of it in any way, and you tell us the truth about what happened, it will make things a whole lot easier for you,' Ashley chimed in. Jackman admired the super's patience with this volatile man.

Bennington hung his head, took a deep breath and began, speaking in a monotone. 'There were maybe twenty of us, all young, all looking for direction, hoping to find something or someone to pin our beliefs on.' He rubbed at his eyes. 'Daemon found us. One by one we joined him at his house, a place called the Hollow.'

Jackman immediately thought of Agatha Christie's book of the same name but couldn't remember much else about it. Bennington was continuing, still in that odd monotone, as if he was reciting a story he'd learned by rote.

'In under a month we were committed to his cause and his beliefs and, after a few more weeks, we came to idolise him.' He looked from Ashley to Jackman and back again, meeting their gaze with his own. 'You needed to see him back then. He was so charismatic, so intense and so passionate.' He swallowed. 'We loved him, we all did. And not one of us realised what was happening. Until it was too late.'

Jackman had many questions to ask, but knew to save them for later. Interrupting Bennington now could stop the flow of memories.

'We were happy to begin with. Daemon seemed to have high ideals — when you listened to him talk, you became convinced that it was really possible to make a brave new world.' Bennington shook his head slowly from side to side. 'Yet I knew, even then, that deep beliefs I had grown up with regarding good and evil were being subtly altered. If I had left at that point and persuaded my closest friends to go too, perhaps the group would have collapsed and no one would have died.' He shrugged. 'But I was hypnotised by him. All I wanted to do was please him. I would have done anything for him, as would my friends. Really, we were enslaved.' He looked at Ashley. 'We did break up, twenty years later, and those of us who are left are still slaves.'

He fell silent. They waited.

Ashley pushed his cooling beaker of tea towards him. 'You've broken away now, Martin. It might not be complete freedom, but you've been brave enough to snap at least one link of the chain by coming here. He won't get to you again.'

Bennington sipped his tea. Jackman could see tears in his eyes. 'We gave him the best years of our young lives and he is repaying us by systematically killing us now we are of no use to him. And don't for one moment believe he can't get to me, because he is in here.' He tapped his head. 'Right here! And he talks to me all the time.'

Jackman thought of Laura. This man badly needed professional help. He'd talk to Ashley the moment they finished here and suggest that a good psych team reach out to Bennington.

'Would you like to take a break, Martin?' asked Ashley.

'No, no, I need to tell you all I can before my nerve breaks. More tea, please.'

Ashley sent for it and Bennington calmed down again.

'Let me tell you about the set-up, so you can get a feel for the life we led.'

Ashley nodded. 'Can you tell us where the Hollow is?'

'It's gone.' It sounded like a personal loss, almost a bereavement. 'It was part of the process, one of the greatest sacrifices he demanded of us. Daemon surrendered his — well, *our* — home to the purifying flames. It burned to the ground.'

'So where did you all live?' she asked.

'In the grounds of some old derelict hospital that Daemon knew of. We made a camp, slept under canvas or in shelters that we built when the weather changed. We were like refugees in the aftermath of a war. But we had to face the hardship to prove ourselves, and we had to build him a church. When that was done and he was pleased with us, Daemon took us to our new home.'

'And where was that?' Ashley asked.

'I don't know. We were taken there in the dead of night, in a coach with shades pulled down over the windows. We drove for hours.' He gave a bitter laugh. 'It could have been a hundred miles away or five miles up the road by a circular route.' He brightened. 'But it was a lovely old house and we had proper rooms that we shared with just one other brother or sister. It was bliss, worth all the pain and discomfort of the months spent out in the open.'

'Was Daemon with you all the time?' asked Jackman.

'Oh no. He shared his time with another group somewhere possibly not too far away. Whenever he was absent, we were looked after by his right-hand man, known as Apostle. At first, he scared us with his fierce loyalty, his utter devotion to Daemon, then as time passed, we began to feel the same and we revered Apostle for his total commitment to the group.' He drank more tea. 'But I was going to tell you about the set-up.' He sat back. 'It was a good life at first. We were self-sufficient, grew our own produce and kept chickens, ducks and other animals, including goats. We spent our days tending the garden and our evenings being taught by Daemon, or Apostle when he was away.'

'Sounds like a hippy commune, the ones that were so popular back in the sixties and seventies,' said Ashley.

'It was. Well, that's how it started. For the first month after we joined, we had to remain celibate, then we were allowed to form relationships within the group, but *only* within the group. He told us we were special, chosen by him, and we must never go with outsiders. It was idyllic and we all embraced it wholeheartedly.' He seemed to be staring at Jackman in particular. 'And then the brainwashing began. I am under no illusion, Detective. I know and accept that I've been brainwashed, but at least some small part of me must have remained undamaged by that megalomaniac, that evil destroyer of youth and love, or I wouldn't be here now.'

Ashley glanced at Jackman, who nodded. Bennington was beginning to shake again, wringing his hands and fidgeting in his seat.

'I wanted to tell you about the first death, but . . .' His eyes darted about the room. 'I can't! Not now!'

'It's okay, Martin. No one is rushing you. We'll take a little break. Are you sure you wouldn't like someone with you? We can arrange a health care professional to sit in, just to give you some support.'

Ashley's calmness continued to amaze Jackman. She had said she wasn't a patient person, but she was certainly being patient now. He shivered, thinking of Alistair Ashcroft. Like Daemon, Alistair was a master manipulator.

'No, no one else in here. No one. I just need a moment.'

Ashley gave the exact time for the tape. 'Interview suspended. DI Jackman and Superintendent Carpenter are leaving the room.'

* * *

Marie had updated Ruth Crooke, given the team a brief overview of what was occurring and assigned their tasks for the day. She had liaised with uniform and added a few bits of info to the whiteboard. Now she was seated with a strong coffee in Jackman's office, gathering her thoughts.

His desk phone rang. 'Oh, I'm so sorry, Harriet, Jackman's out of the office today. Is it something I can help you with?'

'I think we need your people to get out to Solace and quickly, Marie.' Harriet told her what Holly had discovered on her return from the farm park, and that she and the children were with her now.

Marie drew in a deep breath. As Ralph had suggested, this was a clear warning to the Stewarts to get out of that house. 'The message actually mentioned the name Sally Pinket?'

'Yes, who's that?' asked Harriet. 'We don't know anyone of that name, and we've lived in the area for years.'

'Long story, I'll fill you in later. I'll get someone out there straight away. Can they get in to the house?'

'No. Holly locked the door when she left. Shall I meet the police there with the key?'

'No, Harriet, we'll collect it from you,' Marie said. 'He's probably long gone, but I don't want you anywhere near the place until we've checked it out.'

Harriet said she was relieved to hear it. 'I've got the kiddies looking after the ponies with one of my grooms. They are fine, but Holly, well, she's not so good, as you can imagine.'

'I'm going to send a uniformed crew and one of our team, probably Gary Pritchard, since you've met him before. Expect them within half an hour, okay?' She paused. 'Oh, and Harriet? I won't mention this to Jackman until he gets back later this afternoon. He's up to his armpits in a major crime at present.'

'I understand completely, Marie dear.'

'Are you okay with having Holly and the kids, Harriet?'

She laughed. 'I'm fine. The children are blissfully unaware that anything's amiss and are enjoying themselves with Sherbet. Holly and I are just about to have another cup of tea, and then I'll get them all a late lunch.'

'You're a star, Harriet. I'll get this organised and ring you later.'

She hung up, went to the door and yelled for Gary.

He almost ran over, evidently hearing the edge in her voice.

'Someone has just dragged our "unofficial" investigation into Solace House into the present day, my friend,' she growled. 'Take a crew and get over to the Jackman stables. Holly Stewart will give you the key for Solace. They've had painters and decorators in unexpectedly, and they weren't welcome.'

'On my way!'

'And Gary?'

He stopped mid-stride.

'Whoever did it knows about Sally Pinket, or at least knows her name.'

'Bugger! So now, someone is going to have to tell the Stewart family about their family home's even darker past. What a bummer.'

Marie nodded miserably. If Jackman was late back, it would be down to her. Oh deep joy. And it was only two p.m.!

* * *

Jackman and Ashley Carpenter waited outside the interview room.

Ashley groaned. 'Hell, there are so many questions we need to ask, yet we need to let him offload his story at his own pace. I'm terrified of pushing too hard and him cracking. Heaven knows what he has lived through.'

Jackman agreed. 'We have to find out exactly where the Hollow was. And by the sound of it, this maniac Daemon was running two separate cults. Why two? Why not amalgamate them? Surely one bigger group would be even more powerful?'

'My thoughts precisely. Who the hell is Daemon anyway, and probably more to the point, *where*?'

'If we knew the answer to that last one, we'd have our killer,' murmured Jackman. 'And another thing that scares the pants off me is that Martin said Daemon was "systematically" killing them off. That indicates multiple murders.'

'Reinforced by his mention of the *first* death. God. How many are we going to hear about before this is over?'

Jackman had no idea how to respond. Instead, he said, 'I wonder how Martin Bennington managed to resume what seems to be a normal life? You said he has a nice little house in Locksford, friendly neighbours and an old friend who he stayed with sometimes. It's so, well, average; so conventional. After decades of mind control and manipulation he should be a basket case!'

'As to the house, I can answer,' said Ashley. 'His mother lived there until she passed away eighteen months ago. He was an only child — he was actually born there — and it went to him. I think he feels safe there. I haven't seen it myself, but apparently, he's changed nothing, all his mother's things are still as she left them. It's a supposition, but I think he's blocked the cult years from his mind and is back in the days before he met Daemon.'

'That figures.' Jackman looked at his watch. 'How long shall we give him?'

'A few more minutes.' Ashley leaned against the corridor wall. 'I might get Doc Godwin to just check him over again. That bang on the head worries me, even though the doc himself said it's superficial. I know that heads do bleed profusely, but I don't want to deny him treatment that he really should have, like maybe a scan?' She pushed herself forward. 'Yes, I'll do that now. You wait here.'

Ashley hurried off and asked a constable to go and get the doctor and bring him down to the interview room.

Jackman watched her. He liked the way she, a superintendent, treated him as an equal and didn't stand on ceremony, even down to using the odd swear word.

She was back in seconds, followed by the doctor, who bustled past them and into the room. He emerged five minutes later, smiling. 'Relax, Superintendent. There was no actual blow to the head. It was a straightforward laceration from a piece of glass or metal. He won't even have a mild concussion. The gash on his arm was nasty, but again not so deep as to cause him problems. His main problem is mental, not physical.'

She thanked him. 'We know about his mental condition, Doc, and we'll be sure he gets whatever help he needs — we just wanted to make sure he's okay for this preliminary interview.'

When he'd gone, she turned to Jackman. 'Actually, it's a bad time to need psychological help. Our area force psychologist is off on sick leave and the cover we've been getting isn't the greatest. They're very willing but don't have the experience or the knowledge to deal with men and women in custody.'

'No promises, but we might be able to help there,' Jackman said. 'We have a brilliant psychologist in Dr Laura Archer. She, or maybe Professor Sam Page, who guides and advises her, might be prepared to come here and see Bennington. I agree with you that he needs a real professional.'

She smiled gratefully. 'If you can arrange that, Jackman, I'll be forever in your debt.'

'As soon as we're through here, I'll contact her.'

'You're a lifesaver. Now, ready for round two?'

He took a deep breath and they went back in.

CHAPTER TEN

Gary parked in the lane leading up to Solace and went up the drive on foot. He had heard and read so much about the dismal atmosphere of the place that he wanted to get a feel of it for himself. He didn't think he was a particularly sensitive person and thought it more than likely that he'd leave wondering what all the fuss was about.

Halfway up the drive he stopped in his tracks. The image of a young woman rose up in his mind, hurrying, head down, up this same approach. In her arms she carried a tiny child, bundled up in blankets to protect it from the east wind that whipped across the Fen. He felt the anguish pour from her. Somehow, he knew that this would be the last time she would see the baby she had so recently given birth to.

Gary shook his head and blinked fiercely. He was well aware that this vision stemmed from studying Sally Pinket and the Victorian baby farms long into the night, but the force of it struck him like a physical blow. He walked on, trying to concentrate all his attention on the house itself. Goodness, it was austere! Those high, blank walls were screaming out to be given the gift of windows. He'd seen more charm and character in a nuclear bunker. 'Whoever designed this needed shooting,' he muttered to himself.

Before he could think further, he heard the crunch of car tyres on the gravel. The patrol car had arrived.

He was pleased to see PCs Stacey Smith and Jay Acharya climbing out. He waved the front door keys. 'At least we've no need to force an entry.'

'Oh, that's no fun,' said Stacey with a smile, 'I do like to see Jay on the business end of an enforcer.' Her expression became serious. 'So, Gazza, what have you got for us? We were rerouted from another call to meet you here, so we've no idea what's gone on.' She looked around. 'What a dump! I'd get rid of those trees, wouldn't you? They're practically climbing in the upstairs windows.'

'Someone other than a tree has got inside and done a little unauthorised graffiti work on the walls,' explained Gary.

Stacey pulled a face. 'Please tell me it's not drawn in poo. If it is, I'm off!'

'Not to my knowledge.' Gary grimaced. He briefly explained about Holly returning home with her kids to find that someone had been in the house. 'Anyway, let's go and see for ourselves, shall we?'

'After you,' Stacey said firmly.

Gary walked in and wrinkled his nose. He turned to Stacey. 'Well, you got your wish. It's not poo. How do you feel about blood?'

'I'd have preferred good old-fashioned spray paint.'

The three of them went into the lounge.

'Oh my god!' exclaimed Jay. 'That poor woman. Walking in and seeing this, it's horrible!'

'Is it really blood?' asked Stacey. 'Only there's another smell too.'

Gary understood what she meant but couldn't answer. 'I think we need a SOCO in here to check it out. I'll ring it in now. Would you guys mind trying to find how the intruder gained access?'

Gary ended his call and as he did, he heard Jay call from one of the upstairs rooms.

He ran up and found Jay in the children's room.

'The bastard's been in here too, Gary. Look.' He pointed to one wall.

This time it wasn't blood, or whatever that was downstairs — this one was written in thick black marker pen. Crudely drawn, it showed a sort of sinister cartoon witch on her broomstick. Beneath it were the words, "Old Sally is coming for you! BOO!"

Gary scowled, furious. Threatening the parents was one thing but to scare the children was going too far.

Stacey came in. 'He got in through the bathroom window. It was one of those old ones, probably the latch was already weakened. It's wide open, and you'll be pleased to hear that there's a nice juicy footprint on the floor.' She stopped and stared at the cartoon. 'Oh hell! What a first-class shit!'

'My thoughts precisely, only more colourful,' muttered Jay.

Gary was overwhelmed by the urge to scrub the image off there and then, and repaint the wall before the children came home. He felt helpless.

Jay was looking around, a puzzled expression on his face. 'You did say the house is empty, didn't you?'

Gary nodded. 'Yes, the husband is at work and Mrs Stewart took the kiddies to Harriet Jackman's stable. Plus, in case you've forgotten, we've just let ourselves in and searched it. Dimbo. So what's bothering you?'

'Oh, nothing. I'm hearing things, probably a bird, or an animal out in the fields. You know how the wind carries sound out here on the Fen.' He smiled faintly. 'Just for a minute, I thought I heard a baby cry.'

Gary swallowed. He'd had enough of this place. As far as he could recall, he hadn't been really spooked by a house before, but he was now. He wanted out. 'I'm going to ring the sarge and update her. Will you two be able to wait here for forensics?'

They nodded. 'No problem,' Jay said. 'But who is Sally Pinket?'

'As far as I know, she was one of the original owners of Solace House,' Gary said vaguely.

'And she was a witch?' asked Stacey, raising her eyebrows.

'I very much doubt it,' said Gary dismissively. 'And I have no idea why this intruder would want to scare these good people away. It doesn't make sense. Now, I'd better get hold of Marie.' He hurried downstairs and out of the house.

He updated Marie on what they had found. 'They can't come back here tonight, Sarge. The kids would never sleep in that room again. Okay, it was only a cartoon but still, it was loaded with menace. The little girl is only around six, isn't she? It would scare her to death.'

Marie agreed and said it was time to contact the father.

'Can't we hold off a bit longer?' asked Gary. 'When I picked the key up earlier, Mrs Stewart begged me to wait until he finished work. He's in a brand-new job, kind of on probation, and she doesn't want to mess things up for him.'

'Then would you call back at the stables, Gary, and see what alternative arrangements can be made for tonight? If forensics get in and out quickly, the Stewarts might be able to start cleaning up tomorrow.' She paused. 'It was written in blood, you say?'

'Smells like it. At a guess, I would say it was added to actual paint. It'll be the devil's own job to clean it off and then cover it up.' He thought for a moment. 'I'm wondering about contacting that company that we use sometimes who do graffiti removal. They might have something professional that would do the job.'

'That's an idea. But go and talk to Holly, then give me another ring. Oh, and Gary, make sure she does either ring or text her husband when he finishes work. I don't want him driving home and finding us swarming all over his house and his wife and kids gone.'

'Good point, Sarge. I'm leaving Stacey and Jay here and I'll go right now.'

'I'll meet you at the Jackmans' stable at five thirty, unless anything else happens here. The boss won't be back until later this evening, so we'll have to tell Hugh and Holly about Sally Pinket ourselves. I'll see you then.'

He updated Jay and Stacey and hurried back down the drive. He knew it was totally illogical and probably unfair on the two PCs, but another few minutes in that place and he'd be a basket case. So much for being so scornful of those who'd commented on the atmosphere. They were right. He didn't like it one bit.

* * *

Harriet Jackman was disappointed to hear that her son wasn't available to help. There was something about him that made her feel safe, protected. Even when total disaster had struck their family and her lovely boy and Marie had been so badly injured, she had known that Rowan would see it through and make it right again.

She stared out of the office window at the young mother and her two children making a fuss of little Sherbet. What must be going through that woman's head? There was only so much a person could take before something snapped. Even Rowan was unusually concerned about this family, and when he heard this latest piece of news, he'd be furious.

The sound of a car arriving brought her out of her reverie. It was that nice Gary Pritchard. His face was unusually sombre, which could only mean that something else had happened. She hurried from the office, anxious to get to him before he spoke to Holly.

'What's wrong, Gary? You look like you've seen a ghost.'

When he didn't answer immediately, she decided she should have used a different turn of phrase. He had looked quite disturbed by her comment.

'No, no, of course not,' he said. 'Er, it's just that the intruder has left another message and it's on the wall of the children's room. I need to ask Mrs Stewart to find alternative accommodation for tonight, maybe two nights, as the children cannot be allowed to see it. It would scare them further.'

'Oh, the animal! What a dreadful person to do something like that. But accommodation is no problem, Gary. They must stay right here with Lawrence and me. The children can have Ryan and Miles's old room and Holly and her husband can use the guest room. It's always made up in case someone drops by.'

Gary looked relieved. 'That'll be less stressful and a lot easier than trying to book a hotel for a couple of nights. Thank you so much, Mrs Jackman. I'm sure they'll be very grateful.' He pulled a face. 'Now I'd better have a word with Mrs Stewart.'

Harriet accompanied him to the stable yard. 'I'll keep the kiddies occupied while you talk to Holly.'

She threw the two children a big smile. 'Would you two like to meet one of my new horses? He's very special, you know. I rescued him. He was a racehorse and he won lots of races, but then he retired and couldn't make his owners any money, so they didn't want him anymore.'

Aaron looked angry, Poppy incredibly sad.

'But we do, don't we, children? Come and let me introduce you to Rainbow. I think you'll be good friends and, right now, our Rainbow needs all the friends he can get.' With a little wink at Gary, she led them away towards the main stables.

* * *

'But we can't impose on Harriet any more than we are already!' Holly looked distraught. 'And Hughie will be furious. He's so proud. He struggles with accepting help, or charity as he calls it. He says we pay our way or nothing.'

'It's all right, honestly, Mrs Stewart. Mrs Jackman won't take no for an answer, I promise. She'll tell your husband exactly where the best place for those children is tonight, and that's right here, in surroundings they already love.' Gary grinned at her. 'I'm pretty sure that no matter how adamant your husband is, he'll be no match for Harriet Jackman.'

She still looked unconvinced, but Gary was sure he was right. He was also sure the children would come first in the end, and they loved the stables and the horses. To stay here would be the perfect solution for all of them.

'Why are they doing this, Gary?' Holly had tears in her eyes. 'We'd go tomorrow if we could, without all this hatefulness.'

'We have no idea, Mrs Stewart, but sure as eggs is eggs, we'll find out. And, if I have anything to do with it, the culprit will get the book thrown at him. It's a despicable thing to do.' Suddenly he wished he was back in the times, decades ago, when he'd have been able to give the perpetrator a damned good hiding and there'd have been no comeback.

'And this Sally Pinket, who on earth is she?' Holly was asking.

'Look,' said Gary, glancing at his watch, 'why don't you ring Hugh and tell him to come straight here when he finishes work? Say there's a problem at the house and not to worry, no one is hurt, and the police have it in hand, but he must come here directly to be with you and the children. Our sergeant will be on her way here shortly and she'll explain it to both of you.'

Holly hesitated, then shook her head and pulled out her phone. 'Okay, okay, I'll ring him.' She looked up, her eyes still awash with tears. 'This is a nightmare, an absolute nightmare, and I can see no way out of it.'

* * *

Jackman sat opposite Ashley Carpenter in her office. Someone had brought sandwiches and coffee and he was more than grateful for the break. Talking to Bennington was exhausting.

The two detectives ate in silence, both trying to assimilate what Bennington had told them. Finally, Ashley screwed up her sandwich packet and tossed it in the bin. 'How do you come back from that kind of indoctrination, that sort of torture? Because it is torture — deliberate, cruel, mental torture.'

'It's beyond me,' Jackman said. 'I'm just amazed he still retains some remnants of morality and that he's found the courage to tell us what he has.' He managed a smile. 'You do know that "Daemon" is an archaic spelling of "demon" — one that satanists use? According to the ancient Greeks, a daemon was a supernatural being somewhere between gods and humans.'

'Ancient beliefs were never my strong point,' Ashley said somewhat sardonically. 'But it makes sense, doesn't it? If you want to set yourself up as some kind of messianic leader, why not call yourself after a god of some kind?'

'Indeed. That was obviously how he saw himself — god-like but with some decidedly ungodly ways. In any case, he certainly had a hold over those poor young people.'

Ashley had a faraway look in her eyes. 'Hypnotists say that you can never make someone do anything that goes totally against their nature. I always believed that to be true. Now I know I was wrong. Daemon managed it all right, and not just with one or two of his acolytes either. Every single member of that group would have done anything for him.'

'That's how mind control works,' said Jackman bitterly. 'We had dealings with a master manipulator not so long ago. They can convince even the most hardened sceptic.'

Ashley seemed to gather herself. 'So, let's just summarise what we've got so far. Stop me if I go off at a tangent, won't you?'

Jackman nodded.

'They lived in a big old place called the Hollow. As far as we can ascertain, it was outside a village called Wiley Fen, kind of mid-county, south of here. It was possibly owned by Daemon, maybe it was a family home, but we need to check that out. To start with they lived a bit of a hippy lifestyle, self-sufficient, with nookie on tap, so long as they kept it within the group. They met in the evenings when the indoctrination took place.'

'All correct so far,' said Jackman. 'Not forgetting that Daemon split his "educational" activities between two groups. That is still something of a puzzle and needs investigating without delay.'

'Mmm, and over to you for that one, as we believe that the other group was located somewhere in your neck of the woods.' Ashley took a breath. 'Now, one of his doctrines revolved around the idea of a secret knowledge that was known to early civilizations but had been lost down the centuries. Daemon professed to be a descendant of a great nation that had embraced this knowledge and became all-powerful. He told them he alone possessed this knowledge, and he had chosen them as his disciples, those worthy of receiving it. Right?'

'Sadly, yes. He made them feel special, privileged to have such a sacred gift bestowed on them.'

'Except he wasn't giving them anything, he was taking. Apart from their money, he took their principles, their honesty and their fundamental values and practically turned them into immoral savages.' Ashley uttered the last two words with disgust. 'Martin now believes they were often given hallucinatory drugs without their knowledge. He cannot account otherwise for the way he felt when participating in the various "acts" that were said to be rites of passage leading to the next stage of becoming a true follower.'

Jackman recalled what the guilt-ridden and mortified Martin Bennington had told them about these "special" rituals and wondered about the ones he had chosen not to mention.

'Daemon was, or probably still is, a twisted pervert,' spat out Ashley. 'Remember that ceremony on the last day of April, the one he said bound you to him forever?'

'Walpurgis Night, a feast to honour St Walpurgis, a saint of the Roman Catholic Church, said to be the night witches come together to celebrate, and the best night of the year to summon the Devil himself. Saint or Satan, you take your pick.'

'Well, he was a devil all right, and he clearly believed in debauchery. I mean, making an initiation ceremony out of having sex with your adoring followers. How twisted is that?' Ashley was fuming.

'Not only that — the next two initiates, or should I call them victims, were made to witness what they could look forward to on the next satanic feast night.' Jackman exhaled. 'And the awful thing was that by that time, they were so utterly under his influence that they believed it was an honour and celebrated their good fortune at being chosen.'

'Let's move on. The first death.' She frowned. 'And here I'm a bit fuzzy, as Martin was all over the place when he was trying to explain. Am I right in understanding that one of their members died, but it was definitely an accident?'

'Yes, well, *allegedly* he was accidentally crushed when a barn wall collapsed and trapped his legs. From what Martin said, it sounded like acute compartment syndrome, and he could possibly have been saved by emergency surgery. However, Daemon declared that nature must take its course. It was fate, and they could not interfere. The boy died and was laid out on an altar to be revered as their first martyr.' He stopped, frowning. 'I'm now wondering if Daemon had actually contrived the "accident" so as to open the way for what occurred next.'

'Ah, yes, when it turned really primitive,' said Ashley, shaking her head in disbelief. 'I have to admit that at this point in our interview, my whole concept of what is and isn't possible in terms of controlling other human beings went right out of the window.'

'Strangely, this next abomination really does provide a link between the old ritual murder and our present case of the body in the refuse sack.' Jackman paused, looking for the right words. 'What he did was no more than what still goes on in parts of Africa today. I discussed it with my team just a day or so ago regarding the ritualistic killing of Angel. The belief that human body parts are a potent medicine was widespread in ancient times.'

'That doesn't make me feel any better about it.' Ashley wore an expression of distaste. 'Daemon was no godlike ruler, nor was he an uneducated tribal villager. He was an educated modern-day deviant, a weirdo and a sexual predator. If he's still alive, and I'd suggest that he is, given the attempt on Martin's life, it is our duty to stop him before he does more harm.'

'Agreed on every point,' said Jackman calmly. 'I'm just explaining that he very cleverly took an age-old ritual and made it into a ceremony of the utmost significance for his group of brainwashed victims. He turned the death of that innocent young boy into a kind of unholy communion, in which the recipients were imbued with the spirit of their dead martyr.'

'I do get all that, honestly,' Ashley said. 'Martin intimated as much during his agonised ramblings about what he and his fellow devotees were forced to do. But, Jackman, this is the twenty-first century. We are living in a busy farming county in England, not some isolated tropical backwater. Where we live people do not liquidise the organs and body parts of others and drink them.'

'Actually, we're not so "civilised" as all that,' Jackman said. 'I could quote you at least ten cases of modern-day cannibalism. The serial killers Jeffrey Dahmer, Joachim Kroll, Richard Chase, to name just a few. It happens. It goes against everything we believe in, it's abhorrent to us, but it does happen.' He let out a long painful sigh. 'And sadly we've found ourselves digging into one such occurrence. One tiny positive to hold onto — he's not a cannibal. I'd put good money on the fact that his communion ritual was just another trial for his disciples, something to test them, bind them closer to him.'

'Small mercies, I suppose. But what he's capable of still makes me sick,' said Ashley. 'And I won't sleep until we have him locked in a cell. Anyway, what we have to find out from that poor soul downstairs is where Daemon is now.'

Jackman glanced at the clock. 'Whenever you're ready.'

Ashley stood up. 'Then let's get it over with.'

CHAPTER ELEVEN

Marie was relieved to arrive at the stables before Hugh Stewart. She needed an update on the situation from Gary before they tackled what was bound to be a very angry and upset man.

'Harriet Jackman is being an absolute rock,' said Gary emphatically. 'As long as Holly's husband doesn't throw a spanner in the works, she's got everything sorted regarding accommodation and food for the family. She's a brilliant organiser, just like her son. But Holly wants answers, especially about Sally Pinket, and I said you and I would tell her what we know when Hugh gets here.'

'After those messages they have to know, so we have no choice.' She wasn't happy about it. Jackman had wanted that part of the house's history left unmentioned, but things had changed. 'I suggest we play down the possibility that Sally Pinket was guilty and suggest that she was targeted in a kind of witch-hunt. The Stewarts are level-headed townies, let's stick to down-to-earth explanations and not wander into the fanciful.'

'Yes,' Gary said, 'that's the best way to handle it. I just hope Holly is in a fit state to cope with another setback. Harriet confessed to me earlier that she fears for that young woman — she is so stressed out by everything that's happened.'

Marie felt for her. She still failed to understand why anyone would want to frighten the family away from a house that no one wanted.

'I didn't like that place one bit,' Gary said.

'Bit austere, isn't it?' she said. 'Not welcoming at all. And it's not even built in the traditional Fenland style.'

'It's not that. It just doesn't *feel* right. It has a bad atmosphere. You know me, I'm a crusty old cynic, and saying something like that goes completely against the grain.' He shook his head.

'We know too much about the house and its history, my friend,' Marie said. 'It's having a bad influence on how we feel about it. But don't let the Stewarts pick up on that. They have to live there, even after this latest incident, so let's try to keep it cool, okay?'

'Oh, of course. That was just between me and you. And, er, I'd be obliged if you didn't tell the others that it spooked me out. I'd lose all my street cred.' He grinned. 'If I had any to start with, that is.'

A car, driving far too fast, was heading up the lane towards the stables.

'Mr Stewart, I presume,' muttered Marie. 'Time to do our bit.'

Joined by Harriet, they walked towards the car.

'Bring them over to the house, Marie. I'll put the kettle on and make hot drinks and you can talk to Holly and her husband away from the children.'

Harriet hurried off. Marie glanced towards the stables and saw the two youngsters happily grooming a pony, watched over by their instructor, Debbie Quinton. At least they were blissfully unaware of the state of their home — unlike their parents. Marie watched Holly run to her husband, cling to him and blurt out the news of what she had found.

'Come on, Gary,' Marie urged. 'Let's move this conversation to a quieter spot. I really don't want the kids to hear what we have to say.'

She and Gary ushered the couple away from the yard and across to the Jackman family home. Hugh was boiling with rage and Holly seemed on the point of dissolving into tears.

'I know this is a horrible shock, especially for you, Mr Stewart, having just walked in on it all, but I have to talk to you about it and explain a few things.' Marie kept her tone calm and reasonable. 'We have our people out at your home right now and forensics have sent a scene of crime officer. We are taking this very seriously indeed.'

'Where's DI Jackman?' demanded Hugh.

'DI Jackman is currently the officer in charge of a murder investigation, Mr Stewart. He was out of the office when this call came in. I will notify him on his return, and I know he'll want to get in touch with you. In the meantime, I need to get things moving as quickly as possible.'

Her words calmed Hugh's anger somewhat, although he still seemed edgy. Holly asked again who the mysterious Sally Pinket was.

'She once lived in your house, Mrs Stewart, way back in Victorian times,' said Gary. 'She ran a kind of crèche, looking after babies, many of whom were born out of wedlock.'

Marie suppressed a smile at his old-fashioned choice of words. 'It was a perfectly above-board facility often used by the well-off to save the lady of the house the trouble of having to care for a newborn herself.'

'Mmm,' said Gary disapprovingly. 'For a small fee, you could get someone else to do all the hard work for you.'

'And this Pinket woman carried on this kind of business from Solace?' asked Hugh. 'So, if it was a respectable business, why would someone use her name as a threat?'

Marie tilted her head. 'Sadly, this is where local gossip and superstition come into it. We gather from a local historian that Sally might have been targeted, like witches used to be back in the Middle Ages. You know, where a herbalist or a healer was labelled a witch and in league with the Devil, and often ended up tied to the stake.'

Gary added quickly, 'Infant mortality back in Victorian times was unbelievably high. In some areas of London something like thirty-three per cent of children under five died, and even rural areas suffered badly. It seems possible that a perfectly natural infant death may have been viewed by some uneducated and superstitious people as something much darker—'

'Setting off the witch-hunt,' added Marie.

'You mean people thought she was murdering babies?' exclaimed Holly, with a look of horror.

'You know how stories escalate,' said Marie calmly. 'Over the years some completely false legend becomes the generally accepted belief. What you have to know is that there was never one scrap of evidence to incriminate Sally Pinket.'

'In fact,' added Gary, 'the historian that we mentioned has proved that a journalist paid locals to make up stories about the poor woman that all pointed to her guilt.'

'Gary's right.' Marie looked at them earnestly. 'This woman swears that Sally was innocent. She was victimised by this hack, who hated women and was happy to pin murder on them in the press.'

Hugh frowned suspiciously. 'Excuse me for saying, but haven't you done an awful lot of ferreting into the history of our house in a very short space of time? This incident only happened a matter of hours ago.'

Marie raised her hands in surrender. 'Ever since DI Jackman met you, Mrs Stewart, we've been looking into Solace's history for him. He may not thank me for telling you this, but your story touched him deeply. He's bitterly disappointed that you've been treated so badly. Our county has a reputation for welcoming incomers. We recognise that without new blood, some of the old villages would have died. He wants to make things right for you and he's had us all working in our own time to find out everything we can about your home and the reasons for the locals' antagonism.'

Hugh whistled. 'Well! That's over and above.'

Holly looked close to tears again. 'I knew it! I knew he was different!'

'However,' said Marie seriously, 'this latest intrusion into your home was a crime. I have already told you that we have a murder investigation running, but even so, you will now have people looking into your problem on an official basis.'

'And DI Jackman is going to be pretty miffed when he hears about what's happened,' murmured Gary.

Now that they had the Stewarts onside, they discussed the practicalities of what to do tonight. As Holly had said, Hugh refused to accept what he called charity. In the end, Gary was proved half right. Over a second cup of tea, and after Harriet had made a very convincing case for it, a compromise was struck. After the SOCO had got all he or she wanted, Hugh and Holly would return to the house that evening and begin cleaning up, while the children stayed on at the stables and helped with "putting the horses to bed." They would spend the night at the Jackmans'.

'And you're not cooking for us, Mrs Jackman,' Hugh stated firmly. 'It's enough of an imposition having those two for the night. We'll take them to McDonald's.'

Harriet tried once more to get them all to stay but gave up in the face of Hugh's intransigence. At least it solved the problem of what to do with the children.

That settled, Marie was anxious to get back to the station. They all went out to the stable yard, where the children were talking to "their" little pony.

'Aaron! Poppy! Come here for a moment, please,' Hugh called.

The children ran over, hugged their dad and began to describe how to groom a pony.

'That's great,' said Hugh. 'And we've got another treat for you, but first, listen to what I have to say. You see, we think a big bird must have fallen down the chimney while you were out, and it made a terrible mess — soot and dirt everywhere — so Mummy and Daddy are going to clean it up before you go home.'

They looked at each other. 'Oh, I see. We wondered why Mummy was so upset,' said Aaron. 'But we were very happy to come here.'

'Well, that's the treat. Mrs Jackman—'

'Auntie Harriet,' corrected Poppy sternly. 'She's Auntie Harriet, Daddy.'

'Okay, well, Auntie Harriet has said you can have a sleepover here, but first we'll go and have a McDonald's. What do you say?' He raised an eyebrow.

Delight spread over their young faces. Then Poppy looked up at her father anxiously. 'Huggy Bear can come too, can't he?'

Holly smiled. 'We'll collect Huggy with your PJs and toothbrushes, don't worry.'

'And Rory?' Poppy added. 'I can't sleep without Rory by my bed.'

'I consider Rory to be one of the children,' said Harriet. 'Of course he can stay. I do believe he loves the stable as much as them.'

So that was settled.

Back at her car, Marie rang PC Stacey Smith.

'The SOCO's been beavering away for over half an hour, Sarge. He said to give him another hour or so and he should be clear.' Stacey lowered her voice. 'There's not enough in the budget for a full sweep, but he's concentrating on the point of entry and egress, the footprint and samples of whatever medium was used for the graffiti, and generally photographing everything.'

'Best we can hope for, Stacey. When he's through, the Stewarts will be calling by, so are you okay to hang on there until they can lock up?' Marie was doing her best not to have to send Gary back there — it had spooked him so badly.

'No problem, Sarge, although I've spent time in happier places — like a condemned squat or the morgue.' She gave a dry chuckle. 'And Jay here is not a happy bunny at all. He's decided it's haunted.'

'Tell him to get a grip, Stacey. He's been watching too many episodes of *Ghost Hunters*.' But her attempt at lightness fell flat. Nothing about Solace was amusing.

Marie told Gary, 'Stacey's holding the fort, so you get back to base. I'm going to text the boss — he needs to know what's happened, and I want to know when he plans on getting back to Saltern. I've got a bad feeling that this won't end here.'

Gary didn't answer. He didn't need to. She could see he felt exactly the same way.

* * *

After another half an hour with Bennington, the two detectives were beginning to understand the extent of the control Daemon had exerted over his disciples. The story was frightening but Martin Bennington, with the gentle persuasion and support of Ashley and Jackman, held up remarkably well. Jackman came to the conclusion that no matter how terrible the ordeal of the interview had been, it was somehow cathartic for him, a relief to finally be able to share his nightmare with people who could possibly stop the evil for ever.

'The more you tell us, Martin, the more I believe you were being fed hallucinogens,' Jackman said. He had come across this kind of thing in the past and had studied the effects of these dangerous euphoria-inducing drugs. 'I reckon Daemon combined the hysteria he induced in you all with psychedelics. Sadly, you all believed that this state of heightened consciousness was because you were becoming enlightened. Hallucinogens change the way you perceive the world, Martin. They affect the senses and alter a person's thought processes and emotions, their perception of time.'

'That's it, DI Jackman! Daemon said the high we were experiencing was because we were true believers. We were raised up, becoming different, more aware and powerful.'

'Were some of you more . . .' Jackman struggled for the right word, 'More devout? More, well, *fanatical* than the rest?'

Bennington hung his head. 'Thank God I never reached that level. I did things I'm not proud of, Detective, things I don't even want to think about, but there was still a line I didn't cross. I did suspect drugs at one point, but I was young and headstrong and desperately wanted to be part of this new order. Even if I'd believed that drugs were being used, I would have considered it worth it just to experience that rapture. I felt so free, so strong, so formidable, as if I had broken free of all the constraints society imposes on you. I had a sex life most men can only dream of, my life was as good as it could possibly be. Or so I thought.' He laughed, bitterly. 'Free. I was everything but. I didn't have a thought to call my own. My empty head had been filled with Daemon's thoughts, Daemon's beliefs, his demands and wishes.'

He fell silent for a few moments.

'It must have been around then that he chose six of the most "passionate" members of our group, who were to form a special cell under the tuition of Apostle.'

'As in the Bible,' said Ashley.

'I suppose so, yes, it did seem like that,' said Martin. 'They were to be his lieutenants, and they were to lead us when we began our mission.'

'And what was that?' asked Jackman.

But Bennington began to struggle, and Ashley reluctantly suggested another break. This time Bennington refused, saying he had come to make a clean breast of everything, and he would.

'This has to be said. The Six were taken from their rooms and moved into a communal living-cum-sleeping area, where they were to receive intense training. My roommate, a girl who called herself Shona, was one of them. After three days, she asked to be released to return to the rest of the followers, as she wasn't ready for such an exalted position. They gave the others the same option, but no one else backed out, so they chose someone else in her place. When we were alone, Shona told me that she had in fact opted out because, first, she didn't want to be parted from me and, second, because she was beginning to realise that things were not as they seemed.' Bennington's gaze darted between Ashley and Jackman. 'She was reluctant to admit her suspicions, even to me, but I promised not to betray her. I think this was the point when I started to have my own doubts.'

At this, Bennington seemed to slip into a kind of reverie. Jackman said, 'I'm surprised they allowed her to leave this elite group.'

Bennington gave a harsh, painful laugh. 'They didn't. Shona disappeared a few days later and I never saw her again.'

'You believe they killed her?' asked Ashley.

'Without a doubt,' he whispered. 'From that moment on, I was watched like a hawk. Daemon actually gave me counselling for her loss. Even then I suspected his attentions were only a means of sounding out the extent of my allegiance to him.' He heaved a long sigh. 'Somehow I managed to convince them I was still faithful. Daemon was so caring and reasonable that I slipped back into believing that I was special and privileged to belong to the cult.'

Jackman noted that this was the first time Bennington had used the word "cult." It was a breakthrough, an admission that he knew what he had been involved in. Jackman glanced quickly at Ashley, who gave him a barely perceptible nod of understanding.

'Tell us about the cult's mission, Martin,' she said gently.

Bennington squeezed his eyes shut, opened them and said, 'There was a list, called the "List of the Fallen." The fallen were people who had committed various unforgivable sins against Daemon and by default, us, his followers. They were such a serious threat to our progress towards gaining the Knowledge that they had to be removed. It was the job of the Six to locate them and then, in the presence of Daemon and Apostle, ritually prepare them for execution.'

Bennington stopped again. He seemed drained of every last ounce of his energy. Ashley leaned forward, obviously about to thank him and insist that he rest when Bennington fixed her with a glaring, slightly manic stare. 'The first name on the list was Shelley Harcourt.'

CHAPTER TWELVE

When Jackman finally rang Marie, it was almost six o'clock in the evening and he was only just leaving Locksford.

'Hell, boss. You sound exhausted.'

'Oh, Marie! That was the worst interview I've ever participated in, and as yet we're only scratching the surface. What we have got, and it's big, is that he has intimate knowledge of the cult that committed the murders, and he has mentioned the name of Shelley Harcourt along with details about her killing that were never made public.'

'So he's the real deal?'

'Oh yes, he's that all right. Okay, there are things he can't help us with, like actual names and locations, but he has so much other information that we're certain we can piece it all together, a bit like solving a cryptic crossword puzzle.' He sighed. 'It'll take time, but the super here and I both believe it's doable. Oh, and I've spoken to Laura. She's going up to Locksford tomorrow to have an informal chat, prior to assessing Bennington. Their own psychologist is away on sick leave.'

'Well, that's something. She'll be invaluable with a man like that.' Marie was pleased because it meant they would have access to what Laura found out without them having to wait for a report to trickle down through the correct channels.

'I know, and I'll feel a lot better when we have her opinion on him. The last thing we want to do is push him too hard, knowing what he's been through.' He gave a little grunt. 'I don't know, Marie, maybe it's because you and I have had personal, life-changing dealings with a man who was a genius at manipulation that I'm finding this one tough, really tough, to handle. Hearing first-hand what this Daemon has done to what were a group of decent, naïve teenagers makes my flesh creep.'

Despite how he sounded, Marie decided she'd have to tell him about the desecration at Solace. 'Look, boss, knowing how tired you are, I'd love to let this wait until tomorrow, but I can't. There was an incident earlier today involving your friends, the Stewarts. Don't panic, they're all safe, but I'd rather talk this over face to face. I'm waiting for you here.'

'Come on, Marie, just give me the bare bones of what happened.'

'Someone broke into Solace while the family was out and wrote threatening messages on the walls, maybe in blood, we aren't sure. The messages referred to Sally Pinket.'

The silence that followed lasted so long that Marie suspected they had lost the signal. Then Jackman said, 'Okay, Marie, I'm on my way.'

She almost felt his car surge forward.

* * *

Janet sat up straighter in her office chair to stretch her back. When things got interesting, she became lost in her work and the hours sped by. It seemed no time at all since lunch and already it was evening. She stood up, aching and stiff, but very satisfied with her work. John had surpassed himself. How he managed to get the pictures he did and not be seen continued to amaze her. She had a great respect for professionalism and John was nothing if not a professional. He would have made an excellent spy. She pictured him, trilby hat pulled low over his face, in a long overcoat, footsteps echoing in the dark rainy streets of Berlin or Moscow. Janet laughed softly. Instead, he was tramping the streets of little Saltern-le-Fen and what's more, he blended in perfectly. He'd worn work trousers for one job, a grubby sweatshirt and a high-vis waistcoat, carrying a hard hat. For another he'd dressed in a nondescript jacket with a neutral shirt and plain chinos. Mister Ordinary personified, the man who never stood out, the one you hardly noticed, which was what made him so good at his job.

Janet prepared a simple meal, a chicken and avocado salad with new potatoes, while she continued to wonder about John. What drove him? Did he have any passions? She had checked him out thoroughly before Stephen took him on. He was ex-police and had then worked as a bodyguard for around ten years. She knew that he had lost his wife a long time ago. They had one daughter who had never been close to her father and had married young and moved abroad. So what did he have in his life apart from work?

She had always made it clear that there was a firm line between work and their personal lives. They knew nothing about each other beyond the job. Now, in the last month or so, she'd begun to wish that she hadn't been so inflexible. She didn't care for him, had no idea if she even liked him, but she was curious. Did he feel as she did, that the work was all that mattered? Or was he deferring to her senior position in not disclosing more?

Janet ate slowly, going over in her mind the most recent photographs John had provided. They were an exceptionally good character study of the young policeman, Detective Constable Robbie Melton, and his girlfriend, Ella Jarvis, who also worked with the force as a forensic photographer. Rather like John himself, DC Melton blended in. He looked younger than his age, dressed down and would be the perfect detective to place in a situation that required the presence of an average young man who would not attract attention. Yet beneath that commonplace exterior, John had captured a surprising depth of emotion. Janet had had to remind herself that these were covert snaps, not moody studio pictures. Yes, John was a very talented man indeed.

After finishing her meal, Janet decided to do another hour on the Melton file before shutting down for the evening. To date, he was by far the most interesting subject on Stephen's list. Janet was quite fascinated by his life before he came to Saltern-le-Fen, particularly the time he served with the young detective sergeant, DS Stella North, who had been shot in a bungled raid. His rapid deterioration after she was invalided out of the force was thought-provoking. Finding all this out had been a challenge, but that was her job, her forte. Part of that was getting people to talk to her and finding themselves telling her more than they'd intended to.

Janet smiled to herself, saved her work and flagged up Melton for special mention when she next met with Stephen. He would like this one. He was particularly interested in those that showed emotional depth, and DC Robbie Melton appeared to be very deep indeed.

* * *

Jackman rushed into the CID room like a whirlwind, all trace of tiredness gone. 'Okay, Marie, tell me what happened.'

When she had finished, he let out a long, low groan. 'Just what they didn't need! At least my mother saved the day in some respects.'

'Harriet is a real tower of strength, Jackman,' Marie said. 'She manages to be practical and helpful without being bossy. She made our job a whole lot easier, I can tell you.'

'She's always been the same, Marie.' He smiled fondly. 'But this couldn't have come at a worse time for us. We're more or less certain that the leader of this cult has a second group of disciples, located in our area.'

'Oh, bugger! And still operational?' asked Marie.

'From your recent gruesome find, it would certainly appear that way. It's imperative that we locate their base and find this man Daemon.'

'The leader of the group?'

'Yes, and I hate to tell you this, Marie, but he's another evil, manipulating killer, and this one has a whole group of victims gripped in his talons.'

Marie sighed. 'Just as we get rid of one murdering bastard another rolls up. Just peachy!'

'At least this time we have help. Superintendent Carpenter has her entire department tracking Daemon's whereabouts, and traumatised as he is, Martin Bennington is giving us every assistance. Some of what he is remembering really could lead us to Daemon.' He frowned. 'But even though this naturally takes precedence, I won't let the Stewarts' problems get farmed out to some other team. They are my responsibility, and we are going to hang onto them.'

'I thought you'd say that, boss, so I've set it up so that you get all reports directly.' Marie breathed in. 'That blood thing really worries me. I'm pretty sure we're talking animal blood, and from what our Gary said, it was mixed with paint. And that alone is weird. One or the other would make more sense. Why mix them? Using blood is a rather B-movie kind of thing to do, isn't it? *Hammer House of Horror*, or what?'

'Someone's tacky idea of scare tactics,' said Jackman. 'But why the hell go to such lengths to scare them away? If they had anywhere else to go, that poor family would pack a bag and take off tomorrow, without all this shit!'

'Exactly what Holly said. Er, I was thinking . . .' Marie looked at him hopefully. 'Would you have any objections if I set up a little obbo of my own? On a certain car seen heading in the direction of Solace, late at night?'

He chuckled. 'I was thinking exactly the same thing. Maybe I'll join you. How about tomorrow night? Can't do tonight, I'm knackered after those interviews, and I need to prep Laura before her meeting with Bennington.'

'It's a date — sort of. Even if it just crosses this mystery person off our list of unanswered questions, it will be something.' She smiled at him. 'Now go home.'

'I will, after I've gone over to Mother's stable. I need a word with her about those kids and I'll call in to Solace on my way, just to assure them I know what's happened and they are not going to be palmed off or not taken seriously.' He shook his head. 'There's something really nasty going on here, isn't there, Marie? Something we're not seeing.'

'Not yet, Jackman, but we will, I'm sure of it.'

* * *

Stacey and Jay were still waiting for the SOCO to finish up at Solace. The Stewarts had come and collected a few night things for the children and had taken them off to McDonald's prior to returning them to the stables. Holly had told Stacey that they planned to try and clean or cover up what they could so the children wouldn't be frightened.

'That's going to be some mammoth task,' muttered Jay, looking at the scrawled letters on the wall. 'Do they have any idea how to tackle it?'

'Holly mentioned that before all this started, they were planning on painting that lounge wall a feature colour. They'd already bought a dark plum-coloured paint for it. I guess they'll just try to scrub off what they can, then paint over it.' Stacey frowned. 'But it'll take a good few coats, if it ever hides it completely.'

'And they'll not get that permanent marker off the kids' room wall easily either. I know from experience.' Jay looked thoughtful, then suddenly brightened. 'I have an idea!'

'Careful, lad! This sounds worrying.' Stacey looked suspiciously at her crewmate.

'You weren't doing anything special this evening, were you?' He flashed his even white teeth at her.

How could you say no to a smile like that? 'So, what am I about to let myself in for?' she said.

'Our shift is over, so as soon as the SOCO is finished, let's get the patrol car back to the station, pick up a few things from my place and come back and lend the Stewarts a hand to clean up. Much as I hate this horrible house, I think they badly need our help.' Jay beamed at her expectantly. 'What do you say?'

'Will you throw in a KFC, if I say yes?'

'A whole Mighty Bucket to yourself.'

'In which case, I'll go and check with the SOCO right now.'

Stacey chuckled to herself as she went in search of the scene of crime officer. There weren't too many public-spirited young men like Jay Acharya on the force, and she was really lucky to have one as her crewmate. Plus, he was right, she really didn't have anything better to do. She rarely did.

Ten minutes later the forensic investigator was loading his equipment back into his car. 'Sorry I took so long,' he said. 'My next job was cancelled so I spent a bit longer on a few areas that might hold some trace evidence.' He looked around. 'Grim old place, ain't it? Wouldn't want to live here. See you around, guys.' With one last glance back at the old house, he slammed his car door and drove off rather speedily.

'Right! Plan of action.' Jay took out his phone. 'You have Holly Stewart's number, don't you?'

She pulled out her own phone and read the number out to him. A few moments later she heard him telling Holly that he and Stacey were returning the police car but would be back to help them. Then if she and her husband concentrated on the lounge, they could leave the kids' room to them. That done, he pocketed his phone and indicated to the door. 'Let's go, pardner.'

As they drove back to Saltern, Stacey said, 'So what is this cunning plan of yours, Moriarty?'

'You know I live with my brother and sister-in-law and their children?'

'Yes, and you're Ravinder's fourth child, or she treats you like that.' She smiled to herself, remembering Jay's lunchboxes, carefully marked with his name and a kid's sticker on the top. This week it had been emergency vehicle stickers and he had been mortified to be given a fire-engine instead of a police car.

'Well, the youngest, Rahul, went through a stage of drawing on the walls and floor with marker pen. It was a nightmare until I found some amazing spray stuff and a magic eraser that actually worked. I've still got a new one and a couple of erasers, even though Rahul has grown out of decorating walls.' His smile widened. 'And just in case that fails, I've got the very thing to cover all trace of it.'

Stacey shook her head. 'You know, you remind me of a slightly overgrown Boy Scout, Jay. "Be prepared!"'

'Well, that's no bad thing,' he remonstrated. 'You wait and see! The kids will love it.'

Three-quarters of an hour later they were loading what seemed like the entire contents of a workshop into the back of Jay's car.

'Do we really need all this?' Stacey exclaimed. 'What about the kitchen sink, or is that the next trip?'

'Trust me. I'd rather have everything I might need than have to break off and go and find something.' He did a swift inventory. 'Right! Hop in, we're ready. Let's go and be good Boy Scouts — sorry, Girl Guide, in your case.'

'This I have to see!'

* * *

Jay noticed immediately that Holly Stewart had been crying and was even more pleased that they had offered some practical support at this grim time. He was also relieved that their presence seemed to galvanise Hugh into action, which caused Holly to take hold of her emotions and pitch in as well.

To begin with, he and Stacey helped them move furniture out of the way, roll the carpet back and put plastic dust sheets down. Then they filled buckets with warm soapy water. All they could do to start with was try to remove as much of the mess as possible.

As soon as they were into their task, Jay and Stacey carried all his materials and tools upstairs and cleared a space to work in. Jay enjoyed decorating, finding it quite therapeutic.

In no time at all he'd put up a pasting table and unpacked everything he thought they'd need. 'Now for the magic. I'll try the eraser first and if that fails . . .' He threw a cannister of marker remover to Stacey. 'You spray that on, leave it for three minutes and then we wipe it off. It's much harsher, so hopefully these erasers will work.'

To his relief, the thick tough sponge began to lift the black marker pen. He gave another one to Stacey and between them they removed most of the witch's image as well as the message beneath it.

'Oh dear, there's a bit of a shadow left,' said Stacey critically. 'It's almost gone but you can still make it out. I guess the painted wall surface is slightly porous.'

'Never fear, partner, that was just the first stage.' He peeled off a wad of kitchen roll. 'It's not too damp and luckily it's a really warm evening, so let's dry it as much as we can, then while I get ready here, maybe you could go and see how the others are doing.'

While she was gone, he mixed up a bucket of decorators' size, ready to prepare the wall for papering, then found his wide pasting brush. He was grateful that the wall the intruder had chosen to do his artwork on wasn't very large, or it would have taken all night. As it was, they had several hours of hard work to do, but it would be worth it.

Stacey arrived back after a while, carrying two mugs of tea. 'Holly's back on track. Now she's hopping mad rather than tearful and they are doing pretty well, all things considered. She is wondering, as we all are, what you're up to.'

'Well, they're banned from the room until I've finished. Just trust me, this'll make the kids smile, and happy kids means happy parents.'

'Hellfire, Acharya, I'm your apprentice on this job, surely you can tell me?'

He finished sizing the wall, and held up a sachet. 'This is special fast-drying paste — by the time we've sorted out the paper, we can whack it on the wall.' He gave her a big smile. 'Okay, I'll tell you. I bought this special wall covering for one of my nephews, but those kids want for nothing, so I'm reallocating it to Aaron and Poppy. As I see it, their need is greater.' He took a wide roll of paper from a tall box. 'We are lucky, they are in pre-cut sections and this wall is just a little smaller than the one it was intended for, so we can trim it to fit.' He unrolled a section and held it up for Stacey to see.

'Jay! That must have cost a fortune! It's amazing!' Stacey stood and stared at it, wide-eyed.

He'd thought she'd like it. You couldn't *not* like it! It was a mural, a photo-wallpaper of a brightly coloured underwater fantasy scene. Glorious corals and shells and reefs were home to every kind of cartoon fish you could imagine. A smiling whale, a dancing octopus, starfish, crabs, seahorses and brilliant fish of every colour under the sun played and swam happily across the wall. 'The thing is, it's much thicker than normal paper, so nothing is going to show through. We might have even got away with just sticking it over the top, but if a job's worth doing and all that . . .'

'You're something else, you really are. That is *so* kind,' Stacey shook her head. 'You don't even *know* these people, Jay. It's such a lovely thing to do.'

'Oh, shut up, Smith! I'm just trying to ensure a nice comfy place in the afterlife whenever I'm called.' He chuckled. 'Actually, I really do believe in karma — what goes around comes around. But enough philosophy for now. We have work to do before you get your KFC, and as they close at eleven, I suggest we buckle down and get on.'

* * *

Jackman arrived home at Mill Corner just a few minutes after Laura.

'You've been working late too?' he asked as he peeled off his jacket.

She kissed him lightly. 'Typical. I was just leaving when I had a call to attend a possible crisis at Greenborough police station. It turned out to be nothing that a few encouraging words and a cup of tea wouldn't have sorted, but the man did have a history of some quite spectacular episodes, so I quite understood why they called me.' Laura walked into the kitchen, opened the fridge door and sighed. 'God bless Hetty Maynard! I was dreading having to prepare supper. I swear that woman is psychic! She's left a selection of cold cuts, salad and some of that delicious homemade coleslaw she makes.'

Jackman smiled. His cleaning lady-cum-housekeeper was worth her weight in gold. 'Before you came into my life, I would probably have starved, lived in a dump and had grass growing three foot high if it hadn't been for Hetty and her husband.'

While Laura brought out the food and laid the table, he opened a bottle of Chardonnay and poured two glasses. 'I'm so relieved that you are going to see Bennington tomorrow, Laura. I've tried reading up on the subject, but I find the whole concept of cults and extreme ideologies completely bizarre. Some of their views are so crazy that the only thing crazier is that people actually buy into them.'

Laura sat down at the table. 'I'm really interested in your man, Jackman. Not long after I began working profession-ally, Sam and I were involved in assessing a group of college students who'd been indoctrinated into a cult. If it hadn't been for the persistence of one kid's father and mother, they would never have broken free. That incident led us to write a paper on the kinds of people targeted by these radical groups, and the eight steps to mind control. It's still regarded as a go-to reference for students, even now.'

Jackman looked at her with renewed interest. 'I never knew that when I asked you to speak to him, it was just that their psychologist wasn't available. That's really fortuitous.'

'It's a subject that holds a particular fascination for me.' She helped herself to a slice of gammon. 'Oddly, I've been asked to contribute to an online psychology magazine with an article on the differences and similarities between cults that function as an organised group and those led by a solitary person whose aim is to dominate members using psychological abuse.'

'Then I can't imagine a better person to talk to him.' Jackman could hardly wait to tell Ashley Carpenter this news. To have someone with them who really understood his situation could benefit both the investigation and Bennington.

'So, my darling, give me as much of the background as you can.'

When Jackman told Laura that the members might have been fed hallucinogenic drugs, she nodded. 'Did you know that was exactly what Charles Manson did? He gave his followers large doses of LSD, knowing that every acid trip would take them a step further away from reality until they believed everything he said.'

Yet Bennington had managed to escape with most of his sanity intact. That puzzled Jackman.

'It's different from one person to another,' Laura said thoughtfully. 'People don't all react the same way. The ones who suffer most are those who joined the cult quite young, when their self-esteem was still poor, like my college students. It sounds like Bennington was still relatively young but strong-minded enough to have developed some self-belief.' She took a sip of wine. 'He'll be suffering — he must have been damaged, there's no doubt about that. Everyone leaves a cult in a different state of mind. Some are depressed, have anxiety problems, post-traumatic stress disorder and are subject to panic attacks, but common to everyone are feelings of shame, low self-esteem and anger.'

'I saw all of those in Bennington. Especially shame. He was constantly berating himself for what he'd done.'

'He is receiving proper professional treatment, isn't he?' Laura asked suddenly. 'He needs serious help with social reintegration, darling, and his self-blame. He should receive psycho-education from a therapist who really understands that type of mental damage.' She frowned. 'We badly need more experts in this field, we are few and far between.'

Jackman realised he didn't know what help Bennington was receiving, if any. 'He never mentioned any therapy.'

'Then I must check that and urge him to seek help. It's far too much to take on alone.'

'He might well already have someone, sweetheart,' Jackman said. 'It just wasn't mentioned when I was there. And of course, he is a key witness, a member of a cult that endorses and possibly performs ritualistic murder. He could be arrested, he could be placed in a safe house, or he could be hospitalised. There are a lot of uncertainties surrounding him and this case.'

'Then it's good I'm going to see him. I think my assessment will assist your new superintendent quite a bit, don't you?' Laura pushed her plate away and smiled. 'There's a pretty fair cheeseboard in the fridge, so cheese and biscuits and grapes to finish?'

'Absolutely! And I'll make coffee.' Jackman put their plates in the dishwasher. 'And on a different subject . . .' He told her about the graffiti at Solace.

'Odd, isn't it?' Laura said, arranging cheeses on a board. 'One minute everything's calm — I'm dealing with simple problems and you with comparatively petty crimes — then, wham! Back in at the deep end for both of us.'

All at once, Jackman envisioned shadows from a massive thundercloud creeping slowly forward and stealing the sun. Why did he feel so uneasy? It dawned on him that it wasn't the terrible murders and the traumatised Bennington that were making him so uncomfortable, it was the Stewarts and their ill-fated house. He couldn't stop wondering what would come next.

* * *

'This is like the official opening of a new motorway,' muttered Stacey. 'Where's the ribbon to cut? The official with a gold chain around his neck?'

Jay grinned. 'The mayor had a prior engagement. Anyway, this is far more important than a motorway.'

Stacey had to agree with him. 'Can I go and fetch the Stewarts now, or are you going to faff around all night?'

'No, all done, everything's tidied away. Right, Stace, you can go and get them.'

Stacey was quite excited. She looked forward to seeing their faces. Jay had done wonders. She thought again what an extraordinary human being this young man was.

When the Stewarts saw what he'd done with the wall, their mouths fell open. Holly burst into tears and Hugh laughed out loud. 'That's absolutely fantastic! The kids will go crazy when they see it. *Finding Nemo* is Poppy's all-time favourite film too. How on earth can we thank you? It's like a miracle. I mean, we don't have to explain anything now, we can just say we have a surprise for them. Oh, they are going to love that.' He turned to Jay and Stacey. 'But I have to pay for it. That sort of thing doesn't come cheap, I know.'

'I won't hear of it, sir,' Jay said immediately. 'I'm just happy that your children can have some pleasure from it. I bought it for my nephews and niece ages ago but never got the time to put it up. Now they're a bit too old for it and I'm reliably told they want a space exploration wall, with starships and the solar system. Honestly, it's saved it from the bin.'

Stacey knew full well that Jay's nephews were the same age as Aaron and Poppy and he'd bought the wallpaper only recently, but he had saved Hugh Stewart's pride. Another gold star for when Jay Acharya finally checked into the afterlife.

'You've both been so kind,' said Holly tearfully. 'It makes up for what has happened. I'll never forgive the animal that got in here, but at least you two, your inspector and his mother have proved that there are some really good people around.'

'It's time we went,' said Stacey, realising they only had twenty-five minutes before KFC closed. 'We'll call back tomorrow and check on you.'

As they passed through the lounge, she saw that the Stewarts had made good headway with the defaced wall, even though it was a long way from being finished. Still, it was now clean of the foul substance and painted with a grey undercoat.

'I'll get up early tomorrow,' said Hugh, 'and get a couple of coats of emulsion on it before I go to work. That should be enough to disguise the wicked message — well, at least enough so that the children won't see it.'

'Even if we'll always know it's there,' added Holly angrily. Then her face softened again. 'We couldn't have done half of this without your help. We'll be sure to let your inspector know.'

'Oh, no need,' said Stacey. 'Honestly. We're just glad we could help. And it was all Jay's idea.' She winked at Holly. 'His idea of showing a girl a good time when she's off duty. Nothing like a bit of DIY to bring you closer.'

They just made it in time to get their chicken supper and sat in Jay's car to eat it. It wasn't quite what Stacey had had in mind for this evening, but when she thought about it, she had really enjoyed herself. They both felt good about pulling off their impromptu revamp of the kids' room, and for once Stacey was on a high. She giggled. 'You'll get headhunted to join the team in the new series of *Changing Rooms*.'

They joked for a while, thinking up ever wilder careers for Jay, then he said, 'I'm scared for that family.'

Stacey understood what he meant. What had been done was cruel and vindictive and the Stewarts didn't deserve it. 'I reckon you and I should pull out all the stops to find out why someone wants them out of that house, don't you?'

'You have a fine mind, Stacey Smith. I'm with you all the way.'

'Good, because I'm going to suggest a little bit of unpaid overtime. If I can become a decorator's mate until almost midnight, you can be Dr Watson to my Sherlock Holmes. We are going to become secret private investigators in our spare time.'

Jay grinned through a mouthful of spicy hot chicken wing. 'You're on! High five?'

'High five!'

CHAPTER THIRTEEN

A weak and watery dawn trickled slowly across the horizon. Jackman had hoped for one of those glorious scarlet and orange sunrises that lifted the spirits and made you feel good about the day to come. It wasn't, so he left his solitary east-facing spot at the end of the garden in an even lower mood than before.

He wondered if the Stewarts had slept any better than him. He had called into Solace on his way home after work the previous evening and caught them just before they left to take the children out for their meal. They had both looked strung out. Out of Holly's hearing, Hugh had said he was considering moving the family into a low-cost B&B if his wages would cover it. 'The thing is, Inspector, Holly's there alone or just with the children when I'm at work. I'm afraid for their safety.'

Jackman switched the kettle on. If he were Hugh, he'd be afraid too. In fact, he was possibly even more anxious than Hugh. He had too often seen what people were capable of, and their victims were usually innocents — like Holly, Aaron, or little Poppy.

When he got to work this morning, no matter what came up, he was going to assign someone to work full-time on finding the bastard who was terrifying a whole family.

Laura was still asleep. He placed a mug of tea on her bedside cabinet and pulled some fresh clothes from the wardrobe, trying not to make a noise. He tiptoed out of the room and used the shower in the guest bedroom rather than wake Laura at this early hour.

Having dressed, he sat on the spare bed for a while, drank his tea and tried to decide how to divide his time between Saltern-le-Fen and Locksford. Today was no problem. He and Ashley had agreed that he should set up a team specifically to try and locate the second cult. They had a few possibilities, places that Martin Bennington had overheard Daemon and Apostle talking about. Plus, there was one small, possibly very important piece of information that Bennington had given them. He knew exactly how long it took to get from their first Locksford property, the Hollow — the one that had burned down — to the second commune. They would start there. It meant finding the Hollow, then tracing all possible locations an hour's drive from there.

According to Bennington, 'One day, there was a problem at Daemon's other place. The Master was busy for most of the day, so Apostle volunteered to go over there and sort it out. I was working in the house at the time, and I took a call from Apostle asking me to tell Daemon that he'd dealt with the problem and was just leaving to come home. It was two o'clock. Apostle arrived back on the stroke of three. I remember thinking, "One hour away, that's all. Another group, just like us, only sixty minutes from where I'm standing."'

Jackman smiled for the first time that morning. He liked a good solid starting point.

By seven o'clock, he had breakfasted and was ready to make an early start. He went back upstairs and found Laura just getting out of bed. God, she was beautiful, even with tousled hair and her eyes still bleary from sleep. He sighed with longing. There were days when he wished they lived a different kind of life, one that wasn't so demanding, so governed by the clock. Right now, all he wanted was to be with her and not to leave her side for the rest of the day. How precious she was to him.

Instead, he kissed her, wished her a good trip to Locksford and told her he hoped that her meeting with Bennington went well. He held her for a few moments longer than he usually did before letting her shoo him out of the room. She blew him a kiss from the doorway, and waved goodbye.

Oh well, he thought, it could be worse. At least they came home to each other.

* * *

Marie's thoughts were much the same. It was Ralph's last day off and she badly wanted to spend it with him. In fact, she wanted to spend a lot of days with Ralph, from dawn to dusk and right through the night. But they also both loved their jobs, which was good for their relationship because neither complained. Both understood the importance of the jobs they did and what it sometimes demanded of them.

So Marie pulled on her motorcycle leathers, took one last look at the man with the mussed-up hair and sleepy smile, kissed him and went off to work.

Jackman was already in the CID room, staring at the whiteboard. Next to the name "Daemon" he had written, "the Hollow."

'Very Agatha Christie,' she remarked.

'Marie! Sorry, I didn't hear you come in. I was miles away.'

'At the Hollow? Whatever that is,' she said.

'The commune. It's our starting point for today. We believe it was located in a place called Wiley Fen village.'

'Was?'

'It burned down. A ritual cleansing, apparently.' Jackman raised an eyebrow. 'Sacrificing their home and comforts to prove that their only requirement in life was to follow Daemon. Nice, huh?'

'Lovely.' She frowned. 'I don't know Wiley Fen myself. Do you?'

'It's not on our patch but we are free to wander with this case. Not that we'll have to. This search can be done with the help of our very own IT expert, the enigmatic Orac. I need an exact map reference for the area where the Hollow once stood.'

'Sounds like a no-brainer for her. Want me to go and ask her for you?' Marie stifled a smile. He was better than he used to be, but Jackman still grew awkward and embarrassed in the presence of Orac — Orla Cracken to give her her correct name — and would generally get someone else to speak to her for him if he could.

'Please, Marie. And ask her if, when she has found it, she would identify similar-size places that can be reached from it in an hour.'

Marie narrowed her eyes. 'The home of the Second Church of St Daemon?'

'Exactly one hour's drive from door to door, apparently. Daemon commuted between the two.' He paused. 'The thing is, while Daemon disbanded the Locksford group, excommunicating the followers and barring them from attaining his wonderful "knowledge," as well as possibly adding them to his List of the Fallen, Bennington had no idea what happened to the other branch of the cult. As far as he knows, they could still be alive and active.'

'And popping their dismembered victims into refuse sacks for the binmen,' Marie said grimly.

'I'm holding onto the hope that they were disbanded too, but someone is tidying up loose ends.' Jackman put down the marker pen. 'I was just about to work out how to divide up the team. Want to grab a couple of coffees and join me in my office? I'd appreciate your input before you go and beard the lioness in her den.'

'Sure thing, boss.' Marie went down to the vending machine wondering about Jackman. He looked a bit uptight to her, which wasn't usual for him. Solace. It wasn't the cult murders that were getting to him, it was the mystery of Solace House.

Taking a full cup from the vending machine, she wondered what more they could do to help. Between them, she, Ralph and Gary had discovered an awful lot about the place's history in so short a space of time. Apart from lying in wait every hour of the day and night to catch the bastard, she wasn't sure what else they could do. She had thought about suggesting cameras, but if the Stewarts couldn't afford to fell those trees, their budget wouldn't extend to having a CCTV system installed. Unfortunately, from a purely official policing point of view it didn't even come close to being a serious crime. They had a very limited budget for minor infringements like this, and anyway, CID definitely wouldn't be involved. That was why they were all spending their precious off-duty hours helping Jackman in his personal crusade. She smiled to herself. Well, it certainly showed how much they thought of their boss. And to be honest, she was rather looking forward to her late-evening sortie out to Amberley Fen to see if the dirty silver car that the Spriggs had reported seeing appeared.

There were few legitimate reasons for driving onto that part of the fen at night. That lane led nowhere, not to a main road, nor to some vegetable packing factory. Nothing other than Solace and about four other smaller properties scattered along that stretch. Well, tonight might provide some answers, and with any luck Ralph would dig up more information about the mysterious baby farm. He had told her he hoped she wouldn't mind him spending the day with another woman — namely the long-dead Ivy Pettifer.

Jackman looked up as she walked into his office. 'I've changed my mind, Marie. Would you go and see if Orac is in yet, and get her onto that search for me as a matter of urgency? We need to get an early start with finding the location of that commune. Everything else hinges on it.'

She put the coffees on his desk. 'I'll do it now.'

Orac was seated at her bank of screens. She looked up at Marie with a wry smile, the light from the screens causing her mirrored contact lenses to flash.

Marie grinned back. However many years went by, Orac never seemed to change. Those eyes, coupled with her white-blonde spiky Mohican haircut, threw most people, especially Jackman. Marie was the nearest thing to a friend that Orac possessed.

'Ah, the messenger.'

'Morning, Orac. Yes, Jackman sent me, as usual.'

'And what little nugget of information is he yearning for this morning — and so early, too?' Orac spoke in a soft Irish lilt that was at odds with her edgy appearance.

'We have a ritual murder, Orac. Two, actually, possibly three. Two old cases and one very recent. We believe they are the work of a cult. The only thing we know about them is that their headquarters, or whatever you call it, is somewhere in this area, exactly one hour's drive from a village called Wiley Fen and from the site of a burned-out building called the Hollow. Can you find us the exact coordinates of the Hollow?'

'Probably in the time it takes for you to walk back to Jackman's office. Anything else before breakfast?'

'Yes,' said Marie, adding a little request of her own. 'Everything you can discover about the Hollow. Who owned it and when, especially around twenty, twenty-five years ago. I'm interested in the time of the fire and just before that.'

Orac chuckled. 'Well, my friend, this is no challenge at all. Next time, please do better.'

Marie turned to go, then had another idea. She paused on the stairs, then decided to leave it till later. After the morning meeting she might just pay another visit to Orac's underground world. Orac was a bit of a wild card and not much of a respecter of protocol — maybe she could help them with some of the shadier aspects of Solace House's past and its two Victorian occupants.

* * *

When the team had gathered in the CID room, Jackman was pleased to see Kevin Stoner back. That made a full complement of officers, and he had a feeling he was going to need it.

He began by filling them in on what he had learned from the interviews with Martin Bennington about the cult he had belonged to. 'Naturally there is a lot more to be gleaned from him, but there is only so much that you can bombard him with at one time. He was badly damaged by his experience, and the last thing we want to do is cause him further harm. With that in mind, Superintendent Ashley Carpenter and I have made out a list of priorities, and today, while we concentrate on locating the second cult, she'll be working through that list. Her main objective will be to get a clear description of the man who calls himself Daemon, and also of his second in command, known as Apostle. Our own force psychologist is going to Locksford today to meet and hopefully assess Bennington. Luckily, she is pretty knowledgeable on the subject of cults.'

Kevin Stoner raised a hand. 'Excuse me, sir, but so is my father. I can talk to him, and I'm sure he'll be happy to assist the enquiry.'

Jackman was pleased and mildly surprised that they should have two people at hand who were familiar with this unusual phenomenon. Kevin's father was the Diocesan bishop and had probably been concerned with a very different aspect of such cults. 'Thank you, Kevin, that's good to know. I'll certainly keep it in mind.'

He was about to continue when the door opened, and PCs Stacey Smith and Jay Acharya entered.

'Sorry, sir,' said Stacey, 'we just wanted to update you on the situation at Solace as of late last night, but we'll come back when you're through here.'

'No, no, that's okay and please do join us if you have a few minutes. I was just coming to the subject of the intruder at the Stewart house.'

'Yes, sir,' said Stacey. 'The skipper knows where we are.' They pulled up chairs and sat down.

Jackman perched on the edge of a table. 'This seems a good point to mention the problem out at Amberley Fen.

It's not CID business, but I've become rather embroiled in it. I happened to meet the owners of the house in question, and they really need our help. For Kevin's sake, I'll just give a brief overview of the situation.' When he'd finished, he said, 'I'm going to allocate you all specific tasks regarding the ritual murders, but I'm going to ask for one volunteer to concentrate on the intruder out at the house called Solace.'

'I'd gladly volunteer, boss,' said Marie, 'but if you're going to be commuting between here and Locksford, I guess I'm going to be needed to hold the fort on the murder case.'

''Fraid so, Marie.' Pity. Marie knew more about the situation there than anyone, but it wasn't possible. No matter how much he cared about the Stewart family, he understood where his priorities lay. He was also aware that Marie was conducting her off-duty investigation. She seemed as eager to sort the situation out as he did.

'I suppose it had better be me,' said Gary somewhat reluctantly. 'I've been out there and spoken to the family and done a bit of homework on it. It's not my favourite place, I admit, but that family need all the help they can get, so, okay, boss, I volunteer.'

'Good man!' Gary was definitely Jackman's second choice, after Marie. 'Liaise with Stacey and Jay. We need to find that intruder and ask him why he's terrorising those people.' He turned to the two uniformed officers. 'How were they when you left them last night, Stacey?'

Stacey grinned. 'Well, thanks to Jay here, in a heck of a better place than they were earlier. He's worked wonders on the children's room, sir. You should see it.'

Jay blushed. '*We* did the work, sir, not just me.'

'All I did was slap a bit of paste around,' retorted Stacey. 'I know Jay won't thank me for this, sir — we said we wouldn't say anything — but on reflection, I think you ought to know that what he did was above and beyond the call of duty.'

'I'm very glad you did tell me. I'll be calling in later, so I'll be sure to have a look.' He glanced at the clock. 'Now, back to our plan for today. As soon as we hear back from Orac—'

Marie raised a hand. 'I've just had a text telling me she has something for us. Shall I go?'

He nodded. At last, things were beginning to move.

Marie was back in less than ten minutes with several sheets of A4 paper in her hand. 'She's pinpointed four places of interest that fit into that time-distance calculation. One of those is Birch Drove Farm. Now, we know that was not their HQ, but it's rather interesting that it's exactly one hour's drive from Wiley Fen.'

'And the other three, Marie?'

'There's a small plant nursery attached to a big house called Oak Barn at Gibbet Fen. Next is a sort of rambling hotel complex off Blackfriars Lane. And the last one is a big old manor house out on Keldyke Marsh. It's empty and has apparently been up for sale for over a year. Orac has given us the phone number of the estate agent that's handling it. She said that nowhere else that distance away in time is either large enough or suitable for housing a commune.'

'Then we'll split into pairs and tackle them immediately. Make enquiries locally first, don't just go hammering on the front door — we have no idea what we could be walking into. Tread warily and flag up any concerns with me or Marie. Max and Charlie take Oak Barn. Robbie and Kevin, you two look at the hotel at Blackfriars. Marie and I will get hold of the estate agent and go and see if the Keldyke Manor house holds anything for us. Everyone happy with that?'

There was a murmur of assent. 'Okay, off you go and keep me updated. In fact, considering what we are possibly dealing with, I think call in every hour, just so we're sure everyone is safe.'

As the team gathered up their things and prepared to leave, Jackman went over to Gary, beckoning Stacey and Jay to join them.

'Thanks for offering, Gary. I'm anxious to make sure nothing more serious happens out at that old house, especially to any of the family.' He glanced at the others. 'You all know how these scare tactics work. Whoever is doing this could up his game at any minute and I don't want any casualties.'

'We've asked our skipper if we can make Solace a priority, sir,' said Stacey. 'He says that as long as we don't get a shout to anything major, we can assist all we can.'

'Excellent. I appreciate your commitment, all of you. Now I'd better get back to the main investigation.'

The two constables left, but Jackman waved Gary back into his seat. 'Keep a close eye on Holly and the kids, Gary. I'm worried sick about them but I'm saddled with this big investigation. The timing stinks, but I have no option other than to concentrate on the murder.'

'I understand, boss. I'll help all I can, and I'll do my damnedest to find out who is behind it and why.'

Jackman clapped Gary on the shoulder. 'I know you will, and I won't forget that I owe you one.'

On his way back to the office, he saw Marie wave to him from her workstation. 'I've just had a call from Rory, boss. He wants you to ring him as soon as possible. How about I chase up that estate agent regarding Keldyke Marsh while you talk to the Prof?'

He stuck his thumb up, hurried into his office and dialled Rory's number.

'Ah, my favourite DI! Well, my favourite *male* DI. Can't upset Nikki Galena, now, can I?'

'And you are my favourite pathologist. Not that I know too many. Good morning, Rory. You wanted to speak to me?'

'Indeed I do! And I have a nice little piece of information for you, something you probably weren't expecting.' He paused dramatically. 'Drum roll, please.'

If this was anyone else, Jackman would have been telling them to just get on with it, but it was Rory, so he merely smiled.

'Well, it's regarding your unfortunate young woman, the one who turned up in my morgue on two separate occasions, er, due to her being dismembered. All the body parts match perfectly, so you do have a single victim. Hurrah, I hear you cry, but — and here is *la pièce de resistance* — her DNA was on file. Her name is Siobhan Aster, age twenty-five, originally from Hull but had been residing in Locksford for around five years.' He paused. 'This is the bit where you shower me with accolades and extol my prowess. Well, come on, I'm waiting!'

'I hardly know where to begin,' Jackman stammered. 'That's fantastic, Rory!'

'Oh well, I suppose being struck dumb by my brilliance is an accolade of sorts. But listen, dear heart, there's more. I've got hold of the old forensic reports from both historic murders — that of Shelley Harcourt and the one found at Birch Drove Farm— and run a series of comparisons. I can confirm without a doubt that it is not only the same man who butchered all three (he had a very particular cutting technique), but also that he used identical knives for each murder. As we thought, he used a sharp knife and a cleaver. I'll be sending you an image of a similar blade, as I believe I might have identified both the maker and the design. The flesh was cut with a distinctive and unusual boning knife, Japanese, Damascus steel, scalpel-sharp and a favourite of some professional chefs. Then the bone was severed with a cleaver. I could be wrong, but the dimensions of the cuts match pretty well perfectly with the blades in the picture. Find me the knives, Jackman, and I'll prove it beyond a doubt. They are the group's sacrificial knives and only those particular blades would be used for the ritualistic ceremonies. Impressive, eh?'

'Very impressive, Rory. It's one thing suspecting something, but quite another to have actual proof.' Jackman's mind had already started to race. He would need to contact Superintendent Carpenter straightaway. This was confirmation that their original killer was still active. 'What recorded crime was Siobhan Aster on the NDNAD for, Rory?'

'One moment.' There was a pause. 'Soliciting under section 51A of the Sexual Offences Act 2003. I'm afraid our young lady sold her favours for money.'

'Well, that might have been why she found herself on Daemon's List of the Fallen,' said Jackman. 'It would appear that the cult actively encouraged sexual activity within the group, but not with outsiders.'

Rory sighed. 'Ah, free love! Those were the days. Or so I'm told. And on that happy note, I have to leave you.'

'Before you go, Rory, could I ask a favour? It has nothing to do with the murders.'

'I am at your command, dear boy.'

'Last night, a SOCO took samples from some scrawls that an unwanted visitor had made on the walls of a house at Amberley Fen. We believe blood was used, mixed with paint or a similar medium. I know it's not a priority case — in fact it's way down the list — but I'm anxious to know what kind of blood it was.'

'What was the surname of the homeowner and the house name or number?' Rory asked. Jackman could hear him tapping on a keyboard.

'The name is Stewart. The house is called Solace.' He held his breath.

'It's logged in, yes, I see it. A low priority.' Rory paused. 'But if it helps, I'll get either Spike or Cardiff to analyse it later this morning. The rest of the evidence will have to wait, but they can run the blood sample. I'll get them to ring you when they have an answer.'

'You're a diamond, Prof.'

'I know. Bye-bye!'

'Boss,' Marie stood in his doorway, 'I've got a key organised for this old place out at Keldyke. The agent also thinks he might have a bit of history on the house. He's going to look it up for me. If you're tied up here, shall I go and pick the key up, and see what he has for us?'

'I do have a call to make, so yes, if you don't mind. Then we'll head there directly. And, Marie, Rory has found us a name for your dead girl. She was a prostitute called Siobhan Aster and she was from Locksford.'

Marie whistled. 'Wow! And there wasn't even a head to identify her with. That was speedy, even for the Prof. How did he manage it? Or was her DNA on the National Database?'

He nodded. 'It was. The bad news is that the same person murdered both Angel and Shelley.'

She pulled a face. 'Oh my God. Still killing after twenty years. Makes you wonder if he ever stopped, doesn't it?'

'It makes me wonder where the hell he is right now.' Jackman was suddenly afraid for his team. What if they walked into something they weren't prepared for?

'I know what you're thinking,' Marie said. 'Well, that's not going to happen. I've been wondering about this commune and I'm willing to bet it no longer exists. Anyone living nearby would know if there was some odd community on their doorstep. There was a big old house close to my mum's village that was a kind of shelter, they called it a fellowship house. The world and his wife had an opinion on what really went on there. You can't have a sort of kibbutz in a village on the Fens and keep it secret.' She threw him a smile. 'Be honest, have you ever heard of such a place in the last ten years or so?'

'No, I haven't, but it could still exist in the guise of something else, like a hotel. I'm thinking about Robbie and Kevin.'

'Who are two very sensible detectives, boss. And they will do exactly as we would and sound out the locals and the territory, you know that.' She sounded like a schoolmistress, and he told her so.

'Well, honestly! They are hardly going to charge into said hotel and start asking about mind control, are they? Now, make your call and I'll collect the key to our deserted manor house.' She turned to leave and looked back over her shoulder. 'And calm down. The boys will be fine!'

CHAPTER FOURTEEN

Charlie and Max sat in the car park outside the nursery, next to a sign offering fresh organic vegetables and free-range eggs, as well as a selection of garden plants and shrubs grown on-site. They had already checked out a few of the locals — a dog walker, a middle-aged man with a white van who was offloading a mower and some grass cutting tools, and an elderly couple tending their front garden.

They had been told that the nursery had been there for ages. According to the old man, it had changed hands a few times in the distant past, but the Timpson family had owned it for "donkey's years." To all intents and purposes the place seemed above board, but they knew not to go by appearances.

'It's not going to rival the big garden centres, is it?' remarked Charlie Button.

'No,' agreed Max. 'But they must be doing something right if they've kept going for so long.'

'And that old house, Oak Barn, looks like it would take a bit of upkeep too, it's well big.' Charlie looked at the house beside the nursery.

'Big enough for a commune?' Max asked him.

'Depends how many people are in the group, doesn't it? There's outbuildings round the back, but you can't see beyond the glasshouses and the polytunnels. Let me just get a satellite view of this place. I reckon it's bigger than it looks.' He pulled out his phone. 'This is well out of date, but there are definitely some other structures out back, could be store-sheds, it's too fuzzy to make out clearly.' He pushed his phone back in his pocket. 'Let's go and take a look in the shop.'

Inside, they found fresh produce, mainly eggs and honey, all neatly laid out on one side of the area, and on the other, extending back into an outside area, were tables, trolleys and display units full of trays and pots of plants. Max was no gardener, but even he could see that they looked very healthy.

'Just looking? Or can I help you?' The friendly voice came from behind a heap of sacks of potting compost.

'I wanted some fresh eggs,' said Max brightly.

'Certainly. Brown, white, blue or duck?'

'Er, brown please. A dozen.' He'd never eaten a duck's egg in his life and had no idea if the woman was joking when she mentioned blue ones. Then he saw the selection and marvelled at the various colours.

'The blue ones come from our cream Legbar hens. The colour of eggshells depends on the breed that lays them.'

The woman was clearly amused at his surprise at seeing blue and green hen's eggs. She had weathered skin — not wrinkled exactly, just tanned and leathery from long hours spent working outside. She must have been in her forties, he guessed, and had long wavy brown hair with a few threads of grey.

'You're not from around here, are you?' she said.

'No, we were on our way to Saltern and saw your sign. I like to get fresh eggs for my two little ones, but I'm not sure what they'd make of those blue jobs.'

She laughed. 'You throw the shell away, don't you? It doesn't really matter what colour it is, but I'll tell you this, those blue eggs have the most glorious deep yellow yolks and are as tasty as any of the brown ones.'

155

Max smiled. 'Okay, give me six of those as well. You're a good saleswoman.'

'It's just the truth. You'll see when you come to eat them.'

Max was aware that while he was engaging her in conversation, Charlie would be having a good look round. 'I'm glad we saw you, then.' He fished around in his wallet for a note, being careful not to let her see his warrant card. 'My wife would love it here. The twins are old enough now not to take up every moment of her time and she's getting into gardening.'

'Nothing better.' The woman smiled warmly. 'Bring her here one day. We all know our plants, we could help her choose which ones to put where.'

'I might just do that,' he said. 'You have some lovely stock, don't you?'

'Mostly grown here. The whole family are involved in one way or another.' She looked at him with interest. 'My name is Belinda. If she needs any advice, get your wife to ask for me when she comes.'

Max noticed that Charlie was looking through an open doorway that led through to a massive polytunnel.

'It must take a whole army of you to look after all this,' he commented casually.

'Oh no, not really. The watering in the tunnels and the glasshouses is done automatically on timers. The temperature is controlled too, and the roof shades are automated so they come down if it becomes too hot, not that that happens too often, but the sun can catch you out and fry your precious plants. Can't have that.'

He chatted on until he saw Charlie ambling back towards him. 'Better get off, I suppose. Thank you, Belinda, see you again hopefully.'

Back at the car, he put the eggs in the boot, telling Charlie not to let him forget them or they'd end up boiled by the end of the shift. With that, they drove off.

'So? What's the verdict?' he asked Charlie.

'Professional-looking set-up for a small business. All that automation will have cost a bomb. There were very few staff or workers that I could see, but there were quite a few kids' toys and a swing in the area to the side of the house. There were several vehicles parked around the back too.' He paused. 'Oh, and a washing line with clothes of different sizes — men, women, boys and girls. I'd say the Timpsons have a pretty large family. Nothing shouted out commune, just family life. So, what did you glean from the woman?'

Max pulled into the main road back to Saltern. 'She definitely works with the plants, you could tell by her hands, they were quite rough.'

'So, nothing to flag up for the boss? Because it's time to ring in.' Charlie had his phone in his hand.

Max didn't answer for a moment. 'No, nothing really, Charlie, but even so, when we get back, I'd like to check with the land registry and see how big their plot of land is and exactly what is on it. I keep thinking that it's smack bang in the right area, a one-hour drive from the Hollow, and I don't want to miss anything. Sure, it looks dead innocent, but we've seen very little of it, haven't we? Tell Jackman that it seems clean, but we need to look further.'

'Will do, and for what it's worth, I think you're right. The only thing that makes me think it really is just a family business is that the locals aren't bothered at all by the Timpsons. Not one of them suggested that anything out of the ordinary might be going on there.'

Max decided that he'd go back and take Rosie with him. Like he'd said, she was ace at reading people. Maybe she'd see something he'd missed. His in-laws had the twins tomorrow afternoon, so maybe they'd go and buy a few plants.

* * *

'Blimey! What sort of hotel is this?' Kevin was driving slowly past the entrance to the Eastwood Lakes Complex.

'The website wasn't as informative as I'd have expected,' said Robbie. 'And we can see naff all from the road.'

'The entrance isn't exactly welcoming either. I mean, no offers of a carvery open to the public, or even a bar that locals could use.' Kevin frowned. 'You'd think in this day and age they'd be trying every tactic in the book to keep out of the red. The hotel and hospitality business isn't exactly flourishing, especially in a small backwater like Saltern-le-Fen.'

As Robbie had said, practically nothing could be seen of the hotel itself. The drive curved away from the road into tall trees and shrubbery, which edged the entire perimeter. 'There's a few local shops a bit further along. Let's see what the neighbours think of Eastwood Lakes.'

Kevin stopped outside a small convenience store-cum-post office. He looked at Robbie. 'So, what excuse do we make for asking questions? Are we lost?'

'Follow my lead, Kev,' grinned Robbie. He'd been working that one out as they drove.

Inside the shop he picked up a newspaper and two packets of crisps and took them to the counter.

'Mornin' duck! Nice one again.' The woman behind the counter beamed at him. Her florid complexion made him think of children's stories.

'Certainly is.' He smiled back and handed her a five-pound note. While she was getting his change, he asked, 'I wonder if you can help me? That hotel, back up the road a bit, do you know if they do functions? We are looking for a venue for a wedding reception and this location would be perfect.'

'The Lakes? Oh no, me duck, you don't want to go there. It's not that sort of hotel.'

'Oh,' said Robbie dejectedly. 'Shame. It would have been so convenient for the relatives to get to.'

'So, what kind of hotel is it then?' asked Kevin, looking innocent.

The woman gave a little laugh. 'Hard to say, really. It's been a lot of different things in its time. When old man

Hargreaves had it, the Lakes was a *proper* hotel. Had a bit of class, you know? But then the son took over and extended it, and that was when the rot set in. Overextended, more like.' She sniffed. 'They tried all sorts to make it work, but nothing really succeeded. One of the Hargreaves still owns it, but it's more a kind of residential fishing lake now. They put up cabins and got some big static caravans and people rent them, some book in for a long-term stay and some might even own them now. I dunno for sure about that, but we sees a lot of the same folks coming and going.'

Robbie stiffened. Could this really be the commune, right under the noses of the locals? 'Interesting.' He looked at her and grinned. 'No use for what I wanted, but my future father-in-law is always on about finding a nice little place to chill out and do a bit of fishing. Well-stocked lake, is it?'

'You got me there, duck, but I'm supposin' it must be. There wouldn't be so many folk stay there if it were rubbish, now, would there?' Her smile faded. 'But I think your new dad will be out of luck at this place. They aren't taking any more bookings. I had an old fellow in here a few days ago, well upset he was, because he'd gone up there to make enquiries and they were real unhelpful. No vacancies, so sling your hook, was the impression he got.' She shrugged. 'Mind you, since old man Hargreaves pegged it — 'e were a lovely man, 'e were — the rest of the family are a different kettle of fish altogether. Daniel — he's the eldest and the owner of the Lakes — is bloody rude, excuse my French.'

Robbie looked at Kevin. 'Looks like we'll give them a miss, bro.'

'Definitely,' said Kevin. 'And thanks for your help. You've saved us getting told to sling our hook.'

The woman laughed. 'You'd do better to go upmarket if you can afford it, lad. The Saltern Country Club do *beautiful* weddings.'

They thanked her again and left.

Back in the car, Kevin said, 'Will you ring DI Jackman, or shall I?'

'Hold up for a moment, Kev.' Robbie was thinking fast. 'Pull up an aerial map and let's see if we can get a better look at these cabins from above. There might be a back entrance, or at least somewhere that'll give us a better view.' He didn't march in with some bogus enquiry, that would be too risky, but a surreptitious recce would help them make up their minds.

Kevin found a Google map of Blackfriars Lane and converted it to satellite view. 'There are too many trees and bushes to see much, but it looks like there are two lakes and I can make out a few big static caravans, but no cabins. I guess this was taken years back.' He passed it to Robbie.

'Here. See?' He jabbed his finger at the screen. 'Looks like we might be able to get a look at the main house and one of the lakes from here. If any cabins were built since the satellite photos, they'll most likely be close to the lake.' He was pointing at a gated entrance down a narrow single-track lane that was most likely an unused emergency rear exit. It ran parallel to a field and seemed to go nowhere but the rear of the hotel.

'So long as we don't meet anyone, this is our best bet. We can see the place for ourselves and take a few photos for the boss.'

Kevin agreed, reached over to the back seat and picked up a dog lead.

'When did you get a dog?' Robbie said, puzzled.

'I haven't got one.' Kevin smiled at him. 'But what better excuse for checking out places like this than looking for a lost pooch?'

'Nice one. Off we go to look for poor Rover,' Robbie said.

Kevin parked the car in a lay-by, and they made their way back on foot. 'It's been just over an hour, Rob. We should ring in. The boss'll be worried.'

'Okay. I'll tell him we're still talking to the locals and we'll be able to tell him more when we get back.'

About a quarter of a mile along the grass-covered lane, they came to the gate.

'I'd say no one's driven along this track in years, wouldn't you?' commented Kevin.

'And the gate is padlocked, rusty too. But we can see the hotel from here and a few of the cabins. Nothing special, are they? I was expecting some of those nice Finnish log cabins — you know, with a hot tub on the veranda.' Robbie took several shots of the rather unimpressive chalets.

'The hotel's a bit of a dive too,' said Kevin. 'I wouldn't fancy a romantic weekend here.'

They stared at the place in silence for a while. 'What do you reckon?' Robbie asked finally.

'If it was down to me, I'd bring in the uniforms, do an official search,' said Kevin. 'But that won't happen, will it? Too much red tape and we've got nothing to suggest anything more sinister than a seedy hotel that rents out cheap cabins to fishermen.' They turned and strode back towards the car.

'Hey, Rob.' Kevin came to a sudden halt. 'Where were all the people? The old dear in the post office said they were fully booked and it's a nice day. Aren't they supposed to be fishing?'

'You're right,' Robbie said. 'I'm not sure what really is going on here, Kev, but ten to one, it's not what it seems.'

* * *

Marie returned from the estate agent to find that Jackman was yet again on the phone.

The office manager handed her an envelope. 'This came up from IT while you were out.'

They were printouts sent by Orac, written across the top were the words, *"The Hollow. Owners from 1900 to present day. Threw in some images to give you some idea of before and after. Will dig deeper. O."*

Marie looked first at the pictures. The name had conjured up an Agatha Christie novel, but the pictures Orac had found showed a stunning 1930s house in pure art deco style.

In the first photograph it was painted white with a characteristic symmetrical design, broken up by a curved wall and windows and with a balcony above. It might have provided the setting for a Poirot film.

As Marie could see from later pictures, the Hollow remained an iconic building, little altered and obviously well-cared-for. Until, that was, she came to a photograph taken some twenty-five years ago. The gardens, once consisting of rolling lawns and elegant walks and flowerbeds, were now a jungle, a mixture of plants and vegetables amid poultry runs, rabbit hutches, greenhouses, sheds and stores. The white paint on the exterior of the house was peeling and weatherworn. Several panes of glass in the steel-framed Crittall windows had been broken, with pieces of what looked like hardboard jammed into the gaps. It was a sad shadow of a once impressive piece of architectural history. Marie fancied that despite its state of neglect, the house still retained some vestige of its proud heritage, as if declaring, "I'm still here! A coat of paint and some love is all I need."

The last picture came as a shock. Although Marie was perfectly aware that the Hollow had been deliberately burned down, after seeing all those photos of it in its glory days she was brought up short. It was a shell, with only the walls still standing, blackened and looking like they were ready to collapse at any moment. The metal frames of the windows were twisted and buckled. The smell of burnt paint seemed to rise from the paper she held in her hands.

She pushed the pictures back into the envelope. Was there more to this than Daemon had told his followers? Was it deliberate arson? An insurance claim?

Marie scanned the accompanying printout, a list of dates and names with just a short clarification beside each. Apparently, the house had been built for a prominent artist back in the thirties. The woman had been a progressive — a socialist and a Modernist — and her house had been a hub for people who thought the same way about art and politics. Five years after it was built, she died suddenly and the house was purchased by a local landowner called Wilson Nash and from the names beneath his, it had been in Nash family hands until its demise.

She let out a low breath. So was Daemon a Nash? She ran her finger down the list. The last name was Jerome Nash. Was she looking at the cult leader's real name? Marie rang Orac.

'I was expecting a call from you, Marie.' Orac sounded amused. 'And, yes, my comment about digging deeper refers to Mr Jerome Nash and a possible insurance claim. Is that what you are thinking?'

'I could have saved myself the call, couldn't I?' Marie said, laughing. 'I'd forgotten about your telepathic powers.'

'Well, you'll be pleased to know that I've delegated my present commitments to my faithful Philip and am now concentrating solely on your very interesting case. Anything you want traced, send it to me and if I haven't already pre-empted your request, I'll do it immediately. My interest is aroused, and you know what that means.'

Marie did and was grateful. 'How about I throw the whole case to you, the cult and the three deaths?'

'Music to my ears, Marie Evans, and sooner rather than later. I'm positively craving to get my teeth into it. Such a difference to my usual line of work.' Orac was practically purring.

Marie promised she would get onto it as soon as she returned from Keldyke Marsh. Then, chancing her luck, she threw in an unofficial request for info about Solace House, Sally Pinket and Ivy Pettifer.

'Fantastic! Victorian murderesses and dangerous cults, all in one day. How refreshing! Okay, give me what you have and leave me to wallow in my good fortune. Fraud and cybertheft were beginning to bore me, so you've made my day.'

Marie hung up almost overcome with relief — and gratitude. With Orac on board there'd be no more skeletons in cupboards. If there was anything to find, she would find it.

'Oh, Marie, sorry for all the hold-ups.' Jackman was hurrying towards her. 'But if you're ready, we can go and check out our manor house.'

* * *

Laura was alone in Ashley Carpenter's office. The superintendent was out dealing with another aspect of the enquiry and Laura had made use of the quiet to write up her observations on Martin Bennington.

His intensity, his odd mood swings, had been quite exhausting and she was glad of a coffee and a couple of biscuits. Bennington was certainly high-maintenance but extremely interesting. She wished her friend and old tutor Sam had been with her. She liked nothing better than discussing her more intriguing cases with him, and his input was always invaluable. She determined to contact him as soon as she got home. This particular one — recovery from indoctrination — was probably the most fascinating of all the psychological conditions she had come across in her professional life. She had studied it in depth and had become quite an authority on the subject.

She stirred her coffee, watching it slowly revolve and settle. At the end of this investigation she planned to produce, along with Sam Page, a case study that she hoped would become one of the most definitive papers on the psychological effects of indoctrination into a cult. She was fortunate enough to have spent time with an American colleague who had been involved in counselling some of the survivors of the Branch Davidian's "end of days" cult at Waco in Texas. She'd dig out his accounts along with some of the original transcripts when she got back to Mill Corner. She'd only spent one short session with Bennington so far, and he had displayed some of the expected reactions, but there were others that needed careful monitoring. Her colleague's notes and Sam's opinions would be vital in making her final assessment.

She still felt a little drained, but excited too. This was a significant case. Her conclusions about Bennington could have repercussions for the study of psychology but were also important to Jackman and Superintendent Carpenter. When she'd had more time with Bennington she would be able to let them know what questions they could safely ask and the best way to approach the more difficult or emotional ones.

'Sorry, Laura.' Ashley Carpenter hurried in. 'Got waylaid.'

'No problem,' said Laura. 'I needed a bit of time to assimilate my first meeting with Bennington.'

'I needed a good hour and a large whisky after my first meeting with him, I can tell you!'

Laura smiled. 'DI Jackman said much the same.'

'Every time I see Bennington I can't help being amazed at how he has managed to readapt after so many years away from society.' Ashley sat down at her desk. 'He even has a job. Well, he did before it all flared up again.'

'Was it one involving minimal human contact, or very unsociable hours?' Laura asked.

'Yes, it was. Night security, I believe.'

'Then that's how he coped with work. It's quite common in these cases. They are used to working hard and being told what to do, so that part is easy. Social integration is not, so they choose a job where they work on their own.'

'Well, I should get back in there, he's had his rest break.' Ashley pulled a face. 'I'm desperate to get a description of Daemon and I reckon now is my best chance. He's twitchy, as you'll have seen, but he's fairly stable today. I was wondering if you'd like to sit in as an observer?'

'I certainly would,' Laura said. 'I'd be glad of a chance to study his responses. Thank you.' She drained her cup. 'Ready when you are.'

CHAPTER FIFTEEN

Gary gazed at the wall in the children's bedroom. When he remembered what it looked like the last time he saw it, the transformation was little short of a miracle.

'Awesome, isn't it?' said a small voice from behind him.

'Totally, Aaron,' said Gary, and meant it.

The little boy gave a laugh. 'Poppy and I thought something was wrong, but Mummy and Daddy just wanted us out of the way so they could do us our surprise. We had the best time at Auntie Harriet's too — Poppy can't stop talking about Sherbet. He's the pony we're allowed to look after and even ride sometimes.'

'Oh, that's wonderful,' said Gary. 'Do you like riding?'

'Oh yes! I'm going to be as good as Ryan one day.'

They went back downstairs to where Holly was keeping a watchful eye on her daughter, who was sitting on the doorstep drinking a glass of milk, the dog Rory at her side.

When the two children were out of earshot, Gary said, 'You and the others achieved an amazing amount last night.' He raised an eyebrow. 'Their room is a masterpiece.'

'Thanks to your two officers. The children adore it.' She lowered her voice. 'Hugh got up at the crack of dawn and did some more to the lounge before I picked the kids up. I'm going to put a final coat on later today, and then it should be well covered.' She looked down. 'I'm trying to keep busy. If I stop, I begin to imagine all sorts of dreadful things.'

Gary didn't blame her. He too was worried. 'Well, I'm going to check with your nearest neighbours and see if anyone has heard any rumours on the Amberley Fen grapevine. Stacey or Jay, maybe both, will be out here soon, just to keep an eye on things while you're alone.'

Holly squeezed Gary's arm. 'I can't tell you how much we appreciate your help. All we want is for you to catch whoever is doing this and stop him. All right, we made a terrible mistake in coming here — maybe we were greedy, just seeing a bargain and thinking no further — but we would *never* have dragged our children into this nightmare if we'd had any idea of what was going to happen. We sincerely believed that the house was going for such a low price because someone had been killed here, and that didn't bother us. We just looked forward to a new life in the countryside and a happy future for the children.'

'I suppose no one else was trying to buy it at the same time as you?' The thought had just struck him.

'I doubt it.' Holly gave a bitter laugh. 'I've a feeling that estate agent had been trying to offload it for months, maybe years. We were the first mugs to actually put in an offer for it, as far as I know.'

'And do you know who the vendor was?'

'Yes, a couple called Hardy. I think they split up while they were here. They didn't stay long.' She sighed. 'We should have known, shouldn't we?'

'Mrs Stewart, would you mind if I spoke to your solicitor and the estate agent? I'm just wondering if the previous owners were frightened off like you're being, especially if they were only here for a while.'

'Please do. I'll get you their contact details.' Holly took an address book from a shelf. 'Here we are. Millgate and Foreshore were the estate agents — we dealt with John Millgate — and our solicitors are Edwards and Co. A woman called Lizzie Crisp dealt with the conveyancing.'

Gary jotted down the names and telephone numbers. He seemed to remember Harriet Jackman telling him that two other lots of people had moved into Solace in the last five years, neither staying very long. She had put it down to the house's reputation, but Gary was beginning to suspect something darker. He had no idea what, but this went far deeper than a grim old house with a scary reputation. 'I'll check it out as soon as I get back to the station. Will you be okay on your own for a bit? Stacey is due any moment and I'd like to do my tour of the neighbours.'

'I'm fine, Gary. I don't expect you to babysit me all the time, honestly.' She stopped. 'And I think I hear a car. That's probably her now.'

As the engine noise grew louder, Gary realised it wasn't a car at all. 'That's a farm vehicle, Holly.' The noise mounted almost to a roar. 'What the . . . ?'

Gary raced to the door, grabbed Poppy and swung the surprised child into Holly's arms. Rory the dog hurried in after them. 'Get Aaron, Holly, and keep them inside!'

Without waiting for an answer, Gary flung open the back door and ran outside. He had no idea what he'd find out there, but he was certain it wasn't going to be good. He did not expect to run around to the front door and be confronted by a massive and filthy piece of farm equipment being reversed up the gravel drive by a tractor.

'Stop! No! Police! Turn that engine off!' he yelled.

When it was level with the front of the property, the tractor did indeed stop. Just long enough to engage the hopper — which was heaped high with stinking manure.

Just as Gary got level with the tractor cab, it pulled forward again and a great wave of manure shot-blasted the house.

Furious, and unable to believe what was happening, Gary jumped onto the first step of the tractor cab and tried to haul himself up. He managed to make it to the second step and flung back the door. Pulling himself almost level with the cab seat, he bellowed, 'For fuck's sake, stop this thing!'

Instead of obeying, the driver, his face obscured by a scarf, leaned across and shoved Gary backwards. Gary might well have been crushed to death under the massive tractor tyre below, but the force of the thrust threw him onto the ground just out of range.

As he fought for breath and tried to struggle up, he saw that the muck spreader had done its work. The big tractor was accelerating up the drive towards the lane. Bruised and winded, he staggered after it, desperately trying to spot something that would identify the machine.

He got to the bottom of the drive and collapsed onto the verge, helplessly watching the muck-coated wagon roar out of sight.

Stacey and Jay found him still sitting there, four or five minutes later.

'Blue tractor, muck spreader on back!' he gasped. 'That way!' He pointed down the fen lane. 'Try and stop him.'

Stacey directed Jay to go after the tractor, while she knelt down beside Gary.

'Whatever happened, Gary? Are you okay?'

'I think I've bust a rib, Stace. It hurts like hell. The bastard has blasted a full trailer-load of muck over the house.' Gary knew a bit about farming, enough to know that a muck spreader like that one was capable of emptying ten tons of slurry over ten metres in less than a minute. 'I dread to think what state the house is in.'

Stacey helped him up and they made their way slowly back to the house.

Fresh manure clung to the entire frontage, dripping from open windows and windowsills and forming stinking muddy puddles on the path. Forgetting the pain he was in, Gary stood and stared, aghast. He could have cried for the Stewart family.

'Oh my God!' breathed Stacey and gagged at the stench.

'We need to go round to the back. He reversed the spreader round to the front door rather than spray the blank wall.' He groaned. Every breath, every word he spoke was agony. 'Sorry, Stace, but when Jay gets back, I think I need to go to the hospital.'

Stacey helped him inside. Holly gasped when she saw him. 'You're hurt! Oh, Gary, what happened to you?'

'Some meatloaf of a man objected to my trying to hitch a lift on his tractor,' he muttered and forced a grin at the two frightened children, who were staring at him wide-eyed. 'Stacey, ring this in for me, would you? And notify Jackman immediately. He could have killed me. That tractor had its plates covered, all I know is that it was blue and was a New Holland brand.'

'Great, the one everyone uses round here.' Stacey took out her phone. 'Let's just hope Jay can find him.'

Gary doubted it. At the bottom of the lane were three converging fen roads, two of which tied up with the main road back to Saltern. Even if Jay hit on the right one, there were countless farm buildings along those stretches, and the tractor had had about five minutes' start on the police car. Gary hadn't seen much of the machine, but he knew it was the latest model, capable of reaching over forty miles an hour.

Fifteen minutes later he was proved right when an angry-looking Jay returned, saying he hadn't even caught a glimpse of the tractor, but he had found a spreader abandoned in the entrance to a field.

'Ditched it so it could go faster, I suppose,' said Jay, then looked harder at Gary. 'Bloody hell, mate. You need medical attention.'

'I do,' Gary agreed, 'but we can't leave Holly and the children alone, especially with the house in this state. Have you seen the mess, Jay?'

'I could hardly miss it. I came the other way round the house when I saw all that slurry.'

'Look, Gary,' Stacey said, 'I either ring for an ambulance or I take you to the hospital myself and Jay can stay here with Holly. And then, well, there's only one way I can think of to get all this muck off — we shut the house up tight and get the pressure hoses going.' She looked at Holly. 'Half your gravel drive might finish up in the next village, but if we hose the house down, then sweep all the residue into the bushes, I think we can sort it.'

Again, Jay came to the rescue. 'If there's an outside tap, I've got a petrol-driven pressure washer. As soon as Stacey is back, I'll go and pick it up.'

'There's two taps,' said Holly, looking dazed. 'One back and one front.'

'Even better. I'll ring our sarge and get him to send a car with the one from the station too, then Stacey and I can get to work.' He looked at Gary. 'So, what's it to be, Gary? Ambulance, or Stacey?'

But Stacey had made the decision for him. 'Ambulance please, to Solace, Green Lane, Amberley Fen. We have a police officer injured after being pushed from a moving vehicle.' She gave Holly a wry smile. 'That should get 'em here smartish. Do you want me to go with you, Gary?'

'It's okay. You do what you can here, but perhaps you'd ring Gilly for me and ask her to meet me at A & E. I'm a bit breathless and I don't want to frighten her.' He found Gilly's number and handed Stacey his phone.

Stacey assured Gilly it wasn't serious, they just wanted to be on the safe side. 'She'll go there directly, and she'll take you home after you've been checked over. Oh, and I'll update DI Jackman.'

Gary was glad to have had Stacey and Jay there. He had landed on something hard when he fell to the ground, a stone or something. Whatever it was, he was sure it had broken a rib or two.

He felt bad at leaving them all with this mess to clear up, but he had no choice. Indeed, it was a great relief to hear Aaron exclaim that a *big* ambulance had arrived.

* * *

Jackman ended the call and uttered a groan.

'What's the matter, boss?' asked Marie, her eyes on the road as she negotiated a sharp bend.

'Gary's on his way to A&E. Stacey Smith says it's not life-threatening, but the paramedics want him checked over thoroughly in case of a pneumothorax. He's bust a couple of ribs.'

'Oh shit! Poor Gary. Want me to reroute to the hospital?'

'No. According to Stacey he specifically said we weren't to go. His friend Gilly is going to wait there with him until he is discharged. He'll update us then. He's more worried about the Stewart family after this latest stunt.' He frowned. 'Let's get this excursion out of the way and go and see what the hell has happened there now.'

Stacey's earlier report had upset him. This was becoming serious, and now Gary had been hurt on a voluntary job Jackman himself had authorised. It was time to make this official. They couldn't continue pussyfooting around in their spare time. He could see this nasty affair ending up with something really bad happening if they didn't take proper control.

'I don't like that long silence, boss,' said Marie quietly. 'I'm guessing someone is feeling guilty because our Gary decided to act the superhero and dive onto a bloody great tractor. Which,' she threw him a quick smile, 'he is probably thinking better of right now. And I'm willing to bet he isn't blaming anyone but himself.'

Jackman was forced to give her an answering smile. 'I'm sure he *is* regretting it, but so am I. And apart from wanting to see how he is, we do need to ask him first-hand what actually happened. This maniac has gone too far now — we have an injured detective. So, as soon as we are back at base, I'm going to see Ruth Crooke.'

'Absolutely. Oh my! Ritual murders, now this. It never rains and all that.'

Ten minutes later they were making their way up a neglected, overgrown drive. Unlike the places the rest of the team had gone to see, they were going directly to the front door, as the estate agent had assured them the house was empty. He said he'd only been out there a day or so ago and seen no sign of squatters or other intruders.

It took just a brief look inside for Jackman to know that this place hadn't played host to any cult. It was one of those houses that was just too big to sell easily. Having suffered multiple attempts to "modernise" it, the house was too outdated to attract anyone looking for an authentic period home and too damn expensive for what it was. Thick dust coated every surface, the windows needed cleaning and there were no substantial outbuildings. It had not been lived in, or cared for, for a very long time.

'I think we can safely cross this one off the list, don't you?' Marie said.

'Yeah, a wasted journey,' agreed Jackman. 'But we had to see it for ourselves. From the way they spoke, I'm pinning my hopes on Robbie and Kevin. They are well concerned about that weird hotel at Blackfriars. We might just have to pay them a visit.'

'An official one?'

He wondered that himself. 'Remains to be seen. We'll talk to the lads and see what their take on the place is.'

And then his thoughts returned to Gary, and to the family whose house had now been further desecrated. 'Let's get back to base, Marie. It's almost two thirty, I need to tie in with Locksford again, talk to Ruth, and then I want to get out to Solace *and* see Gary. No matter what he says, I won't be happy until I've seen him for myself.'

'I'd better put my foot down then, boss.'

* * *

Ruth Crooke listened carefully to what Jackman had to say. She pursed her narrow lips. 'With anyone other than you, Rowan Jackman, I think you can guess what my answer would be. Of course I feel sorry for the Stewarts, but it's hardly CID's problem, and the fact that you had Gary Pritchard out there deserves a severely slapped wrist. But. It is you, Jackman, and I completely trust your judgement. I too can see this escalating into something much more serious and it does need to be stopped.' She sat back and stared at him. 'My predicament is this. You have a particularly gruesome murder on your hands and from your preliminary report, it was committed by the same killer as two other older murders. This is a major crime and a bloody great headache for me, so you have to stick with it. Now you are a man down, probably only temporarily but even so, with broken ribs Gary Pritchard won't be on full duties for a while. All I can suggest is that I allocate DS Vic Blackwell to you. His DI is in court all this week up in London and they are well on top of their workload, so if that would help, he's yours.'

'Thank you, Ruth. And I won't let the ritual murders suffer for this, I promise. We've juggled two cases before, and we'll do it again.' He looked at her apologetically. 'And thank you for not giving me the bollocking I deserve.'

'I'm fully aware it was done with the very best of intentions. And from a purely selfish point of view, I have to say that you're raising the profile of positive policing single-handedly.'

'Hardly. Actually, there's something you might like to know . . .' He told her about Marie, Ralph and Gary, all working in their own time, and about Stacey and Jay and their late-night stint as decorators in order to help the beleaguered family. 'And now they are organising jet washers and preparing to clean down that whole house. It's awe-inspiring!'

'I'll be sure to make a note of that *and* speak to their skipper about their exemplary behaviour.'

Jackman stood up to leave. 'Appreciated, Ruth.'

'Rowan?'

He turned back.

'Be careful out at Amberley Fen. Maybe it's nothing, but I'm starting to pick up on the menace you're sensing out there. I don't want to be heading up yet another murder enquiry at that cursed address.'

'Me neither, Ruth, believe me!'

CHAPTER SIXTEEN

The rest of Marie's day had passed in a mad rush. She had been relieved to find Gary in one piece, more or less. He did have two broken ribs and severe bruising to his left side and back, but he was lucky to be alive. There was no internal bleeding, which was a blessed relief. But if it had been his head that had hit the rock, it would have been curtains for sure, and it seemed that the tractor driver hadn't been worried one way or the other. Gary had caught a fleeting glimpse of the driver before being jettisoned from the tractor, but all he had seen was a man in dirty overalls with a cap pulled low over his forehead and a scarf obscuring the lower part of his face. He recalled a pair of dark eyes, the stare expressionless and hard as nails.

Learning that he was out of danger and would soon be discharged into Gilly's care, they had then motored over to Solace and assessed the situation there. Somehow, the local grapevine had fast-tracked the news to Jackman's mother and before they left, she had called her son with a proposition. Marie had heard the conversation on loudspeaker and reckoned it was a lifesaver. Jackman just had to find a way to persuade the Stewarts. Harriet had planned to back off a bit as she got older and had decided to employ a live-in manager for the livery stables. To that end, she had converted part of the main stable block into very nice living accommodation. It had two bedrooms and a sunlit open-plan ground floor, with a kitchen and a large modern shower room. And it was empty. Harriet had never let go of the reins and had never employed a manager. 'I know that proud Scot will say no, so it's up to you, Rowan, to make him put his family's safety before his pride. They must come here and stay until you find the evil party behind all this horrible behaviour. We have more security cameras than Buckingham Palace and Lawrence insists, so there. You must sort it, son.'

Jackman put the suggestion to Holly and promised to tackle Hugh. He had also offered to phone his friend Gerry Keane and tell him of the hate campaign that had been launched against his new employee and his family. Gerry and his son were fair men and Jackman was certain it wouldn't jeopardise Hugh's job. Indeed, Gerry was incensed when he heard what had been done to them. Hugh, he said, was a bloody good worker and they had no intention of losing him. The Keane family stood no nonsense from anyone, so if they could help in any way, he had only to ask. He would have a word with Hugh and assure him that his job was safe and that if he needed to be with his wife for a while his pay would not be docked.

Marie was driving Gary's car back to the station for him, her mind on what she had seen at Solace. To her, the mammoth salvage operation Stacey, Jay and a couple of other uniformed officers had undertaken to clean the house up was what policing was all about, though it was rarely put into practice.

She left the vehicle in the station car park and was on her way towards the back entrance when her phone rang, and Ralph's name popped up on the screen. 'Hello you! How are things going with your *other* woman?'

Ralph sounded excited. 'I think I know her better than I know you now, Marie. And she's not a very nice lady at all. Then I had a really lucky break — I found a descendent of hers, and we had tea and chocolate biscuits while the old girl told me what she knew of "Insidious Ivy."'

'Insidious Ivy? Go on.'

'It's too complicated to tell you over the phone, so I'll wait until you get home. Will you be late?'

Marie wasn't sure. 'I'm supposed to be doing a bit of late-night obbo out near Solace tonight, but I'll do my best to get away at the first opportunity. But, Ralph, you're back at work tomorrow. Aren't you wanting to get back to Fenchester to get your stuff ready?'

He chuckled. 'I've already been — after my choccy biscuits. I've brought my work clothes and a bag back with me. I'll stay tonight and leave early tomorrow — if you'll have me, that is.'

'Dead bloody right I will!' she exclaimed, smiling broadly. 'I'll see you as soon as possible.'

Marie hurried through the station door suddenly feeling a twinge of guilt. For the first time since his death, a whole day had passed without her thinking of Bill. Then she sighed and let the guilt go. The past was just that now — past. Finally, after spending years in mourning, she was happy again, and it was all right to be so.

She couldn't wait to get home. To Ralph.

* * *

Ashley Carpenter called her DI into the office and gave him the latest on the interviews with Bennington. 'It's taking longer than we can really afford, but I daren't push him. Dr Archer is being a great help and I'm really glad we have her on board. She, too, is being cautious and I'm following her lead.'

'Well, ma'am, you've managed to extract a description of Daemon from him,' said DI Russ Cooley. 'That's a major step forward.'

'Yes, that's good, but I'm disappointed that he's so vague about this Apostle person. He's the one I'd really like to talk to — if he's still alive.'

'I get the feeling Apostle might even be the executioner,' said Russ thoughtfully. 'For some reason I think Daemon enjoys the sex, the power over others, but uses people like Apostle to carry out the killings.'

'I agree, and so does Jackman, so we do need to discover if he's still a threat, or whether he's been sacrificed for the cause.'

'I've checked out three of the other disciples Bennington gave you the names of, ma'am.' Russ looked at his notebook. 'All dead. Two suicides and another the coroner deemed an accidental death. It was thought she was so distracted by health issues, mostly of a psychological nature, that she inadvertently wrote her car off and killed herself.'

'I have one more name for you and this one really is alive, or so Bennington tells us. It took Laura's gentle persuasion to drag it out of him. It's the friend he spends time with, his *only* friend. He's another excommunicated disciple, and Bennington wants him treated with kid gloves.'

She passed him a name and an address. 'And don't go too late in the day. This person will not answer the door after dark.'

The name was George Ingram. Russ looked at the address. 'Oh, not too far from here.' He looked at his watch. 'I'll go now, if you like. It won't be dark for hours yet.'

'Take Paula with you, Russ. We aren't too sure about this man's state of mind, although since he was a victim of Daemon, he's most probably well damaged. He might respond better to a woman, you never know. And remember, tread warily. No questions about killings, Apostle and the like, just gentle chat to begin with, to test the waters.'

Russ stood up. 'I'll report to you as soon as we get back.'

Ashley was left alone with a head full of unanswered questions. She could almost hear a clock ticking in the background, relentlessly marking the hours until the next death.

* * *

With the exception of Stacey and Jay, who were still up to their necks in muck, the team, plus DS Vic Blackwell, was assembled for what they called a campfire.

'We need to speed things up, and now we officially have two cases running, that's going to take a bit of doing, I'm afraid. I'm not sure how the overtime budget is at present, but I'll do my best to make sure you're paid for any extra time you put in.' He turned to Marie. 'DS Blackwell is pitching in for a week or so, so I'm going to get you to give him an overview of both cases after this meeting, okay?'

'Sure. Really glad you can help, Vic,' said Marie with feeling.

'Okay, let's summarise. The ritual killings first.' Jackman took a breath. 'So, in a nutshell, forensics believe that the same killer carried out all three deaths using a single sacrificial knife and a cleaver. The man is obviously skilled at performing ritual dissections. We have no other reported deaths of this nature since the Birch Drove Farm investigation and the death of Shelley Harcourt in Locksford twenty years ago, until the recent murder of the woman we have identified as Siobhan Aster. We have a man, Martin Bennington, at Locksford who is prepared to talk about the cult he was a member of and that was run by a man who went by the name of Daemon. The participants first lived at a house called the Hollow, on the outskirts of Wiley Fen. Marie has now obtained info that this place, which they subsequently burned down, was owned by several generations of a family called Nash.' He looked at Marie.

'Yes, boss. The last known owner was — or is — someone called Jerome Nash who could possibly be Daemon. Orac is chasing that up as we speak. Daemon insisted that the cult members destroy their home to prove that they needed nothing from life but to follow him — no material possessions, no comforts. They were to prove themselves by sleeping rough, under canvas, until he found a new place for them to stay in. We have no idea where that is — or was. But we do know that Daemon had another branch of his cult which was situated exactly an hour's drive from the Hollow and is right here in our own area. Whether it is defunct or still active is not known, but as they are no doubt responsible for Siobhan Aster's death, we believe at least some of the old cult is still operating.'

Jackman looked over to where Max and Charlie sat. 'You visited the nursery at the house called Oak Barn. What's your opinion? Could it be the place? It's an hour from the Hollow.'

'It appears to be a genuine set-up on the surface,' said Max.

'No one thereabouts had anything other than good things to say about them and no one mentioned any odd goings-on,' added Charlie.

'So why don't I pick up positive vibes from either of you?' asked Jackman. 'Marie and I can categorically discount the manor house at Keldyke. Nothing at all about it gave us cause for concern. You two don't feel the same, do you?'

'I checked with the Land Registry and it's a big parcel of land with lots of polytunnels and greenhouses and other outbuildings,' said Max. 'Although you can't see too much of it from the nursery shop itself. The Google satellite image is out of date and, well, we can't be sure because so much is invisible, but it looks like they really are a nursery, and they have a good stock for a small family-owned business. We are erring on the side of caution, that's all.'

Jackman shrugged. 'Okay, so, any further plans?'

'I'm taking Rosie there tomorrow to buy some plants and hopefully get the owner talking. You know how good Rosie is at reading people. I'd value her thoughts.'

'Smart move, Max. Keep me up to speed on that, okay?'

'Yes, boss, although I suspect this little caper is going to cost me! She's turning into a right little Kim Wilde.'

Jackman frowned. 'I thought Kim Wilde was an eighties pop singer?'

'You're behind the times, guv'nor. She's a landscape gardener now, and my Rosie loves her.'

Jackman shook his head in puzzlement, 'Okay, moving on to Robbie and Kevin. What have you got for us?'

'A whole lot of suspicions, sir,' Robbie said. 'We didn't like the sound, or the look, or the feel of the place. Nothing about the Eastlake Complex adds up.'

Robbie and Kevin explained what they had done and showed Jackman the photographs.

'We want to get inside, sir, but we've got no justification for a warrant, and we're told that if we go in undercover, we'll get told to bugger off.'

'We did wonder about the drone, sir?' said Kevin. 'At least we could see the layout properly.'

That was a possibility. Ruth had secured them one of their own, along with trained pilots. If challenged, they could use the excuse of looking for a suspect who had evaded custody, or a missing child. 'As you have serious concerns, I'll suggest it to the super after the meeting and let you know what she says. Meanwhile, I want the two of you to look into the background of that hotel, find out everything you can about its history and the present owner. Take it to bits.'

'Yes, sir,' they chorused.

Jackman looked down at his notes. 'I had a call from Locksford just before the meeting started. It wasn't good news, although there is one bright light. They have managed to obtain a likeness of Daemon. It will be emailed to me as soon as Locksford have a good e-fit ready, and I'll share it with all of you, especially uniform. Every officer we have should know what this man looks like. The bad news is that we had located another former cult member who was a friend of Bennington's. We had high hopes that he might fill in some of the gaps, things Bennington didn't know. DI Cooley and DC Webber of Locksford CID called round to his home an hour ago and found him dead. He had hanged himself.'

'Maybe,' muttered Marie darkly.

Jackman had been wondering the same thing. The timing was most suspicious, coming just before a visit from the police. 'In any case, it means that every person Bennington has given us the name of is dead. He suggested that if they hadn't already taken their own lives, Daemon was systematically wiping them out.'

'That makes your man a very valuable commodity indeed,' commented Vic Blackwell. 'Are Locksford able to protect him? It's not a very big station, is it?'

'They are very aware of his unique importance, believe me, Vic. It's actually bigger than you'd think and well-staffed. I don't think anyone could do better — other than Greenborough, of course. Now, I want someone to go over the report of the accident in which Martin Bennington was run off the road, and to check out the other two cars involved. It's just a supposition, but we think one of the drivers might be the man known as Apostle. Bennington swears he didn't recognise them, but I'm not so sure. I want local television to put out a call for anyone who witnessed the collision to come forward, especially if they have a dashcam. I've agreed this with Superintendent Carpenter, as it's on her patch, and she's alerted her people to prepare for an influx of calls. I've suggested that they post both divisions' telephone contact numbers, so we can field some of them here. The local hospitals need to be checked as well, for anyone presenting with injuries suggesting a shunt in an RTC. One of the two men was trapped for a while, he could have sustained abrasions, fractures or lacerations, we don't know. So check also for any blood found in the vehicle that was towed to the pound.' He looked around. 'Who's willing to take that one on?'

'How about me, sir?' offered Vic. 'It's a straightforward procedure and since I'm not fully au fait with the investigation yet, it's something I can do quite easily. I'll liaise with Locksford.'

'Perfect.' Jackman was already starting to appreciate the addition of Vic to the team. 'One last thing, all findings should be sent to Locksford as well as to me. They will do the same. This is not a competition, we're working together.'

Jackman then turned to the next item on his agenda. 'Solace, the house in Amberley Fen. Home to Hugh and Holly Stewart.' He told them everything he knew, up until that afternoon. 'And you'll be pleased to know that Gary will be back at the station either tomorrow or the day after, but he'll be flying a desk for a while. He can't drive and we can't risk him doing any further damage to himself, but he insists he can still be a help to the enquiry working in front of a computer screen. There is plenty of info he can collate.' He looked around at them. 'It's fine with me if he's up to it, but guys, please look out for him, okay? He's taken one hell of a battering.'

'Silly bugger!' said Max. 'Fancy trying to stop a bloody great tractor. What did he think he was — the Terminator?'

'I think he thought about those children and their mother and saw the red mist, Max. I would probably have done the same. Which brings us to our aim: find who is behind the intimidation of an innocent family and stop them. The murder takes precedence of course, but I want this sorted, and fast. If any of you have snouts who know that area, contact them. And get over to Amberley Fen and talk to people. People don't get driven out of their homes for no reason. Someone must know something. It could be something relatively recent that's upset someone, or it could go back in history. If he's up to it, I'm going to get Gary and our new office manager, Tim, to act as coordinators on this case.' He shut his notebook with a snap. 'Right. That's as much as I'm going to throw at you for now, apart from telling you to use Stacey and Jay as much as you need to. They're very well up on the goings-on at Solace House — probably more than they intended.' He smiled, somewhat apologetically. 'I'm not asking much of you really, just to catch a ritual killer who has evaded justice for two decades, while at the same time making the world a better place for two little kids to grow up in. Okay with that, team?'

'Easy as falling off a log, boss,' said Max. 'Or a tractor, in Gary's case.'

'Yeah,' agreed Robbie. 'It's a breeze. We've got this.'

'Then let's do it,' said Jackman. 'The starter's pistol has just gone off.'

Back in his office he said to Marie, 'Look, I'm really sorry but I can't join you tonight on the watch for that dirty silver car that the Spriggs saw. Laura has sent me a text to say she needs to talk through her findings about Bennington as soon as possible, and it sounds as if it's going to be a long evening.'

'Forget it, Jackman,' she said. 'That is far more important. I'll take Ralph.'

'If you're sure?'

'Oh yes. I intend to look the driver of that tractor in the eye and tell him exactly what I think of him.' Her eyebrows knitted together in a fierce frown. 'And, depending on the circumstances of that meeting, give him a bit of his own medicine. For our Gary.'

'Anyone ever told you that you can be one scary lady, Marie Evans?' said Jackman, trying to keep the amusement out of his voice.

'Oh, frequently. And now I'm off to terrorise — sorry — *familiarise* Vic Blackwell with our investigations so far. I'll pop in and see you before I leave.'

* * *

Janet had had a migraine headache all afternoon. She had tried to work through it until finally it got the better of her and she gave in, pulled her bedroom curtains and went to bed.

She got up again at around five, remembering that she hadn't eaten, which always made it worse. The thought of food made her feel sick, but it did help to lessen the pain.

Just as she was finishing a slice of wholemeal toast and marmalade, her phone rang. For a moment she considered leaving it — the answerphone would pick it up — but then she changed her mind.

She was glad she did, for it turned out to be one of Stephen's very rare calls. As always, she felt that combination of excitement and nervousness when she heard his cultured voice, and it took some effort to keep her tone even.

'My dear Janet. I do hope that I haven't interrupted your evening, but something has come to my notice, and I thought, *Strike while the iron is hot, Stephen. Dear Janet will forgive you.*'

'Stephen, how nice! No, of course you aren't interrupting anything. What can I do for you?'

'I have another name for your list.'

She grabbed a pen and a memo pad that she kept next to the phone. 'Go ahead.'

'First, I need you to make a few alterations to your work schedule. If you can stop what you are working on as of now and make this one a priority, please. It's inconvenient, I know. I'm aware that you work to a plan and have to tie in with John, but it can't be helped. It has to be this way. It is important to me.'

'I can rearrange the tasks. The order is of no consequence. I can assure you that everything will be completed on time, no matter how I structure it.'

'I am sure you're right. I trust you implicitly. Now, when you have completed the dossier on this new name, it is to be stored as a sleeper and only woken when we reach the final chapter of this enterprise of ours. It is to be added to the intelligence record of our main subject. Do you understand?'

Janet said that she did. She knew each case history and character profile in detail and was perfectly acquainted with what she referred to as Stephen's "pecking order."

'Good, good. And thank you, Janet dear. Your professionalism makes working with you a pleasure. I shall give you the name and wish you a very good night.'

By the time Janet had carefully taken down the name, the line had gone dead.

She stared at it. Another addition to the file on Marie Evans. Hmm. Who, she wondered, was Ralph Enderby?

CHAPTER SEVENTEEN

There was no *MasterChef*-style vegetarian special on the menu for tonight. Ralph had grabbed a couple of ready meals from the supermarket, which they nuked as soon as Marie got in.

'Do you know, Marie, I've been busier here with you than I am at work! I've rushed around like a loon all day today — and this was my holiday, I'll have you know.'

'And you haven't finished yet either.' She told him about their planned nocturnal excursion across the fen to try and spot a dirty silver car.

'Obbo? Oh, just what I wanted. And here was me imagining a long soak in the bath and an early night.' He stuck his tongue out at her. 'Fat chance!'

She grinned at him. 'I'll make it worth your while — later.'

'Then eat up. We have work to do.' They laughed.

'So, tell me all about Ivy Pettifer,' Marie said.

'I can't wait, actually. I had a real stroke of luck there.' He looked at her over a forkful of macaroni cheese. 'You're going to love this, although there is a grim ending.'

'Then get on with it,' she demanded. 'Or are you being deliberately exasperating?'

'Oh, all right, but believe me, this could tick off a lot of unanswered questions for you. Okay. The brief background is that I found an old couple mentioned in an online local newspaper who had recently celebrated their diamond wedding anniversary. Their names were Albert and Beryl Carling and in brackets was her maiden name — Pettifer. So, I took a drive out to where they now live, a warden-controlled housing development about three miles from Amberley Fen.'

'The Church Walk Estate?'

'That's the one. They have a nice little bungalow there. They are well into their eighties, Marie, but you'd never believe it. They're not particularly mobile anymore, but they're both bright as buttons up here.' He tapped his head. 'And Beryl's memory is extraordinary. She told me that they had embarked on a bit of genealogy to keep their brains active and had started with her because she remembered this dark family secret, a massive skeleton in the Pettifer cupboard. She said that the more she thought about it, the more memories surfaced from her childhood. In the end and after a long chat with another elderly relative of hers, she came up with a pretty comprehensive account of what they had been told.' Marie was now well interested and listened intently, wondering what was to come.

'She agreed that such things become distorted over time, but because it was a member of their own family and her parents and grandparents were deeply ashamed that a Pettifer could behave as she did, it wasn't ever embellished or dramatised. She described quite vividly the sombre voices of her parents when they spoke about Ivy. I'm certain that what she told me has more than a grain of truth in it.'

'And the story?' asked Marie.

'Being the eldest girl in a large family, Ivy Pettifer had a lot of pressure put on her. From a very early age she had to care for the young ones, then, as soon as she was old enough, she was obliged to find work to help supplement her parents' meagre wages.' He gave a wry smile. 'But Ivy wasn't particularly employable. Though for the most part she was quite a sweet girl, she occasionally exploded in fits of rage. Anyway, she was finally taken on by Sally Pinket as a kind of domestic servant and nursemaid. Because she had so many younger siblings, the girl had experience with tiny children, so Sally gave her a chance. Old Beryl believes that Sally felt sorry for her. However, not long after she started working there, children began to die.'

Marie was beginning to see where this story was going. 'Oh my! Go on.'

'It wasn't uncommon, of course. Infant mortality was accepted as a normal part of life in those days. All died from natural causes and young Ivy seemed as devastated as Sally, so they continued to take in babies and very young children.' He took a breath. 'Then one day Ivy suffered a complete breakdown and in a kind of frenzy killed four of her charges, drugging them with laudanum, then suffocating them. A young man who did gardening and odd jobs around the place saw what happened and told Sally Pinket.' Ralph took a drink of water. 'Beryl isn't sure why Sally acted in the way she did. She can only guess that she was trying to protect her business and her reputation and possibly also wanted to save Ivy from the gallows, but she covered the whole thing up. She paid the boy to help her and then forget what he had seen. They buried the babies in the garden and spread a story around that a group of rough-looking Travellers had broken into Solace House, terrified her and Ivy and stolen four young children.'

'And that's where it all started,' murmured Marie, imagining the gossips of the time having an absolute field day.

'Luckily for Sally, Travellers had passed through very recently, so her story wasn't beyond the realm of possibility. What she didn't reckon on was Ivy herself. She let the girl go on some other pretext, but it didn't take the Pettifer family long to find out that Ivy was now a very dangerous young woman. She murdered their youngest child.'

'Bloody hell!' Marie said. 'So why didn't that exonerate Sally?'

'Because the Pettifers closed ranks,' Ralph said. 'They imprisoned Ivy in a box room and told everyone she was terribly sick and would probably die. They hinted at small-pox, so no one came near them.' Ralph sighed. 'If they had left it at that, it might all have been forgotten, but they became very anxious about the infant deaths at Solace. They had declared that their own child had accidentally suffo-cated itself with its bedding, but they were aware that some people might start to link their baby's death and those at Sally Pinket's house with Ivy. After all, she was the common denominator. Then they heard that the gardener at Solace was saying that Ivy was mad, not sick—'

'So they started spreading rumours about Sally Pinket,' finished off Marie.

'Exactly. And after paying the gardener enough to be able to leave the village, suspicion fell back onto Sally.'

'Hang on,' Marie said. 'If that was the case, why weren't the police involved?'

'They were. The sergeant was a cousin of Sally's. He did his job correctly, granted no family favours, but drew the line at digging up the massive garden at Solace House. Maybe because he just didn't have the manpower, but more likely because he knew that his cousin was no murderess.'

A cold feeling spread slowly down Marie's spine. 'Oh, Ralph! Are those little bodies still in the garden at Solace House?'

'I think so. Don't you?'

* * *

Laura had just had a hot bath and put on her dressing gown when Jackman's car drew up. He had agreed to pick up a takeaway on the way home, as Mrs M had taken a rare day off and neither she nor Jackman felt like cooking tonight.

She hurried downstairs and found him placing a large brown paper carrier bag on the table.

'I hope it's all right, but I decided on a fish and chip sup-per. I just didn't fancy a great tableful of Indian or Chinese food tonight.'

'Perfect,' she said, going to the cupboard for salt, pepper and tomato ketchup. 'Comfort food. There are plates warming in the oven. Let's eat straightaway.'

As soon as they were tucking into their haddock and chips with mushy peas, Jackman looked at her enquiringly. He didn't need to voice his question, she knew exactly what he wanted to know.

'Well, he's probably the most complicated and intriguing cult survivor I've ever met.' She stopped. 'But before I tell you about our meeting, Ashley asked me to get you to ring her this evening, any time. She said she was going to use their last interview of the day to try to find out the identity of Angel, the body at Birch Drove Farm. She hopes that by the time you call, she'll have a name for you.'

'I'll do it as soon as we've eaten,' said Jackman, dipping a chip in ketchup.

They continued discussing Bennington.

'I'm really grateful to you for getting me in on this, sweetheart,' said Laura. 'I can't wait to talk it over with Sam, as well as my American colleague, Oscar. Martin Bennington is proving an enigma as far as I'm concerned, and I'm itching to know if they think so too.'

'He is what he says he is, isn't he, Laura?' asked Jackman tentatively. 'There's no chance that some of his revelations are imaginary, even fabricated for some reason?'

'Oh no, he's definitely lived in a closed community for a long time, there's no doubt about that. Most of his responses are textbook for a long-term survivor. Although it's possible he might have been more involved and on a much deeper level than he's admitting.'

'You mean he could have taken part in the more violent rituals? The killings?'

She wasn't sure yet. 'The thing is, guilt could be making him deny his part in what happened. If he's now truly appalled at what they did, possibly he just can't face up to the fact. Maybe he won't admit it or maybe he can't, or maybe he's telling the truth and I've got it wrong.' She laid her knife and fork down. 'It's early days yet, my love. At least we seem to have found a modus operandi. He does accept me and the help I can offer, but we are a long way from understanding or trusting each other yet. As I said, I could be very wrong about him, but my gut feeling says that Martin Bennington was a deeply committed member of Daemon's cult back in the day.' She frowned. 'I just wish he'd stop sending out mixed messages. One minute I fully believe he was used and abused, drugged, and subjected to mind control at its worst, and the next,' she shrugged, 'something he says shows a much deeper awareness of what lay behind the cult and what it was about.' She picked at a bit of crispy batter and chewed thoughtfully. 'But there are some things you just can't hurry. This will take time, I'm afraid.'

'I never thought it would be an easy task, Laura, but I firmly believe that if anyone can read that man, it will be you, no matter how long it takes.' He smiled at her. 'Just tell me everything — fact, fiction, even the downright fantastic. It could all mean something as the investigation proceeds. Oh, and I suppose you didn't touch on the subject of the possibility of drugs being administered without the disciples' consent?'

'We — well, Ashley did, when I was observing, and I'd say there was no question about it. He described the euphoria, the conflation between reality and imagination, and I knew immediately it had to be LSD. I've read extensively on its use as an anaesthetic, to support psychoanalysis and treat certain depressive disorders back before production was stopped.' She looked at Jackman. 'It's nothing new, you know. Naturally occurring hallucinogens have been used in rituals for thousands of years to enhance pleasure or induce a state of enlightenment. Daemon just bent the rules and forgot to tell them he was pumping them full of drugs that could leave susceptible individuals with schizophrenia, flashbacks and even severe lifelong disorientation.'

'I should think most of them fell within the definition of susceptible, didn't they?' Jackman asked.

'Generally, but not all were vulnerable. Some of his devotees would have been convinced that Daemon really did have access to an ancient and superior knowledge and travelled his path willingly. He promised them utopia if they followed him. Bennington said that had Daemon told them the world was flat, they would have believed him.' She sighed. 'I've heard that said of most charismatic, self-proclaimed Messiahs.'

They finished eating and while Laura cleared their plates away, Jackman called Ashley Carpenter. After he ended the call, he went over to where Laura stood at the sink and hugged her. 'We've got a name! After all those years, Angel has a name. My darling, that man is our Golden Goose!'

'Who was she?' Laura asked excitedly.

'One of the cult members from the Hollow, a girl called Michelle. She broke the rules and slept with a boy from Wiley Fen village. Daemon himself caught them together. She was made to stand trial and taken away by the four highest-ranking chosen ones to be "cleansed." The other members were told that when she had been purified and had spent time with Apostle relearning their beliefs, she would be forgiven and returned to them.'

'For cleansed, read murdered,' breathed Laura.

'Correct. When she didn't come back, Martin suspected as much but didn't dare speak about it. He said he never forgot her or what happened, and it was a relief to finally tell the police.'

Laura privately wondered if that relief stemmed from something much darker. Maybe Martin had known all along what would happen to her, or even been involved himself in the cleansing.

'And even better, Martin told Ashley that Michelle was her real name. She had always liked it, she said, so she never took another. Ashley's team immediately checked for people who had disappeared at that time and who fitted Martin's description, and they came up with a local girl called Michelle Wilding. Martin identified her from a photograph her parents had given them.' Jackman hugged her tighter. 'This is such a step forward.'

Laura wished she could feel as upbeat, but Martin Bennington was starting to worry her. She had been wanting to talk to Sam about it since she first interviewed Bennington, but he had been feeling under the weather lately and knowing he had a heart problem, she hadn't wanted to worry him. Now, however, she decided it couldn't wait. As soon as she'd made the coffee, she would reconsider phoning her old mentor.

* * *

Ralph and Marie drove along the quiet fen lanes discussing Sally Pinket and Ivy Pettifer. 'I keep thinking about poor Sally. Okay, she was an idiot to bury those babies, but she spent the rest of her life branded a murderer when probably she was trying to save another woman from the gallows.'

'That's my opinion too,' said Ralph. 'I did ask Beryl whether her grandparents had ever considered revealing the truth. She said they were too ashamed of how her family had deliberately lied and shifted the blame to an innocent woman, so they decided to let sleeping dogs lie.' He stared out over the endless fields. 'Beryl's grandparents told her that Sally died in her fifties and her two surviving children immediately sold the house and moved abroad to live, after which there seemed little to be gained by opening up old wounds.'

'And what about the truth — for its own sake if nothing else?' asked Marie.

'Ah, I forgot to tell you the last part of my story about Beryl Carling, née Pettifer. I gave her Anna Baker's phone number and she's promised to supply her with the missing piece of the jigsaw puzzle.' He laughed. 'If the truth is ever to be told, it'll be Anna who'll do it. Especially as it'll be the final nail in Rupert Larkham's coffin. Old Beryl agrees, she thinks it's about time too.'

'Good for you! And it means we can also assure the Stewarts that no matter what crap they hear about Sally Pinket, she was no killer, just a naïve and probably very kind woman who made a mistake and was made a scapegoat.' They were now approaching Amberley Fen and Marie slowed down. 'Although I might omit the bit about the infants buried in the garden. That can wait until we have the person who is harassing them locked up in the custody suite, though it will probably mean that the garden will have to be dug up.' She smiled at him. 'You've been a real star, Ralph Enderby, and I'm so pleased you helped me, even if some of the answers aren't what we wanted to hear.'

He lightly touched her arm. 'I've enjoyed every minute. I'm even beginning to enjoy the prospect of a spot of obbo. That's never happened before.'

'Ah, but you never did it with me, did you?' she purred.

'Well, that's true, but if you want me to observe anything other than the gorgeous Marie Evans, I'd better forget that last comment or I won't be of much help to you.'

'Well, I know just what will throw cold water on that. You're about to meet the rudest couple on the Fens, the delightful Mr and Mrs Spriggs. Those two are enough to knock the ardour out of the most passionate heart.'

'Can't wait. And why, may I ask, are we visiting if they're as odious as you say?'

'Because I want to use the entrance to their field to park in and watch for our target. There's nowhere else on this great open stretch of farmland where we won't be seen. Their gateway has a few straggly trees and bushes that will conceal us from the road.'

'Can't we just park there anyway — police business and all that? Save talking to them,' suggested Ralph hopefully.

'You wouldn't say that if you'd ever met the Spriggs. He'd be right up our arses with his antiquated rust bucket of a JCB digger! And we'd be nose-down in the ditch on the other side of the lane.'

'Better go and say hello then.'

A few minutes later they were back in the car, parked among the trees and hopefully well concealed from any vehicles heading out towards Amberley Fen and Solace.

'I see what you mean about the warm Fenland hospitality. They're both as bad as each other, not a smile between them.'

'She's worse,' said Marie. 'Actually they weren't bad tonight, not much swearing at all. I've heard them at their worst and it wasn't pretty.' She turned to him. 'I'm sorry, Ralph, I feel I've dragged you out tonight on a wild goose chase. Old Mrs Spriggs said he never comes two days on the trot, and he was here yesterday.'

'Well, at least she's certain that he always passes at around ten o'clock, so we won't have to hang around too long. We can give it until just after ten fifteen, then we can go.' He lowered his voice. 'Though I'm perfectly happy to sit here all night with you.'

'Is this the way people our age ought to be feeling?' Marie said. 'You know. Like teenagers?'

'I don't give a damn about how people our age should or shouldn't feel. Do you?' He gazed at her, his eyes shining in the deepening shadows inside the car.

'Not in the slightest.'

She was just about to lean across and kiss him when they heard a car engine approaching up the lane.

'That's not a new car,' said Ralph, back in police mode at once. 'The engine's clapped out, and if it is him, he's bang on time.'

'Now all we need is for it to be a dirty silver colour and we have a spot of pursuit on our hands. All buckled up?'

He grinned. 'Ready to go, pardner.'

The battered silver car motored past, unaware of the eyes watching him from the entrance to the Spriggs's field. Marie gave him a head start, then, headlights off so as not to give them away, drove out after him.

It soon became obvious where he was going. Other than a couple of tiny cottages and a barn, the only inhabited building around was Solace.

'He's pulling in,' said Ralph. Marie coasted to a halt and waited.

The car pulled up at the edge of a field of rape, followed by the sound of a door closing. 'He's going the last part on foot, isn't he?' she whispered. 'But why? What's he up to?'

'We'll find out shortly, won't we?' said Ralph. 'As soon as he's out of earshot, pull onto that grass verge there and we'll follow him.'

Darkness had fallen but there was still enough light to see their way, and soon they were tiptoeing cautiously after the solitary figure. He seemed to know exactly what he was doing and didn't appear worried about being seen — he positively strolled along without a sideways glance. Marie decided that he'd done this so often that he knew he wasn't going to bump into anyone.

'Hold back.' She flung her arm across Ralph to bring him to a halt. 'He's stopped this side of the trees. He seems to be making a circuit of the house just outside their boundary.' Now he was harder to see, half-hidden in the shadows of the conifers.

They followed, keeping well back. After a while he stopped, moved some obstacle from his path and stepped into the garden. It was hard to make him out in the dark, but Marie reckoned he was quite young, though not a kid. He was tall, rather thin, and moved easily, obviously familiar with the tangle of shrubs and conifers.

He stopped and took something from his jacket pocket. A faint light glowed for a moment or two, then went out again. Marie watched, unsure of what he was doing. She felt Ralph squeeze her arm, and when she turned to look, he was pointing through a gap in the undergrowth.

A marked police car waited to the side of the house, the interior light on and two officers inside. So uniform really were taking this seriously. Even so, their man remained in position, seemingly unfazed, though he must have clocked the vehicle.

Like a strange, shadowy tableau, nobody moved for perhaps five minutes, then the light glowed again for a second or two and the man turned and started to make his way back in their direction.

Like two wraiths, Ralph and Marie melted into the gloom and back the way they had come.

Reaching his vehicle, the man found the two of them lounging casually against the driver's door.

'Evening,' said Ralph.

He stepped back. 'What the . . . ? Who the hell are you?'

'I think that question would sound better coming from us, don't you?' said Marie, and they held up their warrant cards.

The man let out a relieved sigh. 'Oh, thank heavens for that! I thought for a moment you might be—'

'Who, exactly?' said Marie.

'The Stewarts. Nasty pieces of work by all accounts. Anyway, how can I help you?' He looked at them steadily, as though he had nothing to hide.

'Are we right in thinking that this is not your first trip out here?' she asked.

'I've been coming here for quite a while now, on and off. But what's wrong?'

She ignored his question. 'And your name, sir?'

'Anthony Bonner.' Now he sounded guarded. 'Why?'

'And your business here?'

'I'm working! Why else would I be creeping about this godforsaken dump at night?' he almost shouted.

'Why indeed?' murmured Ralph.

Marie stared at Bonner. 'We need to talk, but not here. Time we went to meet a couple of friends of ours. Come on.'

They led the protesting Bonner down the lane and into Solace's driveway.

'What a terrible smell,' he exclaimed. 'Must have been spraying the fields with silage, I guess.'

'Spraying the house with it, as a matter of fact,' said Ralph. 'Are you responsible for that too?'

'Me? I don't know what you're talking about!'

They crunched down the gravel drive to the police car. When Stacey Smith and Jay Acharya stepped out, Marie smiled. 'I should have known it'd be you two. Don't you have homes to go to?'

'We were just about to call it a day, Sarge,' said Stacey. 'We've had enough of the stench of manure. We've cleaned the whole exterior down, but it'll take a few heavy rainfalls to wash away the residue from the garden.' She stared at Bonner. 'Who've you got there?'

'Meet Anthony Bonner, PC Smith, a man who is just about to tell us why the hell he's been frightening little kids.'

Bonner's face turned pale. 'I've done nothing of the sort! What are you talking about? First muck-spraying and now frightening children. You guys really have got your wires crossed about me.'

'Oh, I don't think so, Mr Bonner. Maybe you are innocent of the manure but as to those kids, you're well and truly in the frame. Now, from the beginning. What the hell are you doing here?'

Anthony Bonner sighed. 'I'm working. I told you that.'

'Who for?'

'The landlord of this damned place.' He pointed to the dark facade of Solace.

'And who is that exactly?' demanded Marie.

'Mr Isaac Hobbs. He owns a small property leasing company in Saltern.'

In a pig's eye, thought Marie scornfully. 'Details. Address. Contact number.'

He faltered. 'Er, well, he contacts me, actually.'

What a surprise. 'So how come you work for him if you don't even know where his business is located?'

'Okay, okay. He approached me outside the job centre. I'd been there every day for a fortnight, and I was pretty desperate if you must know. He asked me if I'd like a bit of work, cash in hand.' He stared at his feet. 'As I said, I was desperate.'

'And what, exactly, did he want you to do?' asked Ralph.

'Covert observation on some tenants of his who were months behind on their rent. He suspected they were about to do a runner, taking the furnishings with them. He said he believed they might damage the place, set fire to it even.' He reached into his pocket and brought out a small diary. 'Times, dates, comings and goings — in fact, every move they made at night. He told me they'd done this sort of thing before. He said they were a thoroughly unpleasant family, though of course, he only found that out after they'd moved in.'

'You were seen by two little children. You terrified them.'

'He never mentioned kids. I only saw two adults. He said there were some teenagers, and they were as bad as the parents. He didn't care if I got seen, in fact he said it might make them think, but I shouldn't get caught.' He sighed again. 'I'd never scare little kiddies, really. Have I been fed a load of lies?'

'You, sir, are either well and truly gullible, or a barefaced liar,' growled Marie. 'Didn't you find anything about the set-up just a tiny bit suspect? I mean, you know nothing about the man. You can't even contact him.'

He nodded miserably. 'He sounded so plausible. The job was to be completely hush-hush — he wanted to deal with it himself and not use the bailiffs, he said. But even if he did decide to go down the legal eviction route, he wanted to know exactly what the Stewarts were up to and if they were planning anything.'

Marie believed him but wasn't going to tell him as much just yet. 'And you took the money without asking a single question?'

'I've got a wife and a baby, Officer. Look at me! Car that's on its last legs, I owe rent and I'm hardly the best-dressed man about town, am I? I wanted to feed my family, that's all. Look, I've got no nice police salary going into my account — which, by the way, is maxed out with no credit left. So, what would you have done?'

The emotion behind his outburst was genuine. Marie shook her head. 'We need a statement, sir. I'm going to get my colleagues here to take you down to the station, then afterwards someone will bring you back to collect your car.' Her voice softened. 'Mr Bonner, you have been well and truly used. I hope it was worth it.'

'Am I being arrested?' he asked forlornly.

'No, sir. But please make that statement. And we'll want to talk to you again.' She opened the door of the police car and ushered him into the back seat. 'Two things before you go. One, did you ever go inside Solace House and do damage of any kind?'

He shook his head vehemently. 'No way!'

'Okay, and two, you really should know that we suspect your Mr Isaac Hobbs of trying to drive the legal owners of this private property out, by literally threatening them with a reign of terror, which you, possibly inadvertently, were a part of. I'd think long and hard about cash-in-hand jobs in the future.' She closed the door.

'Well, that's one question answered. At least the kids won't be seeing strange men under the trees again,' Ralph said.

'But we're no nearer to finding their persecutor.' Marie frowned. 'Although maybe not. Hold up, Stace!' She stopped Stacey as she was about to drive away. 'Mr Bonner! How did he pay you? And how did he collect all the info you provided him with?'

'He texted me where and when to meet one of his employees. He gave me a cheap phone to keep just for his messages. We usually met somewhere public, like the market square, a café or a pub. It was a different place every time.'

'The phone please, Mr Bonner.' She smiled at him. 'After all, you won't be needing it anymore, will you?' *And guess who is going to turn up at the next meeting.*

He pulled the phone, a burner, from his pocket and handed it to her. 'Dead right I won't.'

'Take him away, Stacey,' said Marie. 'Oh, and I assume the Stewarts are still away?'

Stacey wound down her window. 'Yes, Sarge. Even Hugh Stewart couldn't keep up his proud stance. I'm not sure exactly what DI Jackman told him, but Hugh's accepted Harriet Jackman's offer. No doubt there'll be the usual compromises to keep his pride intact, but at least he's agreed. They'll be back in the morning to collect some of their things.'

The car sped off, leaving Marie and Ralph to return to their own vehicle.

'Interesting evening,' said Ralph, taking her hand. 'As dates go, it was quite unique, even in my book.'

'Life's never dull around Marie Evans,' she grinned.

They wandered side by side under a big, star-strewn night sky. 'So I'm beginning to realise,' he said with a smile. 'And I'm rather liking it.'

'That's fortunate, since I can't see anything changing in the near future. Can you?'

He squeezed her hand. 'Maybe. Maybe not.'

'And what do you mean by that, Ralph Enderby?'

'I mean,' he said slowly, 'that I've come to realise that I much prefer spending my time with you to being alone in Fenchester. I know you come and stay with me too, but so often it isn't possible.' He stopped and looked at her. 'I want us to move in together, permanently.' For a moment she didn't reply. 'No answers right now, just think about it. Give it some thought, take as long as you want and then let's be totally honest with each other. How about it?'

Marie didn't think she needed any time to think but acknowledged the sense in not being too hasty. It was a big step to take. 'It's a deal. And until then, we'll have some more "interesting" dates.'

They walked on in comfortable silence.

CHAPTER EIGHTEEN

Marie arrived at work ten minutes before Jackman.

'You're bright and early this morning,' he said, taking off his jacket.

'As are you, boss. We both like to get ahead of the day, don't we? And I've got a little story to tell you.' She laid Bonner's burner phone on his desk. 'About this.'

'I'm intrigued. Go on.'

'It belongs to whoever is behind the scare tactics at Solace.' She couldn't keep the glee out of her voice.

He raised his eyebrows. 'Do I gather your late-night sortie yielded rich pickings?'

'Sort of, and if nothing else, we now know who the stranger lurking in the undergrowth is.' She told him about the events of the previous evening.

'So, you're waiting for a text from the big cheese behind it all?' Jackman looked as excited as she felt.

'I've been staring at the damned thing ever since I got my hands on it. The moment I get a location, I'll be off like a shot. I'll take a couple of the team, and with your approval, I'd like to try a bit of deception.' She grinned at him. 'Bonner always wears the same jacket and beanie hat, which I've borrowed off him. The hat is pretty distinctive, being emerald-green with a black and gold logo on the front. Our Robbie is the same height and skinny build as him, so he can do a bit of impersonation — Robbie's good at that.'

'And by the time the contact realises his mistake, you'll have clocked him. Then, hopefully, you can get him off the street without too much fuss.' Jackman nodded in satisfaction. 'Well done, Marie! If we can just get the people behind this campaign, it'll be a massive weight off everybody's mind.'

Yours more than anyone's, thought Marie. 'There's something else, boss, and this is entirely down to Ralph.' She told him about Ralph's discovery of a descendant of Ivy Pettifer, adding that there could well be bodies buried in the grounds of Solace.

Jackman closed his eyes for a moment. 'Until all this is over — and I mean both cases — would you mind forgetting that last piece of information? We'll deal with it when the rest is all sewn up. There's a lot more to exhuming bodies than might appear, Marie, it's a complicated legal process. We'll need to try to access any surviving records from Sally Pinket's business at Solace House to see if there are any names mentioned of the infants that were entrusted to her. Then we need to extract those she said were stolen by gypsies. If the story is true and we can get some sort of evidence other than the merely anecdotal, the bodies will have to be exhumed and assigned named graves in accordance with the wishes of their relatives. If there are no traceable descendants, they will still have to be buried properly.' Jackman exhaled. 'It's something I can't even consider tackling at this point in time.'

'Those little souls have lain there for a long time, Jackman. It will do them no harm to wait a bit longer. It's enough to know what probably happened and that all those lies that unscrupulous hack Rupert Larkham spread about Sally were just that — lies.'

Jackman was about to speak when Marie received a message on her newly acquired phone. A smile spread across her face. 'Great. Great spot, too. Unless things go totally tits up, we'll be bringing the messenger boy back with us.'

'So, come on, where is it and when?' demanded Jackman.

'Nine thirty this morning, in that little garden square at the bottom of Fendyke Road, in the east end of town. There are a couple of seats there where Robbie will be waiting for him. I'm off to get him prepared. Luckily, he's in early too. We've got plenty of time, but I want this to run like clockwork.'

'Then take Kevin too, as backup.'

'Will do. See you later, boss. Wish me luck.'

'You don't need luck, Marie. You've got this.'

* * *

Jackman wondered if it was too early to ring Ashley Carpenter but had a feeling that she too would have started early. No one who really cared about the job rolled in on the dot of nine. He was just about to pick up his phone when it rang.

'Ah, I thought you'd be in, Jackman.'

From her brisk tone he guessed she was already on her second coffee of the morning.

'I've just emailed you the EvoFIT image that our IT operator has produced with Martin Bennington. It's not exactly how I'd imagined Daemon, to say the least.' She paused. 'Laura's coming in again this morning, isn't she?'

'She should be well on her way by now. Traffic allowing, she'll be with you shortly,' he said.

'Good, I need her to look at it and tell me that I'm either getting paranoid or seeing something Martin Bennington isn't.'

'Sorry, Super, you've lost me. What's the problem with it?'

'It's not easy to explain, but I'm wondering if because Martin had seen him as a messiah-like figure, he's conjured up an idealised version of Daemon rather than a physical likeness of him. Check it out for yourself and tell me if you think it's the face of a man who could order the dismemberment of a pretty young woman.'

Jackman was already going through his inbox. He found the superintendent's message, opened the attachment and stared at the image. 'I see what you mean.'

'It's not just me, then?'

'No, Super. It looks very much like "rose-tinted spectacles," if you know what I mean. I shall be very interested indeed to hear what Laura makes of it.'

'Shall I get her to ring you later?' offered Ashley.

'If you would. I don't want to saturate the area with a picture that's of no use.'

He hung up and sat staring at the image.

This Daemon had the face of an angel.

Jackman looked closer. He was glad that Locksford had used EvoFIT rather than e-fit and wondered idly how they'd been able to afford it. The image was in black and white as usual, as colour was believed to distract the eye, and was compiled from screens of alternative faces that the witness agreed approximated the actual one. They were not easy to produce because ultimately, the image was only as good as the witness's ability to recall features and describe them to the operator. It was easy, too, for the witness to be led by the operator who had to be careful not to make suggestions.

Despite these caveats, Jackman considered the new technology to be of enormous help. The quality of the final product was almost as good as a photograph and, although it was impossible to obtain complete accuracy, the images were certainly a lot better than having none at all.

What he was looking at now was a picture of a man in his forties or possibly early fifties with thick, long, wavy hair, straight white teeth, a neatly trimmed beard and gentle though penetrating eyes behind a pair of dark-rimmed glasses. There was a hint of a smile on the lips, not malicious or mischievous but almost beatific. 'Well, Martin,' whispered Jackman, 'I'm willing to bet that the day we slap handcuffs on Daemon, he won't be looking half as serene and angelic, if he ever did.'

He decided to hold off on getting it copied until he had had a chance to hear Laura's opinion.

Max stuck his head around the door. 'Boss? Sorry to bother you, but Rosie's here and she'd like to say hello.'

Jackman smiled broadly. 'Send her in! I haven't seen her for ages.'

His ex-detective, who he still thought of as Rosie McElderry, walked in, smiling. Jackman stood up and gave her a hug. 'You look great, Rosie! Married life and motherhood really suits you.' He could hardly believe how much she had changed. She looked a little older, certainly, but now the gritty and determined edge had gone. She looked composed, and possibly even more attractive than before.

'I still miss you guys, though,' she said warmly. 'Well, sometimes.'

She had been a brilliant detective and Jackman missed her too. He told her so in no uncertain terms. 'Now, listen, as soon as those twins are old enough to cope with a working mother, I want you back, my friend. We've got a great team — even if I do have to put up with your little Cockney Sparrow, Max — but you would make it even better.'

'It's a possibility, boss,' she said. 'Although by then things will have changed so much that I'll need retraining.'

'So what? You'd sail through it. You'll always be an "organic" detective — you have the nose, our Rosie. You're a natural.'

'Well, my husband has roped me in as a consultant today, so maybe I'll get the bug again, who knows?'

'We can only hope,' said Jackman.

She glanced back at Max. 'And I get some nice plants for the garden out of it, so win-win, I say.'

He watched them leave with a pang of nostalgia. He was fortunate in the detectives he had in his team, but he always felt they'd lost something special when Rosie left. That, and he just didn't like change.

'Message from Superintendent Ruth Crooke, sir.'

A civilian handed him a memo. He scanned it quickly.

'Against my better judgement, Rowan, you have the drone and a pilot at 11.30 a.m. this morning. Get yourself a plausible excuse

ready, people don't like the thought of an eye in the sky spying on them. Ruth.'

Well, Robbie and Kevin would be pleased, and Robbie should be back from his assignment with Marie in plenty of time. A good look at that strange hotel might provide some answers. Locating the cult's HQ had become of paramount importance now they had a recent ritualistic death on their hands.

As always, his mind bounced back to the Solace investigation, and he checked his watch for the hundredth time. If Marie could bag one of the people involved in trying to get the Stewarts out of that house, they might finally discover what the hell was going on.

Jackman needed coffee. As he walked down the corridor to the machine, he recalled that when he had visited Gary in hospital the day before, he had mentioned the name of the estate agent who'd sold them the house. It was one of several things Gary had been about to deal with when the incident with the tractor occurred. Jackman wasn't sure when Gary would be back at work, but he could at least contact this estate agent. Their name was Millgate and Foreshore, and Gary reckoned Holly had dealt directly with John Millgate.

Back in his office, he looked the firm up on the internet and got their telephone number. Soon, he was talking to John Millgate's secretary.

'John's out on a customer visit this morning, DI Jackman, but I remember that property clearly.'

I'll bet you do, thought Jackman. *The champagne must have been flowing after that contract was signed.* 'Then can you recall if anyone else was interested in the place?'

She sounded quite definite. 'No, no. Mr and Mrs Stewart were the only people to view it.' She lowered her voice. 'The reputation, you understand. The murder of that poor woman. *Normal* people don't want a property with that kind of history.'

Normal people. He'd found Holly's view that it was a whole lot of house for a very small amount of money perfectly normal. A practical person with no time for groundless

207

superstition might see huge potential in purchasing such a place. He bit back his comment about them not wasting any time in offloading it and said, 'And no enquiries after the sale? Even quite recently?'

There was a silence for a moment, then the secretary said, 'Now I think about it, there might have been, though I never dealt with them personally. I seem to recall John mentioning someone asking about it.' She gave a little laugh. 'He was quite taken aback, I think. After having Solace on our books for so long without a single enquiry, it was almost funny.'

Oh, very amusing, thought Jackman. 'I need to talk to John Millgate as a matter of urgency. Can you give me his mobile number, please?'

'I can, but he switches it off when he's with a client, Detective. He'll be back in an hour. Why not try then?'

'The number, please.' This time he didn't conceal his irritation.

She reeled it off. He thanked her rather curtly and hung up.

John Millgate answered almost immediately. 'Solace? Oh goodness, that place! Well, yes, I did have a couple of calls, actually, both from the same man, I think. He wanted to be made aware if any of three properties came onto our books. He said he was looking for something very particular and he was extremely interested in the house out at Amberley Fen.'

'You have his name, sir?'

'I do. In fact I remember it distinctly. It was Carson.'

Jackman felt a stab of hope, which immediately faded. Of course this prospective "buyer" wouldn't give his real name, would he? 'And his phone number?'

'It's back at the office. Shall I ask my secretary to find it and ring you?'

Jackman said that would be a help. It might have been a genuine enquiry, of course. Some people did register their interest in specific properties if they had something very particular in mind. Some even made offers directly to the owners, sometimes very good ones. But Jackman didn't think this was the case with Solace. Not for one minute.

Ten minutes later he had the mobile number. He rang it and, as he suspected, it was out of service. The prospective purchaser, Mr Carson, had obviously dumped it when he embarked on very different tactics. Oh well, it had been worth a try. He scribbled a memo telling Gary what he had done and placed it on his desk. No point Gary chasing up something that had already been ruled out.

The office was now buzzing. Phones rang, printers whirred, and the sound of voices filled the air. Four workstations stood empty — those belonging to Marie, Robbie, Kevin and Gary.

The door opened. 'Morning, boss. Made it.'

Jackman smiled at Gary. He noted how careful he was being in his movements, wincing slightly and gently protecting his ribcage when he sat down at his desk.

'You could have taken just one day off, man. I'd say you look like you've been hit by a bus, but that wouldn't be totally accurate, would it?'

'I must not laugh,' Gary said through gritted teeth.

'Seriously, Gary,' said Jackman. 'If you want to go home, don't even ask, okay? Just go. I really hoped you'd have a rest today.'

'No point, sir. I'd feel as crappy at home, and at least here I can do something more constructive than stare at the goggle-box all day. I've got painkillers and Gilly is on call to pick me up whenever I need to get away, so here I am.' He smiled painfully. 'It's better being at work, honestly. The investigation will take my mind off it.'

'Well, I'm not going to deny I can use you. Are you up to coordinating the Solace affair from here, along with Tim, just as a desk jockey? No fieldwork, of course.'

'Absolutely. Leave it to me,' Gary said.

'Well, I have an update already.' He told Gary about Marie's clandestine investigation of the night before, leading to this morning's operation in the tiny Saltern square. He also told him about the other interested party in the form of the mysterious Mr Carson and his non-existent phone number.

'Mmm,' said Gary. 'He's tested the waters, jettisoned that idea and gone for the jackboot. Let's just hope our Marie and the gang bring home the bacon.'

'We'll know soon enough, so cross your fingers.'

* * *

Robbie was in position about ten minutes before the arranged time. Marie had got Bonner to describe how he felt while he waited for his instructions or his money. Was he excited, unbothered, nervous? Did he sit, looking around casually, or did he read a paper, check his phone? How did he sit? Upright? Legs crossed? Slouched forward? All this helped Robbie do his best to give the impression that he was Anthony Bonner.

And it worked. Marie had carefully chosen a seat that had its back to the lane leading from the town centre and as she had hoped, their target had approached that way. He would have seen Rob from behind, casually checking his mobile phone and wearing that distinctive football club hat and dark jacket.

The man went directly to him, laid a hand on his shoulder, and recoiled in surprise. Then what Marie called a Totally Textbook move ensued. She and Kevin appeared, one at each side of the man, and in moments he was being bundled into a police car. Job done.

* * *

Ashley showed Laura the EvoFIT image before they went downstairs for their first interview of the day with Bennington. Laura was well aware that when you actually knew someone and then tried to describe what they looked like, you "built in" a lot more than just their external appearance, subconsciously adding what you knew about their personality.

Martin had done this in spades. This might be the man that he swore had let him down, turned on him, cast him out and was no longer worthy of his loyalty, but his initial feelings for Daemon, his leader, had flooded into the picture.

'Do we use it, Laura? If this doesn't look like the real Daemon, there wouldn't be much point, would there?' Ashley looked anxious. 'I really thought this would be the kick-start we needed.'

'I wouldn't show it to the public, but it would be a guide for your officers. They'll be able to see through the mask — cut the crap, you might say — and at least they'd be able to eliminate any definite nos.'

'You're right,' Ashley said. 'I'll get it out to the troops, but with a warning not to be taken in by the Christlike appearance.'

'If it helps to reinforce the message, you could remind them of what my colleagues in Saltern found in those black refuse sacks,' suggested Laura.

'Good idea. It'll leave them in no doubt about what he's capable of.' She gathered up her papers. 'Ready for the next stage in the cross-examination?'

'What's today's objective?' Laura asked.

'Apostle. I want a lot more information on that particular devotee. If he's still alive, as we suspect he is, I need an idea of where to look for him.' She hesitated. 'I'm not trying to rush you, Laura, but honestly, how long do you think it will take you to come up with your assessment?'

Laura really had no idea. 'I can do a straightforward psych evaluation to assess mental health in around an hour, Ashley, but that's not why I'm here, is it, nor what you want from me. This is far from straightforward. I know how important Martin is in finding your killer but he's not an easy person to connect with and I don't want to make any recommendations or suggestions until I can establish a rapport with him. We're getting there, but I can't hurry it. You know how complicated he is.'

'Don't I just!' Ashley shrugged. 'Not to worry, but there's something else we have to consider. You see, he can't stay here after today. It has to be either a safe house or a psychiatric facility. We aren't a hotel, and he can't hide here for ever, unless I arrest him and then he'd be remanded at a prison facility where he could remain for as long as eight months if necessary.'

Laura winced. 'I don't think the prison environment would do him any favours. In fact, unless you really believe he might have been involved in the deaths and are obliged to arrest him, I'd advise a health-based place of safety if you want to get the best out of him.'

Ashley looked uncertain. 'Well, I have to decide fairly soon. Anyway, let's go and talk to him now, I'll face that hurdle later.'

Today, Martin Bennington seemed very much in control, so much so that Laura found it rather odd. She wondered how long it'd be before he had one of his strange mood swings and started to fret and become agitated.

Half an hour later it still hadn't happened, but rather than directly answering their questions, he seemed to retreat into reminiscences of the past. Ashley continually tried to direct his thoughts to Apostle, and every time he wandered off into some little happening at the Hollow.

'You can't undo that which has been done, you see,' he said suddenly. 'Apostle did such a very good job, maybe even better than Daemon. He understood how to, how should I put it, "reprogramme" ordinary people and make powerful cult members out of them.'

'You worked with Apostle a lot?' asked Laura. 'Wouldn't you have preferred to work with Daemon?'

'As time went on and I passed through the first stages, I was happy to be with Apostle. There was something very exciting about that man.' He smiled benignly. 'I expect you know all about the way it works, Dr Archer. The group provides an illusion of security, and because you feel happy and safe, you start to believe in the unattainable gifts you're offered.' He laughed bitterly. 'Good health, financial security, peace of mind and even life everlasting. You most likely never knew what little self-esteem you had until they smothered you with flattery and praise. All an illusion.'

His stare was intense, unnerving. It seemed to be saying that he, not she or Ashley, was the one in control.

'And Apostle was very good at this?' she prompted.

'A master. He knew just how to guide and manipulate the new recruits. The way he parted them from their former lives was nothing short of miraculous. Most of us didn't even realise we had joined a cult. Instead we believed we had the good fortune to be part of a group of people with enlightened and powerful leaders.' He looked down at his hands, which lay folded in his lap. 'Now I'm on the outside looking in, I can see that along with the drugs, the paranoia they induced to maintain the illusion was so strong that some members became deranged enough to kill.'

'And this was Apostle's aim? To control the devotees so that they would take a life if the leaders so ordered?' asked Ashley quietly.

'It was Daemon's ultimate goal — that those who were truly worthy would do absolutely *anything* he asked. Apostle's whole reason for being was to assist Daemon in achieving his goals.'

'Did Daemon eventually turn on Apostle, as he did with you and the others?' Ashley asked calmly.

'The last time I saw him he was still by Daemon's side.'

Struck by the odd phrasing of this reply, Laura was convinced that Martin knew exactly where Apostle was now. She shifted a little in her seat and glanced at Ashley, certain that this very astute superintendent believed it too.

'Do you think Apostle is still alive?' asked Ashley.

Martin didn't answer for a while. 'Yes. I think I'd know if he was dead.'

'And where might he be?' chanced Ashley.

'Anywhere he wants. It'll be up to you to find him, I'm afraid.'

'He wasn't driving one of the cars that tried to kill you, then? You did say you saw their faces.' Laura looked at him hopefully.

'No, I didn't know those men at all.' He looked at Ashley. 'I'm tired. Can I rest for a while? I have a terrible headache.'

The superintendent suspended the interview and told one of the officers in attendance to get Mr Bennington a hot drink and some paracetamol.

By this time Laura had begun to have serious doubts about what was going on in Martin Bennington's head. She wished she could have discussed this case with Sam, but when she rang him, he'd sounded so tired she'd decided against it. He'd said he'd ring her as soon as he felt brighter, so it would have to wait until then. Meanwhile she was on her own with this one.

* * *

'Okay, pardner, you know your mission, or shall we run through it again?'

Rosie gave him a baleful stare. 'Really, husband, where do you think I've been all these years?'

With a grin, he led the way into the little nursery shop.

The woman Max had spoken to before didn't seem to be around, instead there was a teenage boy manning the till.

'Hello, mate. Is Belinda around?' Max said.

'She's out back. I can get her if you want,' the kid offered.

'I'd appreciate it, please. I saw her yesterday and she said she could give my wife some professional advice.'

'You've come to the right place then — there's nothing my mum doesn't know about plants.' He loped off into one of polytunnels.

So, they were a family. Max looked over to where Rosie was examining some colourful plants that he seemed to recall his gran growing on the kitchen windowsill. The bright red flowers made him feel quite nostalgic for a moment.

Then Belinda was breezing in. He noticed that she was wearing the same clothes as yesterday, only now they were slightly muddier.

'So you did bring your wife! We must have made an impression.' She beamed at Rosie. 'I'm Belinda. How can I help you?'

As Max watched, it was as if Rosie had thrown a switch. She launched into a stream of chatter featuring loamy soils, a south-facing house and the fact of young children and a dog. *A dog?* Max laughed to himself. He'd forgotten how good she was at this.

Still deep in conversation, the two women moved outside to the open area at the back of the shop, and Max could see some tall climbing plants being stood to one side. This was going to be costlier than he'd thought.

'Not into plants, then?'

The teenager was watching him in amusement.

'Oh, I like them well enough, but I'm lost when it comes to remembering their names.' He pointed to the red flower Rosie had been looking at. 'Like this one. My gran grew them, so I should know what they're called but,' he shrugged, 'I've no idea.'

'That's a geranium, a zonal — see the dark patterns on the surface of the leaves? These ones grow and flower faster than seed geraniums.'

'Hey, impressive,' said Max. 'You know your plants all right. So, what's your name?'

'Ben. I guess I know a bit, but most of the others know more than me. I don't have a speciality like them, I just kind of do a bit of everything.'

Hoping no other customers came in, Max set about getting this likable kid talking. 'What do you mean by speciality?'

'Well, like my two older brothers are in charge of all the composts, fertilizers, pet and animal feeds, then my sisters each have their speciality — alpines, shrubs, bedding and perennials.'

'Wow, so you all work together here. That's quite something. And you're clearly a big family.'

Ben laughed. 'I'll say so. There's aunts, uncles, cousins too, even my grandparents still pitch in.'

'Do you know, I've never ever heard of that before. I love my brothers, but I could no more work with Jim and Howard than fly to the moon. We'd be at each other's throats in less than an hour.' Max made his eyes wide.

'What a shame,' Ben said. 'We all get along pretty well. I guess we have a common goal, it being a family business.' He pointed. 'Would you like a coffee while your wife and my mother spend your money? It's only machine stuff, but it's actually quite good and it's free to customers.'

Max said he would and, glancing at the trolley-full Rosie and Belinda were amassing, began to wonder just how many plants his credit card would stand.

The coffee was good, much better than the stuff they got at the nick, and he was into his second cup when he saw Rosie and Belinda and the trolley making their way back into the shop.

'And they are all supposed to go in my car?' he murmured to Ben. 'This will be interesting. We might have to do two trips.'

'I could get my uncle to deliver them for you, unless you're from out of the area?'

Not wanting to give his address away, Max said, 'I appreciate it, but let's give it a try, shall we? My wife will want to be planting all these as soon as we get home.'

Ben nodded. 'I can imagine. I'll give you a hand. I'm used to packing cars.'

Somehow, they managed. Max was able to drive with only a minimal amount of foliage brushing his face, and he had to admit that it hadn't been as expensive as he'd feared.

When they were out on the main road and heading for home, Max said, 'Situation report, please. All the details.'

'I need to think,' said Rosie, unexpectedly serious. 'I'm not sure whether I'm in awe of their incredible capacity for work or if I believe a word of it. It felt like I'd wandered into one of those true-life documentaries about extraordinary or offbeat families.' She took a deep breath. 'How about you? What did the kid come up with?'

'I'd swear he was perfectly genuine,' Max said. 'I just can't get my head around such a large family all working together. Ben said he thought it worked because apart from him, they all had specific areas they were responsible for.'

'Belinda said much the same. Each one had something to be proud of that they could call their own, and each individual section was part of the whole enterprise. It's far bigger than it appears. They supply plants and sundries to small businesses and landscape gardeners as well as the public.' Rosie lapsed into silence.

'So if that is true, and I have to say that it seems that way simply from the amount of stock they carry, why the feeling that it's all a kind of charade?'

'Pass,' she muttered almost to herself. 'But I'll work it out.'

They drove on in silence. Like a persistent itch that he couldn't reach to scratch, Max's thoughts kept returning to Ben. There was something about that boy. But what? The only thing that had registered as of interest, had been a small tattoo on Ben's wrist. Max had only a fleeting glimpse, as the boy lifted some plants into the back of his car, but it had looked vaguely familiar. Was it that? And if not, what was eating away at him? Max concentrated on the road, but continued to wonder.

CHAPTER NINETEEN

Marie and Kevin sat opposite the man they had so neatly picked up from the little Saltern garden square. They were both excited and trying not to show it. Robbie had dashed off with a couple of uniformed officers and the drone pilot and was preparing to take some aerial shots of his weird hotel complex, and it was still only eleven a.m.

The man, who told them that his name was Mike Coleman, stared back at the two detectives with a rather frightened expression on his face. 'I don't know why I'm here, honest I don't!' he said for the umpteenth time. 'I've done nothing wrong.'

He was in his thirties, of average build, with nondescript features and dark hair, and had no police record.

'Look at it from our point of view, Mr Coleman,' said Marie amicably, 'er, can I call you Mike?'

He nodded and relaxed a little. 'Yes, of course.'

'Look. Something bad happens to a nice family. We make enquiries. We pick someone up who is clearly involved and admits he is. He leads us to you. You admit you are working for the same boss as the first man. So, from our side of the fence . . .' Her smile faded. 'Mike, you are in it up to your neck.'

He swallowed. 'I do a bit of casual work for people, anything I can get my hands on,' he said. 'Even bloody freezing my butt off picking in the fields, and not many locals do that anymore. I'm struggling to keep my head above water without stooping too low.' He swallowed again. 'A few weeks back, this bloke sees me checking out the job vacancies in the little newsagent's in Back Alley. He tells me he was just about to put a card in the window for a runner.'

'And what kind of job is that exactly?' asked Kevin.

'Just a gofer, picking stuff up and delivering it — paperwork and the like.' He shrugged. 'Not regular, but it pays really well, all things considered.'

Marie was getting a slight sinking feeling. She was listening to a rerun of Anthony Bonner's story of last night. Any moment now a familiar name would appear, and they would be back to square one. She looked at Mike shrewdly. Or maybe not.

'This man's name?' asked Kevin.

'Mr Isaac Hobbs, a local businessman, in the property trade, mainly rentals. He did ask if I might be up for a bit of back rent collection, but then he thought I probably wasn't tough enough for that, so I stuck to running errands.'

They questioned Mike Coleman a little longer, but his story never faltered. Abruptly, Marie stood up. 'Excuse us a minute. I need to clarify something with my colleagues. Interview suspended at eleven twenty-two. DS Marie Evans and DC Kevin Stoner are leaving the room.'

'Let's take five for a coffee, Kev,' she said. 'I want to play this differently and I need something from forensics. You go grab the drinks. I'm going upstairs for a few minutes, so I'll see you back here.'

As they hurried down to the big vending machine outside the ground floor messroom, Kevin said, 'Surely he's legit, Sarge? Picked up, just like Bonner was, to do a job for this Isaac Hobbs bloke. He's using innocent suckers who are desperate for a bit of cash but know nothing about their bossman's real intentions.'

Marie looked at him keenly. 'Maybe you're right, Kev, but I'm beginning to think otherwise.' She left him getting the drinks and went up the back stairs to CID, two at a time.

Jackman was writing something on the whiteboard. 'Boss,' she asked, 'have we had anything back from Rory this morning?'

'Yes, a few minutes ago. I'm just about to go through it now. Come to the office and tell me what you're looking for.'

Inside, she said, 'You told me Rory was going to rush through the analysis of the blood and stuff from the lounge wall at Solace. Did he do that for you?'

Jackman thumbed through the reports and notes. 'Ah, yes, but they haven't completed the tests yet. He says more to follow.' He extracted a short printout. 'Oh shit! It was *human* blood, not animal.'

She shivered. 'That's bad, but it's the paint I'm interested in.'

He frowned at her but didn't press her further. 'Er, let's see. Right, they have done that part. It was an oil-based gloss paint, a popular brand, and the colour is listed as Crimson Dawn.'

A smile spread across her face. 'I could be wrong, boss, but I think we have your part-time artist in interview room three.' He looked up sharply. 'Leave him to me, I'll be back shortly.'

Human blood. Hurrying back to the waiting Kevin, her mind was crowded with questions. For a start, it made the situation at Solace House far more serious than just an attempt to scare the Stewarts off. That blood had to have come from someone. Had it been donated willingly, taken by force, or stolen? Only once before had she dealt with a case in which someone stole a bag of blood from a hospital facility. It was very unusual, but it could happen. She pushed the thought away. Someone else would look into that — her concern was the paint.

They drank their coffee standing in the corridor while she told Kevin what she believed.

'Blimey, Sarge, you've got good eyes! But if that's the case, he's a bloody good liar.'

'As are most members of the criminal fraternity,' she reminded him. 'In any case, I'll be arresting him, so we need to get all of his clothing into evidence bags and down to forensics.' She drained her beaker and threw it in the bin. 'Let's do this!'

* * *

Jackman and Robbie went over the footage from the drone for a second time.

'I *swear* this place is not what it seems, boss,' breathed Robbie in frustration. 'But there's still nothing conclusive.'

'I'm inclined to agree with you,' said Jackman. 'I suggest that you look at this yet again and list what you see, like the numbers and locations of those chalets and statics, any signs of life and anything of interest that the drone picked up, okay?'

Robbie nodded. 'Sure. I'll do that now. And if I still find nothing, I'll pay a call. I'll be someone looking for a quiet retreat for a week or so to get over a messy divorce, or some such garbage.'

'If you want to go that route, Rob, do *not* go alone, understood?' While Jackman spoke, Marie came in wearing a big smile on her face. 'I like that Cheshire Cat impersonation, Sergeant.'

'It's Bagpuss actually, boss, because I've bagged a fat cat and if we press the right buttons, he's going to meow like a good 'un, I just know it.'

'Who's Bagpuss?' asked Robbie.

'Before your time, junior. Old kid's TV programme,' said Marie. 'It featured this saggy old cloth cat. He was supposed to be marmalade and white but something went wrong with the dyeing process, and he turned out pink and cream. Don't you know anything, Detective?'

'Apparently not,' said Robbie, shaking his head. 'I'm going back to my drone.'

Jackman indicated his office. 'Come on, Smiley. We'd better update each other. It's been a busy morning.'

Mike Coleman had given them a very believable story and had managed to convince Marie of it — until she spotted a tiny splash of dried red paint on the cuff of his jacket. 'His clothes were sent to Rory, and as they were being processed, one of the officers signing them off noticed a small amount of the same colour red paint deep in the grooves of his trainers.'

'Paint and blood,' Jackman reminded her. '*Human* blood, which worries me a lot. It takes it up a league, doesn't it?'

Marie frowned. 'It does, which reminds me. Last night when we were tracking Bonner through the undergrowth, the thought came to me that someone is going to an awful lot of costly trouble to get their hands on a miserable old property. What if this has nothing to do with the house at all, but with the Stewarts themselves? I mean, what do we really know about them? Where do they come from? Was their sudden decision to up sticks made because of a more critical reason than wanting a rural life for their kids? Were they running from trouble? Was someone after them?'

Jackman let out a low whistle. 'Well, what other thoughts do you have while you're creeping around in the bushes at night?'

'Look, I know you like them — so do I, we all do — but maybe for the sake of good policing we should look more closely at that family?'

She was right. Oddly, that thought had never occurred to him, not for a minute. Suddenly he recalled asking Holly where they came from. She had said "out of the area," from a big town, but omitted to say which. It struck him, too, that he had recommended Hugh for a job purely on his wife's assertion that he was a bloody good worker. *Oh God.* For once, he had let his heart rule his head. Was it going to make him look a complete fool? 'Of course, Marie, we should consider that possibility. I think a check on Hugh would be the place to start. I'll do it myself.'

'Have you heard from them today?' Marie asked. 'I was told they were collecting some things from Solace this morning and taking them to their new accommodation at the stables.'

Oh, Lord! *And* he'd got his mother involved with these strangers in a big way. He hoped to heaven that Holly and Hugh were exactly who he had believed them to be and didn't turn out to have a sinister agenda. 'Er, no, not today, but I might take a run over there later this afternoon.' He tried to push the worrisome thought to one side. 'Oh, you need to see this, Marie.' He handed her a copy of the EvoFIT picture, supposedly of Daemon. 'Laura and the super think we should keep this in-house, for police eyes only and not make it public. Laura thinks it's far from accurate and might be a kind of emotionally induced avatar of the man Bennington used to worship.'

Marie stared at it and laughed. 'Oh my. So we're hunting a JC lookalike, are we? Sorry to sound irreverent, but all he needs are sandals and a halo and he's ready for the Second Coming.'

'So you think it's a bit idealistic?' he asked with a wry smile.

'Frankly that picture doesn't surprise me, Jackman. That poor guy spends years incarcerated in a closed group being shepherded by a man who controls his every thought, and then he's cast out. Poor blighter's either going to hate Daemon to hell or believe that he himself is to blame and continue to venerate his, well . . . whatever that is.'

'Still, there has to be some likeness in that image. At least we know he's not a little bald dumpling of a man or a clean-cut office type. Even if Martin Bennington has elevated him to sainthood, I'm guessing he will be recognisable when we catch him.' Though after Marie's new take on the problem of Solace, even Jackman's enthusiasm about catching the cult leader was waning.

Marie eyed him shrewdly. 'Listen, you. Cheer up. I could be barking up completely the wrong tree, so don't fret over what I said. I'm just being cautious, that's all. If it helps, I too think they're straight as a die, but we do need to look at everything.'

'Thank you, Mother,' said Jackman. 'But to be honest, I'm really mad at myself for not even considering that possibility.'

She smiled. 'Mental overload. It happens to the best of us. Now, what else?'

He was relieved to move on. 'Well, we need to check the forensic reports from Rory. Oh, and Tim gave me a message just before you came back, asking you to drop by Orac at about three this afternoon when she should have something interesting for you about the Nash family.'

'Ah, the owners of the Hollow. Great! Oh, wouldn't it be fantastic to find that the man we are after has a real name. Bloody demon!' Marie said. 'I want to get it right when we slap those handcuffs on him.'

Jackman relaxed a bit. 'Talking about the Hollow, using Orac's coordinates, the Locksford team have found the place at last. Ashley said it was dead creepy, but it must have been quite something in its time, quite a prestigious property. It's just an overgrown and rather dangerous ruin now. No work has ever been carried out on the place — it seems no one has been out there for some considerable time.'

'No point in us trailing up there, then. It sounds like anything interesting to come out of that place will be via Orac.'

He agreed. 'Yes, we'll stick with our checks into the second cult headquarters.' Jackman glanced through the open door and saw Max arrive back. 'And on that subject . . .' He went to the door and beckoned to him. 'Any joy?'

'Well, Rosie has a fortune in garden plants to play with and I'm lighter in the wallet, but we've come to the conclusion that the place needs a further look. It might not be related to the cult at all but there's something a bit fishy about Oak Barn.'

'Just what Robbie said about his bloody hotel.' Jackman rolled his eyes. 'Oh well, you and Charlie push on with that and if any warning signs flash up, back off and get me, okay? However friendly they seem, do not go back there alone, and I mean it.'

Max nodded. 'Gotcha, boss, I'll be careful.'

Marie looked at her watch. 'Gotta go back downstairs. Our painter and decorator should be processed by now and I'm pretty sure he's fit to be interviewed. Want to sit in?'

Jackman would have loved to — Solace interested him a great deal. Regretfully, he declined. Memos and reports were coming in thick and fast, and he had promised to tie up with Locksford again at lunchtime. 'I'll let you and Kevin handle him, Marie, he's your success story. I suggest you let Gary watch through the video camera. He's coordinating all things Amberley Fen.'

'Excellent! I'll do that. See you later.'

Jackman closed the door. His head was spinning. Before he did anything at all, he needed to know if Hugh Stewart appeared on the PNC. If he was known to them in any way, someone would need to do a whole lot of explaining. Jackman took a deep breath and signed into the National Database.

* * *

They went back into the interview room to find a very different Mike Coleman slumped in his seat and rustling in a disposable coverall. He looked terrified.

Having gone through the formalities, Marie looked long and hard at Coleman. 'Mr Coleman, it will be in your best interests if you tell us the truth. We have forensic evidence from your clothing that puts you at the scene of a crime, so I urge you not to attempt to lie. It will only make things worse for you when you appear in court.' She knew full well that no actual proof had been obtained yet — it would take time for forensics to analyse the paint on his clothes — but she wasn't telling Coleman that. When he didn't answer she continued, 'Breaking and entering is a serious offence, Mr Coleman, and even if you didn't take anything, you caused unlawful damage to the building, so you could be looking at a jail sentence of . . .' She glanced at Kevin.

'Up to six years, Sergeant. Assuming Mr Coleman wasn't armed, which would mean considerably more.'

She stared unblinking at Coleman. 'So you need to be upfront, sir, to make things as easy for yourself as possible.'

Various emotions fought for supremacy across his face, until finally, he slumped down further. 'Okay, okay.'

'Excellent. A wise move, Mr Coleman. Now, from the beginning, please.'

'I wasn't lying about how he met me — you know, in the newsagent's? And I was a gofer for him. Mainly taking messages and delivering money to people, like the guy who was watching that old house for him, the one with the bad tenants.'

'What did your employer tell you about these bad tenants?' asked Marie.

'Well, that they owed a lot of rent. He'd discovered that their references were fake, and that they'd ripped off landlords before. He said they were a seriously nasty family and probably had connections to drug dealers. His biggest fear was that they'd do a runner and take all the furniture and maybe even the fittings. He'd recently found out that they'd done that too, stripped a place of everything.'

'All right, so what happened then? What did he ask you to do?' asked Marie evenly, watching him carefully. Coleman's eyes looked strange to her, and she wondered if some of the cash he earned was spent on drugs.

'Mr Isaac told me he was thinking of using some of their own tactics to get rid of them.' He nibbled anxiously on his bottom lip. 'He asked me if I knew anyone who might be up to doing something a bit, er, illegal-like.' He stared at the tabletop. 'Then he told me what he was prepared to pay for a one-off job. Get in, paint some message on the lounge wall, then some scary thing on a kids' room wall and get out again, finito.'

'And it was too good to turn down,' said Kevin.

226

Coleman nodded. 'Didn't see the sense in letting a wedge like that go to some other bugger. It was a simple job, I wouldn't have to hurt anyone or anything like that.'

'And you didn't think that painting something nasty on their bedroom wall might frighten little children?' Kevin said.

'There were no children. He said the family had a couple of teenage boys, real hard cases, and one was using a room the last tenants had done up for kids.'

Marie shook her head. 'Can't see a hard-case teen living with a pretty pink bedside lamp in the shape of a fairy castle, can you, Mr Coleman? Or snuggling up in a Sheriff Woody and Buzz Lightyear duvet set?'

'What? Jesus, I didn't wait to check the furnishings and decor! I just went to the room that he told me about, second door along the landing, did what I had to and buggered off.' Coleman was sweating. 'Look, this is all down to my boss, not me! I was just helping him out.'

Marie ignored the outburst. 'The paint you used, Mr Coleman, the red paint you splashed onto your cuff and your shoe, where did you get it?'

'He gave it to me. Mr Isaac had someone drop it off at my house. He said it was special, stuff you needed a proper cleaning agent to remove. It stank something horrible, but he was dead set on me using it.'

I bet he was, thought Marie. 'And if I told you that the "special stuff" had blood mixed in it, would it surprise you?'

She thought Coleman was going to throw up. 'Blood? You're winding me up!'

'Not at all.' She picked up an evidence bag and held it out to Coleman. 'For the benefit of the tape, I am showing Mr Coleman a mobile phone found in his possession. Is this your phone, Mr Coleman?'

'Yes, it's my work phone.' He still looked horribly shocked about the paint.

'Given to you by Mr Isaac Hobbs?' she added.

'That's right.'

This was beginning to feel like déjà vu, almost word for word what Anthony Bonner had said. 'So, let me ask you about Mr Hobbs. Can you describe him, please?'

Coleman screwed up his face. 'Big chap. Tall. Grey hair — er, thick, wavy hair and a bit of a beard. Wore kind of country clothes, like a wax jacket, and he had these really expensive tweed trousers. He had money, you could tell, but he didn't speak dead posh, just proper, if you see what I mean.'

'And where is his place of business, Mr Coleman?' Staring at the mobile phone Marie knew she was looking at Hobbs's "place of business."

'He never said. He always rang me with whatever he wanted me to do. He must be local, though, or why advertise in Saltern?' Coleman frowned. 'He's lied to me about that family and that old house, hasn't he?'

'Just like he lied to his other employee, Mr Anthony Bonner — you and he passed stuff between you. Well, you and Bonner have been terrifying the life out of an innocent family, including a couple of little children.' Her eyes narrowed. 'Shame you didn't notice that pink fairy castle lamp. If you had half a brain cell you might have put two and two together then.'

Coleman swallowed audibly. 'And it really was blood in that paint? Oh fuck! I think I might need that solicitor after all.'

'Indeed,' said Marie. 'We'll arrange that for you immediately. Meanwhile, is there anything else you can tell us about Mr Isaac Hobbs?'

Mike Coleman shook his head slowly from side to side. 'No comment.'

'Interview terminated at thirteen forty-seven. DS Marie Evans and DC Kevin Stoner are leaving the room.'

* * *

By three that afternoon, and with a lot of help from Laura Archer, Ashley Carpenter had made her decision about

Martin Bennington. She was mighty glad that DI Jackman had arranged for Laura to join her for a while. She was sure his move wouldn't have been arranged so well and so speedily without Laura batting in her corner.

Now they just had to tell Martin that everything was in place for him to leave the police station for the safety of a secure clinic. It hadn't been easy trying to explain that they simply could not hold him for an indeterminate length of time. It was a police station and there were regulations governing who could stay and for how long. Under normal circumstances, he would simply be let go to return home, but knowing the danger he was in and his fragile mental state following his ordeal, it had been decided that he should go to a psychiatric clinic and continue to speak with Ashley Carpenter and Laura from there. It had taken a lot of coaxing to get him to admit that he had already been attending voluntary sessions with a counsellor. When he mentioned the particular facility that this woman worked out of, Laura had thought it probably best to continue his treatment with a familiar face. Plus she had had dealings in the past with both the counsellor and the psychiatric hospital and knew that the place had a very good reputation. And so it was arranged, and this was their last chat on home soil, so to speak.

However, it didn't go quite to plan. Martin was exhibiting signs of extreme nervousness, and Ashley believed they would get next to nothing from him if they continued. Once he was settled in his new place, he would be able to relax and open up more.

'They'll find me,' he said suddenly.

'Your destination isn't known to anyone other than Laura and me — and, of course, your doctor at the clinic, where you will be registered under an assumed name. Even the officers who will be accompanying you will only be told your destination when you're about to leave.' Ashley looked at him earnestly. 'Does anyone else know about your previous counselling sessions?'

He shook his head. 'No one.'

'Where did these sessions take place? At home? Or at the main psychiatric hospital?' asked Laura.

'Neither, they were in a small consulting room in Locksford town. My counsellor uses it for private patients. Several different practitioners have rooms in the building — a physio, an acupuncturist and several complementary therapists.'

'So if by chance someone saw you there, it could have been for any number of reasons.' Laura smiled gently at him. 'There's no connection between it and the facility you are going to, Martin. You'll be safe there until such time as the police either neutralise the remaining cult members, or it's thought prudent to move you somewhere different. They won't have an opportunity to get to you again.'

Martin Bennington stared sullenly into his lap. 'They will find me,' he repeated. He closed his eyes and shivered. 'They have to. Daemon wishes my death and as I told you, his followers do whatever he asks of them. They'll find me.'

Ashley leaned closer to him. 'Martin! Listen to me. You can help us find them and stop them, and then they'll go to prison for life. If you do that, you'll be free of them at last.'

The wild laugh that escaped his throat made her shudder.

'Free? I'll never be free!'

One look at his terrified eyes told her to abort the interview.

CHAPTER TWENTY

Orac was looking unusually pleased with herself, giving Marie a little thrill of excitement. They had to have a name for Daemon. Without that, they were running in circles.

She sat down opposite Orac. 'Dare I ask?'

'Oh, do! Please!' Orac pushed a small sheaf of papers across her desk towards her. 'These are really just an exercise in genealogy and not too interesting unless you are one of the family, but they were necessary to get to the present day. Oddly, there was quite a bit of info on the older Nashs and very little on the modern-day ones.' She leafed through some more printouts and selected one. 'We got to the end of the line and believed we might have our man, until we discovered Jerome Nash.'

She handed a piece of paper to Marie, who recognised a death certificate. 'He's dead?' Confusion swept over her. 'So . . . I don't understand.'

Orac laughed. 'Jerome is dead, yes. But a younger brother who didn't appear in my first sweep is not.' She produced a rather grainy photo, showing a sombre-looking young man with two smiling women. 'Meet Mason Nash, last in line, still alive to all intents and purposes, and the man who made the insurance claim after the Hollow was

231

destroyed by fire.' Her smile broadened. 'Now, although the next piece of information would normally fill you with dismay and probably still will up to a point, it's actually a good indication that we are onto your Daemon. He disappeared immediately after receiving the insurance money, which fits perfectly with the time Daemon was leading his loyal followers through purgatory and on to Nirvana, wherever that is.'

'Mason Nash,' murmured Marie. 'So Mason Nash is Daemon?'

'There's little doubt, Marie. Oh, and the detailed investigation report compiled for the insurance company was very interesting indeed.' She passed her another official-looking letter. 'There was no sign whatsoever of arson or any indication of the fire being started intentionally, so either your witness lied about the cult burning the house down, or someone was cleverer than the fire investigation officers.'

'Wow. I'm not too sure what to make of that one, Orac. Martin Bennington swore they were made to destroy their home. Why would he lie?'

'Why indeed?' Orac shrugged. 'I can offer only one possible explanation and that is the hallucinatory drugs that your reports say were regularly administered to the cult followers. There's an outside chance that the fire started with an electrical fault in the old wiring, as stated in the official report. Daemon probably used the conflagration as a kind of ritual ceremony. If the cult members were high as kites, it wouldn't take much to make them believe they had burned the place down as a form of sacrifice, an act of total submission to their blessed leader.'

It was possible. Martin had said they believed every word that came from Daemon's lips. Even so, it bothered Marie, although she wasn't quite sure why. 'Orac, is this the only picture you have of Mason Nash?' She stared at the newspaper clipping.

'As yet. He seems to have been something of a nobody until he decided to rule the world. Which could explain his desire for power. Jerome was mentioned everywhere, but as for Mason, there's pretty well nothing to find.' Those disconcerting eyes flashed as Orac blinked. 'But I won't give up.'

Marie pulled a copy of the EvoFIT from her pocket. 'This is Martin Bennington's version of Daemon. Our psychologist tells us not to use it, as it doesn't represent a man who mutilates young women and kills at will. Does he look like the person in this picture?'

Orac looked closely. 'It's possible, I suppose. But no way could I work my magic with an out-of-focus photo and an image as unlike the real Daemon as that.'

'Of course you can't. The main thing is that we have a name. Now we can embark on the hunt for him. I'll also scan that early picture of Mason Nash and send it to Superintendent Carpenter. She can show Martin and if he says he recognises him, we're home and dry.'

'And I will endeavour to locate a better likeness for you. Meanwhile, if there's anything else I can help you with, just shout. You know where to find me.'

'I do. And thank you, Orac, you're a star!'

'I prefer genius, but star will suffice.'

The moment she was back in CID, Marie called out, 'Listen up, guys! Daemon's real name is very likely to be Mason Nash, last owner of the Hollow. He claimed the insurance after the fire and did a runner.' She went to the whiteboard, added the name and underlined it. 'We have something solid to go on at last. Orac found an old photo that shows him with a face like a slapped arse. She says he seems to have been insignificant, a nonentity who lived in his brother's shadow. I'm off to tell Jackman the demon has a name, a proper one.' With a triumphant smile she issued the team with a challenge. 'So just find him for me, will you?'

Jackman listened in obvious delight. 'Well done, Marie. You're having a belter of a day, aren't you?'

'That one was purely down to Orac, but it feels good to humanise the bastard — makes him feel catchable, if you get my drift.'

'I do. Being human means you're vulnerable. He's not the invincible Daemon anymore, simply a man called Mason Nash. And what Orac says about him living in his brother's shadow is significant. People who crave adoration and power over others often come from that kind of background. I'm sure this Mason is our man. I'll email the picture to Ashley. They can let us know Martin's reaction to seeing it. I'd like to get actual confirmation — that would really seal the deal on Mason Nash.' He picked up his phone. 'No time like the present. While I call, would you scan that picture and send it to her?'

'Will do,' said Marie and hurried to her workstation. As soon as the image had been sent, she returned to Jackman's office, where he was just setting the receiver down.

'Ashley and Laura are taking it to show Bennington before he leaves. He's being transferred to a place of safety, although the move has been held up for a while as he was feeling unwell. She's going to ring back asap.'

'That sounds like a cue for Marie to go and get some coffees, doesn't it?'

'Wonderful! I've forgotten when I last drank — or ate for that matter.'

'Then I'll throw in a choccy bar. Won't be long.'

She met Vic Blackwell in the corridor.

'Afternoon, Marie. I wish I was having as much luck as you. I thought I was on a simple one with the RTC that saw Bennington knocked off the road, but no such luck. To start with, although there was male blood found in the car at the pound, it's not on the database. Plus, it happened in a spot with no CCTV coverage and the other drivers at the scene were busy trying to save their own hides and missed the actual drama. Typical. Still, that might be about to change as I've just heard that we've found a road user who saw the collision and does have a working dashcam. Praise be!'

'Good luck with that, Vic, and keep me posted.'

He touched her arm as he passed her and grinned. 'Just hoping your luck will rub off on me!'

She laughed, relieved that they were friends again after so many years of animosity between them.

Back in Jackman's office, Marie placed the coffees on his desk, along with a Mars bar. 'Well,' she said, noting his oddly neutral expression. 'Don't keep me in suspense. Has Bennington fingered him or not?'

His face broke into a broad smile. 'He said that it had obviously been taken long before he knew Daemon, but it was him without a doubt. You have your name at last, Marie. Daemon is Mason Nash. Well done!'

'Well done, Orac,' she said. 'It was all down to her. I'll ring her in a minute and tell her.'

'Now we can do some proper police work at last, and trace a murder suspect.' Jackman looked invigorated.

'Sorry to burst this warm fuzzy bubble, boss,' said Marie. 'Regarding our other case, Kevin's been trying to track down this bogus landlord who paid Coleman to deface the walls at Solace. Isaac Hobbs doesn't exist, which is no more than we expected. After all, you don't wage a campaign of terror against an innocent family using your real name, do you?'

'No, you don't,' agreed Jackman. 'I'm afraid you're going to have to approach finding your bogus landlord from a different angle.'

'All I've got is Coleman's description of his erstwhile "employer." Kevin has just checked with Anthony Bonner and his description is very similar,' said Marie. 'I wonder if it's worth trying to get them to work with Orac to produce an e-fit?'

'I doubt whether Ruth will sanction anyone spending the time that would take, Marie. She's letting us work it, but it's still not a high-profile case. Dig a bit deeper with Coleman. Maybe he noticed something else about the man that might help us trace him.'

She nodded. 'Something bothers me about him, boss. Coleman keeps going on about never frightening a child, but the words he was told to write on the lounge wall actually mentioned children, as the message said that Sally Pinket would come for their children, and the one in the kids' room was clearly directed at youngsters. You wouldn't say "boo!" to an adult. He can't be that thick, it's perfectly clear what the message meant.'

'That's a good point, Marie.'

She was just about to leave when Gary appeared in the doorway, still carefully shielding his ribs with one arm.

'Isn't it time you called it a day, my friend?' said Jackman.

'I've already rung Gilly and asked her to pick me up, boss. I need the stronger painkillers, but they make me woozy, so I'll head off home shortly. I just wanted to report that I traced the two previous owners of Solace and asked if they had been frightened off. The first couple said no, they had simply realised that the renovations they'd planned were going to prove too costly and they didn't want to live in the house as it was. The second guy, a chap called Hardy . . .' Gary pulled a face. 'Frankly, sir, I don't think he was being level with me. I'm sure something did go on but he's being cagey about it. He did mention that he and his wife fell out over the place. She packed up and went to stay with her sister and he was left out there alone.'

'Shit. I wouldn't fancy that,' murmured Marie.

'I don't think he did either,' said Gary. 'He moved out shortly after she did, and it was sold as a vacant possession.'

'And along came Hugh and Holly,' sighed Jackman. 'Well, it might be worth pressing Mr Hardy a little harder tomorrow, Gary. Even better, get hold of *Mrs* Hardy and see what she has to say about Solace. You never know, something might have happened that would give us a lead on Isaac Hobbs.'

'Will do. And before I go, we've had no luck at all with trying to find the owner of the tractor and the muck spreader. The owner of the field it was dumped in wants it removed, but no way are we taking that pile of shit to the pound! The farmer might as well hang onto it — they're worth over a grand second-hand, and no one's going to be claiming it, are they?' He glowered. 'Anyway, I'll see you tomorrow, all being well.'

Marie accompanied him out of the office. 'I hope you're being well looked after, our Gary?'

He gave her a big smile. 'Oh yes, thank you, Marie, very well indeed. In fact,' he lowered his voice, 'I could get used to having Gilly around on a permanent basis. We're comfortable together. It seems so natural that I can't think of it being any other way.' He began to laugh, then winced. 'Ouch! That hurts. But honestly, Marie, never in a month of Sundays did I think I'd feel this way, but I do.'

'And Gilly?'

'She feels the same.' He chanced another laugh. 'It's come as a hell of a shock to both of us, I can tell you.'

She squeezed his arm gently, careful not to go near his damaged ribs. 'I'm so pleased for you. I would hug you, but I daren't!'

'Any other time I'd accept that hug happily, but not now.' He looked at the clock. 'Better get myself downstairs, my chauffeur will be here shortly. See you tomorrow, Marie.'

She watched him go, smiling. How quickly the world could turn. It seemed just weeks ago that they were both loners with nothing in their lives but work. Now look at the two of them!

'Marie? Got a minute?' Robbie was staring at his screen. 'What do you make of this?'

He was going over the footage the drone had obtained from the Eastwood Lakes Complex. 'Still at it? You've been looking at that for hours.'

'On and off, yeah. But I do believe I've cracked it.' He pointed to a shot of the cabins. 'These definitely aren't luxury chalets. They appear to be simple cabins for fishermen to chill out in by the lake. They look pretty basic and are all very similar, but I've been looking at the way they're laid out.' He squinted at the screen while Marie peered over his shoulder. 'I'm sure they're all angled so that none of them looks directly into another cabin.'

'That's fair enough. Most places arrange them like that to give the guests privacy,' said Marie.

'True, but look at the rear of the cabins. Every one of them is hidden from view by either trees or bushes so you can't see the small patio and barbecue area at the back. The drone, however, can look straight down on them. Now . . .' He zoomed in on one of the chalets. 'Look.'

Ruth hadn't stinted when she'd ordered their drone. The images were crystal clear. Marie saw a bubbling hot tub and as Robbie moved in closer, two glasses beside it, a bottle that had fallen on its side and several items of assorted discarded underwear. 'Oh dear. Someone isn't fishing for carp, is he?'

'Oh no, not at all.' Robbie raised an eyebrow. 'And there's more.' He closed the film and opened another. 'I asked the pilot to use the thermal imaging camera on a few of the cabins, and this image is pretty indicative of several of the others.' The picture showed the usual flares in different colours, with blue being the coolest spots and reds, oranges and yellows showing raised temperatures. Living sources, animal or human, always stood out well. As did the two particular "living sources" that Marie found herself looking down on. 'Oh. They're in particularly close proximity to each other, aren't they? Or do I just have a dirty mind?'

'These were taken at lunchtime too, not late evening when you could expect a bit of nooky to be going on.' Robbie laughed. 'If I told you we aren't looking at a free love commune as in Daemon's cult, but at some knocking shop, what would you say?'

'So that's why the lady in the local post office said you wouldn't want your wedding reception there!' Marie laughed. 'Well, it's not the result you were looking for, our Robbie, but I reckon it'll be worth uniform paying them a visit.'

'It answers all my concerns. That lady told me the owner wasn't a very nice man. According to her, he had tried everything he could think of to get the place to make money, so I guess this is a last-ditch attempt to keep it afloat. It also accounts for turning "genuine" customers away. The old lady mentioned a regular clientele, now I see why.' He heaved a sigh. 'But it's not helping us any, is it?'

'At least it narrows the search down and if it's not Max's friendly garden centre either, which we all doubt, it'll be back to Orac for another sweep of the famous One-Hour Drive from the Hollow.'

Robbie stood up. 'I'll tell Jackman, then have a word with the duty sergeant downstairs.' He grinned. 'I bet he'll have plenty of volunteers for this one.'

'I wouldn't mind being in on it,' said Marie. 'Nothing like a few bare bottoms dashing for cover!'

She returned to her own desk and sat down. She wanted to think before tackling Coleman again. His story seemed genuine up to a point, but surely he couldn't not have noticed that it was a little kids' bedroom. And he had said he didn't know there were children in the house. Total crap! *Or Sally Pinket will come for your children.* He wrote those words himself. No, he could not in a million years be that stupid. She looked up. 'Kevin! We are going to have to talk to Coleman again. Can you ring the custody sergeant and ask if he can be brought up to an interview room?'

'Yes, Sarge, straightaway.' He made a brief call. 'Fifteen minutes and he'll be in interview room one, with the duty brief.' Kevin went over to her. 'What's worrying you about him, Sarge?'

She explained.

'That bugged me too. I keep thinking that when I was a teenager, I'd rather have slept in the shed than with a pink fairy castle twinkling at me half the night. And that's *me*. I'm not exactly a "hard-case" kid like the fictitious teenagers Hobbs told Coleman lived there, am I?' Kevin was gay, and occasionally he made a passing reference to it that was always amusing.

'So, you don't have many pink fairy castles in your home then, Kev?'

'Er, no. They've never been a favourite, thank you very much. I don't think they're high on Alan's wish list either.' He laughed. 'Anyway, fairies aside, want a coffee while we wait for Coleman?'

'Love one, please.'

After he had left, Marie remembered something else about Coleman's statement that bothered her — its similarity with Bonner's story. It was entirely possible that this Isaac Hobbs person did operate that way, watching for men who were desperate for work and happy to accept cash in hand with no questions asked. It was a common practice among gangmasters gathering up fieldworkers who'd work the land for paltry wages. But these two accounts matched almost word for word. It is universally known that if three people witness the same occurrence they will each give a different account of it. What one notices, another doesn't. What one hears spoken one way, another hears differently. It's human nature. And it is down to the police to sift the wheat from the chaff and find the truth behind them.

Thirty minutes later, Marie was back behind her desk, certain that her twitchiness was completely justified. But it was Coleman himself who really wound her up. Accused point-blank of knowing it was a little kids' room he finally admitted, on his brief's advice, that he had. He said it had shocked him, but the money was just too good to walk away from. If he didn't do it, someone else would and he'd lose a considerable sum. So he'd painted the wall anyway. Well, that was one thing sorted, but still those carbon-copy statements about Mr Isaac and his modus operandi continued to bug her. She read Anthony Bonner's statement carefully, then Coleman's. They could have come from the same person. The odd thing was that she believed Anthony Bonner. She had checked out his background and he was telling the truth about having a wife and kiddie and being on the breadline. It was Coleman's words that didn't ring true.

With a grunt of annoyance, she went over what they'd found on him. No record. Never been in trouble before. Lived in a tiny, rented property in the roughest street in Saltern and had only been there a month or two. Prior to that — nothing. He just seemed to appear from nowhere, hard-up and looking for any work he could get. When she asked, he said he travelled around, doing whatever jobs came up, a statement that was almost impossible to verify.

Then there was his discomfort in interview, and those odd eyes. She'd bet anything he was a user. Maybe not the hard stuff, but she'd seen plenty of people who took drugs in her time, and she thought Coleman fitted into the category of cannabis smoker. Because of her suspicions, she had asked the custody officers to keep a close watch on him and give her their opinions.

She spent another half hour working on the computer, then texted Ralph to see what his first day back at work had been like. The answer was, *No comment. I miss you. Enough said? xxx.* She sent back a text saying that she missed him too, then, feeling like a silly teenager, shook her head and put her phone away, a smile still on her lips.

The smile vanished the moment she saw Jackman come out of his office and head in her direction. Something was wrong. Very wrong.

He leaned over her desk. 'They've lost him.'

It took a few moments to sink in. Bennington? Surely not. 'How? What on earth happened, Jackman?'

'Marie, this is a fucking disaster.' His uncharacteristic use of a profanity made it seem all the more serious. 'Not only that, but Ashley has two of her officers, Bennington's escorts, in ITU. One of them, DI Russ Cooley, is fighting for his life.'

She closed her eyes for a moment.

'I've got to tell everyone,' he said. 'Are the whole team here?'

She glanced around quickly. 'Yes. Except Gary.'

Jackman straightened up. 'Can you all stop what you're doing, please? I need to talk to you.'

The room fell silent. All eyes were on Jackman.

'Just over an hour ago, Martin Bennington was discreetly taken from Locksford Police Station with the intention of moving him to an undisclosed place of safety. He was accompanied by two experienced police officers who were only informed of his destination on their departure. However, twenty minutes into their journey, an ambush occurred. On a narrow stretch of road a mere three miles from their destination, a tractor pulled out in front of the car, forcing it to swerve and brake hard to avoid a collision. In so doing, it skidded and hit a tree.' Jackman took a breath. 'The next part is unconfirmed, but it appears that the vehicle was then set upon by several men, who dragged the car's occupants from the damaged vehicle and into the road. One officer was clubbed with a heavy blunt object and the other, who it appears tried to get back to the car to protect Bennington, was shot.'

There was a collective sound of general disbelief — groans, muffled curses and murmurings.

'They both have serious injuries, and the officer with the gunshot wound was airlifted directly to a critical care unit.' He paused. 'A driver, who pulled off the road some way from the incident and rang it in, said he saw a man dragged screaming from the police vehicle, bundled into another car and driven off. We have no option but to conclude that Martin Bennington has been taken.'

For a while there was silence.

Robbie was first to speak. 'Bennington must have been very important to them to make them do something as risky as shooting a police officer. Shit! They could be in for a sentence of up to forty years in custody. They wanted him back *really* badly.'

Marie's mind was pitching from one thought to another. According to Jackman, Martin had told both Laura and Ashley Carpenter that the cult would find him. He had been adamant, saying it was Daemon's wish that he should die. His followers would do anything he asked of them, so whatever it took, they would obey his command. Marie tried to think logically. The biggest question in her mind was how they knew where he was being taken. She voiced her concern.

'Ashley Carpenter has no idea at all,' said Jackman, despair written all over his face. 'Laura is furious with herself because she was responsible for most of the arrangements for the transfer. Not the logistics of course, but she checked out the clinic, the doctors and psychiatric team and the security arrangements. Bennington had sworn no one knew he'd been seeing a counsellor privately, so there should have been no connection between him and any healthcare professional or facility.' Jackman lowered himself onto a chair. 'They couldn't have been followed because the tractor was waiting, ready to pull out in front of them at that point in their journey. It was carried out like a sodding military operation. Which meant that someone knew exactly where they were going and when.'

'Well, Daemon knew. Mason fucking Nash planned this,' growled Max. 'He's got someone on the inside, hasn't he?'

'Even if he has,' Jackman said, 'I can't see how it would benefit him. Only Laura, the superintendent and the clinic knew where Bennington was being taken.'

'Maybe someone overheard Laura on the phone,' suggested Charlie.

'She swears she was alone in the super's office with the doors closed, and she used her own mobile, not a landline,' Jackman said.

Marie could hear his concern for Laura behind the words. He wanted to be with her to give her his support, not miles away.

He stood up. 'I'll update you all as and when I hear anything.' He turned to Marie. 'If you could join me in my office, please? We need to talk about the repercussions of this for us and our investigation.'

As she followed him from the CID room, she heard someone say, 'Well, that's the last we'll see of our star witness, unless he turns up in pieces in a bin bag.'

She shivered. It was a ghastly thought, but unfortunately probably true.

CHAPTER TWENTY-ONE

Jackman sat at his desk, his head in his hands. He told himself he should be used to having something scupper an investigation — it happened all the time — but this couldn't be so lightly dismissed. Martin Bennington's life was probably in danger and they were all responsible. A man had come to them with possible information about two unsolved murders and they had let him down. On top of that, he had heard the desperation in Laura's voice. She blamed herself, and nothing anyone could say was going to make her feel any different. Of all the worries that crowded in on him, Laura's distress was uppermost.

Marie came in and closed the door. He pointed to a chair and they sat in silence for a moment or two.

'This is going to be tough, Marie. We have to try and distance ourselves from the fact that two police officers have been badly injured. We all must concentrate on being totally professional, take hold of the remaining pieces of this shattered investigation and pull it back together — without Bennington's help.' He puffed out his cheeks. 'Understandably, Superintendent Carpenter is devastated. She had chosen her two most trusted and experienced officers — one of them her own DI — to undertake the move. Both are well-liked and respected, and the one who tried to save Bennington already has two commendations. Ashley is both heartbroken and enraged. All I can say is God help Daemon if she ever gets her hands on him!'

'And you need to cope with all this while wishing you were in Locksford with Laura,' said Marie. 'It's written all over your face.'

He loved Marie for her quiet understanding of him. He nodded. 'I've never heard her so overwrought, Marie. I've seen her anxious, upset, concerned about her clients, in almost every state you can imagine, but this. . .' He shook his head. 'I believed that when she had all that trouble with a referral patient a while back, she was about as distressed as you can get. Seems I was wrong.'

'She'll be fine, Jackman, just as soon as she realises it's not her fault. You know what it's like when we suddenly doubt ourselves and feel the weight of guilt descend. But this was obviously very carefully planned. No matter where he'd been sent or who arranged it, the outcome would have been the same. It had nothing to do with Laura at all.'

'You wouldn't like to tell her that, would you?' he asked, hearing the rueful note in his voice and hating it.

'Damn bloody right I will! I'll ring her the minute we're through here.'

He almost smiled. Sometimes he needed Marie's down-to-earth approach to life to put things into perspective.

'When is she coming home, Jackman?'

'She needs to be there for a while yet. As you can imagine, that station is in a state of shock, and she wants to support Ashley — no matter how shit she feels herself.'

'She would,' breathed Marie. She sat up straighter in her chair. 'So, how do we proceed? All I can think about is how the hell Daemon knew about that transfer.'

'There's little of a practical nature that we can do today, it's close to the end of the shift and I'm going to be asking everyone for an early start tomorrow, so we won't be staying late tonight. I have to talk to Ruth. She already knows the score, but we need to liaise and work out our response for when the shit hits the fan.'

'That will come down fair and square on Locksford, surely?' said Marie.

'It's a joint effort, so we'll be in the firing line too. Don't forget, the public don't know all the rules and regulations that govern us, nor the fact that more often than not our hands are tied with red tape and we can't do things the way we'd like to.'

'True,' said Marie. 'When it gets out that a man who was helping us with a murder enquiry has been hijacked, maybe killed, all hell could break loose. The fact that he was being taken to an undisclosed place of safety won't even register with people.'

'You forgot to add that he was a vulnerable man. That'll make things ten times worse. It's what Ruth and Ashley will be doing their damnedest to conceal. They cannot allow the word "cult" to get bandied about — we all know what the media will do with that.'

'Don't we just,' Marie groaned. 'Well, I guess this means that the Stewart case will be moved to the back burner while we try and cope with the cult.'

Jackman grunted in annoyance. The hunt for Mason Nash and his murdering sidekick would take precedence and rightly so, but once again that poor family would get sidelined. "Fraid so, Marie. But I'm going to leave Gary and Tim with that so we don't lose sight of it, and you must continue with Mike Coleman. I want him charged with burglary.'

'He broke in and he committed unlawful damage to the property, so it's a fair cop. I just think he knows more than he's telling me about the man who paid him to do it. I'm sincerely hoping he gets put on remand, because there's something really odd about him, and I very much doubt he'll turn up for his court hearing. We've still got a bit of time left on the clock, so I'll persevere.' She stood up. 'While you see Ruth, I'll give Laura a ring and tell her a few DS Evans home truths, okay?'

He watched her walk away, feeling as he so often did, eternally grateful to have her as his sergeant. Before she got to the door, his phone rang. When he heard who it was, he held up his hand to stop her leaving. 'A little light relief, Marie. That was Niall. You can cross Eastwood Lakes off your list of possible homes for the cult. It was exactly as Robbie guessed, and the raid has left a whole lot of the "guests" and "residents" with very red faces, and a few coppers with broad grins on theirs. Tell Robbie, won't you?'

She gave a half smile. 'Good news in one way, boss, but it means we're no bloody closer to finding Mason Nash.'

* * *

That evening everyone left the station in sombre mood. Under normal circumstances, Marie would have called into Gary's on the way home and updated him, but knowing he had Gilly there she opted for a phone call later. Right now it was Ralph she most wanted to talk to.

She arrived home before him, which was a slight disappointment, as she had come to enjoy seeing his car in her drive when she got in. She put the kettle on for tea, hoping he wouldn't be too long. As she made her drink, she went over her call to Laura. At least it had been positive. After they'd talked for a while, Laura seemed to realise that someone besides herself and Ashley had to have obtained the details of Bennington's transfer in order to snatch him as they had. She said the general atmosphere of shock and outrage at Locksford police station was quite overwhelming, and she longed to be back in the peace and quiet of Mill Corner. Nevertheless, they had ended the call with Laura sounding much happier, something Marie was pleased to relay to Jackman before she left.

She prepared her and Ralph's evening meal as far as she could, then rang Gary to pass the time. He was as horrified as the rest of them and equally puzzled as to how such a thing could have happened.

'Jackman wants you to keep a hold on the Solace case, Gary. He feels bad about not being able to help that family, but he'll feel a bit better knowing you're still on it.'

'And I can call on Stacey and Jay if I need any legwork done. No problem, Marie. I've got this, so if you speak to him before tomorrow, tell him not to worry. I'll find the person behind this, one way or another.'

'And don't forget you've got Orac,' she reminded him. 'She's working on Mason Nash, trying to find anything she can on him.'

'That's a great help. I'll be sure to keep in touch with her.'

'Oh, Gary, there's one other thing, and this won't be easy.' She recalled the conversation she'd had with Jackman earlier that morning. 'Jackman was going to deal with it personally, but I'm delegating the job to you.'

'Sound ominous,' said Gary. 'Go on then, tell me anyway.'

'I suggested there was a chance that these scare tactics weren't about the house at all but were directed at the Stewarts, Hugh in particular. We know nothing about them, and I wondered if their arrival here meant they had fled some unpleasant situation back wherever they came from.'

'Mmm, it's a possibility,' Gary said thoughtfully.

'Well, perhaps not, because Jackman looked them up, and they are who they say they are. They moved from a rough estate on the outskirts of Nottingham and have never been in trouble with us, so it looks like I was wrong. But we can't be sure that something hasn't happened in either Hugh or Holly's life to cause someone to wish them harm. Do you see what I mean?'

'Like a spurned lover, or an old business partner with a grudge? That kind of thing?'

'Yes, so I wondered if you would ask them tactfully to think back and see if there was any past trouble, maybe a quarrel that was never resolved that could have festered away in a disturbed mind.' She doubted that was the case, but she didn't want to miss a thing.

'I understand. It's a valid point. I had a case once where this really nice bloke was being targeted by some wingnut who turned out to be a cousin who'd lost out on some miserable little inheritance. Leave it to me, I'll be diplomacy itself.' He breathed in sharply. 'Gotta go, Marie. Talking hurts after a while.'

She rang off, saying she hoped he got a decent night's sleep. As she did so, her mobile pinged.

The message read, *On my way! I haven't deserted you!*

She smiled. She needed someone to talk to and who better than Ralph? Even if you didn't know them personally, serious injuries to fellow officers hit hard. Ralph would understand.

You wouldn't dare! she replied and added a smiley face.

He arrived half an hour later. They ate supper and though both were weary, went for their customary walk.

They strolled along the field paths, their conversation a little more subdued than normal. She was struck by how close they had grown, as if words weren't really necessary. This was new to Marie the great talker, yet so right she felt she could cry.

Back home, they turned in early. Exhausted and feeling uncharacteristically vulnerable, Marie just wanted to be held. The attack on their colleagues had made her realise how fragile life was.

Lying in Ralph's arms, she suddenly heard herself say, 'I don't need time to think about what you suggested. None of us know what tomorrow might throw at us, so let's not waste time. I do believe I've found my soulmate in you, and I don't want us to be apart.'

He held her tighter, kissed her shoulder. 'So then we make plans.'

'Yes, Ralph, we make plans. The sooner the better.'

They had just drifted off to sleep when the phone rang. They groaned in unison and laughed.

'Here we go again,' said Ralph.

She hadn't expected to hear Ruth Crooke's voice. 'What's wrong, Super?'

'Marie, there's no easy way to tell you this. There's been an accident.'

Marie held her breath.

'Laura Archer was driving home late from Locksford and her car went off the road.' Ruth took a ragged breath. 'I'm so sorry, Marie, I know she was a friend of yours. You see, I'm afraid Laura is dead.'

Dead? She stared at the phone, uncomprehending, then the meaning of Ruth's words crashed in on her. 'When? Where? Oh my God, Jackman! Does he know? Ruth, does Jackman know?' She was beginning to panic. Behind her, Ralph put his arm around her shoulder. 'Sorry, Ruth, it's the shock.'

'Ah, Marie, I felt just the same, believe me.' Marie did believe her. Ruth, she knew, was fond of Jackman. 'Jackman has been told. He says he'll be ringing you shortly. I just wanted you to know first. He is taking it very calmly — far too calmly, in my opinion, but who knows how a terrible shock like this might affect someone.' She paused. 'Sadly, you've been there yourself, so I don't need to say anything further.'

It was a surprise to hear this austere woman speak so gently.

'Be there for him, Marie. At the moment he is all business, demanding to know the facts of the case, the official verdict, but when the reality hits him, he's going to need the support of us all, you especially.'

Yes, thought Marie, this was exactly how Jackman would react. He would need to know every detail of what happened. He would be clinically detached — until he had gleaned every single fact about how, why and in what circumstances Laura had died. 'Of course I'll be there for him, Ruth. You don't need to ask.'

'I know.'

'Can you tell me what happened, or is it still unclear?'

Ruth sounded more herself. 'Oh, it's clear, the whole thing was caught on camera. What we don't know is why.

She was a few miles from home, on the main road and approaching the roundabout at the junction for Cartoft. She didn't slow down, Marie, she just veered to the left, went over a grass verge, down a bank and into the dyke that ran alongside the road.'

'Brake failure? Something catastrophic happened to her car?' Marie asked, trying desperately to understand.

'It's too soon to know for sure, but it doesn't seem that way. We'll have to wait, I'm afraid. The crash investigators are there now and so is Jackman.'

'I'll go straight there, Ruth.' With the phone still held to her ear, Marie was out of bed and rushing around looking for clothes.

'Take a moment, Marie, he won't be going anywhere for a while yet,' said Ruth. 'I don't want you flying off on that bike of yours and finishing up in some ditch too. That's an order!'

Ruth was right. 'I'd not be much help to him if I did that, would I?' She took a deep breath. 'When did it happen?'

'Around an hour ago. A young man who works in the garage on the roundabout witnessed the whole thing. He and a driver who had been filling his car at the time ran over, climbed down the bank and got her out of the vehicle. I think they were frightened of a possible fire.' She paused. 'She was already dead. Her rescuers tried to resuscitate her but there was nothing they could do. When the ambulance got there ten minutes after being called, it was already too late.'

An odd feeling of uneasiness stole over Marie. Laura didn't speed, she always drove with care, a little too slowly in Marie's opinion. Bumping up a kerb and crossing the verge would have slowed the vehicle even further. Marie had seen dozens of cars nosedive into ditches. The occupants mostly clambered out practically unharmed — those that were injured had nearly always been speeding and even so, were rarely very badly hurt. But dead? Very, very few.

'I know what you're thinking,' Ruth said. 'But don't try to work it out by yourself, you'll drive yourself mad. There will have to be a post-mortem, of course. I'm about to take

251

the liberty of ringing Professor Wilkinson, as he is a friend. He will provide the truth.'

At least that was something. Rory would look after Laura.

'I'll let you get ready, Marie. Ring me any time, day or night, it doesn't matter. You have my mobile number so don't be afraid to use it. Now, as you will realise, Jackman will be relieved of duty and, considering the case he has running, I'm going to put a suggestion to you.'

Marie waited.

'I don't want to farm it out to another team — anyway, that wouldn't be feasible at this stage. I'll take it over myself. Jackman has kept me updated all along, so I know just where you are with it, but I want you leading the team. Are you all right with that?'

It was the best she could hope for. Jackman would be fine with it too, she had no doubt. 'Absolutely, Super.'

'Excellent. I'll call an early meeting. I'm sorry, Marie, a whole load of emotional baggage is going to be landing on your shoulders in the weeks to come.'

'They're broad shoulders, Ruth.'

For Jackman's sake, they would need to be. But for the first time in many years, she wouldn't have to carry the weight alone. With Ralph's support, she would be strong enough to bear it.

As soon as Ruth ended the call, Marie pulled on some clothes, hugged Ralph and texted Jackman.

I'm on my way.

The answer came straight back.

Good.

No more needed to be said.

CHAPTER TWENTY-TWO

Marie dismounted from her bike and saw Jackman standing, still as a statue, staring down into the ditch at Laura's car.

She went and stood beside him and gently squeezed his arm. She didn't speak — there was nothing she could have said. Any words of comfort would have sounded trite. She stared at the familiar vehicle and, suddenly, she was gazing not at a car, but a vintage motorcycle and the person carried off in an ambulance wasn't Laura but Bill, her husband. All the anguish of that moment flooded back.

Jackman seemed to sense what she was feeling. 'If anyone knows what I'm going through at this moment, it's you, Marie. I'm sorry. This must be terrible for you.'

Jackman's selflessness brought tears to her eyes. He spoke again, his voice flat and unemotional. 'As you can see, there's very little damage, except to the front bumper and the bonnet. She wasn't speeding. She rarely did.' He paused. 'And there are no skid marks, Marie, none at all.'

She looked back at the road, now cluttered with cones, police cars and emergency vehicles. He was right. The RTC investigation specialist would normally be measuring skid marks, assessing speed and distance travelled, checking for a dead or injured animal that she had perhaps swerved to avoid, but tonight they were doing none of that, for there were no marks to measure.

'Looks like she just drove off the road. Intentionally.' He sounded desolate.

'And you know as well as I do that that would *never* happen,' Marie said, 'so there's a likelihood of brake failure or some serious malfunction of the car. There must be.'

'And if it isn't that?' He turned and looked at her. 'Marie, I've a bad feeling, very bad, about what might have happened.'

She squeezed his arm tighter. 'I'm not going to lie to you, Jackman, so have I, simply because of the case we are dealing with. But all we can do is wait for forensics. We can't keep speculating, it doesn't provide answers.'

'You heard that they tried to save her, the two lads?'

She nodded. 'It sounds like they acted very quickly. They gave her the best chance, didn't they?'

'Oh yes. And I've thanked them. They're in shock too, very upset. Nice lads. Caring.'

His voice sounded oddly distant, then she felt him start to tremble. 'Let's go and sit in your car for a while.'

He allowed her to lead him away, giving the crashed car a final look before turning his back on it.

As soon as they got into his vehicle, he said, 'I need to go to the hospital. I want to see her.'

'Of course, but you are not driving. I'll get one of the uniforms to take you, and I'll get your car collected later.'

He laid his hand on her arm. 'I can drive, honestly. I learned long ago how to compartmentalise. But I'd like you to come with me, if you would?'

'Of course.' She knew not to nag him. It wouldn't do any good.

'I have another favour to ask. It's Sam Page. I can't give him the news over the phone and I'm going to be tied up at the hospital with bureaucracy. But he has to be told, he can't hear about this from anyone but us. He thinks of Laura as his daughter, he loves her dearly. He lives alone and he has a heart condition. I want him to come back to Mill Corner with me.' He sighed. 'We can grieve together.'

'You want me to go and break the news to him?' she asked.

'Yes. And don't worry about leaving me on my own. I'll ring my mother. She'll come and wait with me. Apart from you and Sam, she's the only other person I can bear the presence of right now.'

'I know how you feel.' Marie had felt the same after Bill was killed. Her mother had been the one rock she could cling to. 'I'll go home after the hospital, collect my car and ring him to let him know I'm coming. I'll break it to him as gently as I can and stay with him until he's ready to be taken to your place. You should be through by then, and if not, just ring me.'

They sat on in silence, until she sensed he was beginning to recover from the initial shock. Looking ahead through the windscreen, he said, 'What were those bad thoughts you had, Marie? Did they by any chance touch on murder?'

'I don't know what to think, but as a police officer . . . let's just say that if Daemon can snatch Bennington right out of our hands, it wouldn't be too much of a stretch to imagine him killing Laura.'

'Thank you for being so honest, my dear friend. Now, shall we go and visit my beautiful girl?'

* * *

When Marie got home sometime after three thirty in the morning, Ralph was awake and waiting for her. She fell into his arms, sobbing.

As they lay in bed, she told him everything that had happened — almost worst of all being Sam's reaction.

'It was the saddest thing I've ever had to do,' she whispered into his shoulder. 'And like you, I've delivered plenty of bad news in my time as a copper. It was like a light went out. He held it together incredibly well, wanted to know how it happened and how Jackman was. But,' she struggled for words, 'it seemed as if his spirit left him. I can't put it any other way.'

'But he agreed to go to Mill Corner with you?' said Ralph.

'He said he knew Jackman would worry about him being on his own after hearing the news. But he didn't want to go, Ralph. He wanted to be alone, I know he did.'

'I can understand that, but as it starts to sink in, it'll be better for both of them if they're together. They both loved her, and I'm sure sharing the grief will help.'

'I just cannot believe she's gone. In the blink of an eye, just not there.' Marie raised herself up and looked at Ralph.

Her question hung in the darkness. 'But why were there no skid marks?'

* * *

The night passed slowly, the blackest night Jackman had ever known. He hadn't expected to sleep, and none came. He lay in bed, periodically reaching across for Laura and finding only a cold, empty space. After a while, he nestled into her pillow, smelled her perfume and worried about what he'd do when it faded.

When he had first seen Sam, he'd wondered if he had done the right thing in bringing him here. Then they had fallen to talking — reminisced, laughed and cried. At times they held onto each other like frightened children, afterwards smiling again at some shared memory.

Yet lying in the darkness, he was nevertheless dimly aware that devastated as he was, he was still Detective Inspector Rowan Jackman. That man, that professional, would carry him through.

A kind of strength returned — possibly a survival mechanism, but that was no bad thing. He had a problem to solve, and the detective in him was already looking for answers. In his mind he pictured the road to that ditch. The road without a mark on its surface. Oh yes, he wanted answers, and he was determined to find them.

He closed his eyes, and as dawn stained the sky outside his window, exhaustion finally granted him oblivion.

* * *

Holly was just preparing the children's breakfast when Harriet Jackman appeared in the open doorway, her face paper-white. Holly was stunned at her news. She had only met Laura a couple of times but had taken to her at once. She would have liked to have that lovely, gentle woman as a friend. And now she was gone. My God, was this whole place cursed?

'I wanted my son to come and stay with us, be with his family,' said Harriet. 'But he said he needs to watch over their old friend, Sam Page. He was reluctant to leave the home he'd shared with Laura.' She sighed. 'And of course, he has a lot to arrange, things that are best done from home.'

'Please do give him our sincerest condolences, Harriet. He must be devastated.'

'He is, my dear. He loved her very much, as did we. We couldn't have chosen a better partner for our son.' She swallowed. 'This is the second time the family has gone through a tragedy like this, you know. Rowan's brother, James — his wife also died in tragic circumstances. I thought we'd just got over that and now . . .' She shook her head. 'Sometimes you wonder just how much a person is supposed to take before something gives.'

Holly understood and said so.

Harriet rallied. 'Listen to me. Laying all this on you, my dear! I'm sorry. I'll be as strong as an ox again in a couple of minutes. I just wanted someone to talk to, and I did want you to know what had happened.'

'Thank you, I appreciate it. And, Harriet, you can talk to me any time. You've been so good to us that if we can do anything to help, just ask.'

After Harriet had gone, Holly suddenly realised that they had also lost their champion. Jackman wouldn't have any time for their problems now. Holly didn't mean to be selfish, it was just a thought, but nonetheless it scared her.

* * *

This second blow, coming immediately after the attack on their Locksford colleagues, hit the whole of Saltern station very hard indeed. Laura had been well-known and well-liked. She had seen many of them through difficult and emotional times after they had suffered a trauma in the line of duty. It felt personal. One of their own had fallen, and should it turn out that someone else was to blame, they'd have a whole army of vengeful officers on their trail. Word of the absence of tyre marks at the crash scene had spread around the station like wildfire, and Marie was thankful that Jackman hadn't been around to hear some of the theories.

As each member of their team came into work, she had taken them aside and told them what had happened. All were shocked to the core, but it seemed to hit Gary particularly hard. Whether it was because he was unable to function fully, or because he was a bit older than the rest of the team, he appeared deeply moved for Jackman. He told Marie he felt guilty. Here he was, so happy, while his dearest friend and colleague had had all the joy ripped from his life.

'I feel exactly the same, Gary, but think of it like this: it means you have to live for the day, grab whatever life offers and enjoy it while you can.'

'I know, and I realise it could have happened to any of us, but I still feel bad.' He shook himself. 'Anyway, enough of my feelings, where do we go from here? We need to knuckle down and sort these cases, don't we? For the boss and for Laura.'

She glanced at her watch. 'Ten minutes and Ruth will be addressing us all. She's going to take command but I'm in charge at ground level, and I intend to keep the cases running exactly as Jackman would.'

Gary nodded. 'Thank heavens she's left them with us. I could see the cult one going to another team.'

'We've done too much already, and we're too tied in with Locksford to change things at this juncture. We're going after this bastard, Mason Nash, and we'll make sure we nail the son of a bitch.'

My, that came out a bit strong, thought Marie. Nevertheless, she meant every word.

'And I'm going to sew up the Solace mystery,' said Gary. 'It'll be one less weight off Jackman's mind. I know what he's like, in spite of all his hurt and grief, he'll be worrying about the Stewart family and their cursed property.'

They had a crusade. Marie was certain that the whole team would be behind them, carrying their banner for Jackman and his Laura.

* * *

After the meeting, Ruth and she drew up a plan of action. Marie then phoned Superintendent Ashley Carpenter and explained how she intended to proceed. She found Ashley icily in command of her side of the operation. She too had set all emotion aside. 'Time for all that when we've nailed this bunch of murdering lunatics.'

Marie had wholeheartedly agreed. No one was going to fall to bits on her watch, especially not her, and she made sure Ashley was aware of it. They ended the call with considerable respect on both sides.

Her mobile rang with a call from Jackman, and she found herself talking to a very different man to the one she'd left the night before.

'Okay, Marie, this is how it is at this end.'

She couldn't help smiling. This was the man she knew and loved. The man who would always be a policeman above all else.

'Sam and I have talked a lot, as you can imagine, but we are in a more grounded place this morning. We both

259

agree that we can't sit at home and be morbid — for a start, it would be the last thing Laura would have wanted. So,' he paused, 'we have formulated a strategy. Initially, of course, there's all the necessary arrangements to make — visits to solicitors and undertakers and people to notify, but I've just phoned Mum and she's offered to come with me. She's such a good organiser we'll be sure to get it right between us.'

'Oh, I am relieved to hear that. It's not something to do alone.' Marie recalled her own mother, Rhiannon, holding her together when she had faced the same horrible tasks.

'I know.' She heard a tremor in his voice, and then it was gone. 'And Sam has made an offer that is above and beyond the call of duty. He has volunteered to go to Locksford and act as consultant psychologist in Laura's place. But to do that, I need Laura's laptop, which was in the car. He needs her notes. Do you think you could get it released from the property store for me? We can then download her files to Sam's laptop. It would help enormously — otherwise he'll have to start from square one, and Ashley won't have the time for that.'

'There's no reason why you can't collect her things, Jackman. It's not like they're evidence or anything. I'll go and speak to the property officer as soon as I get off the phone.'

He thanked her. 'Please don't think I'm being unfeeling plunging into all this, Marie — it's simply my way of coping. I have to be doing something. I know Ruth was obliged to relieve me of duties for a while, but I can't do nothing, I'd go mad. I still can't believe what has happened. It's just not possible. Laura was so . . . oh, so alive, and now . . .'

Marie wished that she was with him, not at the end of a phone line. 'I know, I know. In my opinion, you're doing the right thing. You must cope in whatever way feels right for you, sod everyone else. You'll come through it, I promise.'

'I have to, don't I?' He sighed. 'She'd never forgive me if I gave up.'

'Talking about not giving up . . .' Marie told him that the teams, both his and Ashley's, were hell-bent on bringing the two investigations to a successful conclusion. 'We're going after them, Jackman, you can rely on that.'

'I know I can.' He sounded brighter. 'And talking about that other investigation, when Mum and I have done all the grim stuff, I think I might spend a little time out Amberley Fen way — you know, just talking to a few people, listening to the gossip about Solace.'

Again, Marie wasn't surprised. But she did urge caution. 'If that's what you think you need to do, just be sure to take care of yourself, my friend. Be kind to yourself, don't take on too much. You know as well as anyone that there are a lot of stages to go through in your grieving.' *He has a long way to go yet*, she thought sadly. Right now he was almost denying that anything had changed. She recalled the rollercoaster ride of emotions that had swept her away after Bill died, and her heart went out to him. 'I'll get that laptop, Jackman, and bring it round after work, okay?'

'That would be great, then Sam will have somewhere to start. We'll see you then.'

Marie had hardly ended the call when an excited Max burst into the office.

'Sarge! I think this is important! I mean, well, I could be wrong, but . . .'

'Max! Slow down.' Marie had rarely seen him so keyed up.

He screwed his eyes tight shut for a moment. 'No, I'm not mistaken. We have to follow this up.' He looked at her intently. 'The garden centre. The boy who helped me load the car — Ben. He leaned into my vehicle to pack one of the plants, and I saw he had a small tattoo just above his wrist. It didn't register at the time and his shirtsleeve quickly covered it up again, but it was the same as the symbol carved into that dead girl. Sarge, I swear it was.'

'The cult symbol?' Marie stiffened. 'We need to know for sure, Max. We can't drive up mob-handed and raid the place and find out it's some Japanese symbol for love and affection.'

'I thought of that too,' he said, his eyes sparkling. 'Which is why I've just remembered how much I need zonal geraniums. While I'm there I might get him to reach me something from off a high shelf. If need be, I'll keep buying stuff until I get to see that tattoo.'

Marie thought quickly. 'Max, are you absolutely certain that no one there suspects who you are or what you do for a living? I can't have you walking into a dangerous situation. We've got enough to cope with on the emotional front right now.'

'No, they're cool with me, I know it. And my Rosie was a star. She even had me believing some of the things she was saying. I'm fine with going back there alone.' Max looked at her hopefully.

'And what if your Ben isn't there?' asked Marie.

He pulled a face. 'Yeah, well, it could go a bit Pete Tong if that's the case. I'll have to improvise.'

Marie wasn't happy but understood the significance of that tattoo should it turn out to be what Max believed. 'Okay, but no way do you go alone. Take the least obvious detective with you.' They both stared at Robbie.

Robbie Melton chanced to look up. 'Er, what?'

'Could you develop a deep interest in garden plants, Robbie?' Marie asked.

He shrugged. 'I walked round RHS Wisley once with my Aunt Hazel. I was only ten, but I've got a good memory.'

'That'll do,' said Max. 'Got a job for you, mate.'

CHAPTER TWENTY-THREE

Beneath the cool, efficient facade, Superintendent Ashley Carpenter was shattered.

Two of her most trusted officers were in critical care. She had lost the man, probably forever, who had vital information about the cult murders, and now Laura was gone. Unable to bear even thinking about the injuries done to Paula and Russ, she turned her mind to Laura Archer, who had been a comparative stranger until a day or so ago. She had liked the psychologist from the start, and the way Laura had dealt with the mercurial Bennington added both admiration and respect to Ashley's initial impression of her.

Sitting alone in her office, Ashley went over every detail of Laura's reaction to the events of the previous evening. She and Laura had been together since the news of Bennington's disappearance reached the station. Laura had been a massive support, a tower of strength, and try as she might, Ashley could not recall the slightest sense of anything being wrong.

There was only one indication that Laura might have been troubled. She told Ashley she felt responsible for the incident because it had been she who'd organised things with the clinic that Bennington was on his way to. Ashley told Laura that even if she hadn't been there to advise, he would still have been sent elsewhere. No, that wasn't it. Laura's misplaced feeling of guilt couldn't have been bothering her so badly that she lost concentration and drove off the road.

Ashley began to pace around her office. There were four possible causes for that accident — mechanical failure, a distraction such as an animal running out in front of her, falling asleep at the wheel . . . or someone had tampered with her car.

Had she been that tired? If she was, she hadn't shown it. She had promised to be back in early the next day and had seemed, if anything, energised by the disaster.

Was she the kind of person to swerve to avoid an animal? Probably, but then she would have braked and there'd be skid marks on the road. There were no marks.

Ashley stared out of the window. So mechanical failure then, principally the brakes, the answer to which would have to wait for the car to be examined. That left the question of foul play.

Bennington's old friends, now his lethal enemies, were fond of using the highways as playgrounds, weren't they? First, Bennington had been driven off the road, then their escort car had been forced to crash. Had they played with Laura's vehicle too?

She was pretty sure her last assumption was correct — Laura Archer had been eliminated. But why? Ashley returned to her chair and flopped down. And what then?

* * *

Gary had spent a good half hour going over what they knew about the threats to the Stewart family. True, they had made remarkable progress in a very short time, but it wasn't nearly enough. They had apprehended the two men who had scared the children and vandalised the house, but their mysterious boss, the rental property businessman, Isaac Hobbs, remained elusive. It was obviously a false name, just like the Mr Carson who'd offered to buy the property should it come on the market again. Carson had turned out to be just as real as Isaac Hobbs.

He skimmed down his list and ticked off *Previous owners and possible threats to them*. He had now spoken to Mrs Hardy, the estranged wife of the last owner of Solace. Far more forthcoming than her husband, she had said that although there had been no direct threats, she had twice seen a couple of shifty-looking men who seemed to be watching the house. She said how relieved she was to be living fifty-six miles from Solace. 'I hated the place, DC Pritchard. I hated it every second I was there. My ex had all these highfalutin ideas that I knew would come to nothing the moment we moved in. And I was right. Thanks to that house even our marriage fell apart.'

Gary suspected her marriage was well on the rocks by the time they arrived in Amberley Fen — Solace had probably dealt the final blow. Her description of the "shifty" men was a bit vague. In their forties, both tall, one heavier built and one skinny, both a bit rough around the edges, unshaven and badly dressed. Not too much to go on there.

He needed to have that talk with Holly, as Marie had asked. He would have liked to drive out there and see her in person, but driving was just too painful, and he didn't want to ask for a lift. He picked up the phone.

Holly seemed relieved to talk. She admitted she'd feared that their case would be dropped following the tragic death of Laura Archer. 'Of course, we'd completely understand. I mean, it's totally unthinkable. That poor DI Jackman. Our hearts go out to him.'

Holly was right. It *was* unthinkable, and Gary still couldn't believe they'd never see Laura again. He pushed the thought aside and hastened to ask his question. Did she think there could be someone with a personal grudge against them?

'Funny you should say that. Hugh and I asked ourselves the same question only last night,' said Holly. 'We racked our brains to recall anything in our past lives that could have aroused that much resentment, but we couldn't think of a thing. We considered whether we might have offended anyone, or whether someone might have misunderstood something we said. The only thing I could remember was an old friend of mine who fancied Hugh and made a bit of a fool of herself over it, but she's in no way dangerous or vengeful, and anyway she apologised for having been such a prat, so it's not her. No, Gary, we can't think of anything. It *has* to be the house.'

'Well, we had to ask, just to rule it out,' said Gary. The house it was, had to be.

After Holly assured him they were very comfortable in their stable accommodation and the kids were over the moon, Gary rang off.

Now all his boxes were ticked, apart from one. Last on the list was a comment from Marie asking if he could look into why Mike Coleman's story bothered her so much more than that of Anthony Bonner, the man who had been paid to watch the house at night. The stories matched perfectly, but Coleman's just didn't ring true.

Gary rang the custody sergeant and asked for Coleman to be taken to an interview room. Luckily the duty solicitor happened to be on the premises that day, which just gave Gary time to find out from Stacey and Jay whether anyone else had been seen hanging around Solace since the incident with the muck spreader.

Stacey answered almost immediately. 'It's quiet as the grave out there, Gary, excuse the analogy.'

Her words made him think of the babies buried somewhere in that wilderness of a garden. For some reason he wondered if someone else knew about them, someone who didn't want the ground dug up because there were more bodies there than just the original four.

He finished the call and phoned Tim, wondering what his theory would sound like to a different pair of ears. 'Tell me if you think this is totally improbable, but what if one of Ivy Pettifer's other relatives isn't happy about her story coming to light? Maybe someone besides Ralph's lady, Beryl Carling, knows about her propensity to do harm to kids.'

Tim Jacobs looked pensive, but then he often did. He was a young-looking, rather studious man, very thin, with a shock of dark, curly hair, left full on top but cut short at the sides and back. With his floppy hair and heavy, dark-rimmed glasses he looked like a bookish student. In fact, he was almost thirty five and a very capable office manager, who had never been to university and came into their office by way of an apprenticeship as a business administrator. 'I'd say it's very possible. The older Fen families tend to be very protective of their own — present and past, good and bad.' He smiled, revealing teeth that a film star might have been proud of. 'So, are you suspecting that our Ivy could have bumped off a greater number of her little charges than Sally Pinket knew about and buried them secretly in the gardens of Solace House?'

'Maybe,' said Gary ruminatively. 'Or someone else buried bodies of their own along with the babies that they knew of.'

Tim puffed out his cheeks. 'Phew! Then that place needs to be dug up.'

'They'll want a whole lot more than my wild guesses before anyone will authorise that. It'd take a big chunk of our budget to clear a garden that size, even if we brought in the techies with their ground-penetrating scanner.'

'Still, your hypothesis would answer the question of why someone wants the Stewarts out of the place. They'd started to clear the garden before they ran out of money, and might well start again now Hugh is back at work.'

'Good point, Tim. So they up the ante and really put the frighteners on the family.' Gary suddenly noticed the time. 'Oh, hell, I have to get downstairs — we'll carry on when I get back.' He grabbed his notepad and pen and hurried off to talk to Coleman.

* * *

Laura Archer's body had been taken to Rory Wilkinson's main mortuary facility in Greenborough. There would be no jokes around the autopsy table today.

267

Rory cleared his throat. 'I'm grateful that we have been granted the privilege of attending to our dear friend and colleague,' he said quietly. 'As we did in her life, in death we shall accord Laura our utmost respect and affection.' He looked from Spike to Cardiff. 'There are any number of people who are wondering how this terrible thing could have come about. I believe it will be down to us, not the vehicle inspection team, to provide the answer. Let's do our very best, my friends.' He nodded to Spike, who started recording: 'This is Case Number 37-SLF-03, Laura Archer. This is the body of a well-developed, well-nourished Caucasian female . . .'

* * *

Ruth Crooke was on her way out of her office when her desk phone rang. She listened and let out a gasp. 'Are you absolutely sure, Rory? Sorry, of course you are. It was just so unexpected.' She sank into her chair. 'And Rowan certainly won't have considered that either. Will you tell him, or shall I?'

'I suggest that it would be better coming from you as his superintendent, Ruth, and then I'll talk to him and explain the details.' Rory gave a sad little laugh. 'And knowing Jackman, he will want them all, down to the minutest.'

'You're right, Rory. I'll ring him immediately.' She thanked him for contacting her so quickly and hung up.

Jackman's phone was switched off. He was probably with the undertakers or solicitors. Ruth hung up without leaving a message. He needed to know this as soon as possible, but not via a text.

Ruth rang down and asked Marie to come up to her office. She should be the next to know.

As soon as Marie was seated, Ruth said, 'I've just heard some news which shook me at the time, but now I've thought about it, I realise it's actually a huge relief.'

Marie shifted in her chair, clearly impatient, but Ruth was silent for a few moments. The fact was, it was difficult to put into words. 'The call was from Professor Wilkinson, who had just completed the post-mortem on Laura Archer.' Marie leaned forward. 'There is no mystery behind her death, Marie, no conspiracy at all. Laura suffered a seizure and lost consciousness while at the wheel of her car.'

'A seizure?' Marie whispered. 'But why? She wasn't epileptic, or—'

'If you recall, she took a blow to the head at the hands of one of her patients not very long ago. She was taken to hospital, unconscious, having suffered a serious concussion. Well, Rory tells me that people who have suffered a head injury like that can often have a seizure, even months later.'

'And that was the case with Laura?' Marie's voice was shaky. 'And it could have happened anywhere, at any time?'

Ruth nodded. 'Rory said that the head injury was much more serious than originally believed. I think Laura had been on borrowed time for several months.'

'So that's why there were no skid marks. It's that simple.' Marie exhaled loudly. 'I do hope Jackman can get some peace of mind from that outcome, Ruth, although he'd probably like to kill the man who hurt her in the first place. God, this is all like some kind of weird dream. I dread to think what's going to happen next.'

'But this is good news, Marie. No more wondering or speculating about how she died, no severed brake lines, no slow-acting poison, no evil drivers forcing her off the road. She simply died. Heartbreaking, yes, but murdered, no.'

'Yes, yes, Ruth, of course it's good news and, as you say, we can stop going over possible causes and simply mourn our sad loss.' She paused. 'And concentrate all our efforts on catching the remaining members of this damned cult, especially Mason Nash and his sidekick, Apostle. I wanted to talk to you anyway, as a matter of fact. Max has an idea that a lad working at that nursery has a tattoo in the same design as the cult symbol. He and Robbie are going to see if they can check whether what he saw is correct, and if it is, I want to launch a surprise raid on that place. As one of those two officers at Locksford was shot, I suspect there are firearms on the premises, so I'd like an armed unit as well.' She gave a little shrug. 'Max could have been mistaken — he only caught a glimpse of it — but if he's right, we could have them, Ruth.'

'All right. I'll find out how the land lies with calling in the Tactical Armed team and get an estimated response time from them. Let me know the minute you have confirmation. In the meantime, I have to contact Jackman. His phone is switched off at the moment, but he has to be made aware of Rory's findings.'

Marie stood up. 'Thanks, Ruth. I appreciate you telling me about Laura, and I'll be back the minute I've spoken to Max and Robbie.'

Ruth tried Jackman's mobile again and this time he answered. She took a deep breath. This wasn't going to be easy.

* * *

'Bugger! He's not in the shop,' cursed Max. 'This calls for a bit of improvisation. Oh well, here goes nothing.' He pushed the door open and strolled in, looking around hopefully. 'Ben not here today, mate?' he enquired cheerfully.

The man behind the counter put down a watering can he was holding. 'Er, he's out back helping Belinda with some new stock, I think. Can I help you?'

'I'm sure you could, but I was chatting to Ben about something the other day, and rather than go over it all again . . .' He paused. 'You couldn't give him a shout for me, could you? Tell him it's the bloke who nearly got bankrupted after his wife and Belinda got their heads together.' He laughed and rolled his eyes in mock exasperation.

'I'll see if I can find him.' The man headed out towards the sliding back doors.

'I wonder if they're on commission here,' muttered Robbie. 'He didn't look exactly happy.'

'I doubt it. Apparently, it's a family business — all for one and one for all, as they say.' Max looked around the shop, by now quite familiar to him, and noted a couple of items placed just out of reach that he could ask Ben to take down. 'Rob, if I give you the nod, go back to the car and start the engine. I'm not feeling the love like I did before.' He handed Robbie the car keys. 'Could be my imagination but I'd like a swift exit strategy in place, just in case.'

Robbie took the keys from him. 'Got it. Sensible move, Max. I'm feeling a little hinky myself.' He looked around. 'Not exactly packed out, is it? Like, no customers?'

'Probably don't need them after what I spent thanks to my Rosie, but you're right, Rob. There weren't any last time we came either. They certainly don't survive on passing trade, although the locals all say they do well here, are good neighbours and all that.'

'Doesn't add up,' mused Robbie, his eyes glued to the back door. 'And I'm not too happy about the fact that a chap has just gone out to that big white van and is just sitting in it, watching us.'

'And several men are approaching the shop from the house out back, and Ben isn't one of them.' Max strolled around the shop, pretending to admire the plants, then made an exaggerated gesture towards a small bank of flowering shrubs just outside the entrance door. 'Time to admire whatever they are, Rob, then abort the mission, fast.'

They ambled over to the display, lifted a plant to examine it, then, at a word from Max, turned and legged it back to the car.

Rob was gunning the engine and accelerating toward the exit before Max's door had even closed.

So was the white van. Its intention to block the gates was obvious.

Max was eternally grateful that he had reversed into the parking space by the door, so they had a straight run to the exit. They slipped through the open gates only just before the van, which clipped their rear bumper.

'Shit!' Rob fought to keep control of the car as they started to skid into a tailspin, but he managed to correct it, put his foot down and roared off down the road.

'Nice one, Rob.' Max swallowed hard and pulled out his phone. 'I'll ring this straight in. The sarge needs to get something in motion before they pull down the shutters and raise the drawbridge. We were clearly not going to get one of those nice coffees today.'

* * *

Jackman, Harriet and Sam sat around the kitchen table at Mill Corner. For once in his life, Jackman had allowed himself to shed tears, only because he was with two of the three people he most trusted and cared for.

'It's the relief, Mum. Sam.' He sniffed. 'My Laura wasn't murdered, and I didn't send her into a situation that caused her death. At least that won't haunt me for the rest of my life.'

After Ruth's initial call and soon after they had returned home, Rory had called and explained very gently that Laura wouldn't have suffered. It had been a catastrophic occurrence that might have happened at any time. He said that most people were unaware of what could happen following a head injury, and considering some of the other possible outcomes — being left terribly brain-damaged, for one — it was a blessing for Laura.

Even Sam's spirits seemed to lift at the news, though he still expressed regret. 'If only it had been me and not Laura. Life is so unfair sometimes.'

'I think tea is required,' said Harriet, standing up and making for the kettle. 'And then we should check the to-do list and see how we are progressing. Sam, have you contacted that superintendent at Locksford yet?'

Jackman looked fondly at his ever-practical mother. There were few people who could read a situation better than Harriet, and she had changed the subject at just the right moment. Jackman's pain began to subside, and now the dreadful possibility that Laura had been deliberately harmed was gone, he felt he could face the future with a lot more optimism.

'Yes, Harriet,' Sam was saying. 'I rang while you were both out. She is extremely grateful, believe me. I just need to read through Laura's notes on Bennington this evening and then I'll go to Locksford tomorrow morning.'

'Marie is going to be here by six, work allowing,' said Jackman. 'Mrs M has left us a meal for tonight, so we could eat and then go over everything together, if you like? I know a fair bit, having met and spoken to him, so perhaps I can add my thoughts.' Anything to stop dwelling on Laura's death, he added to himself — work, problems to occupy his brain so that his thoughts didn't drift back to that crash site.

Sam was nodding. 'That would be a great help, especially as I'll no longer be able to meet the man himself. Your take on him will be important. I just hope I can be of some help — that station is in tatters after all that's happened. Superintendent Carpenter is being an absolute trooper, but I could hear from her voice that she's only just holding it together.'

Standing behind him, Harriet squeezed his shoulder. 'Then you're the best person to help her, even if you do nothing except be there and listen. I'm sure she knows only too well how to organise her team, but sometimes even the strongest leader needs a listening ear and an encouraging voice.' She gave his shoulder another squeeze. 'And it'll help you too. You need to be doing something positive, and what could be more positive than helping someone else?'

Sam reached up and held the hand that rested on his shoulder. 'I know and I'll do my best, Harriet. It's exactly what Laura would have done in my place. I'm going to be strong for her and finish the job she started.'

'That's the spirit!' She hurried to the fridge for milk. 'And I have to pour this tea before it stews.'

They sat drinking tea, going over Harriet's to-do list. Then, with his capable mother at his side, Jackman ploughed through the difficult task of informing as many people as he could find from Laura's address book. Her mother was the most difficult, as she had gone abroad, and he could find no address for her. Sam then took over, contacting Laura's colleagues from the psychology world.

After almost two hours, they were all drained.

'It makes it real, doesn't it?' said Harriet softly. 'I felt that way when our Sarah died. All those shocked voices on the other end of a phone, all the outpourings of sorrow.' She shook her head. 'But you've done most of it now. That's a big hurdle behind you.' She stared down at the list. 'Flowers we can't do until we have a date for the funeral, neither can we arrange a venue, but hopefully now we know what happened, it shouldn't be a long wait.'

'Rory said that as the death was due to natural causes, the coroner should release her to us any time. Even if there is to be an inquest, we can still get a cremation certificate, as the post-mortem is complete.' *Listen to me*, thought Jackman, and shivered. Here he was, calmly arranging the funeral of the woman he loved, the woman he had laughed with and made love to merely a day ago. Everything felt unreal, as if he had slipped into some nightmare world and would soon wake up. All at once, he wanted to talk to Marie. She had lived through the same nightmare. Marie would truly understand.

Jackman stood up and, saying that he needed some fresh air, went into the garden. He made for his favourite spot with the view out over the Fenland fields and rang Marie.

The call didn't exactly go as he had planned, but it certainly galvanised him. Marie, Ruth Crooke and a uniformed superintendent were about to lead a team of officers into Max's garden centre, which could well prove to be the cult headquarters.

He ended the call cursing the fact that he was stuck at home when he should be with them on the front line. Marie had sworn that the first call she made after the operation would be to him, and he was to hang on in there. *Hang on in there?* How the hell was he going to do that?

Before an answer came, he heard a vehicle approach. A marked police car drew to a halt outside the mill's front door.

Jay Acharya climbed out. 'DI Jackman. Sergeant Evans sent you this, sir. She said what with everything going on right now, she might be held up or forget, and it was important to you.'

He handed Jackman a sealed bag containing Laura's laptop.

'You missed out on the action so as to bring me this, did you?' said Jackman. 'Sorry about that. I can offer you a coffee, though.'

Jay grinned. 'Well, as you say, I've missed the handbags at dawn, so maybe a quick coffee would make up for it.' He lost the smile. 'I'm so sorry for your loss, sir. Stacey and I both want to say that if there's anything we can do, we are there for you.'

Unable to speak, Jackman patted the young officer's arm. After a few seconds he swallowed and managed to mumble, 'Er, thank you, Jay. I appreciate it very much. Now, since Mother is on catering duty, I should think the kettle was boiling before you even turned the engine off. Come in and bring me up to speed on what's occurring.'

CHAPTER TWENTY-FOUR

A council of war was in progress outside the Saltern-le-Fen police station. Ruth, Marie and Superintendent Fred Marsh of uniform were conferring on the best course of action.

'Armed backup cannot get to us in under three-quarters of an hour. The central hub has had three major call-outs today, so the timing is not in our favour.' Ruth looked enquiringly at Marie. 'But from what you say happened to Max and Robbie, we cannot afford to waste that amount of time. If Mason Nash is based there we should act without delay, or he'll be gone. Are we all agreed?'

'We've had units watching both the entrance and a back exit of the nursery and seen no one attempting to leave. In fact they report that it all seems very quiet. Bit odd really,' Fred Marsh said. 'They could be battening down the hatches to prepare for an attack, although I did put the helicopter up a while ago and they saw nothing out of the ordinary.'

'Could we be wrong about the place?' asked Ruth.

'Not from the shunted fender on the back of the car Robbie was driving. That van was all out to stop him, no question,' Marie said.

Ruth thought long and hard. If she sanctioned an action without due consideration she'd be in deep shit, but if she procrastinated and a killer got away, she'd be in it up to her neck. 'Okay, we go in, but not heavy-handed. Reasonable force if necessary. What numbers have you got, Fred?'

'Four units, Ruth, each with an officer trained in Tasers. Two go in the front, two in the back, round up all the staff and occupants of the place and hold everyone in one area — I suggest the shop. Then Sergeant Evans and her team can talk to them. We've all seen that e-fit likeness of Daemon, or Mason Nash as we now know him, and if we see anyone who even vaguely resembles that man, we immobilise him immediately.'

'I'll use the front car park as the command post,' Ruth said. 'And no heroics. If anyone gets the slightest whiff of a firearm, retire to the vehicles and await the ARVs. I don't want to see anyone from this division airlifted to a critical care unit. Okay?'

'We're ready when you are, Ruth,' said Fred.

'Us too,' added Marie.

'Then we move out in five.' Ruth checked her watch. 'Brief your officers, Fred, and remember, we want a smooth and effective raid with no casualties.'

* * *

The adrenaline running high, they all piled into vans and cars. Marie kept Max close to her. He was her link. He had met three of the people there, and she particularly wanted to know what the role of the woman called Belinda was. She seemed to be a proper matriarch: several of the people who worked there were her offspring, and her son Ben certainly looked up to her.

As they neared the nursery, she suddenly wondered whether Apostle might be a woman. They had assumed a male, simply from what Bennington had said to Ashley Carpenter and Laura, but what if he hadn't liked to admit that he had been in thrall to a powerful woman? Apostle could just as well be female. And why not? Women were equally as capable as men of a fanatical devotion, maybe even more so.

She mentioned it to Max, who whistled softly.

'I'd not thought of that. Belinda certainly has presence, Sarge. She's kind of charismatic, despite the wellies.' He shrugged. 'It's possible, I suppose. Either that or she's a kind of front.'

That was possible too. Well, they would soon know one way or the other.

As the vehicles poured in through the nursery gates, Marie realised how much she missed Jackman's presence.

* * *

The CID room felt like a ghost town to Gary, empty apart from a couple of pool detectives at the far end and he and Tim at the other.

He would have liked to pull on a stabby himself, but it was out of the question given his damaged ribs. He shouldn't really be here at all but he was glad to be able to play a part, however minor, and most importantly, support Jackman.

Gary stared at the notes he had made during his interview with Mike Coleman and compared them to another set of notes made during a telephone conversation with Anthony Bonner. He was now in complete agreement with Marie. The only downside was that he had no more idea than she did as to why one story rang true and the other didn't.

He ambled off to get a coffee and found Vic Blackwell at the machine.

'Any joy with those cars that rammed Bennington the first time around, Vic?' he asked, fishing in his pocket for change.

'Not really, mate. Both nicked, that's for sure, although the other road user's dashcam did give me a couple of half-decent shots of the two drivers. I've just been down to leave them with Orac so she can play with them.' He removed his beaker from the machine. 'I could be wrong, but I don't think they were trying to kill Bennington, just get him off the road. They wanted him alive for some reason. Bennington's car wasn't supposed to spin and knock seven bells out of his assailant. That was certainly not in their plan. Especially when he took full advantage of it and legged it while the driver of the second car was attending to the one he'd hit.' He shrugged. 'The getaway car has been found north of Locksford, burned out in a lay-by. End of story.' Vic leaned against the wall while Gary got his drink. 'I wonder how Marie's doing.'

'Yeah. You didn't fancy getting stuck in, then?' Gary said.

'I was out.' Vic pulled a face. 'I missed the shout, but they've probably got a full complement out there in any case. I just hope no bugger pulls a gun on them.'

Gary didn't miss the shudder. Vic had been on the wrong end of a gun in the past and had almost died. 'Me too, Vic, especially as the ARV isn't anywhere nearby.'

They returned to their workstations, and Gary continued to try to fathom out why Mike Coleman gave him warning signals and Anthony Bonner didn't. Their stories were so very similar. Well, that was the problem, wasn't it? They should vary somewhat, but they matched almost word for word. He stared at the name Mike Coleman and started absentmindedly doodling down the margin of his notes — weird trees and little boats, and names that stuck in his mind. Why were those stories so similar?

He kept doodling, elaborating on the name Isaac Hobbs, adding loops and swirls. Then he stopped and stared at the name. Funny, that . . . his cousin lived in a place called Hobbs Lane in Harlan Marsh. She had told him that back in the sixteenth and seventeenth centuries Hobb meant Devil — it was another name for Satan. Gary froze. So did Daemon! Jackman had said it was an archaic spelling of demon. Was Mason Nash not just Daemon but Isaac Hobbs too?

Gary stood up so quickly that he almost knocked his chair over. A sharp pain seared through his ribs. He swore, took a few shallow breaths, then called out to Vic Blackwell. 'I think I've just made a connection here that has scared the shit out of me.'

Vic hurried over to him and Gary explained what the two names meant. 'Tell me this is a coincidence!'

'Oh shit!' murmured Vic. 'Sorry, mate, no can do. We need to tell someone, fast. Unless we are both barking up the wrong tree, it's Mason Nash who is trying to drive the Stewart family out of their home!'

* * *

It took less than ten minutes to gather all the residents and staff of the nursery together and herd them into the shop area. No one had put up any resistance, although Belinda kept demanding to know what the hell was going on.

Marie stared at her, trying to make out exactly what the set-up was here. She had a creeping feeling that it wasn't quite what they'd believed.

Ruth joined her and, addressing Belinda, who was clearly in charge, demanded to know why two of their officers had had their car deliberately rammed in an attempt to stop them leaving the car park.

'Your officers?' Belinda looked perplexed as Max stepped forward.

'Yeah, what exactly were you trying to do, Belinda?' he demanded. 'Hadn't I spent enough money this time?'

'You're a police officer?' She let out a cry of exasperation.

'Sorry,' said Max. 'I didn't know I had to provide details of my profession before I could buy a few geraniums.'

Marie took over. 'Have you ever heard of a man named Mason Nash, or Daemon as he prefers to be called?' From Belinda's startled reaction she certainly had, and from the shuffling and obvious discomfort of some of the others in the shop, so had they.

'I think it's time we took this down to the station, don't you?' said Ruth. 'We need a long talk with you.'

'No!' Belinda said. 'I'll talk, but let's do it here. I don't want to leave my family.'

'Oh, we can *all* go, if you like,' growled Ruth. 'We've got just enough holding cells.'

'No, please.' Belinda's voice was suddenly softer. 'You don't understand. I promise I'll tell you everything if we can just talk here. Maybe in the house?'

Marie glanced at Ruth who gave an almost imperceptible nod. 'Okay, but if we are at all concerned about your story, you'll have to come to the station with us.'

Leaving the rest of them in the shop, Marie, Ruth and Max followed Belinda out the back and across to the house.

It was big old place, probably originally a farmhouse, and it still had some of the features of those times. It was clearly home to a sizable number of people. The kitchen shelves were stacked with plates, bowls, mugs and various other bits of equipment. On the huge old table sat an overflowing fruit bowl, a stack of table mats and coasters, books and various bits of gardening paraphernalia — twine, plant labels, secateurs and the like.

Belinda pushed it all aside and indicated a couple of chairs.

'Let's start with Daemon, shall we?' said Marie, taking a seat facing Belinda.

'Yes, I do know of him. And I wish to hell I'd never heard his accursed name.'

Belinda clearly wasn't acting. She stood with her fists clenched, tears in her eyes. 'Can I ask you something before I continue?' she asked Max. 'What were you doing here today? Why did you come in the first place? It certainly wasn't to buy geraniums.'

Marie answered for him. 'On his previous visit, my detective constable noticed that the young man, Ben, has a cult symbol tattooed on his arm. And since you seem to run a very unusual establishment here, we became concerned.'

Ruth turned to Max. 'Go and get him, please.'

Max returned a few minutes later with a white-faced Ben.

'Please be kind enough to roll up your sleeves,' demanded Ruth.

Ben looked anxiously at Belinda.

'It's all right, Ben, you can show them. And don't worry, my darling, you're still safe here, I promise.' Belinda's voice was calm now and she smiled encouragingly at the lad.

Slowly, Ben pulled up his shirtsleeves to reveal not one, but two identical symbols, one on each forearm.

Marie breathed in sharply. They were exactly the same design as the one etched on the arm she had seen protruding from the black sack in the ditch. She swallowed hard. 'Please explain why we shouldn't cart the whole damned lot of you down to the nick.'

'Because this is not what you think,' said Belinda. 'Yes, Ben was in the cult. It took me nearly six months to get him out. And,' she added accusingly, 'another six to try and heal his damaged mind, plus a year or two to show him what genuine love is and that he is finally safe. He's a lovely boy. I was not going to let that evil bastard ruin his life any more than he had already.'

'He really is your son?' asked Max.

'Every single one of the younger ones here are my children, but I didn't give birth to any of them. I rescued them and I gave them work and a home and a proper family.' Her eyes bored into Marie's. 'And responsibility and purpose.'

'So this is a kind of shelter?' Marie asked in amazement. 'And are they all former cult members?'

'I don't see it as a shelter,' said Belinda. 'I see it as a home, a place they will always be safe in, for as long as they want. And no, only Ben belonged to the cult. The others were victims of, oh, many different forms of abuse — familial or social breakdowns, drugs, or all three.'

'But if that's the case, Belinda,' asked Max, 'why did your people deliberately drive at our vehicle to try and stop us from leaving?'

Belinda laughed, bitterly. 'Because we thought Daemon had sent you. We thought *you* were from the cult, come to take Ben back!'

Marie was certain Belinda was telling the truth. So, what now? If the cult weren't here, where were they? Not at the hotel, nor the old manor house she and Jackman had visited. That left them with nowhere to look. Desperation suddenly gave way to excitement. Ah, but now she had Ben!

She decided to get all the facts in place before she plunged in. If it had taken so long to put Ben's head back together, she didn't want to undo all that work through her own impatience.

'How does this place work, Belinda?' she asked. 'Max mentioned brothers, sisters, aunts, uncles, even grandparents.'

'It's the best environment I could think of for allowing damaged souls to heal.' Belinda looked at her across the table. 'It started when my parents, who owned this place, fostered an abused child and brought him up as my little brother. The transformation in him was miraculous. As our small family business grew, I started to see that working with nature in the form of caring for plants was just what other lost children might need. I knew I couldn't do it alone, so I took on four dedicated helpers. One was a social worker, one a Samaritan, one an occupational therapist and the last one was an army veteran. Each brought a specific skill set to our home, providing guidance and protection and restoring normality to the children we took in.'

'Ah, the aunts and uncles,' breathed Max. 'And the young people you take in become brothers and sisters — a family unit.'

'Exactly.' Belinda was practically incandescent with fervour as she described her project.

Marie could hardly bear to demolish even the smallest part of the good Belinda had done, but she had a killer to catch. 'Belinda, I have no doubt that what you have built up here is exceptional, but there is a bigger picture to consider. People are dying because of that cult and its murdering leader. I don't want to upset him, but Ben has to tell us what he knows about Mason Nash and his set-up or more people will die.'

She heard Ben whimper. Belinda jumped up and ran to the young man, clasping him tightly to her. 'No, Detective! You must not question Ben. He has told me everything he can. It's me you talk to, and not in Ben's presence either.'

Marie glanced at Ruth. They both nodded.

'As you wish,' said Ruth. 'But we have to do it now.' She indicated to Max to take Ben away.

'Don't leave him with the police, please. Give him to his Uncle Trevor,' said Belinda. 'He'll look after him from now on. He'll be able to cope with Ben should he regress.' She returned to her chair. 'All right, Officers, what do you want to know?'

* * *

Ashley Carpenter had just received the latest reports from uniform and traffic. Nothing new had come in regarding the car that had carried off Martin Bennington. After the incident it had simply slipped into the side roads, where there were no cameras, and disappeared. No sightings, no reports and, as far as she was concerned right now, no hope.

Regarding Bennington, she was feeling about as guilty as it was possible to be. She knew he couldn't have remained at the station, he had to be moved to a place of safety, but even so, his pleas to be allowed to stay in the one place he had a chance of survival kept echoing in her head. She heard herself assuring him that no one knew of the route or their destination, which at the time she believed to be true. As it turned out, she was wrong, someone had known all right. It was the not knowing who that was and how they'd managed to convey the information to the cult that kept eating away at her. If only she could talk it over with Laura. *Well*, she thought bitterly, *that's never going to happen*.

Ashley was usually a positive person, remaining optimistic even in the gravest situation, but this had shaken her to the core. The one bright spot was that the eminent psychologist, Sam Page, a dear friend of Laura's, had offered to come and assist her. It was an incredibly magnanimous gesture, considering that he must be in pieces over Laura's death. She guessed at a fierce wish to finish what Laura had started, a desire not to leave a human being unaided, a problem unresolved.

He would be with her in the morning, which, as far as she was concerned, couldn't come soon enough.

CHAPTER TWENTY-FIVE

Marie was just about to begin questioning Belinda Saunders when her phone vibrated in her pocket. A message from Gary: *Ring me asap, urgent!*

'Forgive me, please. I have an urgent message from the station.' She looked at Ruth. 'I need to take this.'

'Go,' said Ruth. 'I'll make a start.'

Outside, she rang Gary. He began without preamble.

'Sarge! I think that the cult is behind the scare tactics on the Stewart family. I think it's them who want Solace. There is no Isaac Hobbs. Hobb means devil, as does Daemon.' He took a breath. 'And if that's the case, I know why Mike Coleman bothered you so much and Anthony Bonner didn't. Coleman's a cult member, sent in to paint that message. He was given the same background story as Bonner's in case he got caught. Bonner really was picked up outside the job centre and offered well-paid, off-the-books work. He is what he says he is, but they didn't dare send an outsider to paint those things on a kid's room wall, so they sent one of their own. They probably thought we wouldn't finger him, but thanks to you, we did!'

So the two cases were actually one and the same. But Solace House wasn't big enough to house a whole commune.

Marie realised that if what Gary suspected was true, they now had two cult members in their care.

'Whatever you do, Gary, don't let Coleman go! And don't let it be known to anyone, especially him or his brief, that we suspect he's connected to the cult. There's a lot he could tell us, if we can only find a way to get it out of him. Is anyone there with you other than Tim?'

'Vic Blackwell, Sarge.'

'Brilliant! Ask him to help you with whatever you need. We'll be back in a while, but, well, there's no commune here. However, we do have a very vulnerable lad who was a member of Daemon's clan. We're getting there, Gary. Every hour brings us a step closer.'

'Er, Sarge. I know it's a really bad time for him, but shall I tell Jackman about my theory? After all, the Stewarts are staying with his mother. Maybe they should be kept in the loop?' Gary said.

'Yes, and tell him I'll ring him with an update as soon as I've interviewed the woman in charge here, okay? And, Gary? Ask Jackman if Sam Page could give us an hour of his time to talk to Coleman. If he's been indoctrinated or programmed by this bloody Daemon, he needs careful handling. Sam could help us, now that we don't have . . .'

'Laura to call on,' Gary finished the sentence for her. 'I'll ring him now.'

Marie ended the call, her head spinning. They had lost Bennington, who had been their only living connection to the cult, but now they had Mike Coleman, most likely an active member, and Ben, who must have been a very young disciple, given that Belinda rescued him two or three years ago. Soon they could have descriptions of Daemon and Apostle and maybe even find out where they were based.

She hurried back inside.

* * *

Harriet had gone home to prepare dinner and check on the stables. Sam was deep into sorting through the notes Laura

286

had made on Martin Bennington, and Jay had left. Jackman found himself wandering aimlessly around the garden, unable to find the joy and peace he usually found there. Instead, he was confronted by a black hole, a horrible void. Suddenly he was alone. He kept telling himself that he'd always been a loner, and perfectly content to be so. But of late, he'd come to see that after all, the insular life wasn't for him. With that realisation, he had worked hard to bring work, home and relationship together to make a life that was whole, fulfilling. Now, it was as if some great force had just stopped time and he was left dangling in limbo.

He hated how empty his life now felt. He had been so positive earlier, where had that determination gone?

His phone rang. He was grateful for the interruption, even muttering 'Saved by the bell' before he answered.

'Boss? Is this a bad moment or have you got a few minutes? I think this is really important, else I wouldn't have called.'

Was Gary anxious or excited? Jackman wasn't sure. 'It's fine, Gary. What have you got to tell me?'

As Gary spoke, the void started to recede, and he grew alert and energised once more.

'It didn't make sense to start with and of course I've no proof yet, but the more I think about it the more likely it seems,' said Gary. 'I mean, a house with a history like that one would be perfect for a madman like Daemon. With no interested buyers and neighbours who avoided the place like the plague, he'd be sure of being left alone to get up to whatever he wanted. Okay, it's not big enough for a whole commune, but he probably wants it as a bolthole for himself and possibly his closest disciples.'

'And you think the reason that Coleman made Marie so twitchy is because he's actually a cult member?'

'I do. I'm sure of it, boss. Marie thought he was — or is — on drugs, which ties in perfectly with Daemon feeding his followers hallucinogens, don't you think?'

'What you say reminds me of the time he made his followers live under canvas and sleep rough, to prove their loyalty. He could be about to do that again, you know, test them, send them into the desert for forty days and forty nights before taking them back,' Jackman said, now totally focussed on the investigation.

'As in, he has the house, and they survive in that wilderness of a garden?' asked Gary.

'He's done it before. He's quite capable of doing it again.'

'That reminds me of the other question I was going to ask. The sarge wondered if Sam Page could spare an hour to talk to Coleman and give us his impression. She says we need to tread very carefully if he's under the influence of that maniac, Daemon.' Gary paused. 'Oh, and there's also the Stewarts. Can I leave it to you to decide how much to tell them, boss?'

'Of course. I don't want to scare them, especially as we don't know for sure if your theory's correct, but I really don't want them anywhere near that place until we've caught Daemon. Even the thought of him being in the same area gives me the creeps. I'll ring my mother, then go over a bit later and talk to Holly and Hugh personally.'

'Thank you, boss, and the sarge says she'll contact you as soon as she's through at the nursery.'

By the time Jackman ended the call all trace of his earlier despair had disappeared. He hurried indoors to talk to Sam.

* * *

Belinda Saunders related the story of her first attempt to free someone from the clutches of an evil cult. It was a harrowing account, involving the son of a friend of hers. She had heard of a sort of hippy commune in the local area, and after the boy ran away from home, she traced him to their centre. It was an enormous struggle to get him away.

'Where is this commune exactly?' asked Marie.

'The group disbanded a while ago. The place is empty now, but it wasn't far from here. Called Arden Fleet Farm, it was a ramshackle old house with several decrepit barns set around a yard. It belonged to an old woman and her husband.

After he died, she refused to let the place go to anyone else.'
She thought for a moment. 'What was her name now? Ah,
yes, she was called Edith. That's right, Edith Pettifer.'

Pettifer. The name ignited a flash of warning in Marie's
brain. Ivy Pettifer, who went to work for Sally Pinket and
killed the infants. Hellfire, what was this? The pieces of the
puzzle began to slot into place. 'So, Belinda, this Pettifer
woman. Did she allow Mason Nash to move into the farm
with his followers? And if so, how did he know about her?'

'She was some kind of distant relative, I believe. And
yes, she gave him the run of the place. He did the house up,
made two of the barns into dormitories and the third into a
kind of meeting hall — he called it his church.' She curled
her lip in disgust. 'He and his cronies lived and fornicated
in the relative luxury of the house while the kids — like our
Ben — slept in the barn.'

Marie looked intently at Belinda. 'This is important. I
have a picture, it's a composite but a good one, and we need
to know if it's a reasonable likeness of Mason Nash. Did you
ever see him?'

'Not face to face, no.'

'Without upsetting him, do you think you might be able
to show it to Ben? To get him to say if it's really like Daemon
or not?' Marie said.

'It's of the utmost importance, Belinda,' added Ruth
solemnly. 'Or we wouldn't ask.'

There was a long silence before Belinda said, 'I want to
help, of course, but in all honesty, if you were a young lad
like Ben, how would you react to being shown a picture of
the man who raped you?'

There was little point in taking it further. They still had
Mike Coleman, and Marie had fewer concerns about causing
him psychological damage. Ben was younger, vulnerable, and
trying to rebuild his life. Mike, well, he might fight them all the
way or he could fold under pressure. They'd just have to see.

'Point taken. I'm sorry, we won't push it,' Marie said.
'But tell me, did he ever mention a man called Apostle?'

Belinda stiffened. 'Yes, Officers, he did. And I beg of you, on no account must you mention that name in Ben's hearing. That animal was the worst of the lot. He was obsessed with Daemon and would do anything for him. He was a very dark angel indeed. He could charm the young ones, be the inspirational leader they craved and worshipped, and could just as easily take a knife and slit their throats.'

'We believe they sacrificed some of the members, Belinda,' said Ruth gravely.

'If they did, and I think you're right, it would have been Apostle who performed the rituals.'

'Did Ben ever describe him to you?' asked Marie.

'Only to say that he was tall and thin. He was a chameleon, Ben said — one minute bright, charismatic and captivating and the next utterly terrifying.' Belinda wrung her hands together. 'Apostle was the one Ben feared most.'

Then our friend Martin Bennington is very likely already in bin bags and awaiting collection at some roadside, thought Marie. 'So, according to what you say, the commune disbanded, yet you're still afraid they'll come for Ben. How do you work that out?'

'The commune doesn't exist anymore but its rotten heart still beats. Daemon, Apostle and four acolytes are continuing to function. They intend to start a new group. When they're ready, they'll begin recruiting again, but first, they need to build up their power and resources. It's those men we fear.' Belinda looked wrung out. 'Please, can my family be allowed to return to their home and their work now? We're a community of care, not a cult.'

Ruth stood up. 'Of course. Thank you for telling us all you know. We have to find these evil people and lock them away, Belinda. Then your Ben can finally get some peace.'

'If you can do that, I'll be in your debt forever, and so will he.'

'Oh, we'll get them, Belinda, one way or another. We won't give up until we do,' Marie said.

Marie hurried back to her car, then sat and watched the police vehicles move out as she gathered her thoughts. She then rang Jackman and gave him the whole story.

He whistled softly. 'If Mason Nash is a distant relative of the Pettifers, he'll know all about the murders at Solace House — and about the bodies buried in the garden. Hell, Marie, exactly what *is* his reason for getting hold of that old property?'

'We are told there are six of them. Solace is plenty big enough for six people to live in. I think he wants it as a sort of sacred place to found his cult in, you know, like when great cathedrals were built on early holy sites.'

'Only his sacred site will be built on evil,' murmured Jackman. 'Solace is perfect for him. Marie, now the two investigations are one, I can't be shut out any longer. I know things that Bennington and Laura told me, and at the same time I've been in at the start of everything that's happened at Solace, plus I've also developed a close rapport with the Stewarts. I need to get back! Nothing I do will bring Laura back, but I can help to put these killers behind bars.'

'Then talk to Ruth, Jackman. She's on her way back to base right now. And I'm one hundred percent behind your decision.'

* * *

Detective Inspector Jackman was back in control. Maybe not yet in an official capacity — Ruth had to make a decision on that — but at least his head was in the right place. He and Sam grabbed a light supper to keep up their energy, though neither had any appetite. Having eaten, Jackman dropped Sam at the station to talk to Marie about his forthcoming interview with Mike Coleman, then drove to his parents' house.

He found his mother in the outside porch struggling to extricate herself from a pair of mucky boots.

'Rowan, darling! Have you eaten?'

He smiled at her. That was so like his mother! 'Yes, Mum. Sam and I had supper before we came out.'

She looked at him suspiciously, decided he was telling the truth and led him through to the kitchen. 'So, tell me what you know about these awful people who are trying to drive that poor family from their home.'

Jackman needed his mother and father to be fully aware of the seriousness of the situation while not putting the fear of God in them. 'Is Dad around this evening? I'd rather like him to hear this too.'

'He'll be here in a minute, Rowan. He's just finishing a call to someone in his network in the education sector. You know what your father's like when he gets the bit between his teeth. Right now, it's the treatment of young Aaron and Poppy and the bullying that's still going on, especially on the school bus.'

'Ah, the one-man-radical-change dynamo is in action, is he?'

''Fraid so, but probably all for the best in the long run.' She gave him an affectionate hug. 'Are you feeling better this evening, son? You look different to when I left you just a matter of hours ago.'

He kissed the top of her head. 'Thanks, Mum. The mood swings are going to have me in their grasp for a while yet, but something has happened in an investigation that both Laura and I were involved in. It's one case I need to see through to a satisfactory conclusion. There must be no mistakes and not one single guilty person must get away without paying dearly. So . . .' He held her at arm's length and looked into her eyes. 'I have to keep it together until I know they are locked in a cell and will never walk free again.'

'Only then can you mourn.' She nodded. 'I understand, and we'll be there for you when the time comes, all of us.'

Jackman was almost relieved to see his father enter the room. His mother's professions of love and support had him verging on tears again, and he couldn't let that happen, not yet.

They sat around the kitchen table while he told them about the last remaining members of a cult who wanted

Solace as a base and, if the police's assumptions were correct, would stop at nothing to get it. He saw a look of indignation spread across his father's face.

'Right, son. Well, you can relax about the Stewarts' safety. I'll make a couple of calls. I didn't think I'd need those fellows again after last time, but I can get my security men out here in a matter of hours. I know it's the house they want, but they might well attempt to intimidate the family to get it. I'm not leaving anything to chance.' He stood up. 'I'll do it immediately.'

His father's no-nonsense response to every situation never ceased to amaze Jackman. The man's desire to put things right, and as quickly as possible, was unrelenting. They hadn't been close when he was younger — work and business always seemed to come first where his father was concerned — but now Jackman was older, he saw they weren't so very different after all.

'Are you going to tell Hugh and Holly?' Harriet was asking.

'I'll go over there shortly. The last thing I want to do is frighten them, but they need to be on their guard.' He pulled a face. 'I know Hugh is anxious about his new job, but I've let Gerry Keane and his father know the score and they are perfectly happy to give him time off to be with the family until this is over. I just hope he realises it's a genuine offer and keeps his wife and kids close, at least for the next few days. Marie thinks we are within striking distance of these men and with two divisions hunting them, I hope it won't be long.'

'And every man and woman out looking for them will have their injured colleagues on their mind, so they'll be giving their all, I have no doubt,' said Harriet. 'Shall I come with you to see our little family of refugees?'

'Please, Mum, I'd appreciate that. What time do the children go to bed?'

'In about half an hour, I think. They've already said goodnight to Sherbet and Rainbow.' She gave a little chuckle. 'They don't know this yet, but should they stay in this area

293

when this is all over, your sweet, thoughtful nephews have said they'd like to give them Sherbet as a present. Ryan is riding so well he's onto more difficult horses now, and Miles said that as long as he can have visiting rights and sometimes assist with grooming, he thinks it's the best idea ever.'

Jackman felt a rush of love for his two nephews. They had suffered more than most kids their age, and he believed that made them sensitive to other youngsters who were troubled or frightened. 'I think it's a great idea too, Mum, if you're happy with it.'

She laughed. 'What do you think? I'm positively delighted.'

* * *

After his talk with the Stewarts, Jackman drove to the police station, picked up Sam and continued on to Mill Corner. Marie looked exhausted, so he told her to get off home while she had the chance, and they'd talk in the morning.

He was just unlocking the front door when his phone rang. Ruth. He took a deep breath and offered up a silent prayer.

'Look, Rowan, speaking as a friend, I want you to be absolutely certain that you're up to handling such a difficult and distressing investigation while you're coping with your sad loss.' She took a breath. 'But listening to you earlier, I realised that it's the only way forward for you, so if you're quite sure you're fit to work, I won't stop you. In fact, knowing that I would feel exactly the same, I'll welcome you back with open arms. This is not a time to be without my best officer.'

'Ruth, I could hug you!'

'Then it's fortunate this is a phone call, isn't it?'

He didn't miss the hint of amusement in her voice. 'Thanks, Ruth, I appreciate it.'

He informed the superintendent that he'd spoken to his parents as well as Hugh and Holly Stewart, and that his father had arranged security for the house and stables areas. They could do no more in that respect.

'I'll see you tomorrow, Rowan. Then the hunt will really begin. If we have two viable connections to Mason Nash, we have a greater chance of catching him than ever before. Now, try to sleep — although that's probably a stupid thing to say.'

He ended the call and hurried into the kitchen to find Sam. 'I'm back at work tomorrow, Sam, so we'll both have plenty to keep our minds occupied.' He lifted a bottle of malt out of one of the kitchen cupboards. 'I think we've earned this, don't you?' Somewhat absently, Sam thanked him. 'Didn't go too well with Mike Coleman?' Jackman inquired.

'Hard to say really, I only observed. Though I commend your Gary's observational skills. Coleman has most definitely been manipulated, and I sense he's a very damaged man. I can foresee a problem arising when he realises we know about the cult connection.'

'We desperately need to know things that probably only he can tell us,' said Jackman, pouring whisky into two glasses.

'He's bound to shut down on us, so I need to consider how best to deal with him.' He took the whisky Jackman handed him. 'Now I wish I hadn't said I'd go to Locksford — my time would probably be best spent here. Coleman needs the skilled handling of an experienced professional.' Sam's eyes suddenly lit up. 'Ah! I've just had a thought.' He set down his glass. 'I might just know someone who fits the bill a treat.' He pulled out his mobile and scrolled through his contacts. 'Ah, here she is.' He held the phone to his ear. 'Cross everything, this woman could well be the answer to all our prayers.'

Jackman listened to him speak to someone called Julia and wondered who she was. It had to be a colleague, but the way Sam was talking to her indicated that he knew her very well indeed. Jackman sipped his drink and waited.

The conversation didn't take long and then Sam was pushing his phone back into his pocket with a satisfied expression. 'We are indeed honoured.'

'Your colleague is going to assist us?'

Sam gave a laugh. 'Well, she's not exactly a colleague, Jackman. Julia Tennant is my ex-wife, and although it pains me to have to say so, probably the finest psychologist I've ever known.'

'Ex-*wife*?' Jackman exclaimed. 'I had no idea you'd been married.'

'My dark secret.' Sam chuckled again. 'We married in haste and repented at leisure, as they say. We were both young, driven, just starting out in our careers. Work consumed our every waking moment. We just didn't have the time for each other, and it didn't take us long to realise that although we did love each other very much, no way could we live together. We were like chalk and cheese, both in the same profession but opposites in every other way. We parted amicably after a year. It was a sadness and a blessing. We both went on to achieve everything we had hoped for in our careers, but neither of us married again — neither felt the need.' He looked at Jackman, a rather wistful smile on his face. 'I sometimes wonder if . . .'

'Did Laura know? She never mentioned it,' Jackman asked, still amazed at this revelation.

'No, it's been years since I've mentioned it to anyone. And I only told you now because I wanted to ask her help. She *will* help, by the way. She'll drive over tomorrow morning and will go directly to the police station and ask for you.' He took another mouthful of whisky. 'Only last year, Julia was involved in counselling indoctrinated people rescued from a cult that used similar mind-controlling techniques to your Daemon. It's hard to believe, but experts think there may be over five hundred cults operating in the United Kingdom and up to half a million people who are, or have been, involved in a cult.'

'I had no idea it was so prevalent,' said Jackman.

'Most people don't — they associate cults with the big horrific American tragedies, like the Manson killings and Waco in Texas. But they are here all right, and Julia is involved in trying to raise greater awareness of the dangers. They vary from huge organisations masquerading as religious orders to small, highly dangerous groups with very twisted ideas indeed. Most use psychological coercion to indoctrinate mainly young, vulnerable people.' He shook his head sadly. 'If Laura had told me what was going on, I would have immediately suggested that she liaise with Julia, but bless her heart, she was worried about my health. What a terrible irony.'

For a while they sat in silence, drinking their Scotch, lost in their memories of Laura.

After a while, Jackman said, 'It's getting late, old friend. Why not turn in? You have a bit of a drive in the morning.' He frowned. 'Are you sure you're okay to do that?'

Sam nodded. 'Oh yes. I still love driving. I'm over the initial shock, and now I know that you have the best possible help here, I can go and support the other team in Locksford. I gathered from that superintendent's tone that they could really do with some assistance.' He started to get to his feet, then sat back down. 'By the way, you were asking if I felt bad about my observations of Mike Coleman — well, my concerns weren't actually about that interview, they were about *that*.' Sam pointed to Laura's laptop. 'Her notes on Bennington and his treatment at the hands of Daemon. I know how she thinks. There was something troubling her that she didn't include in the notes. I need to hear the actual recordings so that, hopefully, I can pick it up from that.' This time he did stand up. 'I'll say goodnight. Try to sleep, Jackman. You're going to need every ounce of your energy to tackle Mason Nash.' He squeezed Jackman's shoulder affectionately as he passed him on his way out.

Jackman sat on, feeling an overpowering need to be close to Laura. Bed wasn't the answer, so he went outside into the moonlight and unlocked the door to her consulting room.

At once, he was in her presence, surrounded by all things Laura. He walked around, touching the various objects, picking them up and replacing them where they had stood. He looked at the pictures.

Finally, he adjusted the lighting to very low, unfolded a soft fleece blanket that had been lying on her chair and, pulling it around him, curled up on the sofa.

He closed his eyes and slept.

CHAPTER TWENTY-SIX

When Janet awoke at around six o'clock, she saw that she had a message on her mobile. She read it, read it again and sent a carefully worded reply.

She got up and showered, made her breakfast and rang John. She read him the message. 'This is a first, isn't it?' she said, with a wry smile. 'Can I throw that one at you and ask you to make it a priority?'

'Certainly,' said John. 'As you say, it is a first and something of a surprise too. It never ceases to amaze me how quickly our client learns about whatever's going on. This is certainly not common knowledge yet.'

'He has a considerable network working for him,' she said. 'We're only small cogs in his great wheel.' *Albeit very important ones*, she added to herself. Soon her task would be complete, and she hadn't yet come up with a plan to keep herself close to Stephen. He was so much more than a client to her that she hated the thought of losing contact with him. Well, that wasn't going to happen, was it?

They agreed on their new plan of action for the next few days, then Janet hung up. She cleared the breakfast things, made a cup of herbal tea and took it through to her office.

Soon she was staring at her screen, and the photos in the file attachment. 'Funny old world,' she murmured to herself. 'Who'd have thought it?'

With great care, Janet typed the single word "Deceased" across the bottom of Laura Archer's record.

* * *

By eight o'clock, Saltern-le-Fen police station was humming. Jackman must have got in at some ungodly hour because when Marie went in, his desk was already piled high with reports, his printer churning out reams of paper.

'Well, boss, you've certainly hit the ground running, haven't you?'

'Morning, Marie. You know how it is. Leave this place for a couple of hours and it all builds up.'

He smiled at her, the old Jackman — a tired and gaunt version, maybe, but it was Jackman, nevertheless. They were back on track.

'Sit down and bring me up to speed, then I'll give you some news. You first.'

Anxious to hear his news, she gave him a brief account of all that had occurred while he was away. 'So, boss, what are you itching to tell me?'

'We have some help with Coleman. Sam has referred a specialist to us, a woman who knows all about mind control, cults and indoctrination. Her name is Dr Julia Tennant and she's a forensic psychologist. She will be with us,' he glanced at his watch, 'in about an hour.'

'Ah, that's a relief. Sam told me he was committed to Superintendent Carpenter today but was rather anxious about Coleman. He's our way in, if we can only get him to tell us where Mason Nash and his remaining cohorts are living.'

'Sam reckoned that if anyone can get him to open up, it'll be this woman.' Jackman bit his lip. 'But that kind of thing takes time, which is something we don't have too much of.'

'Coleman's our best hope, though,' said Marie. 'We can't press that lad Ben too far after all the work Belinda has done to give him a life back, not even to stop a killer.' She paused, realising that her phone was ringing. 'Excuse me, boss.' She looked at the display. 'Talk of the devil — it's Belinda.'

Belinda sounded agitated. 'I'm wondering if you might be able to come back to the nursery, Detective, preferably as soon as possible. And bring that other officer with you, the Cockney one.'

'Max? Well, yes, of course. Has something happened, Belinda?'

'It's Ben. He wants to talk to you — well, to your Max, actually. I think that now he knows Max hadn't intended to harm him or take him away, Ben feels he might be able to help, and he liked Max.' Belinda took a breath. 'Ben has come to realise that if you catch Daemon and lock him up, he'll be free of the cult. He just wants to be like other kids and enjoy himself without looking over his shoulder for the rest of his life. It's a big thing, DS Evans. He's never been able to open up before.'

'I just have to find Max and tie things up here, so I reckon I'll be with you in around twenty-five minutes. I'll see you then.' Marie ended the call. 'Well,' she said to Jackman, 'forget what I just said about counting Ben out. Shows what I know. The kid has come up trumps. Can I leave you with the new psychologist and get straight over there, boss?'

'Go,' said Jackman. 'I need time to fill Julia Tennant in anyway, and I'll take Robbie or Gary with me when I talk to Coleman.'

About twenty minutes later, Marie and Max were back in the big farmhouse kitchen nursing mugs of tea. This time, only Belinda and Ben were with them.

The young man was clearly anxious but looked determined too. Marie was pinning her hopes on Max and his open, approachable manner.

The first thing Ben said was, 'If you catch them, they'll go to prison, won't they?'

They both nodded, and Marie said, 'Oh yes, Ben, you can be sure of that. And with the right evidence against them, they'll get life.'

Ben rubbed his hands together as if he was cold. 'I know stuff.'

Max leaned across the table towards him. 'Then tell us, mate. We have to get the rest of this cult behind bars before anyone else gets damaged or killed.' He looked him in the eye. 'They do kill people, don't they?'

Ben shifted around in his seat. 'Yeah, they do.'

'Then tell us everything you can,' urged Max. 'You want rid of these evil people as much as we do, but without you we're stuffed. We know sod all, so help us, Ben.'

Ben swallowed several times. 'I'll tell you what I can but if I can't finish, like it gets too much for me, you need to know something.' He tore a sheet from a memo pad lying on the table among some gardening magazines and wrote a name and an address on it. 'They think this woman is dead, but she's not. She faked it. She looked after me for a while in the commune. I don't know for sure, but I think she knows where they are now.'

'They?' asked Max.

'Him.' Ben rubbed his hands faster, clearly very agitated now. 'And the other one.'

Belinda touched Max on the shoulder. 'Don't push him. You know very well who he means. He just can't say their names.'

They knew all right. Daemon and Apostle.

Max took the paper, read it and handed it to Marie. It was a name and an address: *Emma Knott. Four, Cranley Court, Saltern-le-Fen.*

Marie knew Cranley Court. It was a small block of flatlets on the edge of town. Low-cost rentals mainly — one-bedroom, minimal space but not run-down. An anonymous kind of place.

'She's much stronger than me,' whispered Ben.

'You, my man, are a hero.' Max grinned at him. 'I've got the greatest respect for you, so don't knock yourself. Just tell us what you can, okay? And when this is all over, I promise to bring my wife back here and let her wipe my bank account clean on your ruddy plants. Deal?'

Ben managed a smile. 'Deal.'

They left thirty minutes later with more information than they'd expected and drove directly to Cranley Court. The journey passed mainly in silence, both of them still trying to assimilate what Ben had told them. It had been a horror story, a sequence of terrible events such as no one would believe could happen in quiet, rural England. But it had all happened, and if they didn't find a way to stop those two sadistic psychopaths, it would flare up again, either right here, or in some other backwater.

The woman who answered the door was around forty five, with long dark hair drawn back severely in a ponytail. She was so thin as to be anorexic, but Marie didn't think that was the case — there was a wiry strength to her. Set in the planes of her angular face was a pair of startling, enormous, washed-out, pale-blue eyes.

The stare she gave them was neither enquiring nor antagonistic, but it was most disconcerting. Marie cleared her throat and said, 'Ben sent us.'

The door opened. 'Come in, quick!'

Inside, they showed her their warrant cards.

'So, the day has finally come.'

Marie noted the hint of an Irish accent. 'We need your help, Emma.'

'First, tell me how Ben is,' she said.

'Brave, that's how,' replied Max. 'Actually, all things considered, he's good. He's with kind souls who're protecting him. And if we can just get the last remaining cult members behind bars, he'll thrive again, I know he will.'

Emma nodded slowly, then exhaled. 'I hoped that would be the case with Ben. He was worth saving. I took the risk of telling him what happened to me. It was worth it — he cared about me as I did him. I suppose I was a substitute mother.' She sighed. 'Since then I've seen him a few times, always in the distance, but I've never dared approach him. I have no intention of raking up old memories for him, I'm just happy he's surviving.' She pointed to a shabby sofa and sat facing them on a large beanbag. 'You know about Daemon then?'

'And Apostle.'

She visibly recoiled. 'I see. So you want to know where they are.'

'We *have* to know,' said Marie. 'They must be stopped. We've been informed that they're regrouping with the intention of rebuilding the sect.'

'Like a dark phoenix, rising from the ashes,' Emma whispered. 'That was always his intention. He was looking for a sacred site, somewhere that would enhance his power so that he would become unstoppable. I believe he has found it, and it's quite close by.'

Marie watched her and wondered about the long-term effects on this woman of the drugs Daemon had administered. She had a strange, other-worldly air and a dreamy way of speaking, as if she was thinking out loud rather than addressing them directly. 'He has, Emma, and he's terrorising an innocent family in order to drive them away and make it his.'

The eyes narrowed. 'But if you know about it, you can stop him, surely?'

'Oh yes. If he goes anywhere near it, he'll be picked up, but we're worried about how he'll react now he knows we've thwarted his chances of ever getting hold of the place.'

Emma gave a brittle laugh. 'Hell hath no fury doesn't always refer to scorned women, Detective. This family — do they have young children?'

Marie felt a sliver of ice slide down her backbone. 'Two. One aged seven and the other eight.'

'Then guard them with your lives. He will want compensation for what you've denied him. He will take a sacrifice, no doubt about it.'

The matter-of-fact way Emma spoke of sacrifice chilled Marie even further. 'Please excuse me a minute.' She pulled out her phone, rang Jackman and passed on the message. He had said his father had security in place, but even so, Marie didn't entirely trust it. Having emphasised just what danger the Stewart children were in, she ended the call.

Max was asking Emma how she had escaped.

'I "drowned," right in front of their eyes, in a fast-flowing river.' She gave a satisfied sigh. 'They didn't think I could possibly survive, but they had no idea what a strong swimmer I am, or how long I could hold my breath under water.'

'But you didn't go far. Why not?' Max frowned. 'If it was me, I'd have got as far from them as I possibly could.'

'It crossed my mind, of course, but it was always my intention to find a way to stop them. I couldn't go to the police — every single former member who has tried that is dead, and that's a fact. So I decided to alter my appearance, hide in plain sight and keep watch on them.' She gave an odd little laugh. 'I had what was once called a "fuller" figure, so I starved myself, exercised constantly and lost ten stone in weight. Even I wouldn't recognise my old self now. Anyway, I knew that one day someone would come asking questions and I'd have the answers, and then that special someone would finally end Daemon's reign of terror.' Emma looked down, apparently in deep thought. Then she looked up. 'Are you those people?'

'Dead bloody right we are,' growled Max.

Emma smiled. 'I do believe you might be.'

Marie kept thinking about what Emma had said, that every single person who had tried going to the police was dead. She drew a line under any possible hope for Martin Bennington. He must have been aware of the probable outcome too, which was why he had begged to be kept safe. The only comfort was that Martin had at least initiated an enquiry and there was now a manhunt in progress. So his brave efforts had not been in vain.

Marie fastened her gaze on the gaunt frame of this woman, her hollow cheeks. 'We have to ask some hard questions, Emma. Do you think you can help us? Do you have the strength?'

Her pale eyes grew even paler. 'You have no idea how strong I am, Detective. Ask away.'

Marie produced the EvoFIT picture and showed it to her. 'Is this an accurate likeness of Daemon, would you say?'

To her surprise, Emma burst out laughing. 'Not when I saw him last!' She took the picture and looked closer. 'I suppose there is something of Daemon in there . . . all I can say is whoever gave you this description must have been high at the time.' She shrugged. 'I suppose you know that's possible.'

Marie said she did. 'So, how would you describe Daemon?'

'Unremarkable, ordinary, rather nondescript — until he started to talk to you. He could wheedle his way into your brain from the first words he uttered. Then he embodied whatever you wanted from your leader — power and the key to knowledge beyond the average person's understanding.' Her eyes glittered briefly, touched by the old fervour. 'This picture. Is that how one of the followers saw his Master? Who was it?'

'A man named Martin Bennington,' said Marie.

'We didn't use our real names. Do you know his chosen name?'

'No.' Marie tried to recall if one had been mentioned but came up empty-handed. 'He might have told someone at Locksford, I suppose. I'll find out.'

'No matter. If he was from our twin group, I wouldn't have known him anyway. We knew of its existence, but we weren't allowed to meet. We asked why we couldn't join together — it would have made our church even more powerful — but Daemon declared it wasn't the right time. He said the day would come when the Knowledge had passed between all of us and then we'd unite, and do battle with Armageddon.'

'But now you know what an evil, manipulating, mind-bending psycho your Daemon really is,' Max interrupted.

She fixed him with an icy stare. 'Don't underestimate his power, Detective. You do so at your peril. Believe it or not, after just one hour with him even you would see what every other victim saw. Consider that I was once an up-and-coming young lawyer with a glittering career ahead of me. Not every one of his converts was a hopeless case, believe me!'

'I'm sorry, Emma,' Max said. 'Can you tell us where Daemon and his group are?'

'I'll have to take you there. Well, as close as I dare. I can't risk being seen.'

Gripped with excitement, Marie leaned forward. 'You don't have to risk anything, Emma. Can't you show us on a map?'

'It's not easy to find, but I suppose I can try.'

'How many of his followers are left, Emma?' asked Max.

'Six. The two of them and four disciples.'

That tied up with what Ben had told Belinda. Marie felt around in her pocket and found a second likeness. This time it was a mugshot taken of Mike Coleman when he was brought into custody. 'This man. Is he one of them, Emma?' She handed her the picture.

'That's Michael. Yes, he's one of Daemon's staunchest followers. He was one of the special ones, chosen to do Daemon's dirty work. He's dangerous, Detective, despite his rather innocuous appearance, so be very careful around him.'

Marie rang Jackman a second time, warning him to take care in Coleman's company. None of them had considered Coleman to be much more than a pathetic victim coerced into doing whatever Daemon asked of him. Well, Emma certainly didn't see him like that, and she should know.

'Do you know about the List of the Fallen, Emma?' she asked.

Emma looked down into her lap. 'Those who went against Daemon or indulged in unacceptably sinful behaviour were added to the List to be ritually cleansed.' She looked up. 'Sacrificed.'

'By Apostle,' Marie said. Like Ben, Emma hadn't once uttered that name. It seemed he inspired more fear than Daemon himself.

'That's right,' Emma said. 'Find him and his ceremonial knives and the killing will stop.'

Marie was sincerely sorry for this woman. Clearly highly intelligent, she had lost everything through a chance meeting with a psychopath.

She took out her phone and brought up Google Maps. 'So, what area is he living in, Emma? Let's see if we can pinpoint his lair.'

'Between Rainham-le-Fen and a village called Eastern Bank. It's about twenty minutes' drive from here up the coast.'

Marie located the two places and the interconnecting roads and handed her phone to Emma.

After scrolling up and down for a while, Emma said, 'It's here. Off Pot Belly Lane. There's a small terrace of farm workers' cottages, three of them. Daemon occupies two and the third is empty. It had a burst water pipe years ago and had to be abandoned. It's still awaiting repair — the farmer has no interest in doing it up. Too costly.'

'You've certainly done your homework,' commented Max.

'I've had plenty of time, haven't I? Waiting, watching and gathering evidence all these years.'

And all the while boiling with anger and hatred, thought Marie.

'They never leave the place empty, Detectives,' Emma went on. 'There's always at least one cult member at home. Maybe they have something to hide, I don't know. What I do know is that even if I'd wanted to get inside, which I didn't, I couldn't have done it without being discovered.'

Marie was already planning the raid. The tiny terrace of houses stood alone, with nothing but fields around it. Apart from an old, dilapidated barn, there was no other habitation for at least half a mile. Perfect!

Emma suddenly looked pensive. 'Did you mention a man called Martin?'

'Yes, Martin Bennington. Why?' asked Marie.

The dreamy faraway look had returned. 'I was mistaken. I *have* heard of him. We had a girl brought in one night. I had a feeling she was on the List from the way she was treated. We weren't supposed to speak to such people, but I felt so sorry for her that I smuggled in some food, and we talked. She said she had declined an invitation to become one of the Six, which was considered an insult to Daemon and the whole brotherhood. So she had been brought there to be reindoctrinated.' Emma sighed. 'I knew what that meant, but I didn't say. She told me she hadn't wanted to be parted from "Mark," whose real name was Martin, so had rejected the offer to move up the hierarchy. She said that as soon as she got back to Locksford, they would run away together. I knew she would never go back. She would never see her Martin again. It was heartbreaking — he sounded such a sweet guy. I always wondered about him and whether he got to know what really happened to her.'

'He knew,' said Max. 'He's the one who blew the whistle on the cult, but sadly—'

'Say no more. I've always believed that even your police stations aren't safe from Daemon, which is why I didn't go to the police myself.'

Marie was now seriously concerned for Emma's safety. Only she had first-hand information, and she'd just passed it onto them. If Daemon could track down a police car when even the drivers didn't know their destination until they got behind the wheel, he could certainly trace Emma. 'I think we need to get you to a place of safety, Emma, I really do.'

'No way! I'll take my chances out here, thank you.' There was a glint in her eyes. 'I've given you what you need, now catch those devils. Then, when the trial is over, I will disappear for ever.'

'You'll testify?'

'It's why I'm still alive, DS Evans, still here. Oh yes, I'll testify.'

CHAPTER TWENTY-SEVEN

Julia Tennant made an immediate impression on Jackman. A sense of calm and tranquillity seemed to flow into the room with her when she walked in. She had the stately bearing of one of those timeless British dramatic actresses, but at the same time he felt at ease with her, as if he'd known her for years.

She was of medium height with silver-grey hair, worn short and layered. Probably in her late sixties, she still looked stunning despite her age and the fact that she wore almost no make-up.

That she had once been married to Sam Page was actually not as surprising as Jackman had initially believed. They shared something, although he wasn't sure exactly what. It certainly wasn't their looks. But something about her was strongly reminiscent of Sam.

She offered her condolences with an empathy that made Jackman think she must have gone through a similar tragedy at some time in her life.

Having accepted the offer of tea, she sat and drank it while he told her what they knew about the cult. Julia listened carefully, interjecting the occasional question. Nothing he said seemed to surprise or shock her. When he had finished, she said, 'Mind-control techniques don't vary much whether the groups are large and radical or small with a single self-proclaimed leader. The trend these days is to masquerade as a group promoting a wellness regime or addiction treatment programme. It is sometimes difficult to differentiate between a genuine course or a cult until you are inside it, and by then you're invested in it and the indoctrination begins. Though we may not think so, every one of us is susceptible, and sometimes those people who believe it could never happen to them are the easiest to "convert." Sadly, they are the last to know that they have been brainwashed. It's heartbreaking for their families, who often have to watch their loved ones undergo a devastating personality change.' She gave him a searching look. 'What do you make of this man, Mike Coleman?'

'Well, we originally believed him to be a rather pathetic chap, someone who had fallen on hard times and would do any job he was offered just to get enough money to make ends meet. Then one of my detectives, noting his odd behaviour, realised that he could belong to the cult. Then my sergeant called just a few minutes ago and told me he is actually very dangerous. Apparently, he's a senior member of the cult, a kind of elder, answerable only to Daemon and Apostle.' He sat back in his chair. 'Initially he was our only way in, but now we have discovered another former member still alive who's willing to divulge whatever we want to know in order to get Daemon and his remaining henchmen arrested. So, if Coleman clams up, all is not lost.'

'That's good to know, so we don't need to put too much pressure on him too soon. Perhaps we should go and take a look at him now?'

'Certainly. We haven't yet told him of our suspicion that he is part of the cult. He thinks he's just being charged with burglary and causing criminal damage, so I thought that for today you might observe from outside the interview room. We have a video link you can watch him through. We can't allow him to suspect that you're a psychologist — we'll save that one for later.'

Julia agreed. 'Good. It's best I observe him first. Will I be able to speak to you through earphones and suggest a few questions of my own if I think they might be useful? Not in this first interview, but maybe the next one.'

'Yes, we can do that, no problem.' Jackman glanced at his watch. 'He'll be in the interview room now, so shall we go? I'll be very interested to hear your opinion of him. It seems he's a very good actor — at least he had us all fooled.'

Julia smiled. 'They usually are, DI Jackman.'

* * *

Jackman was still in the interview room when Marie and Max left Emma's flat. Marie had called him as soon as they knew the location of Daemon's temporary home, but his phone was on mute. She left a message, then decided it couldn't wait and rang Ruth Crooke.

The superintendent sounded almost excited, which was quite unusual for this cool woman. 'Good work, Marie! I'll pull Jackman out of his interview immediately. This takes precedence over everything. Get back here as soon as you can, and I'll get the ball rolling. I need to take it upstairs first, then we'll all meet in the CID room to plan our next move. And once again, good work.'

'It's Max who should be congratulated, Super. He established a rapport with Ben, the lad at the nursery, who gave us Emma Knott's name.' She ended the call, and they sped off.

'Thanks for putting in a good word with the super, but it was hardly down to me. It was Ben finding the courage to open up.'

'Come on, Max, credit where credit's due. You were great with him.' Already, Marie was beginning to feel the adrenaline surge through her veins. In just an hour from now, Daemon and his murderous devotee Apostle could be in handcuffs, on their way to a cell.

If only she could talk to Ralph, share her excitement with him. She pushed the thought away, and at the same time doubts began to creep in. These were dangerous people who were hardly likely to give in without a fight. Any attempt to apprehend them had every chance of going terribly wrong. She thought about the disastrous outcome of some of the more infamous cult sieges. She recalled some of the newspaper headlines declaring how many people had died, and she involuntarily shivered. Then she steeled herself and thought, *Well, Marie Evans, this siege is not going to be like that! Today, one way or another, we are going to put an end to this murdering cult!*

* * *

Bedlam raged in the station, with officers shouting to each other as they pulled on protective gear and checked their equipment belts in preparation for the raid. Jackman, Marie and Julia sat in Jackman's office, waiting. They could do nothing until everything was in place and the relevant checks had been made. From her observations of Coleman, Julia had come to the conclusion that he was indeed an indoctrinated cult member. She had sensed a very frightening undercurrent in the interview room, almost a hum, that suggested serious mental imbalance. In her opinion, he was indeed potentially dangerous, and the advice they'd been given was sound.

Jackman passed this on to the custody sergeant, and then they turned their attention to what they might expect to happen in the next few hours.

'Ruth has gone into overdrive and has managed to get the raid sanctioned as quickly as possible,' said Jackman. He turned to Julia. 'All the red tape these days puts a stranglehold on any spontaneous actions. If we actually adhered to all the health and safety regulations, we might as well give up.'

Marie grunted. 'It's so bad that if someone is drowning, H and S regulations declare that we mustn't jump in to save them. There is not an officer I know who is able to swim who would abide by that. Imagine having to face the relatives, for a start. You'd have to live with letting someone die when you

312

knew you could have saved them. It goes against everything we're here for.'

Tim Jacobs came in with some papers and laid them on Jackman's desk.

'Confirmation of five men living in the terraced cottages on Pot Belly Lane, sir. The farmer letting the cottages has positively identified one of these as Mike Coleman, so we are pretty certain your intelligence is correct and we have the right location.'

Jackman thanked him. 'And Ruth has brought in the Ditch and Watercourse people to assist. They are sending a ditch-clearing dredging machine out to Pot Belly Lane supposedly as part of regular maintenance operations. Luckily, it was due to be done quite shortly anyway, so it won't appear strange. It's usually a one-man job but he's taking a trainee today in the form of PC Simon Laker, whose groovy headphones won't be playing music. He's going to let us know what he sees out there.' He looked at Julia. 'We're very glad you could be with us on this. If these cult members prove difficult, we could well need your expertise.'

'I'm happy to help in any way I can.' She leaned forward and addressed Marie. 'Could I ask a question?'

'Fire away,' said Marie.

'Do you trust this woman, Emma Knott?' Julia asked.

Marie didn't hesitate. 'Yes. She gave us no cause to doubt her.'

Julia nodded slowly. 'Only I've seen something like this once before. A willing cult survivor suddenly materialises with all manner of helpful information, but it turns out to be a trap. The survivor is in fact still a devoted follower and a lot of people are placed in danger.' She smiled rather apologetically at Marie. 'Your Emma may be nothing like that, of course, and I'm not saying I don't trust your judgement, but I've learned to question everything where unstable minds are concerned.'

'Very wise,' said Marie. 'But I'll go with my gut instinct on Emma Knott. I'd swear she was on the level when she spoke to us. And it's rather interesting that she can't even mention the name of the man called Apostle. Young Ben was the same.'

Julia exhaled. 'Sometimes the fanatically converted are far more frightening than the leader they idolise. Many years ago now, I had a patient with very dangerous tendencies. If he had stayed in the real world, these might have remained harmless fantasies, but joining a satanic cult gave him free rein to live out some of his darker imaginings. There is always the chance that the innocent believers who do the recruiting can accidentally bring a true psychopath into the fold. Maybe that's the case with this Apostle.'

Marie went out to get some coffees, possibly their last hot drink for a good while.

While Julia made notes on her observations of Mike Coleman and read through the reports on Daemon and his cult, Jackman phoned Superintendent Ashley Carpenter and told her about the planned raid on the cottages in Pot Belly Lane. She asked him if she could assist with men on the ground. It wouldn't take long to deploy a couple of teams from Locksford. He told her that Ruth had it in hand and had called in backup from Greenborough and Saltfleet. 'There will be five males maximum in the cottages, so that's two officers per suspect and plenty of support waiting outside. Since your officer was shot, she has an armed unit on its way. We can't do more than that.' They also had a trained negotiator and two police dogs with their handlers, plus his own detectives. As this was a surprise raid, the odds should be in their favour.

'I was actually about to ring you, Jackman,' Ashley went on. 'We've found a headless torso not too far from the nick, dumped on a bit of waste ground that's awaiting development. Its gender and approximate age all point to it being the remains of Martin Bennington. The forensic tests haven't come back yet, but I sense it was probably a message for us.'

Jackman said how sorry he was. The superintendent was most likely right about it being left to taunt the police.

'Anyway, I'll keep you updated on that, but I have to thank you for sending Sam, Jackman, he's an absolute godsend.' She sounded very low, nothing like the positive and forthright woman he had worked alongside. 'Things are pretty dire here, as you can imagine, and having him around has made it a lot less lonely.'

'How are your two officers, Ashley?' Jackman asked.

'Paula is responding pretty well. She might be out of intensive care tomorrow, but Russ, well, he's in an induced coma, and his chances don't look good.' There was a catch in her voice. 'He's a great officer, the best, so when you go after these killers, remember that, will you?'

'Every single one of us will be thinking of our comrades, believe me.'

'Then good luck, Jackman. We'll all be praying you nail those bastards.'

After he'd finished the call, Marie came back with the coffees. 'It's like the eye of the storm out there now. Everyone has gone quiet, waiting for the hammer to fall.'

'It's a big thing when you know the men you're going after hurt your colleagues. There's a lot at stake.' He told her about Ashley's sudden mood change and how disconcerting it had been.

Marie sighed. 'She sounded like a powerhouse when I spoke to her yesterday — shocked, obviously, but full of determination and very angry.'

'Something's not right there. Maybe I'll talk to Sam when this bust is out of the way.' He glanced at Julia, who was deep into a report on the earlier ritual killings. 'You okay about coming along with us, Julia? If it came to a stand-off and a negotiator was required, your advice on how to tackle them could be vital.'

'Oh yes.' She looked up. 'As long as someone can find me one of your lovely protective vests.'

Jackman assured her he'd not let her get anywhere near the front line without one. He looked at his watch. 'Not long now. Ruth will be mustering us any minute.'

He'd barely finished speaking when Ruth hurried into the office and shut the door behind her.

'Before we move out, a couple more bits of info have just come in.' She looked at them with a tight-lipped, anxious expression. 'Hell, I'd dearly love to leave this until early tomorrow and do a dawn raid before they're even out of their beds — those are always more successful. But we can't afford to waste another hour. This Daemon seems to have ears everywhere, and if he gets the slightest hint that Emma is still alive and has blown the whistle on him, she'll be dead by supper time, and they'll be long gone by morning.'

'You're right,' said Jackman. 'We have to strike now. So, what's this info you have?'

'PC Laker has identified four occupants. Presently they're all together in one of the two cottages. The fifth might be there too, but hasn't shown himself, so he can't tell. But four out of five would be very satisfactory and it means the odds of overpowering them just went up in our favour. And I've been granted permission to put the helicopter up, just in case any of them manages to escape in a vehicle. So we'll be hitting them with everything we have.'

'We go in mob-handed, hard and fast?' asked Marie.

'It's the only way. Silent approach, then straight in and immobilise everyone in the house.' Ruth smiled at each of them. 'Time to gather the troops. Let's make this work.'

* * *

Hugh Stewart's new employers had insisted he take time off until he was sure his family were no longer under threat. Nevertheless, he couldn't help worrying that he was becoming either a burden or a nuisance. He really enjoyed the work and dreaded the thought of being unemployed again. They'd been through some rough times, but nothing had affected him more than not being able to support his family. It had been degrading and humiliating. Hugh had inherited his father's intense pride in being the family breadwinner, so it had hit him hard.

If it hadn't been for Harriet and her husband Lawrence, he might well have bundled Holly and the kids into the car, left them in some cheap hotel and gone back to work.

As it was, they were comfortable and safe, and the children were having the time of their lives with "Auntie Harriet" and her horses and dogs.

Hugh still couldn't believe that Lawrence had arranged a professional security company to look out for them. Even now, as he looked across to where Poppy and Aaron were sitting watching Ryan put one of the bigger ponies through its paces, he saw a very muscular man surveying the stable area from a distance.

How had they come to this? And where would it end?

He felt Holly slip her arm through his. 'Harriet says DI Jackman sent a message earlier. He says none of us are to leave this area and to keep within view of the security operatives. It appears they are very close to arresting those people but should any of them get away, there is a chance they'll come here.'

Hugh understood what that meant. Whoever had failed in their task of getting them out of Solace would be looking for vengeance. 'Makes sense,' he said, and drew his wife closer. 'Means we're going absolutely nowhere for a while.'

Automatically, he stepped a few paces closer to his children.

CHAPTER TWENTY-EIGHT

Rarely does a raid proceed entirely to plan, but the one on Pot Belly Lane was practically textbook.

They approached from two directions, blocking off both exits, and stormed the two cottages. Pivotal to the operation was a clear diagram showing the layout of the buildings, courtesy of the farmer who leased them. The clinical execution of the operation meant that there'd been no need for negotiators, Tasers or excessive violence. Not a shot was fired. In fact the armed response unit's presence hadn't been necessary. The helicopter was rerouted back to base.

Marie stood and watched as four handcuffed men were bundled into the waiting vans. It seemed her quick word with the angels before it all kicked off had paid dividends. She would remember that for the next occasion.

Even so, there was one aspect of the raid that made it less than perfect in Marie's eyes. Instead, it left her feeling uneasy and pensive.

When Jackman appeared at her side, along with Julia Tennant, she guessed they were both thinking along similar lines.

'Any guesses as to which one was Daemon?' she murmured. '*If* he was there at all. We still have one disciple at large — it could be Daemon, Apostle or a simple minion.'

'I have no idea. But it was their reaction that stunned me,' said Jackman. He turned to Julia. 'Was that what you'd have expected — you know, the kind of, well, weird acceptance of their arrest? I mean, it was almost like they saw it as a triumph, not a failure.'

That was exactly what had puzzled Marie. She had never seen a group of suspects behave so oddly. They had shouted encouragement to each other, cheered. They called out that being taken by the heathens had been prophesied, and that they'd rise again.

'I imagine that their leader had always known that arrest was possible,' said Julia, 'so he planned for it, feeding it into his prophecies, making it appear as if it was an inevitable stage in their evolution to higher things. That it was meant to be.'

'Just another step up the ladder to world domination,' muttered Jackman. 'Very clever. Take a defeat and make your brainwashed acolytes believe it's a victory.'

It had seemed that way. When they were asked their names, each one of them had chanted, 'I am the privileged son of the True Knowledge!' One even sang a kind of protest song as he was hustled into a cage in the back of one of the vans.

The whole thing had a slightly comic, unhinged quality to it. On the surface, this had been one of the most successful operations she'd been part of, but to Marie it felt tainted.

She saw Julia looking at her. There was a kindly look on her face and a touch of amusement. She was sure Julia could read minds.

'It's still a major coup, DS Evans, don't let them ruin it for you. Remember, it could have been a bloodbath. Instead, you now have five out of six of the last remaining members of this cult under lock and key. I think you can afford a little time to bask in the glory.'

But Marie didn't feel like basking just yet. The whole thing felt incomplete, and until they had Man Number Six in a cell with his brethren, there was no glory for her.

* * *

While the adrenaline ran high in the police operation — fast and furious and played out against a background of engine noise, shouting, splintering wood, thundering of boots on old cottage floorboards and screams of excitement — the woods around the Jackman stable were an oasis of peace. Birds sang, a gentle breeze soughed in the leaves of the trees and the muffled, rhythmic thud of cantering horses and the occasional relaxed snort of a contented animal rose and fell on the air.

It seemed idyllic.

It was. Except for one thing.

Unnoticed even by the birds, an evil man with a twisted mind was stealthily inching his way ever closer.

* * *

'Of course there is one simple way to know exactly which of our suspects is Daemon,' stated Jackman, glancing anxiously at Marie. 'The question is, will Emma Knott have the courage to come into the station and identify him?'

'And do we have the right to even suggest she get within a mile of the men who destroyed her life and sent her into hiding like a hunted animal?' added Marie.

'And Ben?' He looked at Marie hopefully. 'He was brave enough to open up to Max. Maybe he could at least look at the mugshots.'

'It's not going to happen, boss. Because they aren't all locked up, are they? One is still free, which negates everything. Both of our victims will remain in a state of terror until there are no more cult members roaming the Fens.'

She was right, but he'd had to ask.

'If I might interject?'

He had almost forgotten about Julia. She seemed to possess the ability to blend into the background, watching and listening in silence. Jackman looked at her eagerly. 'Of course.'

'If I could speak to each of them, I'd be able to tell you which one is Daemon.' This was a simple statement of fact — she wasn't being boastful. 'He'll give off very different vibrations. He'll have a distinctive quality about him that he won't be able to conceal, or indeed wish to.'

Sadly, there was one fly in the ointment. 'The problem there,' Jackman replied, 'is that we already have Coleman and now two of the others here, and our custody suite isn't big enough to cope with them all. That, and it was considered prudent to split them up anyway. Greenborough have taken two of them.'

Julia was unperturbed. 'No matter. Greenborough is only half an hour or so away. Let me see the two you have here and then, if necessary, I'll drive over to Greenborough.'

Suddenly Jackman felt afraid for Julia. It was reminiscent of the fear that had overcome him every time Laura had had to deal with a badly deranged patient. It was a kind of primeval instinct in him that signalled danger.

'Now that would work,' said Marie.

He realised that she was staring at him, waiting for confirmation. 'Yes, and the sooner the better. We need to know exactly who is still out there — and if it is Daemon, then he'll have a plan, won't he, Julia?'

'Oh yes. He'll have every eventuality covered. Free or incarcerated, it's all irrelevant to him. Nothing, other than death itself, will get in his way.'

'Then I'll ring down and arrange interviews with the two we have here.' He picked up the receiver, then stopped. 'But you should never go in alone. You must always be accompanied by one of us and a uniformed officer. Marie? Would you oblige?'

She grinned at Julia, then at him. 'Leave it to us, boss. We've got this.'

* * *

His progress was slow and deliberate. This was to be the culmination of all he had worked for. His footfall was so measured, so light, that he didn't even startle the birds. Not a twig snapped beneath his bare feet.

The ceremonial belt was heavy around his waist, but the weight of it felt good. It would assist him in accomplishing the final act, and then he would ascend to the higher realm and be welcomed to Mount Olympus as a god. Two further sacrifices were all that were needed before the knowledge of the gods was revealed to him, the second of which, the final act, would be to surrender his earthly being. The first, before that exquisite moment, would be a last offering. One more martyr and their precious blood.

Blood. He could almost smell it.

Slowly, oh, so slowly, he moved nearer.

* * *

'Result!' Marie smiled at Julia but refrained from offering a high five — Julia seemed a little too refined for one of those. 'It saved you a trip to Greenborough too.'

Mason Nash had been the second man Julia had interviewed. That he was indeed Daemon had been immediately apparent when he began to speak, and his megalomania showed itself.

'I'd still like to see all the suspects, of course,' Julia said, 'but I expect there'll be plenty of time for that. Right now, we know who Daemon is, and that's a big step forward.'

Insignificant, until he spoke to you, Emma had said. She was right.

At first sight, Marie had immediately dismissed him as a possible Daemon, he made such an unremarkable figure in his scruffy jeans and khaki shirt. Then Julia had got him to talk, and a very different man emerged. His voice drew you in, seduced you into believing his words. It was extremely disconcerting, even for a tough nut like Marie.

'It wouldn't do to spend too long in his company, you know.' Julia was not joking. 'He has a gift for oration, and he uses clever techniques to engage you. Even his simple ordinariness and his plain looks serve to lower your guard, he appears so completely unthreatening. I'd suggest a word about him to your custody sergeant, Marie. Thick-skinned coppers believe themselves immune to anything some nutter might say. But he would only have to draw them into conversation and . . .' She shuddered. 'Tell your custody sergeant to warn his officers to on no account engage with Mason Nash, not even as a dare.'

They returned to the CID room and Jackman's office. 'I wish we'd been able to get some idea of where the last remaining cult member might be,' said Marie.

'I'm afraid none of these people will tell you that, my dear,' said Julia. 'It'll be tough enough even getting their names. Your best hope would be Emma Knott, but I know how you feel about involving her while one of them remains at liberty. I'm forced to agree with you there, although I think you should consider that should the man on the run be Apostle, he is the most dangerous of all. If Emma could look at the mugshots of the men in custody we would know for sure if Apostle is among them, or if he's the one that's out there somewhere.'

Marie nibbled on her bottom lip, trying to decide. Finally, she said, 'If I did ask her and she agreed, would you be on hand to counsel her?'

Julia touched her arm. 'Of course I would, my dear. She'll need someone, especially if she does find herself looking at an image of the man who frightens her so badly.'

'Right, so let's tell Jackman.'

* * *

He wished he had a little more time, the warm sun on the back of his neck felt so pleasant. He had been standing perfectly still for some time now, just watching. The security guards had been something of a surprise. He smiled. Big apes. Confronted with a man who fought with his gods

323

beside him, what could they do? Nothing. He would have his sacrifice.

Almost without thought, his hand moved to his belt and he gripped the handle of his ceremonial blade. The knife felt good, eager to do its work. It was also good to be out in the world without the others. Free of the group at last, free of Daemon. Poor deluded Daemon. The perfect showman. But to believe himself to be the Chosen One and the receiver of the True Knowledge, really, it was laughable. Daemon was the magnet, useful for drawing in the army, but he, Apostle, was the real leader, the one destined for glory. And now the time for that glory had arrived.

He stood for a few minutes, watching his sacrificial lamb. He studied the guards and their movements as they patrolled the yard, the entrance from the lane and the woods beyond. They were like cameras, like lenses, their heads turned this way and that, but they kept to a regular pattern.

Leaving the cleaver on the belt, he slipped the sacrificial knife from its sheath.

* * *

Hugh was talking to one of the riding instructors who was full of praise for Aaron's horsemanship considering how new he was to riding. He recalled later the pride he had felt as he gazed around at the tranquil pastoral scene. And stopped.

It must have happened in a flash, but it felt like slow motion.

A man, wearing some kind of loose top, ragged jeans and a wide decorative kind of belt emerged suddenly, seemingly out of nowhere. A terrified scream rent the air — Holly, imploring him for help.

Then everything seemed to happen at once. Before Hugh could even move, three men and a dog sprang forward.

* * *

To Marie's surprise, Emma Knott offered to come to the station so long as she could be assured of not coming into contact with the men they had arrested.

Marie seated her in Jackman's office and placed the photographs one by one in front of her. Greenborough had emailed their two photos over, so they had the full contingent, minus of course the missing man.

Michael Coleman they already knew. The others were Raphael, Bracken, Rufus, and Daemon.

Emma looked at Marie with wide, sad eyes. 'So the one who is missing is the one I prayed would be locked up, hopefully until the day he died.'

Their worst fears had been realised. 'I'm afraid so, Emma, but we'll get him, believe me.'

'I'd like to, DS Evans, but you don't know that man.'

Marie gathered up the photographs and put them back in their file. As she did so, another picture slipped out onto the desk.

Emma gasped. 'You said you didn't have him! But you have! Is he here? God! Tell me he's not here!'

Marie and Jackman stared down at the picture he had brought back from Locksford. That of Martin Bennington.

'That's him! That's Apostle!'

'No, Emma,' Marie said. 'That's the man who came to us in the first place, our whistle-blower. That's Martin Bennington.'

Emma gave a strangled laugh. 'Then . . . oh dear. I'm sorry to say that you've been had. It was Apostle you had at the station, not Martin Bennington.' Her laughter continued, gradually becoming hysterical. Julia hurried forward and knelt down in front of her.

'It's all right, Emma, he's not here, I promise. Now, look at me, take some deep breaths.' Julia looked up at Marie. 'Would you be so kind as to get this girl a drink?'

Marie opened the door and shouted for someone to get a glass of water and some hot tea with sugar, and to hurry. Back inside, Jackman's expression was unfathomable. His phone buzzed, and he read the message. He read it again, mumbled, 'I simply don't believe it,' dropped his phone and put his head in his hands.

'Boss! What is it?' Marie asked.

'That was Sam. He's found some more notes on Laura's laptop. She had begun to mistrust what Bennington was saying. Apparently, she was going to consult Sam as soon as she got home and tell me of her suspicions. She wondered if Bennington might still be involved with the cult, possibly occupying a high position.' He swallowed. 'A few more hours and she would have made the connection and he'd have been arrested. Instead . . .'

Emma was looking utterly perplexed now as well as frightened, and Julia was opening the door to a concerned-looking Robbie who handed her the drinks.

Marie knew exactly what Jackman was going to say before he opened his mouth, and her heart sank.

'We need forensics to look at Laura's car again, don't we?'

She was forced to agree. 'Even if what happened was inevitable, we need to know if that man intended to kill her.' Another thought came to her. 'Well, if nothing else, we now know who arranged the pile-up that left two of our colleagues critically injured. There was no inside mole, no information leak. None of our people were to blame. The whole thing was a scam. Bennington himself told Daemon exactly which clinic they were heading for. I bet if we check with Locksford, we'll find he made a call before he was transferred. What a bastard!'

'But to what end?' asked Jackman. 'Why do all that? Why put the remaining members of the cult in the firing line?'

'Because he wanted to finish it,' said Emma, clutching her drink with both hands to hold it steady. 'He was trying to take control even before I left. He thought he didn't need the commune at all, didn't need anyone. He had his own agenda and considered himself to be all-powerful, to a point where he obviously believed he could fool the entire police force. He was all about manipulation. Getting into the heart of the police station and feeding you all the lies he no doubt did would have been the most incredible power trip imaginable for him.'

And he did it with bells on, thought Marie, recalling all the things that Jackman had told her about poor Martin Bennington, the brave victim who had found the courage to blow the whistle on the cult. What a crock of shit! 'So he and other cult members would have staged the initial car crash that brought him to Locksford police station. Vic Blackwell said it didn't look like an attempt to kill Bennington, just to drive him off the road. Only it went a bit wrong when Bennington spun and hit the other car.' So it had all been a fabrication, from beginning to end, the idea being to feed the police enough information to hunt down Daemon and the others and get rid of them. Marie wondered what story he would have concocted to get them to help him. She put the question to Emma.

Emma laughed bitterly. 'Oh, DS Evans, they would have believed anything he told them and gone along with it. He probably said it was decreed that he must enter the citadel of the heathens and come out again, victorious. That it was all part of the grand journey to Nirvana.' Her laughter died away and she stared down at her feet. 'We lost our way, Detective Inspector Jackman. At the start, I think Daemon really did dream of establishing a better, more holistic way of life, but Apostle slowly insinuated the idea of sacrifices into Daemon's mind. Ha! Daemon, the mind-bender, fell prey to an even darker manipulative mind than his own. It would be laughable if it wasn't so tragic.' Emma started to cry.

While Julia comforted the girl, she whispered to Jackman and Marie, 'I think she is absolutely right, you know. This man is a psychopath, and you have to catch him before he does any more damage.'

The shrill ring of the office phone made them all start.

Jackman took the call. 'What? When?'

Slowly, he lowered the phone. Marie went up to him and touched his arm. 'Tell me!'

'There's been an incident at my mother's stables. The emergency services were called. Three men are injured. That's all I know, except that one might be my father. There are no more details as yet.' He leaped to his feet. 'I have to go!'

'I'll look after Emma,' said Julia.

Marie ran out after Jackman. 'Hold up, Jackman. This time I insist on driving!'

* * *

The scenarios that played out in Jackman's head as they drove across the Fen to his parents' home were the stuff of nightmares. How could his father be hurt? He rarely went to the stables. And how bad was his injury? He wondered if he could take much more on top of losing Laura. He was as close to the edge as he had ever been.

The yard was a scene of frenzied activity.

'Over there!' Marie pointed to a spot not far from the saddle room and the forge.

His mother was busy directing her stablehands and instructors to move the horses away from the commotion. He ran over to her and hugged her tightly. 'How's Dad? Is he all right?'

'You mean the hero of the hour?' She gave him a tight smile. 'Don't worry, my darling, he'll be fine. He's not badly injured, there was just rather a lot of blood, and he's making the most of it.' Then she gripped his arm. 'To tell you the truth, the whole thing was frightful. That terrible man! He tried to kill her!' And she burst into tears.

Jackman took her in his arms, looking helplessly over her shoulder at Marie. The scene had a slightly unreal, almost farcical quality to it. He wished he could work out what had actually happened.

'I've just spotted Stacey and Jay,' said Marie. 'Stay with your mother, I'll find out what's occurred.'

He couldn't remember ever seeing his mother break down in tears. She was a rock, the family's solid foundation. Harriet just didn't cry. And his father? Hero of the hour? His father was a thinker, a man of words who operated behind the scenes. Desperate to find out what had happened, he held onto his sobbing mother and waited for Marie to return with some kind of situation report.

Marie soon hurried back with Stacey in tow. 'We were called to a fracas involving a weapon — a knife, to be precise,' Stacey began, 'and when we got here all hell had broken loose. It's your cult member, sir. Jay and I recognised the knife from pictures we'd seen of the ritual murders.'

By now Harriet had rallied and was fast becoming her old self again. 'Go, Rowan. Tell your father I'll be with him as soon as all the horses are safely inside. And make sure no one allows that psycho to get free again. He's quite insane.'

When they got there, the exercise yard looked more like a field hospital than a place to put horses and riders through their paces.

'What the f—?' Jackman was having difficulty working out just what he was looking at.

It appeared that there were four separate groups on the stage, playing out four different scenes.

The first featured his father, lying on an ambulance trolley with a large bloody dressing across his left arm, while two paramedics monitored him, chatting cheerily.

The second was a kind of set piece, with Holly and Hugh centre stage, both sitting on the ground with their children between them and Rory the dog at Holly's side. Holly had a thermal blanket wrapped around her, and two police officers were taking notes.

The third involved a security guard on another trolley, with a bloody pad pressed against his side and two medics preparing to ship him off to hospital.

The final scene, a much larger one involving some ten or more people, was taking place some distance from the others. Jackman noted the presence of a policeman, more paramedics, a motorcycle first responder, security guards and a dog handler with his German shepherd.

Jackman stood and stared. Was he finally going to see the dread Apostle? Or was he going to see Martin Bennington, the man he had spent hours with, and for whom he had felt such sympathy? The man who had been strong enough to survive the mind-control techniques of a cult leader. His eyes narrowed. He was pretty sure which one it would be. He took a deep breath. *But first to Father.*

'It was a team effort, son. You should have seen it, happened in a flash! He just appeared out of nowhere, waving this damned weird knife. Then he had Holly in his clutches, she screamed, and, well, we all simply reacted.'

His eyes were too bright, and the words tumbled out too fast. Jackman looked at the paramedic who pointed to the blood pressure monitor. His father was in shock, his blood pressure was sky-high. Jackman said a few encouraging words and told him Harriet would be with him as soon as the horses were all safe. 'I'll be back soon, Dad, I just need to check in with my colleagues.' He half turned to go, and then added, 'I'm proud of you, Dad.'

His father gave him a beaming smile. 'I'm beginning to see why you like your job so much, son.'

For a man who had ridiculed his son's chosen career for most of his life, this was quite something.

Jackman then went to the Stewarts and found Marie sitting on her haunches, talking to them. She looked up at his approach. 'Our Holly has had a narrow escape, boss. But a couple of real superheroes came to her rescue. Didn't they, Aaron?' She winked at Aaron, who nodded furiously.

'And my dad is one of them. He was epic! He saved Mum's life!'

'A lucky break,' said Hugh dismissively. 'It was a team effort.' He looked at Holly and swallowed hard. 'As for me, the moment I saw the one I love with a knife at her throat, I didn't think twice. Well, none of us did. We just piled in.'

Jackman was still none the wiser. He wondered who to ask for a coherent account.

Marie read his thoughts. 'Talk to Debbie Quinton, boss, she saw it all.'

Jackman said he would. He turned to Holly, who seemed remarkably unshaken considering what she'd been through.

'I'm okay,' she said, 'honestly. For one terrible moment I thought I was a goner, but it was all over so fast. And it *is* all over now, isn't it?'

'Yes. All of it. You guys won't be troubled again.' Echoes of the voices of Sally Pinket and her dead children called out to him, and he added, 'Though there are some issues we have to talk about when things have calmed down.'

'Oh, and for the record, DI Jackman, there were *four* heroes.' She ran her hand through Rory's fur and tickled his ears affectionately. 'I think this one did as much damage as all the others combined.'

'Brave Royal lineage,' he said, and bent down to stroke the dog's back. 'Good man, Rory.'

Now, finally, he would lay eyes on the person who'd unleashed all this mayhem. For a moment Jackman held back.

He felt Marie take his arm. 'Are you up for this, boss?'

Was he? Well, it had to be done. 'I'll be interested to see what someone capable of carrying out multiple human sacrifices over the course of many years looks like. And I sincerely hope I never live to see another.'

Martin Bennington was a mess. Plastered with dressings on various parts of his body, bruised and battered, with one eye swollen and fast closing. He sat on the ground, his head bowed, handcuffed wrists in his lap. The reason they were not behind his back, which would have been usual, was because his right hand was thickly bandaged and clearly causing him severe pain. Two burly police constables flanked him, and another stood at his back.

Before he approached Bennington, Jackman spoke to one of the three medics who were treating him and asked what the score was.

'He needs hospital treatment, sir, no question. He has multiple cuts and abrasions, has sustained a blow to the head and has a deep wound in his right hand that will require surgical intervention or he may lose it.'

Excellent, thought Jackman. No more precision dissecting of innocent victims' bodies.

'Your colleagues are arranging a police escort for the journey to the Greenborough Emergency Department and a twenty-four-hour security watch on him while he's there. Saltern Hospital doesn't have a vascular surgeon available or the facilities to house him securely, so it's Greenborough, I'm afraid.'

DI Nikki Galena would no doubt be delighted to receive such news on a Friday evening. Jackman reminded himself to ring and apologise. He thanked the medic and turned back to Marie.

She gave him a small smile of encouragement, and they approached the seated figure and stood looking down at him.

Jackman didn't miss the evil glint in his one functional eye. 'Sucker!' Bennington hissed. 'They don't come any more gullible than you, do they? You and those two stupid women. Professionals? What a laugh! It's no wonder we got away with doing what we did for so long. You're all nothing but a joke!'

Jackman reined in an overwhelming desire to beat the man to death, right here, in front of everyone. With the greatest effort, he smiled coldly down at the killer. 'Joke, you say? Well, I do believe we get the last laugh. Have they told you you could lose your hand? Speed is of the essence, apparently, but there don't seem to be any theatre slots available. Shame, that. Oh well, prosthetics are so good these days, aren't they? But I'd look after it if I were you, they nick anything in prison.' He looked at Marie. 'I think we're done here. Let's go and talk to your witness.'

His howls of rage followed them across the yard.

CHAPTER TWENTY-NINE

Debbie Quinton proved to be that rare asset, an observant and reliable witness. She even seemed to have noted where everyone was and what they were doing immediately before the drama unfolded.

'I was talking to Hugh Stewart about the way young Aaron has taken to the saddle. While we chatted, we couldn't help glancing at those security guards. It's rather off-putting to have men like that around in a place like a stable. I mean, I know they should make you feel more secure, but their presence just makes you feel you might be in danger.'

Marie agreed.

'The two children were with Ryan and a groom, over by the forge.' She pointed across the yard. 'Ryan was explaining how the farrier shod the horses.' She then indicated a spot close to one corner of the arena. 'Holly was standing there looking at Mr Lawrence Jackman, who had just called out to her. He said he had some good news about the children's schooling.'

'So that's why he was here,' breathed Jackman.

'He doesn't come very often, but it was lucky he did today.' Debbie frowned, concentrating. 'Then everything happened at once. This man leaped out from the side of the hay barn and grabbed hold of Holly. She screamed for help. I think that's when we all saw he had a wicked-looking knife in his hand.' She looked at Jackman and smiled. 'I'd never have believed your father could move so fast! Ryan had just been showing the children a hoof pick, it was on a multitool.'

Jackman knew it well. He'd bought the pocket grooming kit as a gift for Ryan himself.

'As Hugh and the nearest security man leaped forward, I saw Mr Jackman grab the hoof pick from Ryan and rush at Holly's assailant. The security guard got there first, but without letting go of Holly, the man stabbed the guard in the side. Then he raised the knife to stab Holly, but your father was already on him. The knife cut your father's arm, but he didn't even flinch. As the man raised it again, Hugh grabbed him around the waist and held him fast, and your father dug the hoof pick into the hand holding the knife and dragged the curved metal pick downwards. Blood spurted everywhere. At that point I dialled 999 on my mobile.' She puffed out her cheeks. 'Oh my! It was chaos, but I saw the knife fall and Mr Jackman kick it away. Then Hugh and the second security guard overpowered him. He kept fighting until the guard punched him in the face and he fell back and hit his head. I think he was out just long enough for them to secure him until the police arrived.'

'I've never seen my father move any faster than a slow walk around a conference table,' said Jackman in awe. 'He really did that?'

'Without hesitation, DI Jackman,' said Debbie. 'They were all quite fearless!'

Marie wondered if they would have been quite so fearless had they known they were tackling a ruthless multiple murderer, and decided yes, they would. Holly's life had been in danger. She thanked Debbie, told her that someone would take her statement and assured her that if any of them felt they needed to talk about what they had witnessed, counselling could be arranged.

Debbie thanked her but said they were a tough bunch at the stable. Once your horse had thrown you and rolled on you a couple of times, you could take most things in your stride.

Marie followed Jackman over to the ambulance crew tending to his father but remained in the background so he could talk with his mum and dad alone.

The yard was swarming with police personnel and vehicles, and a uniformed superintendent was barking orders. Marie felt a sick tiredness descend upon her. She should have felt elated. They'd done it — all the members of the killer cult had now been rounded up. But she could only feel sad. Apart from the mountain of paperwork that would shortly land on her desk, this case had left heartbreak in its wake. After all the furore had died down, Jackman would have to return to an empty house and face the loss of the woman he loved.

Marie walked away from the hubbub and sat on a seat outside one of the livery stables. A chestnut head appeared over the half-open door and gave a soft little whicker.

'Hello, mate. Sorry, I've got nothing to give you.'

Seeing there was no food on offer, the head withdrew, and Marie was left alone.

She recalled that first day, when they had been handed a twenty-year-old cold case. How fired up they'd been at the prospect of solving a crime that had had everyone foxed for so long — the kudos, the celebrations there would be if their team managed to crack it. Well, they had achieved that and a lot more besides, including finding answers to a terrible crime from Victorian times and restoring the good name of a long-dead woman who cared for children. But there was no triumph in it and certainly no cause for celebration. Marie just felt sick at heart.

Her mobile buzzed. She opened the message.

Are you safe?

She typed back '*I'm safe.*' But even this was tinged with sadness. There would be no caring messages for Jackman, no one to go home to now it was all over.

Her own experience told her that he had a very long road to travel. All she and the others could do was be there for him. He still had the job he loved, a loyal team, good friends and a loving family and, although it might not mean much to him at the moment, that was what would see him through.

Are you coming home soon?

Sorry, not until late. Jackman needs me.

EPILOGUE

One month later.

Driving out to the house called Solace, Jackman, Marie and Gary wondered what they would find. It was a strange time for the Stewart family, and Gary, who had kept in regular contact with them, knew they had struggled to make a decision about their ill-fated property.

Today, a police team, along with a technician and his ground-penetrating radar system, were to start work on locating and uncovering whatever was buried in the garden of Sally Pinket's old home.

'They took the news that the house had been a Victorian baby farm really well, didn't they?' said Gary. 'I'd have probably turned tail and run, but Holly and Hugh said they found it almost cathartic. They were fascinated by the fact that Ivy Pettifer's crimes had been laid at the door of the innocent Sally Pinket and could only feel sorry for her.'

'At least they know the house wasn't the centre of a series of brutal Jack the Ripper-type murders,' added Marie. 'Knowing that would be far from cathartic.'

'They said they have something to tell us,' Jackman said. 'I'm guessing it's their final decision about whether to keep the place.' He turned into the lane that led to Solace.

'Oh, I say!' exclaimed Gary as the house came into view. 'I wouldn't have recognised it. It looks completely different.'

The dark, untidy old conifers had gone, felled and carted away. Now the house looked out over miles of fields and across to the village church at Amberley Fen.

'Well, for once the Stewarts had a real stroke of luck, and it was courtesy of Ruth Crooke of all people,' said Jackman. 'Before we could get the geophysics boys in with their GPR, the ground had to be cleared. If it had only been the Victorian baby deaths, I don't think even Ruth could have sanctioned that amount of work, but she insisted that as Daemon had been so desperate to buy the house, there was a good chance we'd find evidence of more bodies buried here. And she had her way. The whole area had to be stripped.'

'So those awful half-dead trees have been cleared courtesy of the Fenland Constabulary.' Gary laughed. 'Nice one!'

They had to park in the lane as the drive was full of cars and official vehicles.

'They're treating it like an archaeological dig,' said Marie, picking her way between the vans and 4x4s. 'All the relevant licences have been obtained should they actually need to exhume any human remains, and if they do turn up anything, it has to be reported to the coroner's office. It's a big day in the macabre history of Solace.'

'Is there really a chance they'll unearth more than just the children?' asked Gary. 'Only, I got the feeling that Daemon only wanted this place for the bad energy. After all, apart from Ivy Pettifer's contributions, there was the more recent murder that took place here. It would have been the perfect little family home for when he fancied time away from his commune.'

Jackman didn't answer immediately. The intensity of the threats made against the Stewarts in the attempt to get them out still bothered him. 'I doubt it, Gary, but,' he shrugged, 'who knows? He wanted this place very badly, so I can't help but wonder if there was more to it than met the eye.'

'Well, we'll know later today, boss — there's enough people here to excavate an entire Roman villa,' said Marie. 'Look, there's Holly!'

Holly Stewart was standing in the kitchen doorway, waving to them.

'It's like manning a cafeteria here today,' she said, pointing to a line of freshly washed mugs on the table.

For the first time since Jackman had met her, Holly looked happy. Which, given the massive operation underway just metres from the house, was surprising to say the least.

'You'll get your tea too, don't worry, but first, let's just go into the lounge.' Holly pushed open the door and they trooped in.

The first thing that hit Jackman was the light. The whole room was awash with bright morning sun. He remembered how even at midday they'd had to have the lights on. Not now.

'It's incredible,' he breathed. 'I mean, I always thought the trees shut out a lot of the light, but this is amazing.'

Holly beamed with delight. 'The whole house is the same. It's like it can breathe again.' She laughed. 'The morning after they finished clearing, we got up and came down here just as the sun rose. It was a revelation. And it made our minds up. We're going to stay.'

Everyone said how delighted they were, although Jackman guessed they were all secretly wondering if it was the right thing to do. So many bad things had happened here. Could the Stewarts really put so much behind them?

'Now, drinks. What can I get you?'

Back in the kitchen they sat and drank tea while outside, the garden was alive with men and women busy with their equipment.

'Where's Hugh?' asked Jackman.

'He'll be back shortly. He's taken the children to the stables — they're mucking out today. I'm dreading the state their wellies will be in when they get home. Harriet insisted they spend the day with her so they don't have to witness what's going on in the garden. It's no place for young children today. She also suggested that if it goes on too late, we all spend the night in our little flat at the stable.'

'I hope you don't mind me asking,' said Marie, 'but are you really both okay with living here, knowing what could be found today?'

'You probably think we're mad, I know, but we've talked it over and weighed up our options. It wasn't easy, as you know, Gary — I've bent your ear often enough in the last six weeks. Well, we don't believe in ghosts, but we do respect the dead, and if there really are little children buried out there and they can finally be given proper burials and maybe get their names back, then we'll be happy. We're going to completely redesign the garden and reroute the drive so that it comes in from the side of the property and up to the front door, so people won't be faced by a blank wall when they arrive.' She laughed. 'Our muck-spreading friend actually did us a favour, Gary. When the ground is all properly turned over, it'll have a lovely mulch of free manure.'

'Well, he did *me* no favours,' muttered Gary. 'My ribs still ache.'

'Wimp!' said Marie, grinning at him. 'What do you expect if you try to climb onto a moving tractor driven by a psycho?'

When the laughter had subsided, Jackman asked, 'No nightmares over what happened at the stables, Holly?'

She shook her head. 'I'm just thankful that my saviours weren't too badly injured. It happened so quickly it hardly had time to register, and the children think it was the coolest thing ever, so no, no nightmares.' She threw him a grateful smile. 'We could never have got through this without you, your family and your friends. Your father has even arranged a new school for the children. It's close to where Hugh works, so he can take them in of a morning, and now I've got a little car of my own, I can pick them up at the end of the day. No school bus, no bullying.'

Hugh arrived a few minutes later, and they all went to see how the dig was progressing. Finding themselves alone at one point, Jackman said, 'I gather that nothing was disturbed when they took the tree roots out — as in human remains? Seeing as how no one knows where those infants were buried, I did wonder.'

'Nothing at all.' Hugh looked across at the GPR operator wheeling what looked like a mower with a monitor on the handles up and down some carefully measured lines. 'They've divided the whole garden into grids so the data collected will be accurate.' He pursed his lips. 'I hope we aren't wasting someone's money here. Suppose they don't find anything at all? It could all just be some local folktale.'

'Marie, Ralph and Gary would disagree with you there, Hugh. They did extensive research into the Pinkets and the Pettifers and are absolutely certain there are remains here. They're just not sure how many.'

The first child was discovered thirty minutes later, and shortly after that three more, all in close proximity to the first.

'Ralph was told that Sally and her gardener buried four babies,' said Marie in a hushed tone. 'It seems they were right.'

A new team took over, digging along the exact coordinates shown by the GPR reading. Everyone else stood around, waiting and watching to see what would be found.

An hour later, just as the soil was being scraped from the first small bones, a shout went up from another part of the garden. The technician called out that he had located something else.

Jackman hurried over to where the man was staring at his monitor.

'Another child?' asked Jackman.

'No, sir. I'm not sure what this is, but the readings are different to the remains we've just found. It's something else, and it's not buried so deeply.'

Jackman beckoned to two police officers standing nearby. 'Time to start digging again, boys. With great care, please. Our expert here thinks that whatever this is, it's only buried about eighteen inches down.'

'Looks like Ruth's gamble has paid off,' whispered Marie, who had appeared at his side. 'She'll be relieved to hear about this.'

'Let's see what it is first.' Jackman's mind was throwing up any number of possibilities, not the least of them being a dead cat.

They didn't have long to wait, though it felt like forever.

'We've got something, sir! It's solid and it's wrapped in some kind of material.'

'Then stop digging, lads, and thank you. We'll get forensics in now.' Jackman turned to Marie. 'Rory sent two SOCOs in case they were required. Bring them here, if you would. This is too delicate for us plods to tackle.'

Jackman stared into the hole. He had an idea of exactly what they'd find. A shiver crept across his shoulders. 'Oh, yes, you wanted this plot of land and its accursed house for a damned good reason, didn't you, Daemon?' And drifting across the fields on the breeze, he heard the whispered sound of someone cursing him.

'What do you think it is, boss?' Marie was back, accompanied by two SOCOs.

'Unless I'm very wrong, it's the last piece in Rory's jigsaw puzzle, Marie, that elusive piece that completes the picture.'

By three o'clock that afternoon they had uncovered three skulls. Jackman believed one of them to be that of Michelle Wilding, the girl from Birch Drove Farm they had known for so long as Angel. He was sure that tests would prove one of the others to be a match for the headless body that resided in Rory Wilkinson's cold storage cabinet — that of Siobhan Aster.

But the third, well, that was a mystery and was the reason he insisted that the GPR operator keep going and survey the whole area. The only other headless body that he knew of was the recently found male victim dumped close to Locksford police station that he now knew to be the real

Martin Bennington. But that had only happened a day or so before the cult members had been captured, so they wouldn't have had the time or opportunity to get here and bury it. No, number three was a much older skull. It caused Jackman to ask himself how long the cult had been using Solace as an unofficial burial ground for severed heads. Did this one belong to someone on the List of the Fallen? Thinking of this, he remembered there was another unsolved mystery, that of the human blood used to decorate the Stewarts' lounge wall. Whose was it? If it had been blood alone then DNA might have been extracted, but the paint had seriously contaminated it. That was something that they might never know the answer to.

Deciding he badly needed a hot drink, he made his way back to the kitchen to beg a cup of tea. He couldn't help but think this latest discovery might impact on the Stewarts' decision to stay on.

To his surprise, Holly laughed when he mentioned this to her. To his further surprise, she gave him a hug.

'Dear Jackman! Do you know, with every single bone that is lifted from this soil the house feels lighter and so does my mind. This place is being cleansed of the shadows of the past. We're going to make this our forever home, and we will bring up happy children here. One day Solace will mean just that, a place of comfort, you see if it doesn't!'

Jackman smiled. Her enthusiasm gave him no option but to believe her. No matter what was going on outside or what they might find in the hours to come, it wouldn't take away the peace and happiness in that bright and sunny kitchen.

* * *

Janet lowered the receiver and replaced it in the cradle at the end of her final call to John. They had wished each other well, hoping they might work together again one day, but neither mentioned meeting up socially. Their job for Stephen was now complete. He had been pleased with their work and would be transferring a very generous amount into their respective bank accounts.

Janet had gone to see him to let him know that all had been tied up just as he had requested. She also said that knowing what she did now, it would be unfortunate if her work for him was to come to an end. She had assured him this had nothing to do with his very generous wages, in fact she would be happy to work for a pittance if he would consider keeping her on. He had said that he would indeed consider finding a position for her.

That done, she could do no more than hope, and she turned to her glass of Rémy Martin.

She sat in her favourite chair, sipped her brandy, and wondered how to use her forthcoming payment. She might take a holiday, a luxury cruise perhaps, with fine dining and elegant comfort. She had always had a hankering to see the Caribbean.

The sound of the doorbell jarred her out of her reverie. Amazon, most likely. She had recently ordered some cleaning materials.

She was shocked to see John standing at the door, an indecipherable expression on his face. But when she saw the long slim-bladed knife in his hand, her look of enquiry turned to one of terror.

The pain was like nothing she could have ever imagined, but it didn't last long.

Then John was gone. Slowly she slid down the wall and sank to the floor, the dark blood ruining her pristine cream carpet.

* * *

John contacted his client. The message was short. *Mutual friend sadly deceased. Computer backup erased. Commission complete. Awaiting next assignment.* An hour later he received a reply.

John smiled. Phase Two looked interesting. Very interesting indeed.

* * *

It had grieved Jackman to do so, but he had purposely held back Laura's funeral until, with the help of Orac, he had located her mother and stepfather. Marie had given her their details, and she finally traced them to an isolated spot in the high Massif Central area of Aveyron in France. As the funeral had already been postponed while further forensic checks were carried out on Laura's car to determine the possibility of foul play, Jackman waited until they were on their way back before he set the date.

The night before the service, he and Sam sat in the kitchen at Mill Corner. They had a lot to discuss, so Jackman had opened a bottle of his favourite brandy.

'Something I forgot to mention,' said Sam. 'I know you rang Locksford to tell Ashley Carpenter that Laura's car hadn't been tampered with, and I think she gave you an update on the two injured officers, who are now both on the road to recovery.'

'Yes, Ashley did tell me. Sounds like it'll be a long haul for young Russ Cooley, though. Life-changing injuries, she said, but she didn't elaborate. It's upset her badly, hasn't it?'

'Her daughter is engaged to Russ. He's her prospective son-in-law and she adores him. She blames herself for sending him and his colleague Paula on that particular trip. She still finds it hard to talk about it, or she would have spoken to you. It's all too much for her to cope with at present. I've suggested she take some leave as soon as possible, so as to try and come to terms with her grief and her guilt issues.' He took a sip of brandy. 'But like all you pig-headed coppers, she wants to see the case through to the bitter end before she'll admit she's running on empty.'

'I'm afraid it's how we roll,' Jackman said, 'to use the vernacular.'

'Don't I know it!'

'She did answer one other question that was bothering me,' said Jackman. 'Although he was much older, of course, Ashley identified the man we thought was Martin Bennington as the one who had been brought in in connection with the first enquiry into Shelley Harcourt's murder. I thought she'd made a mistake when we discovered that he was really Apostle, but it turned out she was right. It was Apostle the police had picked up all those years ago, but he cunningly gave Martin's name instead of his own. He knew everything about him, and since the lad had never been in trouble before, he got away with using him as a fall guy. That's why he fooled Ashley so easily this time. My God, he really did take us for a ride.'

They sat quietly for a while, then Jackman said, 'So, regarding the main issue on tonight's agenda. Your decision, please, Professor Samuel Page? I hope you've made one.'

'I accept, Detective Inspector Rowan Jackman, most graciously.'

Jackman was pleased. He had done the right thing both for him and for his old friend, Sam. He and Laura had been trying for ages to convince Sam to move into the converted mill, especially after he had been injured. There was a spacious living area above the consulting room, and, above that, another large space that could be made into guest rooms or a study. Hitherto, feeling that he'd be intruding on Jackman and Laura's new life together, Sam had opted to remain in his lonely cottage on the edge of the marsh. Now that had changed.

Jackman lifted his glass in salute. 'Welcome to your new home, dear friend.'

'I admit I was starting to dread the coming of winter. I love my old cottage, but the passing years and my deteriorating health were beginning to make me feel rather vulnerable. I shall put it on the market after we've said goodbye to Laura.'

Jackman knew selling the house would be a wrench, even if it was the most sensible thing to do. 'You can do whatever you want with the mill, Sam. I'm really glad we had that snazzy domestic lift fitted. The staircase isn't steep, in fact the way it climbs gently around the curve of the mill, you can still manage it easily, but if mobility does become a problem, you'll still have access to all the floors.'

The mill would give Sam independence while not being isolated. When Jackman was at work, Hetty and Len Maynard would be around to help Sam out should he need it. And Jackman would have a friend close by. A win-win situation.

'And Julia? Have you heard anything from her?' Jackman said.

'Nothing definite yet. It would be a major change for her but,' he looked at Jackman over the top of his glass, 'I think she'll see it as a challenge. A small wager says you could have a new force psychologist any time soon.'

'How would you feel about that, Sam? Would you be okay with it?'

'You couldn't do better, my friend, and I'd be delighted.'

Jackman grinned. 'Do you think you and Julia, er, well, you know?'

'No way!' Sam exploded into a laugh. 'We know each far too well for that! But I'd love to have her around more.'

They lapsed into an amicable silence.

Jackman pointed to the brandy bottle. 'Top-up?'

Sam shook his head. 'I think I'll turn in now. We've got a long day tomorrow.'

With a sigh, Jackman agreed.

One more day to get through. Then what?

As he trudged upstairs to the big, empty bedroom, he already knew the answer: work. And then more work. It was how Marie had made it through so, somehow, he'd do the same.

Somehow.

THE END

ALSO BY JOY ELLIS

Thank you for reading this book.

If you enjoyed it please leave feedback on Amazon or Goodreads, and if there is anything we missed or you have a question about, then please get in touch. We appreciate you choosing our book.

Founded in 2014 in Shoreditch, London, we at Joffe Books pride ourselves on our history of innovative publishing. We were thrilled to be shortlisted for Independent Publisher of the Year at the British Book Awards.

www.joffebooks.com

We're very grateful to eagle-eyed readers who take the time to contact us. Please send any errors you find to corrections@joffebooks.com. We'll get them fixed ASAP.